FAR
and
AWAY

ALSO BY AMY POEPPEL

The Sweet Spot
Musical Chairs
Limelight
Small Admissions

FAR
and
AWAY

A NOVEL

by Amy Poeppel

EMILY BESTLER BOOKS

ATRIA

New York   Amsterdam/Antwerp   London
Toronto   Sydney/Melbourne   New Delhi

EMILY BESTLER BOOKS

ATRIA

An Imprint of Simon & Schuster, LLC
1230 Avenue of the Americas
New York, NY 10020

For more than 100 years, Simon & Schuster has championed authors
and the stories they create. By respecting the copyright of an author's
intellectual property, you enable Simon & Schuster and the author to continue
publishing exceptional books for years to come. We thank you for supporting
the author's copyright by purchasing an authorized edition of this book.

No amount of this book may be reproduced or stored in any format, nor may it be
uploaded to any website, database, language-learning model, or other repository,
retrieval, or artificial intelligence system without express permission. All rights
reserved. Inquiries may be directed to Simon & Schuster, 1230 Avenue of the
Americas, New York, NY 10020 or permissions@simonandschuster.com.

This book is a work of fiction. Any references to historical events, real people,
or real places are used fictitiously. Other names, characters, places, and events
are products of the author's imagination, and any resemblance to actual
events or places or persons, living or dead, is entirely coincidental.

First Emily Bestler Books/Atria Paperback edition June 2025

EMILY BESTLER BOOKS/ATRIA PAPERBACK and colophon are trademarks
of Simon & Schuster, LLC

Simon & Schuster strongly believes in freedom of expression and stands against
censorship in all its forms. For more information, visit BooksBelong.com.

For information about special discounts for bulk purchases, please contact Simon &
Schuster Special Sales at 1-866-506-1949 or business@simonandschuster.com.

The Simon & Schuster Speakers Bureau can bring authors to your live event. For
more information or to book an event, contact the Simon & Schuster Speakers
Bureau at 1-866-248-3049 or visit our website at www.simonspeakers.com.

Interior design by Lexy East

Manufactured in the United States of America

1   3   5   7   9   10   8   6   4   2

Library of Congress Cataloging-in-Publication Data has been applied for.

ISBN 978-1-6680-2285-6
ISBN 978-1-6680-2287-0 (ebook)

With love to Alex, Andrew, and Luke,
my German-Texan sons

PART 1

He is happiest, be he king or peasant,
who finds peace in his home.
—Johann Wolfgang von Goethe, German writer

Whenever you feel homesick,
just remember what a lucky girl you are.
—Dorothy Turner Mitchell, Texan grandmother

The students involved in the scandal that spring may have been Rockwell's best and brightest, but most kids at the school didn't even know who they were. Lucy found out who was involved when her son texted: D + R + S + me = big trouble.

She was having lunch at Haywire on McKinney, sitting between Bryn and Harper, the impressive young CEOs who had hired her only six months before. She found them intimidating. Lucy worked remotely, and twice this powerhouse duo had flown her to their chic headquarters in LA for an in-person meeting. But today they had come all the way to Dallas just to see her. Lucy had no idea why.

She read Jack's message under the table and texted back a question mark and a smiley face, thinking that if he and his friends were in some kind of trouble, it couldn't be all that bad. Lost keys maybe. Or a crashed computer.

Lucy looked up to see Harper twisting a lock of her highlighted hair around one finger. "Should we have drinks?" she said, sounding not rebellious, but rather as if she'd just learned of a new custom, one she might dare to try herself.

"Like a cocktail?" said Bryn, intrigued. "Like . . . champagne?"

The waiter arrived. Lucy closed her notebook and sat up straight in the tufted U-shaped booth, smoothing her napkin over her lap.

"Did I hear champagne?" the waiter said as he placed their salads in front of them.

"Sure," said Lucy with a shrug. "Heck, yeah." This was, after all, the start of a momentous family weekend.

The waiter nodded and turned to her bosses. "Are we doing three glasses or a bottle?"

Harper was tapping her lips with her finger. "On second thought," she said, "I think I'll stick with mineral water."

"Same," said Bryn, adjusting her sleeveless top, which emphasized razor-sharp collarbones. "Day drinking wrecks me. But I love this for you, Lucy. You should celebrate."

"A glass then," said the waiter.

Lucy immediately regretted the order.

She assumed the celebration Bryn was referring to was Jack's high school graduation. But the women exchanged a glance then, as Harper leaned forward and said, "We came to tell you in person, the Laurel team *love*-loved your pitch."

Lucy started, knocking her bare knee into the table leg. "Really?" she said. "As in . . . ?"

"As in," said Bryn, "we got the contract for their six West Coast hotels. It was your concept that sold them, that whole Scandinavian, clean look you presented."

"I worried it was giving hospital vibes," Harper said. "Bland, sterile even. But they absolutely adored it."

"Great," said Lucy, unable to contain her smile. She loved her job with this boutique firm, so much more than the low-budget hotel chain where she'd worked before. It was awkward, though; she'd fought for this aesthetic against her own bosses, who were gunning for their signature, edgy boudoir theme that always included an obscene amount of red velvet. "I'm on it."

"Good," Harper said, "because they want to launch as soon as possible."

"Onboarding starts Monday," Bryn said.

"I'll be ready," said Lucy.

"Are you sure?" Bryn said, pouting slightly. "Because we know you've got, like, a whole *thing* this weekend."

"It's fine." Lucy opened her notebook again and clicked the top of her ballpoint. In addition to the graduation, her visiting in-laws, and a backyard party for fifty, she would find time to prepare a kick-ass presentation. "It's no problem."

"They're our biggest client," Harper said with a bit of surprise, as though she could not believe Lucy had delivered this win. "So we need to earn their confidence right off the bat."

The waiter came back and set the lone champagne coupe on the table, just as Lucy's phone started to vibrate on the seat beside her. She glanced down, seeing the dreaded word "School" on her screen.

"I'm so sorry," Lucy said. "I wouldn't normally take this, but Zoe wasn't feeling well this morning and—"

"Who?" said Harper.

"Her daughter," said Bryn, sliding out of the booth to let Lucy out.

"Just . . . a sec," Lucy said, holding up a finger and stepping away from the table. She heard a voice saying, "Hello? You there?"

Lucy recognized the drawl of the principal's secretary. "Donna," she said. "Yeah, I'm here."

"Phew," Donna said, sounding breathless. "We need you to come in to discuss the accusations."

"Sorry?" Lucy put a palm over her free ear to block out the background noise from the bar. "What accusations?"

"It's about Jack," she said. "He participated in a . . . sexist activity."

Lucy's first reaction was to laugh. Jack was many things, most of them nerdy and some of them astonishing, but *sexist* he was not. He was a teenage boy, so he did things from time to time without thinking them all the way through. He was late for everything. His posture was bad and his feet smelled. He was a terrible driver; these were all accusations Lucy herself would level. But sexist? No.

"Principal Neal wants to know how fast you can get here."

"What happened?" Lucy said.

"I can't say anything more," she whispered, "but Jack is in serious trouble."

"Shit," Lucy said, glancing over at Bryn, who was poking at her salad suspiciously, and Harper, who was looking around the restaurant, taking in its southern decor with bemusement. "I'll be right there."

Lucy walked back to the table and apologized profusely to her bosses. They stared at her blankly when she explained that she absolutely had to leave.

"*Now?*" Bryn said.

"I'm so sorry," Lucy said. "There's some kind of emergency—"

"Rotten timing," Harper said, putting her fork down. "We have so much to go over."

"Could we meet later today?" Lucy said, stuffing her notebook in her tote bag. "Like in an hour or so? I could come to your hotel?"

"We're flying back this afternoon," Harper said.

"But do what you have to," said Bryn. "Family comes first."

Lucy thanked them, but she was pretty sure neither one of them really believed that.

⊶

She picked up her minivan from the valet and broke the speed limit as she took the tollway from downtown to her kids' school. On the way there, she called her mother, who picked up on the first ring.

"Aren't you supposed to be in a meeting?"

"I had to leave," said Lucy. "I'm heading to the school."

"Uh-oh," Irene said. "Who got sick?"

"No one. Jack's in some kind of trouble." She remembered what Donna said. "Serious trouble."

"What did he do?"

"I don't know yet. Probably nothing," Lucy said. She could hear her mom's manicured nails tapping on her keyboard. And then the clicking stopped.

"Jack's a smart kid," she said, "but his frontal lobe has a ways to go."

"Donna said he did something . . . sexist."

"Sexist? Jack? I don't think so."

"Yeah," Lucy said, "me neither."

"But you should probably call Mason anyway."

Lucy swerved to dodge a busted tire in the middle of her lane and then swerved back to avoid a pickup truck on her left; the driver honked and shot her the finger.

"Hello?"

"I'm not going to bother him," Lucy said. "Mason is on Mars."

"Mason is in New Mexico."

"Potato, po-tah-to," Lucy said.

"It's a theater set. Get someone to holler over the chain-link fence."

"It's not theater; it's a *simulation*."

"Potato, po-tah-to," her mother said.

"Please don't belittle NASA," Lucy said, "or the biosphere or Mason. I'll call you when I know something. I'm almost there."

"Jack's a good boy," her mom said. "He probably pulled a senior prank. Something dumb but harmless."

"Yeah," Lucy said. "I bet you're right."

"Wait," Irene said, "how did it go with Happy and Brie?"

"Harper and Bryn. I got the client," said Lucy.

"Good for you, I knew you would. And what about your in-laws? Is their flight on time?"

"They land at six, and Henry gets in from Chicago at six fifteen."

"Thank God he's not bringing the crew. His children are hellions."

"The reservation's at seven thirty."

"We'll meet you there," her mom said, "unless you want Zoe and Alice to ride with us."

"Yes, definitely."

What Lucy didn't know as she was driving to the school that afternoon was that nothing was definite. The story of what Jack had done—or what people thought he'd done—was already sloshing out into the world, a toxic glob taking on a life of its own, sprouting hairy legs and developing bad breath, growing monstrous. No matter how fast Lucy drove or what she did or didn't do when she arrived at the school, there was no motherly act that could contain the fallout, and everything she knew to be set in stone was already falling to pieces.

She got off the tollway and drove by the Preston Royal shopping center, turning into the campus. She passed impossibly green athletic fields and the state-of-the-art glass and steel science pavilion, parking as close to the columned entrance as she could get. It was ninety-seven degrees that afternoon, and yet she grabbed her cardigan from the back seat, anticipating the frigid air-conditioning in the school.

A cluster of seniors in their blue and white plaid uniforms eyed her as she passed them.

"Hi, Madison, Becca, Allie," Lucy said. "Congratulations."

None of them answered. Not a single "Thank you" as she walked by. She'd known these girls since they were in elementary school, not that they were friends with Jack exactly, not that they'd ever come over. But the class was, on some level, tight-knit. Lucy could not imagine what had happened to account for such rudeness.

Through the atrium—filled with balloons and a giant banner that said *Hooray, Graduates!*—Lucy arrived at the glassed-in, navy-carpeted administrative suite. Donna, the normally cheerful school secretary, nodded at her curtly, coral lips in a tight, straight line, and pointed her sharpened number-two pencil at the corner.

There was Jack, looking ashen, hunched over his closed laptop, the top of which was covered in stickers: *Github Rules. Dogs believe they are human—Cats believe they are God. Let's Go Solar.* And *Lefties are the besties.* Jack was right-handed, so that last one had to be a nod to his twin sisters. Or a sticker ambush committed by one of them.

"What is going on?" Lucy said, sitting down in the chair beside him.

"It's not what it sounds like," he said. He was jiggling his foot at top speed.

"What does it sound like?" she asked. "And where are the others?"

"They were sent home," he said, his eyes on the floor. "They might get suspended."

Lucy could feel her heartbeat quicken. "Are *you* getting suspended?"

"Probably."

"But why?" she said. "And how can anyone be suspended? Y'all're graduating tomorrow."

"It was a stupid . . . thing," Jack said. "I thought the others would have cleared it up by now."

"Look at me, Jack," Lucy said, her exasperation and panic growing. "How stupid? What did you do?"

"Really stupid," he said, glancing over at her, looking more like a scared ten-year-old boy than a young man heading to college. "But I can explain."

She hoped so. She hoped he could fix whatever this was the way he could remove a bug from glitchy code or stop a fight between his sisters. She put on her sweater, a bit of armor for what was coming, and said, "Tell me everything I need to know."

Before he could answer, the door to the principal's office opened, and Janice Burton, queen of the senior class moms and Lucy's neighbor from two streets over, walked out with her daughter, Cynthia. Lucy was relieved to see an ally; the Burtons had known Jack since he was a toddler. But on spotting Lucy and Jack in the corner of the room, Janice wrapped her arm around Cynthia as if to shelter her from some encroaching danger, hurricane winds or a pack of coyotes. "Shame on you," Janice hissed as they walked by.

"Excuse me?" Lucy said. "Shame on . . . ? Don't we get to explain?"

But what, Lucy wondered, were they explaining? Janice and Cynthia were already out the door, marching down the school corridor, when the principal—former Texas Tech running back Kevin Neal—hulked out of the office. Kevin's hairline was damp with sweat. His shirtsleeves were rolled up to reveal muscular forearms and a heavy watch that looked like it was rated for deep-sea exploration, even though they were three hundred miles from the Gulf of Mexico. Lucy put a hand on Jack's shoulder, hoping that whatever he had to say in the next few minutes would fix what was going off the rails here and that Kevin would calm himself down before he had a heart attack, which would not be his first. Jack might be disorganized and socially clumsy, but the fact remained, he was a dream student, especially in the eyes of a principal. He was a Rockwell lifer, he was not a troublemaker, and he had an MIT acceptance for the fall, a win that the school administration had not only celebrated but happily touted as their own in a recent newsletter.

Kevin exchanged a grim look with Donna before turning to them. Lucy stood, and as Jack got up, he stepped back to let her go in first, whether out of gallantry or fear, she could not say. She looked at the open door and then at her good-natured, earnest son, and she felt an impulse to grab on to anything fixed around her, anything known. *Here we go*, she thought.

She reached out and took hold of Jack's arm.

BERLIN

On the rooftop deck of the Schultz Foundation offices, with its view of the verdigris cupolas of the Berliner Dom, Greta moved through reception, chatting with guests and reveling in her newfound milieu. That these people had invited her, that they even knew who she was, was in itself a kind of fantasy fulfilled.

The events that day—a culmination of a full year of high-stakes decisions and one especially thrilling purchase—had started with the signing of documents at the auction house. There was the unveiling of the seven paintings for a select audience at the National Gallery, followed by a private lunch with members of the Schultz family. After a flurry of interviews with various media outlets in the early afternoon, the family and their close friends had gathered at the foundation offices. Greta was thanked for her calm, steady guidance. She was complimented for her expertise and aesthetic sensibilities. She wanted to hold on to the day forever.

After the last speech had been delivered and the final trays of wine and *Häppchen* had been passed, she said her goodbyes, starting with the family's patriarch, Sebastian Schultz. He shook her hand, smiling more warmly than he ever had before. One of his matronly daughters, always in florals and pearls, opened her arms for a stiff hug and handed her a bottle of Taittinger in a gift box.

And then Sebastian's granddaughter Vanessa, the family member who had shown the most interest in the art itself, the woman who had made this all happen, stopped her at the door.

"*Ich habe einen Vorschlag,*" Vanessa said. "If you'll take me on, I want to be your next client. Only me this time around, so no family quarrels. And unlike my grandfather, I say *Alte Meister* be damned! I want contemporary art."

Greta's pulse quickened at the idea of starting a project. She'd quit her job at an auction house to work for the Schultz family and needed new clients now that their collection was complete.

"Of course my budget is a lot lower," Vanessa went on, "but I think we could have some fun. Can we meet sometime next week?"

"I'd love to, but I'm leaving for New York Sunday," Greta said, hoping that the distance between them wouldn't put off her potential new client.

"Lucky," she said. "When are you back?"

"In a year," said Greta, and she loved the sound of it. "My husband's taking a sabbatical. But there's no reason we can't—"

"*Perfekt,*" Vanessa said, waving her hand as though an ocean between them posed no obstacle. "Let's catch up with each other in the fall. Meanwhile, you can keep me in the loop with all the galleries there."

Apparently, whenever Vanessa appeared, doors opened.

"In that case, yes," Greta said, "I'd love to work with you."

Vanessa smiled with an air of wealth and possibility. "You and I," she said with a spirited nod, "are going to shake things up."

⊶

It was still light out when Greta's taxi dropped her in front of her building in Charlottenburg. She climbed the stairs to the top floor and turned the key, stepping out of her high heels in the entry. The apartment was quiet, making her miss the days when she would have been greeted on a Friday night with the sounds of pop music and the high-pitched voices of Emmi and her friends. She walked down the hall to find her husband in their bedroom, packing a large suitcase. He'd closed the curtains, and the bedroom felt like a cave.

"Well, *hallo*," Otto said as she walked in. "How went it today? All was okay?"

From the moment Otto's New York sabbatical had been approved, he'd insisted on speaking only English at home. Greta was happy to oblige because—while she spoke English almost as well as she spoke German, thanks to her American mother and years of summer camp in Maine—Otto needed the practice.

"The Schultz family was very happy," she said.

"I hope they are, given how much euros they have spent." He patted her shoulder affectionately. "You look changed."

"They had a hairstylist and makeup artist at the television station," she said.

Otto turned his attention back to his suitcase. "I can't find my blue and white sleep-suit," he said.

It was mostly Otto's vocabulary that needed work; he had a habit of relying on direct translation, which often failed. Other times he picked the wrong word out of thin air.

"In the laundry," she said. "I'll have it all done tomorrow."

"*Schau mal,*" he said, indicating his mostly full suitcase, "a good start, yes? I have not so much to do before we are leaving."

Greta had already finished packing; her two suitcases were in the entry, ready to go.

"I thought you were having dinner tonight with one of your symposium speakers," she said.

Otto checked his watch. "Yes, and he is so impressive," he said. "He made a very good lecture today."

"And your talk?"

"Tomorrow morning," he said. "I wish I had time to practice with you. My slides are, mmm, *gut genug*, but some of the English is *schwer*. I will never be as . . . liquid as you."

"Fluent. And you'll be fine," she said, relieved not to be subjected to an hour-long presentation on the removal of bunions, at least not while she was still buzzing with energy from the day's events.

"I must make myself ready for dinner," he said, and went into the bathroom.

Greta talked to him through the closed door. "I called Emmi this morning," she said. Their nineteen-year-old was at the university in Freiburg—as far away from Berlin as she could have gone. But this summer she would be living with them in New York. Greta was so happy to know they would have coffee together every morning before Emmi's internship and go to concerts and plays on the weekends. "She says the firm is somewhere in midtown on the East Side—Weiss, Watkins, and something or other. It's not the easiest commute, but she'll manage."

Greta kept thinking they must be overlooking some detail for the trip, but it seemed they were really ready to go. They had passports, plane tickets to Newark, and a furnished two-bedroom faculty apartment waiting for them on Riverside Drive. While Emmi and Otto were at work, Greta would get fully versed on the American contemporary art scene, visiting galleries and meeting artists. A former colleague, now working at Sotheby's, had already invited her to the opening party for a sculptor who was having a solo exhibition at an art space in Brooklyn.

She straightened a frame on the wall that held a small woodcut by Kirchner that she'd found in Prenzlauer Berg. "Otto," she said brightly, over the sound of running water, "the Schultz granddaughter wants to hire me to build her art collection." She could hear Otto gargling. "Vanessa is a force. She has such confidence." Confidence and very expensive-looking jewelry. Greta ran her hand over her hair, still stiff with hair spray from the photo shoot where she'd smiled alongside Sebastian Schultz and the museum director in front of *Girl with a Red Turban*, a Vermeer that had been presumed forever lost and that Greta had managed to acquire. "She's only in her early thirties," she said, "but she has great instincts, and she's very"—Greta paused, trying to find the right descriptor for her new client—"bold."

From inside the bathroom, Otto made a guttural yelp, half bark, half cry. Greta's first thought was that he'd fallen.

"Otto?" She knocked on the door. "What happened?"

He didn't answer.

"Are you okay?" she called out as the sound of running water stopped.

He pulled open the door, his eyes wide. He was holding a washcloth in one hand, his phone in the other. "He can't do this." He dropped the washcloth on the floor and walked off, staring at his phone.

"Who can't do . . . what?"

"My new boss—the *Arschloch*—he halted my sabbatical funding."

"Halted?" Greta felt the joy of the day evaporate in an instant. "That's not possible. We're about to—"

"'*Aufgrund von Budgetkürzungen,*' blah blah blah . . ." Otto said, scrolling through the message. "He says I can't go."

"No, but . . ." Greta's face flushed in anger. "It's too late—"

"He's *sorry* for any problem this might cause." Otto dropped down on the foot of the bed and put his head in his hands. "I thought I would get *eine Pause* from the politics of my work, and have more nicer colleagues at last."

"Otto," Greta said, overcome by a wave of disappointment for them both.

Otto stomped his foot on the floor. "Thirty years at the same institution, and I'm all the time disrespected."

She had heard this refrain many times of late and had not wanted to believe it was true, but maybe Otto had seen the situation accurately.

"They have been looking for a way to push me down for months," he went on, "and Moritz the Monster and the new *Arschloch* department chair have finally done it. *Wie peinlich!*" he said.

"No, Otto," said Greta, but it *was* embarrassing; they'd told everyone their plans. She put a hand on his shoulder to steady herself.

One of them needed to keep calm. "*Schatz?*" she said. "As terrible as this is, I don't think we can solve this crisis right now."

"I will write a letter of protest—"

"Yes, but what about your dinner?"

"Dinner?"

"Your dinner with the symposium speaker?"

Otto looked at her, panicked. "*Scheiße.*" He jumped up. "What time is it? *Oh Gott, Oh Gott,* I have to go."

"Try to breathe," said Greta, following Otto to the front door.

He put on his raincoat. "I feel like I'm being demolished."

Diminished? she thought. But that was almost worse.

Sliding his phone in his pocket, Otto stepped into his loafers, adjusting the arch inserts. "At least the man I'm taking for dinner is *ein guter Typ*. Friendly and . . . *großzügig?*"

"Generous," Greta said.

"Yes, *he* is the kind of colleague I wish to have."

Greta patted his back. "Too bad you can't join his lab," she said sympathetically.

Otto gave her a nod and rushed out.

Greta closed the door and made tight fists with her hands, reeling from the dramatic shift in mood. It couldn't be possible that New York was being stolen away from them, after all the planning, all the anticipation.

And she had no one to share in what had been—up until now—a most remarkable day, a day that had made news not just in Berlin, but across Europe. She poured herself a glass of wine and took it out onto the balcony, where she saw Otto disappear into a cab and speed away. Across the street, a young couple kissed under the light of a doorway.

A breeze caused Greta's silk skirt to flutter against her knees, and she heard music coming from her American neighbor's apartment below. The base was thumping.

She leaned over the stone balustrade, and there was Adam, sitting on his own balcony. He looked up and smiled at her.

"Hey, you," he said, getting to his feet. "How did it go today?"

Now that her night had taken an epically unpleasant turn, Greta found herself at a loss for words. "It was . . . fine," she said.

"*Fine?* No need to be humble. You know, you were in the *New York Times International Edition* today: Under the careful guidance of Greta von Bosse, the Schultz Collection is a national treasure that . . . totally kicks ass, I'm paraphrasing. I'd demand my personal tour if you weren't leaving," he said. "New York ho!"

For a split second, she thought he was calling her a ho. "Yes, westward ho," she said.

She couldn't bear to talk about Otto's lost sabbatical, so she held up her phone, miming an incoming call, and ducked back inside. She felt completely unmoored and tried to remember the pride and pleasure of the past weeks as the Schultz family, museum directors, and the press acknowledged her for having formed a collection of European masterpieces—all portraits of women, from every walk of life, from the lowly to the sublime. The sixteenth- to nineteenth-century paintings, depicting femininity in every form, were now on display in a single room bearing the Schultz name, and she had done her part to create that.

She would not let the change of plans derail her. She looked around her beloved apartment. She'd recently had the old herringbone floors restored to a beautiful finish. The apartment had all its original fixtures, the hardware on the doors, the medallions on the ceilings. They'd lived here for fifteen years, and she had everything the way she liked it. Leaving this apartment to go to New York had seemed worth it; she had hoped that she and Otto would find a new kind of joy there, on their own and, more important, with each other.

And that's when the worst part of Otto's news dawned on her: Emmi! Greta was losing the gift of a summer with her daughter living under her roof.

Madison	$1,278.26
Nell	$6.09
Katie	$3,247.90
Cynthia	$337,221.20
Lilly	$17,620.37
Allie	$743.99
Maggie	$347.52
Becca	$73,247.00
Grace	$24,872.21

DALLAS

Lucy's phone pinged to announce that today was graduation at the Rockwell School. But Jack would not be graduating, and none of the Holt family festivities surrounding the event were happening. Lucy would not tap her foot along to "Pomp and Circumstance" as the students marched in procession. There would not be a big lunch at Mesero, nor would they gather in the evening at her house for a celebration with Jack's friends and their families, even though Big D Party Rental had already dropped off linens and set up six round tables and fifty folding chairs in the backyard. It was impossible to believe that it was all canceled, including MIT in the fall.

Jack had been so close, and now everything was grievously and hideously bungled. Lucy punched a fist into the mattress.

She hadn't slept. The scene in the principal's office had replayed over and over in her head while she tried to think of a way out of this mess. She had a house full of guests in town for graduation—Mason's divorced parents, along with his brother, Henry—and sometime around midnight, she was sure she'd heard something, raised voices and a thumping on the front door. When she'd gotten up to look out the window, there was no one there. Her heart was pounding even now as she stared at the ceiling of her bedroom, watching the blades of the overhead fan spin, feeling crushed. The evening before, Jack—all chin stubble and leg hair, taller than she by six inches—had cried on her shoulder for the first time since he was a little kid. And all she could do was pat his back and tell him that somehow—although she had no peg on which to hang this promise—things were going to work out.

At least his friends would rally around him. They were superstars. A band of misfits, sure, unpopular by whatever metric high schoolers use to calculate popularity. But they were a nice group. Smart, generous; they had one another's back. Rosie was an aspiring environmentalist. Drew, who had arrived at Rockwell in second grade, was shy, painfully so. He and Jack volunteered every Wednesday afternoon, socializing animals at a local shelter, which is how the Holts had ended up with a pit bull, a something-doodle, a guinea pig named Piglet, and three still-unnamed tabby cats, one of whom was downright aggressive, though no one could tell them apart. Sam was the last to join Rockwell and was the most outgoing of their group, recently wowing them all as Howie the milkman in the spring production of *Our Town*.

And then there was Jack: fan of bad puns and Torchy's Tacos, member of a climbing gym, highly sensitive, and seriously into math.

All nice kids. None of them perfect. Only one of them expelled.

⚷

Lucy climbed out of her side of the bed, and the dogs, Bunny and Tank, followed her out of the room as she went to wake the twins. Instead of decorating graduation cupcakes for their big brother that morning, the girls were going to Saturday swim practice. They were groggier than usual as they ate their cereal. But then came the usual morning chaos, conducted in hushed tones rather than at normal volume. The girls ran around in pajamas, searching for goggles and dry pool towels, and then went to brush their teeth.

"Is my hair green in the back?" Zoe said, twisting to see for herself in the bathroom mirror.

"Yes," said Alice.

"No," said Lucy, sniffing the chlorine that emanated from her daughter's head. "Your hair's fine. But let's put it in a ponytail."

"A green ponytail," said Alice snidely.

Lucy hustled them into the hallway, just as Uncle Henry came out of the guest room in a bathrobe, his hair standing up on end the same way Mason's did. He put out a hand and high-fived the girls on their way downstairs.

"You're up early," Lucy said quietly. The last thing she wanted was to wake Jack or Mason's parents, given how late they'd all been up. "Did you sleep okay?"

"Until the sunlight nearly blinded me," he said, pointing a thumb over his shoulder. "Adding that huge east-facing window was a bad move." Henry had designed the house, and people either loved the architecture or despised it, as her mother did. "I had a nightmare that the doors were all the wrong sizes and were falling out of their frames. It was like that dream where your teeth fall out."

"It wasn't a dream," Lucy said, patting Tank, who was leaning heavily against her leg. "The dogs heard it too and went completely bonkers."

"Or we're all experiencing a collective anxiety," Henry said, shaking his head. "Poor Jack."

"Ellen took the news pretty well," Lucy said.

"As you know, my mother is a pathological optimist. But she'll be sad if it turns out that Jack isn't moving to Cambridge."

For Lucy, the very words "Jack isn't moving to Cambridge" were like a punch to the gut.

"I called home last night," Henry said, "and tried to tell the gang what happened, but I got confused about the math part."

Of course Henry would tell his wife and kids, but Lucy hated to know the story was spreading and probably mutating, all while Mason knew nothing about what had happened. She dropped her voice to a whisper. "Jack wrote a complicated formula to calculate how much the most popular girls in his class would have to be paid to invite him to their graduation parties. Someone found the list and claimed he was putting prices on them."

"Too smart for his own good," Henry said, putting a hand on her shoulder, "like father, like son. I'm sorry Mason isn't here."

Lucy was too. Very sorry.

"My brother picked a hell of a time to go to New Mexico."

"Mason is on Mars," she said.

Henry shrugged. "Whatever you say."

He returned to his room, and Lucy went downstairs, where she found the girls in the kitchen with her father. He'd let himself in the back door and was crouched over, patting Bunny on the rump. When he straightened up, he stepped on a plush dog toy that let out an absurd squeak under his sneakers. Alice was getting Go-Gurts from the fridge to take along in the car. Even the twins were trying to act as though everything were perfectly normal when absolutely nothing was.

When she saw that the girls still hadn't put on their bathing suits, Lucy sent them back upstairs to change, hoping Alice could keep Zoe on task.

"How's he doing?" Rex said, putting a hand on the counter next to the plastic-wrapped tablecloths and napkins she'd rented for the party.

"Oh, Dad," said Lucy. She sat down on a barstool, feeling the fatigue in her legs. "I'm freaking out. Drew's mom heard the Burtons might try to press charges. There's talk about a restraining order—"

"The Burtons, our *neighbors*?" her dad said, his face flushed. "They're demonizing a boy over a piece of paper. Why can't they let him explain the math and apologize?"

"It was easier to kick him out," Lucy said, "than to make sense of datasets."

"You want me to go over to the Burtons'," Rex said, "and give them a talking-to?"

Lucy was also tempted to try to talk to Janice, mother to mother, but she'd been instructed by the principal not to make contact. "No, you can't," Lucy said firmly, "and neither can I without making things worse."

"I don't see how things can get any worse," Rex said.

He had a point. "Thank you for taking the girls this morning," she said. "Who knows what the swim team parents have heard." She got up to make a pot of coffee.

"I meant to congratulate you," her dad said.

She turned back to him and coughed out a laugh. "What for?"

"Your mom said you got that client, for the Danish design you pitched."

Lucy had forgotten all about Laurel Hotels. The lunch at Haywire seemed like ten years ago. "Right," she said. "It isn't so much Danish as Scandinavian in a more general way."

"Whatever you want to call it," her dad said. "It wasn't easy to go against your bosses and their brothel theme—"

"Boudoir—"

"—but your good taste prevailed."

All the more reason Lucy felt tremendous pressure to deliver. She wanted not only her bosses but the whole team to believe in her vision.

She was washing out the coffeepot when Alice ran in, dressed in her swimsuit and jelly sandals. She grabbed on to Rex's leg and yelled "safe" so Zoe couldn't tag her. But Zoe paid no attention; she was playing a different game altogether. She came spinning into the room wearing Jack's cap and gown, her stuffed rabbit, Fred, under her arm. Behind her one of the cats was chasing the black fabric as it dragged across the kitchen floor, his claws tearing the hem into ribbons.

⚬⊶

After they left, Lucy hid the cap and gown on a shelf in her closet. She checked the time; the ceremony would be starting in three hours. She was still—for no good reason—holding out hope that the principal would call and tell her he'd changed his mind, that Jack was off the hook. She kept her ringer on, just in case.

Alone in her bedroom, she sat cross-legged on her bed and called NASA. Sandra picked up right away. "Good morning, Lucy. I guess congratulations are in order."

"Unfortunately not," Lucy said. "We've had a crisis here."

"Oh, I'm so sorry to hear that," Sandra said, as sweet as could be.

"I need to talk to Mason."

There was a long pause. "Well, bless your heart," Sandra said, with an uncomfortable laugh. "You know that's not going to happen."

"No, seriously," Lucy said, shifting to make room for the dogs, who joined her on the bed. "There's a problem with Jack, as in 'Houston, we have a problem.' I need Mason to call me," she said.

Sandra cleared her throat. "He can't *call* you. Mason is on Mars."

"Mason is in New Mexico," Lucy said.

"Lucy," Sandra said, scolding, "this is a commitment. And you're asking to break sequestration in week three? This doesn't speak well for your ability to handle the stress of a partner in space."

"Mason is not *in* space and he's never going to space, so just tell him that Jack's in big trouble, okay? Do whatever you have to do. But tell him I need him. *We* need him." The dogs were watching her, cocking their heads at the intensity of her voice.

"Is this a health-related matter?" Sandra said. "Like, is your son *physically* okay?"

"Would that make a difference?"

"Not necessarily," she said.

"Seriously, Sandra?" Lucy said. "This is stupid. Just give Mason a phone."

"There's currently a glitch in the Mars Reconnaissance Orbiter UHF antenna. And unfortunately, Mason and the crew cannot be reached at this time."

"*Please?*" Lucy said, indignant that Sandra would be so stubborn. "Make an exception? Just this once?"

"You signed up for this mission too," Sandra said, as if Lucy were a child, "and you were told very clearly that communication blackouts would be an anticipated occurrence."

"How long," Lucy said, trying to keep her cool, "will this particular blackout be in effect?"

"I can't answer that," Sandra said. "But I can tell you that communication with Earth at this time would destroy the integrity of the entire project."

"Wow. This is so not okay. And Mason's going to be furious when he finds out," Lucy snapped, and she hung up. Bunny and Tank were still watching her, waiting. "Mars, my *ass*," she said.

The doorbell rang, and the dogs started barking. Lucy let them out in the backyard and went to the door, worried there might be an angry mob. Instead, through the window she saw a stranger, a woman in cowboy boots and a long, tiered denim skirt. She opened the door, taking in the smell of her neighborhood in early summer, cut grass and magnolia blossoms.

"Hi, I'm Sylvie," the woman said. "I just bought the house next door to you."

"Oh, hi," Lucy said. "Welcome." She'd seen the "For Sale" sign go up and the "For Sale" sign come down, all within a matter of hours and had been impressed by whoever made such a big decision in such a hurry. Now she knew. "I'm Lucy," she said, realizing she hadn't brushed her teeth or her hair yet. The timing for an introduction to her new neighbor could not have been worse.

"Real nice to meet you," Sylvie said, putting out her hand. She had turquoise bracelets on her wrist and pretty, silver rings. "Sorry to come by so early. I'll be moving down from Plano in a couple of weeks, and I just wanted to say a quick hello. I'm planning on having a few people over for drinks to welcome myself to the neighborhood, once I get here and unearth the wineglasses. No offense to the husbands," she added, "but I thought it might be nice to meet the ladies around here first."

It occurred to Lucy that this woman had to be the only person in a ten-mile radius who had not heard about her son and the infamous list he'd made. "My husband's out of town anyway," she said, "on a work thing. He'll be gone awhile."

Sylvie nodded sympathetically. "My ex traveled all the time," she said.

"Come on in," Lucy said.

"Only for a second. We don't want your AC to escape." Sylvie did a graceful little leap over the doormat and then looked around the entry.

"I just love y'all's house," she said as Lucy closed the door behind her. "So unusual. I hope it's okay if I ask for a few recommendations, like who cuts your grass and cleans your pool. This is my first time living alone, not that my ex was much help around the house, but I'm sure as hell not climbing a ladder to clean my own gutters." Sylvie laughed, though Lucy thought she detected a little sadness.

From the kitchen she could hear Mason's mother and her own talking in the kitchen and realized she'd never turned on the pot of coffee.

"I've always found meeting people easy, through school and whatnot," Sylvie was saying, "but my kids are grown and flown. I've got a daughter in her last year of business school at Oklahoma State and a married son living in Atlanta. So I'm pretty much a one-woman show now."

Lucy looked down at her pajamas. "Sorry about my appearance," she said. "Today's a little hectic. I've got relatives in town, busy eight-year-old twins, and a son who's"—Lucy paused and glanced up the stairs—"considering a gap year," she said.

"I remember what that's like," said Sylvie, nodding. "Anyway, I just wanted to say hi. I'll drop off an invite for my party after I move."

"Thank you," Lucy said. But she doubted she would be going to Sylvie's party, or to any party, or to anywhere else around town, including Starbucks or the Tom Thumb. What the hell was she going to do?

"I'm hoping this is as nice a neighborhood as everyone says, but I admit," Sylvie said, glancing behind her at the front door, "I'm having my doubts this morning."

"Sorry?" Lucy said.

"Oh, I figured you knew. I hate to be the one to tell you this," Sylvie said tentatively, "but somebody egged your front door."

Lucy remembered the thumping she'd heard the night before and clenched her teeth.

She opened the door and stepped outside—eggshells and slime under her bare feet—and looked at the outside of the door. "Well, how about that," said Lucy. "I think—this must be one of those end-of-school pranks." There had to be a dozen eggs smashed against the wood and puddled up on the doormat. Lucy felt a stinging behind her eyes. "Kids," she said, putting her hands out in a cartoonish shrug.

"That's going to be a real pain to clean," Sylvie said, carefully hopping back over the doormat. "You need a hand?"

"No thank you," Lucy said, "I can manage. But thanks for telling me."

"Sure. I guess you know already about the other . . . prank?"

"The other . . . ?"

"Your car?" Sylvie said, and pointed toward the driveway.

Lucy stepped away from the broken eggs and saw Jack's Prius sitting off-kilter, three of its tires slashed.

As bad as she'd thought the situation was, it was far, far worse.

To: Otto von Bosse
From: Troy Judson

Hi there, Otto,

    Thanks so much for inviting me to the symposium. And thank you for dinner last night! I really enjoyed the chance to talk about robotic surgical solutions for metatarsal tumors and other exciting developments in our world of feet. And let me say again, I was real sorry to hear about your sabbatical falling through like that. But I'm hoping your department head's bad decision will be our gain! I called the dean of my university, and we'd love to host you in Dallas. As I said before, the research you do has inspired my own, and I think there could be a real benefit to a collaboration. Let's do this!

    Down to brass tacks: We can provide you with lab and office space, a postdoc to run studies, and all the equipment you could need. Since you've been denied a sabbatical salary by your institution, we can finagle the budget to kick in some kind of stipend. We don't have any housing to offer, but might I suggest you consider a house swap? I know people who swear by them. Could be a win-win! I'm attaching a map, indicating the neighborhoods you may want to consider.

    It would be an honor to host you in our department! How soon can you come?

Best,
Troy Judson, MD
UT Southwestern Medical Center

Girl with a Red Turban	€60,000,000
Bathing Woman	€27,000,000
Prostitute in Repose	€4,000,000
A Lady Reading	€3,300,000
Dancer in Yellow	€876,000
Madonna del Parto	€750,000
Noblewoman with Parakeet	€650,000

BERLIN

Otto—who wore pressed gingham shirts to work, who listened to Beethoven in the bathtub, who read widely and ate narrowly, who loved soccer with its yellow cards and red cards—was, like many Germans, a stickler for rules. And yet he'd broken one of the most important marital ones. Greta was gobsmacked.

She met him at the door when he got home. "How could you agree to something like this without discussing it with me first?" she said.

"I apologize. You are correct," Otto said as he stood on the doormat, rain dripping off his umbrella. A brightness in his eyes showed he wasn't all that sorry. "But it happened so fast. And I thought we did talk about it, *zufällig*. When I was leaving for dinner last night, you said I should be part of a lab that has more friendlier people."

Greta crossed her arms as Otto came into the entry, taking off his wet coat and shoes. As he was closing the door, she could hear Adam's laughter in the stairwell below them.

"The playboy," said Otto, "is entertaining a group of people who look like . . . *Diebe*."

"They're not thieves," said Greta. "They're more likely rock musicians from his studio."

"Well, I don't like him," Otto said. "I have never liked that man." He slipped his feet into his slippers.

"Please, Otto," she said impatiently, "explain yourself."

"Can I eat something first? It's been a long day."

They went to the dining room. Greta was meeting her sister for dinner later, so she had *kaltes Abendbrot* arranged on the table for Otto. There was a basket of bread and a board with cheeses, ham, tomatoes, and olives. She'd gone shopping that morning, thinking they were staying in Berlin and she might as well fill the fridge back up again. She'd also unpacked her clothes and taken her empty suitcases back down to the *Keller*. And then Otto had called to tell her his big news. Her outrage was causing her entire body to stiffen and her head to ache.

"I thought you'd be happy," Otto said, sitting in his usual seat at the dining table and placing his linen napkin across his lap. "You wanted to leave Berlin, to have an adventure, *ja?*"

She poured herself a glass of wine and handed him the bottle. "Yes, but not just *any* adventure."

"Please, Greta," he said. "My institute was wishing to . . . spool me into the sewer—"

"That's not really—"

"But I found a solution. I am crawling myself back out of the toilet. I am being welcomed, most kindly, by this Texan doctor who saved me from looking foolish to my colleagues. Oh, the *Arschloch*'s face when I told him about the offer! It was after the symposium was *vorbei*, and—"

"I'm sure that was very satisfying, Otto. But this is all too fast. You're giving me whiplash."

"Whiplash?" he said, reaching for the breadbasket. "What is whiplash?"

She was so annoyed with him then, she could feel her face turning red. In her desperation, she played the death card. "I'm already dealing with the loss of my father and my mother's decision to sell my childhood home. And now you're throwing a completely unexpected change at me. It's too much."

"Lillian is doing the right thing," Otto said, patting her hand before selecting a roll that he began to slice open. "Why would she need such a large house anymore?"

Greta couldn't argue with that. "Why Texas?" she said.

"Dr. Judson is offering everything I need to do my research."

He pronounced Judson *Yudson*. Greta did not correct him.

"There's only *ein kleines Problem*," he said.

There was a gust of wind outside, and rain spattered against the windows. Greta got up to close the transom above the balcony door, seeing a lot more than one little problem. She was struggling to reconceive the next twelve months of their life, starting with the fact that she wouldn't be with Emmi this summer. She'd never been to Texas, and it was not on any bucket list she'd ever made. And she doubted Vanessa Schultz would have the same enthusiasm to work with her from Dallas.

She sat back down and held her hands together on the table. "And the one little problem, as you see it, is what?"

"This hospital in Dallas can only pay part of my salary," he said. "*Ein Stipendium.*"

Greta closed her eyes and tried to breathe steadily. "Otto," she said, "I don't have a job anymore. How much is the stipend?"

"I don't know yet, but probably not much." He took his fork and stabbed a piece of prosciutto. "But maybe we could be . . . How do you say *sparsam*?"

"Frugal," said Greta, her voice flat. She took a big sip of wine.

"Yes, like my grandmother after the war. We have saved some money," said Otto. "And Dr. Judson had a wonderful suggestion—*sehr interessant*. He said it is *win-win* if we make a 'house swap,' because then we are not paying to live there. A good idea, *oder*?"

"A house swap?" Aghast, Greta sat back in her chair, looking around the room, her eyes settling on the expressionist still life painting she'd hung beside the curtains. "And have strangers living in our apartment? Absolutely not."

"Why are you so quick to say no? A stranger is not always a bad person. What about the last stranger you met? Herr Schultz's granddaughter? That was also win-win."

He was right about that; a year ago, Greta had stopped for a cup of coffee at the Gendarmenmarkt and sat next to a woman who asked for the sugar packets from her table. Greta had noticed, under the young woman's left elbow, the catalog from the Museum Barberini in Potsdam that featured the Impressionist collection of the billionaire philanthropist Hasso Plattner. After passing the sugar, Greta mentioned a Morisot painting she'd seen there, and they began a conversation that had changed everything. Vanessa Schultz had simply appeared in her life that day, and it felt like she'd cast a spell over her, one that made people warm to her and trust her.

But that did not mean Greta wanted some random stranger living in her house, using her Fissler pots and pans, sleeping in her bed. Soaking in her bathtub! She took a sip from her Lobmeyr glass, imagining someone else drinking out of it. She hated the idea.

"You aren't eating," Otto said, his fork in hand.

"I'm going out with Bettina. And anyway, I'm not hungry," she said, sorry for how sulky she sounded.

"I wish you could keep your mind open. If we could make this work," said Otto, "I am being so happy. Dr. Judson is brilliant. And his work on soft-tissue masses is the top-notch. This hospital, Southwestern, has six Nobel Prize winners. Six!" He held up five fingers on one hand and his thumb on the other. "When we come back in a year, my colleagues here will respect me."

Greta didn't answer. She knew nothing about Dallas, good or bad. Otto might have a purpose there, but what was she going to do?

"We have already our tickets to Newark," he said, "and I discovered an airline called Spirit that has very cheap prices to Dallas."

"And where do you propose we stay when we get there?"

"There's a Holiday Inn one and a half kilometers from the hospital; we can stay there until we make our house swapping."

The room darkened, and there was a low rumble of thunder. Greta could not help but glower at him.

"We're leaving our beautiful home," she said, refilling her glass, "to stay in a Holiday Inn by a hospital?"

But Otto looked at her then with pitiful hope in his eyes. "*Bitte*, Greta, please, I need this," he said. "I'm so tired of the people here, my colleagues who are always penetrating me in the backside, and the rain, rain, rain. All the time, the rain." He reached over and took her hand. "I know you're disappointed about New York and Emmi. *Ich auch*. But I think we could have a nice time in Texas." He rubbed his thumb over her knuckles. "Maybe enjoy the Wild West together. *Ja*?"

⚯

"The *Wild West*?" Bettina said. "Did he actually call it that?"

"He's romanticizing a horrible situation," said Greta. She and her sister were drinking martinis at Hildegard, sitting at a high table across from the crowded bar. At their feet, Til, Bettina's enormous Bernese mountain dog, named after the film star and heartthrob Til Schweiger, was sleeping soundly despite the noise.

"Well, I think it's kind of adorable," Bettina said, tossing her long hair over her shoulder. "He's got the wrong idea, though; Dallas is very sophisticated." Bettina was turning heads in her skinny jeans and sheer, low-cut top. She looked thirty but was fast approaching forty, a fact she vehemently denied.

Greta stabbed her vodka-soaked olive with a toothpick. "I thought we were going out for dinner," she said. "I need to eat something other than nuts."

Bettina studied Greta over the rim of her almost empty glass. "Years ago," she said, "I secretly thought Otto was too old for you."

"Secretly? You *said* he was too old for me, multiple times," Greta said, "even on our wedding day."

"But maybe I was wrong. He's the one acting young at heart. So spontaneous!—and in the face of a major letdown. I'm kind of impressed with him. Maybe you need to loosen up. It's only a year."

She reached over then and tried to undo the top button on Greta's tailored van Laack shirt.

"Stop," said Greta, brushing her hand away.

"Why are you dressed like Mom on her way to a luncheon in Wannsee? No guys are going to try to pick us up—"

"I don't want guys to—"

"*I* do," said Bettina. "And you're sending the wrong message. Where did you get that heinous shirt anyway?"

"From Mom," said Greta, "in Wannsee. I went to say goodbye to her, and I salvaged it from a pile of clothes she was giving away. She seems almost too happy."

"What are you, the grief police?" Bettina said, resting her chin on her hand. "Is she not mourning sadly enough for you?"

"You aren't supposed to make significant changes in your life for a year after a partner dies," said Greta, "and she's already sold her house with practically everything in it, including"—and she held up her index finger—"Dad's drafting desk, which he promised to *you.*"

Bettina squinted. "I really don't think you should be *more* upset about that than I am. My level of upset should kind of set the bar."

Greta desperately wanted the Bauhaus sconces from the hallway of her childhood home, but she didn't mention it.

Over Bettina's shoulder two men appeared to be having a lovers' quarrel, one holding on to a fistful of the other's shirt.

"The suburbs are a bad place for a single woman," Bettina said, leaning down to check on Til. "And anyway, it's better for us to have Mom in the city."

"I know. I just worry Tobias is having some kind of anesthetizing effect on her. He's the last person I would have chosen to be her helper."

Greta's most vivid memory of Tobias Meyer was when he was ten or so, and his parents invited them to go sailing on the Wannsee. Tobias thought it was a fun joke to fling himself into the lake, forcing his father to shout "*Klar zur wende!*" and turn the boat around to retrieve him. They spent most of that summer afternoon sailing in circles until Tobias's mother became enraged and threatened to tie her son to the mast. Greta's mother had hired that reckless boy—now a grown man—to help sort out their father's clothes and papers, to go through the attic and the basement, and to pack up for her move.

"She says he's a godsend," Bettina said, "which is over-the-top maybe, but at least he's being a help."

"If Tobias's own father doesn't trust him enough to work in the family business, then why should we trust him to work for our widowed mother?"

"As soon as she moves," Bettina said, "she won't need him anymore." She raised a finger to the bartender, ordering another round.

"No, I can't," Greta said. "I've got a flight to hell in the morning."

A young man in a suit was angled away from his finance pals at the bar, making eyes at Bettina; she winked and smiled at him.

"Can you focus on *me* for one night?" Greta said.

"So needy," Bettina said, rolling her eyes.

"I always hoped at some point in my life I'd have the chance to live in Manhattan like you did, and it will probably never happen." Bettina's time in New York had completely erased whatever minimal German accent she'd had, while people often asked Greta where she was from.

"At least Emmi still gets to go," Bettina said.

Greta took the last sip of vodka. "If she can find a place to live."

"She will." Bettina shifted on her barstool, crossing her long legs. "You can live vicariously through her. And as for a house swap, it's not as impossible as you think. There are websites for these things."

"I'm not having a complete stranger live in my home," she said.

"Then post something on Instagram, I'll share it with my friends."

Greta picked up her phone and scrolled through pictures of her apartment, its high ceilings and cozy lighting. "I don't want to," she said.

"It's this or a Holiday Inn on the side of a freeway," said Bettina flatly.

Greta breathed in deeply and opened Instagram. "What do I say?"

Bettina took a cigarette out of her purse. "Something like 'Seeking a house in Dallas beginning ASAP, ideally for one year but flexible.'"

"I thought you quit smoking," Greta said, composing a message. "It's so bad for you."

"*In exchange,*" Bettina said, "*a gorgeous 'altbau' apartment in Berlin's most boring, bougie neighborhood.*"

"Charlottenburg is not boring," Greta said.

"Fine," said Bettina, "*in Berlin's . . . safest neighborhood.*"

Greta wrote *most desirable neighborhood.* "Anything else?"

"*Perfect for anyone evading arrest.*"

Greta typed *Perfect for anyone in need of an escape,* adding three exclamation points at the end.

The bartender brought their new drinks and a dog bowl filled with water. After he walked away with the empty glasses, Greta pushed her martini toward the middle of the table. Bettina slid it back toward her, her eyes still following the handsome man who was mingling as if he owned the place.

"Do you know that guy?" Greta asked.

"And add a picture of your balcony," Bettina said. "Americans get such a hard-on for a good balcony."

Greta reviewed the photos, hating this entire idea. "What if I get squatters? I've heard about people who find these seemingly perfect tenants and then they can never get them out."

"You won't get squatters."

"What if they don't use coasters? What if they wear their shoes inside?"

"So you'll refinish a tabletop and clean the floors," Bettina said, untying the leash from the table leg. "Not the end of the world."

She was wrong about that; it was never a good idea to tamper with the original finish of antiques unless you absolutely had to. Greta took a breath and tapped *Share.*

She put her phone down on the table. "But New York," she said sadly. "Mom has so many stories about growing up there. I wanted to feel more connected to it, more at home."

"New York's not going anywhere," Bettina said. She was on her phone, typing rapidly with her thumbs. "Okay," she said. "I just re-posted. Let the magic begin." Then she stood up and took her leather jacket from the back of her chair.

Til sensed a change and got to his feet as well, his big body knocking against the table leg. Greta patted his head.

"I'm going outside for a quick smoke," Bettina said. "I'll only be a minute."

"You can leave Til with me," said Greta.

"It's okay," Bettina said. "He needs to *pinkel* anyway." She started to follow the good-looking man to the door.

"Bettina," Greta called after her, a knowing lilt to her voice.

"*Sei kein Baby.* I'll be right back."

Greta watched her go and then waited, taking small sips from her drink, getting more and more annoyed the longer she sat there. Her phone pinged with an Instagram notification, and she opened the app to see a message: Hey pretty lady sexy you want sugar daddy pay money?DM me!

Trolls. Greta blocked the account.

The bar was getting louder, and Greta drummed her fingers on the table, turning to the door in search of Bettina. The two men ar-guing at the next table were deep in conversation, their foreheads pressed together. Whether this was an escalation of their feud or a reconciliation was impossible to tell.

A man walked up to her, and Greta prepared to gently rebuff his attention. But he was only asking whether he could take Bettina's barstool.

Again, she got a notification, this time from someone who fol-lowed Bettina: My son and his six friends are looking for a place to hang in Europe while they take time off college. No home to exchange, but interested?

No, Greta was not interested. She reached for her drink and took a bigger sip this time. She folded and refolded her cocktail napkin. She considered leaving, but she had no desire to talk to Otto, to re-pack her bags, or even to sleep. She wondered whether Bettina was coming back at all; it would not be the first time her sister had ditched her in a bar.

She was curious to know whether the two men would patch up their disagreement or go their separate ways. One minute they were kissing, and the next they were gritting their teeth in anger. How would it end?

Greta finished her drink and then started in on Bettina's.

DALLAS

The yolks were still runny, but the egg whites had dried like glue onto the door and seemed almost resistant to water. Lucy scrubbed with a hard-bristled brush until her arm ached, hoping to get the mess cleaned up before Jack saw it. She stepped back and let her mom spray the door down with the hose, soaking the stones under her bare feet and the hem of Lucy's pajama pants.

"Who can we murder for this?" Irene said. She had taken off her shoes and cuffed her khakis.

"I just can't understand what Jack was thinking," Lucy said, scratching at a piece of eggshell with her fingernail. "He was this close to launching the next big stage of his life. This close." Lucy held up her thumb and index finger to show just how close her son had been.

"If you ask me, the dumbest thing he did was tell the truth," her mom said. "Why he felt the need to throw his whole self under the bus is beyond me. He should have lied."

"Mom!" said Lucy, flicking the piece of shell to the ground. "You don't mean that."

"I most certainly do," Irene said. "What good did confessing do?"

"I'm proud of him for telling the truth," Lucy said, but she too wondered whether Jack could have told some version of the story that might have allowed him to graduate with the rest of his class. "He was the one who did the math, and he didn't want his friends to get in trouble. But what I don't understand is why no one is letting him explain what he really meant by it."

There was a knock on the door from the inside, and her father-in-law cracked it open, poking his mostly bald head outside. Irene pointed the hose away in the direction of the petunias so he could come out without getting his loafers wet.

"Henry called AAA," Graham said. He was wearing corduroy pants on this brutally hot day. "They'll be here in the next thirty minutes."

"Thank you," said Lucy, "and thanks for scraping the shoe polish off the car windshield."

"About that," he said, interlocking his fingers together, "what is an *incel* anyway?"

"An incel," said Irene, "is a boy who spends all his time playing video games in his parents' basement."

"Not exactly," said Lucy, "although that's incel-adjacent."

"This house doesn't have a basement," Graham said, as though he'd outsmarted them.

Graham was a Harvard professor who had published three books of poetry, and as tuned in as he was to the human condition, he did not have much of a grasp on the practicalities of life, which had driven Ellen completely up the wall when they were married. He did not own a cell phone; he carried a Moleskine notebook in his pocket instead, which he insisted served the same purpose.

"Incel," said Lucy, taking a break from scrubbing the door, "stands for involuntary celibate."

"Ah," said Graham, "I love a portmanteau."

"Not this one," said Lucy. "May I be blunt? Mom, cover your ears." Irene did not.

"They're actually self-imposed, unfuckable—excuse me—males. They despise women and can't grasp why women hate them back. Jack is not in any way, shape, or form an incel. He respects women; he loves his sisters. His very best friend is a girl."

"Ahhh," said Graham, taking a pencil stub from his pocket and jotting notes. "Then I wonder why that term was scribbled on his car."

"He was misunderstood," Lucy said.

"Unfortunately," Irene said, "that's exactly what an incel would say."

Lucy shot her a look.

"But no," Irene added, "the term does not apply to Jack."

As Lucy swapped out the brush for a sponge, she noticed a Mercedes sedan coasting by slowly, a middle-aged man in the driver's seat eyeing the house. Lucy recognized him as the dad of a fourth-grade Rockwell girl. "I really don't know what to do about all this hate," she said to Irene and Graham, "other than fortify the castle walls."

Uncle Henry cracked the door open and then came outside as well. "I have good news," he said.

"We're too depressed to process it," said Graham, and he began to recite: "*When, in disgrace with fortune and men's eyes, I all alone be-weep my outcast state—*"

"Dad," said Henry, "must you?"

"It's very fitting," said Graham. "*And trouble deaf heaven with my bootless cries—*"

"I just wanted to tell you that Jack's up," Henry said. "My mom got him to sit outside with her. That's a good thing, don't you think?"

Lucy dropped her sponge in the bucket, wanting to see Jack, while dreading the state he might be in.

"You go on," said Irene. "We'll finish up here and wait for the tow truck."

Lucy looked at the three of them, so grateful for the support of her family.

⚷

Jack was sitting with Mason's mother at one of the bare rental tables set up in the backyard. His face was pale and his blond hair was wild and lit up in the sunshine, making him look like a cross between a zombie and an angel. Ellen had put a plate in front of him with a piece of buttered toast, the crusts removed. He hadn't touched it. He was antsy and fidgeting, digging his toes in the grass.

"Did you get any sleep?" Lucy said, putting a hand on his back.

"We're feeling a little fitful," Ellen said, using "we" to mean Jack. Ellen was wearing the outfit she'd packed for graduation, a linen dress and matching jacket, and Lucy wondered whether she was still holding out hope or that was her only option. "But I'm sure there's a way to fix this problem. We just have to put our heads together."

Lucy wasn't sure of that at all.

Jack looked terrible. He had dark circles under his eyes, and he was twitchy with adrenaline. "Should I call MIT?" he said. And then he turned to look up at Lucy. "Or email the admissions people? I really think I can make them understand what happened."

"I don't know," Lucy said. She'd been wondering whether *she* should call MIT, to defend Jack from whatever Kevin Neal was going to tell them, or whether that would only make things worse.

"Or I could go there in person," he said, "and show them the math, and they'll see I'm just a kid and not some kind of . . . predator." He was frantic. "I mean, I satisfied all the requirements for graduation. Even if they won't give me a diploma, I still technically graduated, didn't I?"

"That's a good question," Ellen said, turning to Lucy. "Did he?"

Lucy would have to ask the principal when she could face him without either yelling at him or bursting into tears.

"And what about my summer job?" Jack said.

"I don't see why you can't tutor," she said. Jack had gotten a job at a community center in Oak Cliff working with middle school kids.

"Maybe Principal Neal is going to call my boss there," he said.

"I'll have to ask him first thing Monday morning."

The kitchen door opened, and Lucy saw her dad standing in the doorway, motioning for her to come back inside. He was home at least an hour too early, and that couldn't mean anything good.

"Hang on," she said, and walked quickly back to the house, bumping into one of the fifty folding chairs crowding the yard.

Her dad was getting himself a glass of water.

"Where are the girls?" she asked him.

"Upstairs, and I don't want you to worry," he said, "I handled it."

"What—what did you handle?"

"Some kids told Alice and Zoe that Jack's going to jail for the rest of his life, and they got pretty upset. I got some nasty looks and comments from the parents, but it's okay, I told them off and got the girls out of there as quick as I could."

Lucy wasn't sure that telling people off was the right approach. "Are the girls okay?"

"They are now," he said. "But I don't think they can go to swim practice anytime soon."

"Until when?" she said. "I mean, this will blow over eventually, right?"

Rex screwed up his face, as if to say no, he did not think there was a chance in hell of things blowing over. Lucy looked back outside at Jack. He was pacing around the yard now, making figure eights around the tables.

"What are we going to do?" she said. "Seriously, Dad, I don't know what to do."

And then her phone pinged with a message from the senior class mom group chat. Apparently, no one had bothered to remove Lucy's number. She looked down to see that Cynthia's mom, Janice, had written:

Woooo hoooo, Mamas! Happy graduation day to our awesome kiddos!! - and congrats to us too! (Reminder: group pic on the school steps right after the ceremony.) I know we're all relieved that *sicko* Jack won't be there. That pervert better stay away from our girls. Here's to a great day, ladies!

Sicko? Pervert? Her Jack?

Lucy dropped her phone as if it had sent an electric shock through her hand.

8—⚡

The day passed in a blur, as Lucy kept the girls busy, the relatives fed, and Jack from falling into a pit of despair. Through it all, she waited for a miracle.

Instead it was the caterer who arrived. Despite all the tables and chairs in the backyard calling attention to a party, Lucy had forgotten to cancel. A staff of uniformed helpers marched through the house, carting the makings of a surf-and-turf banquet into the kitchen and unloading tray after tray onto the countertops. Lucy watched in stunned silence as they fired up the grill, preheated the oven, and boiled a cauldron of water large enough to cook forty pounds of jumbo shrimp. They tossed salads, warmed appetizers, and chilled wine. It was the wine that spurred Lucy to get herself dressed and gather the family. No matter how dark the mood and how dire the circumstances, she would not let the opportunity to spend time together pass them by.

It felt absurd, but when the food was ready, Lucy got the girls downstairs, Henry away from the television, Jack out of bed, and the grandparents from their various corners, and sat them all together at one of the tables.

Lucy hated giving toasts, but she stood up anyway and clinked her glass. "So," she said, "this isn't the day or the weekend we expected, but the important thing is we're a family and we're together to support Jack through this tough time. We love you, Jack, and we aren't going anywhere." *Heartfelt*, she thought, *but lame*. Mason would have done better.

"Hear, hear," said Henry. "But just as a reminder, I *am* going somewhere. My flight's at noon tomorrow."

"Ours is at two," said Graham, "is that right, Ellen?"

"I don't think that's the point Lucy was trying to make," Irene said.

"I'm sorry, Jack," said Rex. "This is a really tough situation."

"But you never know," said Ellen, "something good may come of it."

What good, Lucy thought, could possibly come of this cluster-fuck? She could not imagine a silver lining.

Lucy turned to look at Jack. He was staring off into space, his teeth clenched, a scowl on his face. Lucy had a feeling he'd gone from the denial stage of grief to anger in the course of the day.

As the catering staff milled around, refilling water glasses, they all picked at their food. Tank got on his hind legs and stole a steak off Zoe's plate, and no one even bothered to reprimand him.

After the dishes were cleared, Lucy tipped the servers and sent them home, telling them to take the extra-large sheet cake with them.

⚷

In the middle of the night, Jack came into her room and handed her his phone, open to a *Dallas Morning News* article: *An empty chair at Rockwell's graduation*, the subheading read, *represents Gen Z's failure to form healthy friendships*. Lucy sat up to read the article while Jack flopped on his back.

"What fresh hell . . . ?" she said, spotting an image in the article of the very list Jack had created.

"Rockwell's least popular senior," Jack recited, "serves as an example of the breakdown in adolescent socialization. Apparently, my generation can't forge platonic bonds or relate to peers in a way that isn't transactional. This phenomenon is a result of isolation during Covid, overindulgent parenting, excessive use of social media, and violent video games. And porn."

Lucy glanced at him, noticing little spots of Clearasil dotting his face. It was a good sign, she thought, that he still cared about his skin at a time like this. "The article seems like a psych analysis rather than a news piece," Lucy said, scrolling through it, feeling oddly relieved. "Hey, you aren't named."

"Right," Jack said dryly, "my identity in this scandal is a total mystery."

"This article's bullshit. You formed very solid friendships."

"It doesn't matter. MIT will never let me come." He put an arm over his face and took a shaky breath.

"We don't know that," she said, and handed him his phone. "What I really don't understand is why everyone is jumping to think the worst about you."

"Everyone listens to Cynthia," he said quietly. "So now they all think I'm an asshole."

"But why?" she said. "And how did Cynthia even get the list?"

"I wish I knew." He curled away from her on Mason's side of the bed.

"It's going to be okay," she said, feeling the hollowness of her words.

"I don't see how." He was completely still. "I'm really sorry, Mom."

Lucy felt her heart break into a million pieces.

⚬⊤

She couldn't go back to sleep.

While Jack was breathing quietly on the other side of the bed, she read the *Dallas Morning News* article again, wondering how many people had seen it already. She googled Jack's name, scared to find what else might be closing in on them, and then she checked Cynthia's TikTok. There she was in a new post, her pretty, tear-streaked face up close to the screen. Lucy put in her earbuds.

"I'm healing, y'all," Cynthia was saying, blinking her fake lashes, "but it's so hard. I know I was given, like, a really high value on that list he made, but that's not even the point. To find out there's a guy in our class who thinks he gets to decide what we're worth? He thinks he can put a price on me? On any of us? It's so messed up. Where does *he* get off judging *us*? Fuck that asshole loser."

The story was not blowing over; it was gaining steam.

Lucy opened Instagram next, where she saw post after post of graduation pictures, caps, gowns, and bright smiles. She clenched her teeth, hating the bitterness she felt.

She scrolled past, stopping short when she saw a reel from a German woman she hadn't seen since she was in college and hadn't thought of in years. Bettina had written: *"My sister and her husband need a place to live in Dallas, Texas—ASAP! Hoping for a one-year arrangement. In exchange: her swanky apartment in Berlin. Check out her post! —>"*

Lucy did and read the caption that ended with the line *Perfect for anyone in need of an escape!!!*

Lucy stared at her phone. There was not a person on this earth more in need of an escape than Jack was at that very moment. Berlin! She had not been in almost twenty years, and she felt flushed at the thought of it, the scale of the city, the energy, the fun. Berlin's motto had been "Poor but sexy," which fit the city (and Lucy and her friends at the time) perfectly. She glanced over at Jack; no one would know him there. And Berlin was, most definitely in fact, a city Jack should know.

Lucy went to the woman's profile, her finger hovering over the message button. What would Mason think if she packed up all three kids and fled this snake pit? Would leaving be an act of cowardice? Or an act of courage? Courage, she decided. It would not be easy to leave the comfort of their home. She couldn't fathom how Mason had done it. She was proud of him, but she could not understand how he could be away from them and miss out on six months of their kids' lives. When she'd asked him, he'd said it was about the betterment of humanity.

"What about the . . . worserment of your family?" she'd said. "We'll miss you."

"I'll miss you too. Terribly," he'd said. "But this is so much bigger than us."

Lucy could never in a million years muster the willpower to live in a small, enclosed habitat with strangers, to be separated from her family, to give up access to regular pleasures like good food, sex, and hot showers. She knew she wouldn't last a week. But Mason had given up all of that and then some—even handing Lucy his phone and wallet before leaving—to test out whether his trademarked Dust-Bunnies, the robots he invented to clean dirt off solar panels, might have a role in a future colony on Mars. Mason couldn't even talk about the possibilities without getting flustered with excitement.

When she and the kids had said goodbye to him, he'd waved and blown kisses so fervently, it was as though he actually believed he was about to board a rocket ship and blast into space. Instead, he'd climbed into the back of a gray van that jolted off in a plume of dust.

He may not have been on Mars, but Lucy was on her own nonetheless. And some part of her felt lit up by the idea of taking the kids and blasting out of this hellscape.

She looked at the pictures again on the Instagram post. There was a balcony! Lucy loved a balcony. She wanted this escape so badly that it surprised even herself. It was the one thing she could do: give Jack the gift of time away from a community that had not granted him the slightest benefit of the doubt.

Lucy clicked.

BERLIN

Greta had been up most of the night, drunkenly repacking her suitcases. At dawn, she had two cups of strong coffee and called Bettina, who answered with a groggy "*Hallo*."

"I can't believe you," said Greta. "You dumped me at Hildegard—so *unhöfflich*—although I shouldn't be the least surprised. *And*, you ordered two more drinks before you left, expensive martinis, which I drank because I hate waste. And third, you left me with the bill."

"Who is this?" Bettina said.

"But I've got to hand it to you," Greta said. "You actually did it."

"What did I do now?" Bettina said. "And why are you calling me at the crack of dawn?"

"I just got a message from an old friend of yours. Lucy Holt. Does that ring a bell?"

"Lucy . . ."

"Holt," she said. "You knew her in college."

"Riiiight, Lucy Hope . . ."

"Hol-*t*," Greta said, emphasizing the *t*. "Please tell me you remember her." She heard the click of a lighter, a swift inhale of breath, a slow exhale.

"Sure, okay," Bettina said. "What about her?"

"She's moving into my apartment tomorrow." Greta could hardly believe she'd made such a big decision so rashly, and after a whole lot of vodka.

"Good. Glad to be of help. Can I go back to sleep now?"

"You have to keep an eye on her, okay?" Greta said, scanning her room for personal items that would need to be packed away before they left, anything that could get broken or, God forbid, stolen. "It all happened so fast, and I don't know the first thing about this woman. Promise me you'll make sure she's not trashing my apartment?"

"Is she coming alone?"

"I think so, but . . . to be honest I'm still a little drunk. She loves Berlin and always wanted to come back." Her messages were mostly a string of emojis and exclamation points. "I don't know a thing about her house except that she has a swimming pool!"

"Everyone in Texas has a swimming pool," Bettina said before coughing loudly in Greta's ear.

"And something about her parents living in her backyard? If I get there and there's a yurt behind the house, I'm leaving. But it's a temporary solution anyway, just to get us through the summer."

"Lucy . . . ? I do remember a Lucy something," said Bettina. "She had a very hot boyfriend. A real Viking. I was jealous."

"This was almost too easy. She gave me her address and told me where she would hide a key. Do you remember her being . . . impulsive?"

"I barely remember her at all. Listen, I gotta go. Prince Charming is leaving, and the least I can do is walk him to the door."

"The guy from the bar? Really, Bettina?" She squeezed her eyes shut and tried to imagine what it would feel like to have a complete stranger unbuttoning her van Laack blouse, touching her skin. She shuddered, thinking it wasn't much more intimate than having this Lucy person sleep in her bed and touch all of her things. She had a lot of clearing out to do.

"Don't be judgmental," Bettina said.

"Sorry. It's just been a long time since I had a one-night stand. I honestly can't even picture it."

"You've *never* had a one-night stand," Bettina said, "and it's been a long time since you had any sex at all. So how about you work on you?"

"Touché," said Greta. It was sad, but very true.

"Lucy . . . ," Bettina said. "Actually, I remember liking her, if that helps? She was a lot of fun."

Greta felt a little flash of jealousy. She didn't think Bettina would ever use the word "fun" to describe her.

⚷

Otto was rushing around the apartment looking for his keys when he jammed his toes on a box that had yet to be moved down to the *Keller*. He spent a good deal of time hopping up and down, justifying his pain level by reminding Greta of the vast number of nerve endings in the feet.

He limped to the door, collecting his wallet and phone. "I'll be *schnell*," he said. "I had no idea the *Arschloch* would demand my *Schlüssel*." The frenzy of the morning was making Otto forget his English.

"Why would he want your key?"

"I don't know. And he says he needs to talk to me about something. I worry he's going to give my *Büro* away to someone *anders* in my *Abwesenheit*. I don't want anyone in my space."

"I feel exactly the same way," Greta said resentfully.

Otto turned and faced her. "*Danke*, Greta," he said. "Thank you for doing this and for finding the house swapping."

"Don't thank me yet. Who knows what I've gotten us into," she said.

After Otto walked out, she brought an empty box into Emmi's bedroom. She packed up some clothes her daughter had left behind, pajamas and T-shirts, but decided the books on her shelves—the Pippi Longstocking novels, and all of Harry Potter and Tolkien— could stay. On top of the bookshelf was an antique Meissen plate holding seashells Emmi had collected over the years at her grandparents' Baltic summer house. It was too fragile to pack, so Greta left it there as well. She emptied the pens, scissors, and notebooks from her desk drawers, realizing that when Emmi had moved to Freiburg, she'd taken almost everything with her.

Greta was left feeling very nostalgic. She sat on Emmi's bed and called her.

"Hey," said Emmi, sounding a little breathless.

Greta could hear street noises in the background.

"*Hallo, Schatz,*" Greta said.

"I hear you're going to Texas," Emmi said. "That was quite an *Überraschung.*"

"No one was more surprised than me," said Greta. "*Es tut mir sehr leid.*"

"Why are you sorry?" Emmi said. "I thought this was a good thing. Dad sounded excited."

Greta looked out the window at the treetops, thinking "excited" was not a word she would choose to describe her current frame of mind. She was upset. Angry even. "I was looking forward to spending the summer with *you,*" she said.

"Sure, but Dallas sounds great too. Dad's getting me a ticket to visit you."

"Is that okay? Will you come?"

"Sure. I've never been to Texas."

"But what about your New York housing this summer?" Greta said. "I feel terrible that we promised you a room—"

"I can find something else," Emmi said. "Maybe a sublet closer to where I'm working. My hours are going to be brutal."

Emmi did not sound in the least bit disappointed to spend the summer in New York *without* her parents.

"Mom, can I call you later? I want to go for a run before Karl and Monika and I are meeting for lunch."

Emmi and her best friend, Monika, shared an apartment in Freiburg, and Greta knew that Karl, Emmi's boyfriend, spent every waking and sleeping minute there. She was glad Emmi would have some time away from both of them this summer, a chance to spread her wings and meet new people.

"Tell them I said hello," Greta said, standing up and straightening the covers on the bed. "Where will they be this summer?"

"Berlin first," Emmi said. "But then Monika is spending eight weeks in Heiligenhafen."

"Really?" Greta said. "Without us there?"

"I know," Emmi said quietly. "Weird, right?"

This was the first year that no one in the family was going to her mother's leaky summer cottage on the Baltic Sea. Greta could still picture Monika at eight years old, spending two weeks with them, taking her first swim in the ocean and scouring the sand for shells. She went with them every summer after that.

"Where will she stay?"

"She rented an apartment near the square and got a job at the bookstore."

"Ton und Text?" said Greta, feeling a longing for the village and its shops. Not only had she taken Emmi there every summer, but she'd also spent her own childhood vacations in the town. "Are you sorry you're not going too?"

"Yes, but this isn't the summer for a beach trip. I still can't believe my advisor picked me to intern with her; she's the most impressive woman I've ever met."

That stung a bit, but who was Greta to argue? Emmi's mentor was a lawyer who fought relentlessly for women's rights all over the world, especially for the poor. She was, indeed, a hero.

"But I hope we can go for Christmas," Emmi said.

"Good luck with that," Greta said. Her mother hated the Baltic in winter. "If anyone can convince your grandmother to open the house in December, it's you."

After they said goodbye, Greta finished tidying Emmi's bedroom, feeling resentful of Otto, who was robbing her of precious time with their daughter.

Greta checked the time and carried the box to the door. In a neatly organized kitchen drawer, filled with rubber bands, batteries, clothespins, and matches, she found the key to their basement storage room right next to the key to the car. She put both in her pocket.

Once she'd stacked the boxes next to their winter tires and bicycles, she walked upstairs to the ground floor and braved the drizzle in the back courtyard. Parked there, in all its classic glory, was the yellow Volkswagen Beetle, the car she and Otto bought at the end of the summer when they'd first met. She adored this car for its design, of course, but more for all the memories it had helped create. They'd had a lot of fun together over the years, but something between them had gotten lost along the way. As she sat behind the wheel of the parked car, her hands at *zehn* and *zwei*, she could feel what that lost thing was, even if she didn't have a word for it, not in English or in German.

She and Otto had paid cash for the car, secondhand when they'd bought it twenty years ago, splitting the cost between them, a sign of partnership. The first time they took it for a drive, they'd gone all the way to Potsdam, parked by a lake, and *knuddel*ed until it was dark out. Otto couldn't keep his hands off her that night, but that was a long time ago.

Greta closed her eyes, kissed the steering wheel, and said goodbye.

MESSAGE TRANSMITTED FROM MARS VIA NASA DEEP
SPACE NETWORK

To: Lucy Holt
Planet Earth

Dear Lucy—

Greetings from Mars. According to ground control, there's a "satellite snafu," so we aren't receiving any communication other than essential information on the mission. I knew this was a likelihood, but it's not nice to be over 225 million kilometers away from home and completely out of touch with you and the world.

I hate hate hate that I missed graduation. Send pictures, please, and, who knows?—maybe I'll get them in the next data dump. Did my dad recite poetry? Did your mom tell Henry she hates the house? Were the girls so proud of their big brother? A college kid! Wow. Tell Jack I am very proud of him. Here's a joke he'll appreciate: How does NASA organize a party? They *planet*. How are the girls? I bet Zoe's happy to be done with school.

I don't mean to complain, but our space here is objectively tight and everything is red. Like everything because they've covered our entire outpost with dust that gets under our nails, and sticks to our scalps, and even winds up in our food. It occurred to me today that I've given up my freedom(!), and although I knew that and came here voluntarily, it's still a shock.

My DustBunnies survived the "journey," and yestersol I prepared them for deployment on the solar panels. I really want them to be a success, so I am working hard to ensure they function optimally. My fellow crew members and I are getting along well. We have our daily assignments (group and solo), and we're maintaining protocol in the midst of all manner of unpredictable conditions. (We experienced an equipment failure this morning, nothing imminently life-threatening, but a glitch with the toilet system that was quite a to-do.)

NASA has impressed upon us the need to keep up morale in isolation, BUT—*how* one goes about that is up for debate. I want and need time to myself, so I can rest up and work well in our little society. But I seem to be the only introvert in the group. The others want to do communal activities—games and team-building exercises—and they've suggested singing together in the evenings and, as this is the most international mission of its kind, sharing stories from our varied cultures. Let me just say: if I have to participate in sing-alongs for 177 Sols, I'll go mad. You know that's not my thing. It's embarrassing and I don't even know where to look. Our medical officer Yağmur brought a yaybahar from her homeland, and the sound that it makes is haunting and makes me homesick for you and the kids.

I can't wait to hear from you.

Peace and love,
Mason
Science Officer, MARS (ALPHA RED CANYON 6)

PS Did Mickey fix the pool drain?

BERLIN

Greta checked her face in the mirror and walked out of the apartment, touching the keys in the pocket of her cardigan as she went down the stairs, her hand sliding along the varnished banister. She stopped at the door of the apartment directly below hers and rang the bell, the sound echoing off the marble walls and floor.

Adam opened the door immediately. "Hey, you."

"I'm sorry to come so early," Greta said, stepping over the threshold.

He kissed her on the cheek. Adam was dressed in his usual attire, faded jeans, hip sneakers, and a well-worn black T-shirt. "Look at you," he said, "never a hair out of place." But he must have noted something in her expression because he frowned. "Everything okay? You look stressed."

"Just a last-minute change in our plans," she said. "And a few too many martinis with my sister last night."

"Come on in," he said in his deep voice, "and take a deep breath. Coffee?"

"No, thank you," she said, hesitating for a brief moment before following him through the set of double doors into the living room. His apartment was an Ikea showroom, but with flea market touches that made it cool. She stopped in front of a photograph of a seminude burlesque dancer.

"I got that last weekend," he said, brushing a bit of dust off the carved, antique frame. "I think it's from the twenties. Do you like it?"

Greta leaned in and studied it. From the silvery sheen and texture of the paper she could tell it was not a reproduction. "Very much," she said. "You have a good eye."

They walked by his matte-black Steinway in the living room alcove; Greta would often sit on her own balcony, just so she could hear him play, sometimes a little Gershwin, other days Alicia Keys.

On his balcony, situated diagonally beneath hers, he had chairs with stretchy cords that formed a kind of hammock and always left horizontal marks across the backs of her thighs when she sat long enough.

He picked up a heavy glass ashtray from the windowsill and placed it on the little table next to her chair. Greta did not smoke. But she had told Adam the first time she came over that she'd smoked Marlboros back in the day and sometimes missed them. Adam had bought her her own pack so she could enjoy a few drags in secret. Bettina would be appalled by her hypocrisy.

He offered her a cigarette then, but Greta shook her head, a bitter taste filling her mouth. "Too early," she said.

The pack was almost empty. Had Adam been giving *her* cigarettes to some other woman? Silly, but that stung.

"Tell me how I can help," he said, his palms open before her. "Can I water your plants?"

"We don't have plants," Greta said.

"Not even on your balcony?"

Adam had a few geraniums perched in the window box beside him. His flowers were blooming.

"We're not going to New York after all."

"Oh, lucky me," he said, without missing a beat. "That's great—I mean, you're pretty much my only friend here."

He leaned back in his chair and put his sneakers up on the railing.

"I've seen you with a friend or two since you moved in," she said. More than once, Greta had walked down the stairs in the morning to find Adam kissing a woman goodbye in his doorway.

He blushed. "We both know, I like your company better than anyone's. And sure, I hang out with musicians now and then, but they're not friends; they just want something from me. But you . . . Will you take me on a tour of your collection this week?"

"That will have to wait," she said. "I'm still leaving Berlin."

He looked over at her, cocking his head. "Now I'm confused."

"We're going to Dallas, Texas, instead," she said. "We leave in about an hour."

"Wow," Adam said. "That's a big change."

"Otto has a better opportunity there, and he's very happy about it."

"And you?"

"Not so happy," she admitted.

"You were looking forward to seeing your daughter, right?" he said. "She was going to stay with you all summer?"

Greta nodded, surprised he remembered.

"I guess you can visit her instead," he said.

"I'd like to, of course," she said, but she knew that visiting Emmi wouldn't be the same as living together.

Adam held up a finger, got up, and abruptly went inside. Greta reprimanded herself for sitting down with him at all; there was still so much to do upstairs and no time left to do it. Out on the street, she could see the bakery on the opposite corner, the smell of bread wafting up to the balcony. The trees had sprouted pale green leaves, and Greta felt instantly, prematurely homesick for her neighborhood in summer.

Adam returned with two champagne flutes and a damp bottle tucked under his arm.

"What's this?" she said.

"Your goodbye party."

"Adam," she said, so pleased he would do this for her.

He filled the glasses.

"It's a little early in the day, no?" she said.

"Champagne is a breakfast drink," Adam said. "I won't let you get sloppy or anything, but cheers: To a big . . . Texan adventure, I guess."

She clinked her glass against his as he sat back down. "*Konterbier*," she said.

"Sorry?"

"Hair of the dog." The bubbles made her shiver.

He took a new pack of Marlboros from his pocket. "And I bought you these to take with you since you won't be able to sneak them from me anymore."

She smiled. "Thank you, Adam."

"So tell me everything. Texas." He was looking at her so intensely, she had to look away. "Have you been to Dallas before?"

"No," she said, "and I'm keeping my expectations low."

"Why? Dallas is great," he said.

"It is?"

"Oh, you'll love it there. I've only been a few times, but the people are nice, there's a good bar scene, and some of the best food you'll ever eat."

"But I don't know anyone there," she said, "and I have no idea what I'll do with myself all day long."

"Hmm," he said, "I can think of quite a few things."

"Really?" she said. Adam wasn't flirting. They'd become comfortable together, but he'd never crossed a line and neither had she. She took a big sip of champagne. "Meaning . . . ?"

Adam looked up at the sky and said, "You'll get hooked on country music. I see you wearing cowboy boots and riding a Harley."

She laughed and put a hand to her head. "*Nein, nein.* All that noise? I'd get *Kopfschmerzen*."

"No! Not koffshmurshen, whatever that is. Okay, fine," he said, "no motorcycles. Then how about"—he threw back half his champagne, his eyes full of mischief—"you'll hang out at a fancy country club, sipping margaritas by the pool. You'll stretch out on a chaise and pretend to read a book while a lifeguard flexes his muscles in front of you."

"What book?" she said, wanting the full picture of this fantasy.

"You're asking for details of the book and not the lifeguard? This is why I love you, Greta. Okay, it's an erotic paperback from the supermarket," he said. "A steamy bodice-ripper."

Greta laughed again but it came out forced, because what she really wanted to do in that moment was sit in his lap. She scolded herself and shifted in her chair, trying to appear more relaxed. "Anything else?" she said as coolly as she could.

"I'm just getting started," he said, looking at her more seriously. "I can imagine you having a torrid affair."

"What? *Me?* Never."

"Yes," he said, "with the lifeguard. Or with . . . a grizzled cowboy."

"Grizzled?" she asked. "Why grizzled?"

"It's a trope," he said. He picked up the bottle to refill their glasses. "He's handsome, but in a rugged, leathery way. He'll rescue you from a stampede, tip his hat, and call you ma'am. And then he'll seduce you under the stars."

"Adam!" she said. If only Otto had such an active imagination. She brushed a piece of lint from her pant leg. "I don't think you have a very clear picture of who I am."

"I don't think *you* have a clear picture of who you are. You're glamorous and, wow, sorry, but that picture of you in the newspaper?—at the auction, where you were holding up that paddle like a . . . You have no idea how cool your whole *vibe* is." He put his glass down, catching the edge of the table and spilling his champagne. "See," he said. "You make me nervous."

"No, I don't," Greta said, leaning back in her chair, crossing one ankle over the other. If anything, he made her nervous.

"You know what else you should do?" he said. "Speaking of paddles?"

"I don't think I want to know," she said, but in truth she was very curious.

"Pickleball," Adam said.

"Pickleball?"

"Pickleball!"

"Oh," she said.

"It's fun and very social. It's perfect for a woman your age."

"*My* age? I hate to tell you this, Adam, but I'm not *that* old—"

"God, no, I meant . . . *our* age. I think it would be a good way for you to meet people, that's all." He looked down at his hands. "Take it from me: it isn't easy being in a new city, far from home. You've been really great to me. I'm going to miss you."

"Well, there's no need to miss me," she said, "because I've re-placed myself. There will be a woman living in our apartment this summer."

"Who?" Adam looked appalled. "Why?"

"We're swapping homes," Greta said.

"Really?" Adam said. "Wait, she's American?"

"Yes, her name's Lucy," Greta said, reaching in her pocket and holding up her spare keys. "Lucy Holt, and she's arriving tomorrow. I'm hoping it's okay if she rings your bell. She'll get here at around eight in the morning. Could you let her in?"

He took the keys from her, his fingers touching hers, and placed them on the wet table next to the champagne bottle. "Sure. No prob-lem."

"And tell her not to wear shoes inside my apartment."

"Ever?"

"And if she's a bad neighbor—noisy or whatever—let me or Otto know."

"Otto?" Adam scoffed. "Otto and I never speak. The most I ever get from him is an obligatory nod when we pass each other on the stairs. He can't stand me."

"Oh, that's not true," said Greta. It was true, absolutely.

"In six months, Otto and I have never had a single conversa-tion," said Adam. "He's got that formal, German male thing to the extreme—I'll never get used to it. He calls me *Mr. Lance*, and he backs away from me like I might infect him with something."

Otto was stiff, and it worried Greta that he was going to fare no better with his colleagues in Dallas than he had in Berlin. Possibly even worse. But she didn't like anyone putting Otto down. "Formality is part of German culture," she said primly; by nature she too was formal.

"Well, I hate it—no, I'm sorry," Adam said quickly, noticing perhaps her change in posture. "I take it back. I shouldn't speak badly of your culture or your husband. Shame on me. I sometimes forget you're half German."

She felt much more than half. She felt, in spite of her proficiency in speaking English, at least eighty percent German. "Germany has many good sides, you know," she said, "and so does Otto."

"Tell me," said Adam. "What are they? Otto's good sides? Of course he's different around you. It's just, from the outside, you two seem . . . different."

"Oh, not at all," Greta said, and she took another big sip of champagne. "Otto is very . . . I was only twenty-two when we met. I was working as an assistant at Ketterer Kunst, the auction house, and he was already a doctor and very attractive, and he swept me off my feet."

"Well," Adam said, "he is a foot guy. . . ."

"Clever," she said, smiling. "Otto says I've damaged my toes wearing high heels." The champagne, this early in the day and on an empty stomach, with alcohol already coursing through her system from the night before, was making Greta very tipsy. "And he's, well, we're very attached to each other." She polished off her champagne in one gulp. It was time to go. "So, don't forget," she said. "Lucy Holt, eight a.m. tomorrow, the keys. And Adam, maybe don't have an affair with her. It could get complicated, you know."

He laughed and gave a little salute. "Understood," he said. "Dallas ho!"

For a split second, she thought he was calling Lucy a ho. "Ah, right," she said. "Westward ho."

She stood up as Adam was trying to top off her glass again. "No more," she said, laughing. "I've got a flight to catch—" She placed a hand on Adam's shoulder to steady herself, looking out at the street for a fixed point on which to focus. And there was Otto, standing in front of the corner bakery, staring up at her with his mouth agape.

DALLAS

Lucy blinked her eyes open and remembered—with great alarm—that she had bought four plane tickets to Germany sometime in the middle of the night.

Jack was sound asleep on his dad's side of the bed and the sight of him at peace, even temporarily, comforted her. She sat up, found her phone, and saw she'd received her first message from Mason. She skimmed it—*A college kid! Wow . . . Did Mickey fix the pool drain?*— and then read it again from the beginning. Mason was utterly, blissfully unaware of the crisis, which meant Lucy had to manage it all by herself, which made her all the more glad to be blowing town.

The doorbell rang, and the dogs jumped off the bed to see who was there. Lucy followed behind, noting that the whole house smelled like boiled shrimp.

Jack's best friend, Rosie, was on the doorstep. Lucy was so pleased to see her, she stepped outside and wrapped her arms around her. It felt as if she were hugging an ironing board. The dogs circled her in happy greeting, licking Rosie's fingers.

"Congratulations," Lucy said, noticing a bit of celebratory graduation glitter in Rosie's hair.

"I'm on my way to the airport," Rosie said. She pointed to an idling car in front of the house. "My thing in New York starts tomorrow."

Rosie's "thing" was a summer internship with Hudson River Park. She would be a freshman at Brown in the fall. Her life was moving forward. Lucy did not begrudge her any success or happiness that came her way, but her big plans didn't make Jack's situation any easier to bear.

"I'm happy to see you," Lucy said. The doormat was still wet under her bare feet, and she stepped back, opening the door wider. But Rosie did not come in. She was fidgeting with the elastic band that was holding her braid together and would not look Lucy in the eye. She cleared her throat. "Can you tell Jack I came to say good-bye?"

"Do you want me to get him?"

"No, that's okay, maybe just tell him—" Rosie's face crumpled as she started to cry. Lucy tried again to bring her inside, at least to get her a tissue, but Rosie refused. "Just tell him it's so . . . *unfair*," she said. "It was supposed to be funny. He didn't mean anything bad by it, and then—how did that stupid list get out there?" Rosie's nose was running. "He won't even answer my texts," she said. "He's my best friend, and he hates me."

"He doesn't hate you at all," Lucy said. "He's just too upset to talk right now."

Rosie wiped her face on her sleeve and then looked at Lucy for the first time. "What's he going to do?"

"He'll be fine," Lucy said, nodding her head to feign confidence. "Don't you worry."

"Will you tell him . . ." Rosie was gasping, taking quick, jerky breaths between words. "Make sure he knows we're friends," she said, "no matter what. Tell him I'm sorry. And tell him I hope he'll talk to me again when he can." She turned around and rushed off to the car.

"Good luck," Lucy called after her. "We love you!"

She felt relieved that, like Rosie, they also had a flight to catch, a place to go.

Lucy went back in the house to find the three identical cats and Lucy's nonidentical twins in the kitchen.

"Tic, Tac, and Toe," said Zoe with her mouth full of Cheerios.

"No cat wants to be called Tic," said Alice. "And nobody at *all* wants to be called Toe."

"Eenie, Meenie, and Miny," said Zoe.

"Good morning," Lucy said. "Are the grandparents up?"

"They're packing," Alice said.

"What if I were to tell you guys," Lucy said, "that *we* need to pack today too?"

"Why?" said Alice. "Is Jack getting arrested?"

"Jack is not getting arrested," said Lucy. "We're just taking a little trip on a plane."

"I don't like planes," said Zoe.

"Are we going to Costa Rica?" said Alice.

"Not this time," said Lucy. "Somewhere better. Can you get the suitcases out of the hall closet upstairs? I need to go talk to Reenie."

"In your pajamas?" said Alice.

Lucy looked down. "No one's going to see me."

"You always say that," said Alice, "and someone always does."

Lucy went out into the backyard, only to find that Alice was right as usual; Mickey, the man cleaning dead leaves out of the pool, waved as she walked by in her pajamas. She waved back.

He took off his headphones and nodded his chin at the rental tables. "Did you have a good party?" he said.

"Fewer people than expected," she said. "Any interest in leftovers? I have enough steak and shrimp to feed an army."

"I'm a vegetarian," Mickey said.

"Ah," said Lucy. "Never mind then. Is the pool drain working okay?"

But he'd already put his headphones back on and was bobbing his head to some beat as he ran the skimmer across the surface of the water.

She opened the gate in the fence between her parents' lot and theirs.

The house Lucy grew up in was a 1940s bungalow with crepe

myrtles lining the walkway to the street and a front door and shutters painted, as her mother liked to say, the color of Texas bluebonnets. Lucy rarely saw the front of her parents' house anymore. When Mason came along, with his unwavering certainty, his love of kids and pets, and a vintage engagement ring, he bought the lot that abutted the backyard of her parents' property and—with his brother's architectural plans—built a modern, solar-powered house in the place of the one-story ranch that was there before. Irene and Rex loved having them close by, but her mom had never forgiven them for building what she called the "Cruise Ship" on the other side of the fence.

Irene came out onto the patio to greet her, coffee in hand, her hair in curlers. "You look like crap," she said.

"I barely slept." Lucy sat down at the mottled glass table. "But I'm feeling a little better now actually because—"

"You need to take a nap today."

"No nap," Lucy said. "Too much to do."

"It's for the best the in-laws are leaving, under the circumstances," Irene whispered, although there was no possible way anyone could overhear. She sat down next to Lucy and patted her leg.

"They're not the only ones leaving," Lucy said, thinking her plan just might sound unhinged in the light of day, while it had seemed like such a reasonable choice in the dead of night. "We're flying to Berlin today. The kids and I are spending the summer there, maybe longer. I haven't actually thought that far ahead."

"Excuse me?" Irene put her coffee down. "Germany? Have you lost your mind? You're not even dressed, and you're going to *Germany*?"

"In, like, three hours," Lucy said, checking her phone. "Two, actually. Plenty of time."

"Lucy," said her mom sternly, pushing back her chair. Irene did not like to go farther than LBJ Freeway if she didn't absolutely have to. "You can't do that."

"But we have to," Lucy said plainly.

"No, it's too far. And what about the dogs? What about the cats?"

Rex came around from the garage then, carrying a ladder.

"What are you doing with that?" Lucy said.

"Gutters," her dad said.

"Be careful."

"Excuse me," said Irene, snapping her fingers in front of Lucy's face, "but you are the one who needs to be careful here."

"What's going on?" Rex said.

"Can you drive us to the airport in a couple of hours?" Lucy said. "We're going away for the summer."

"Sure." He sounded relieved. "Great idea. Where're you headed?"

"To *Germany*," her mom said, and then she turned on Lucy. "Why Germany?"

"Because I know it," Lucy said. "And we sure as hell can't stay here."

"Who's going to take care of all those animals you adopted?"

"I found a pet sitter," Lucy said. "Sort of. A house sitter. I mean, people. German people. They're coming to live here. In fact, they're already on the way and should be arriving sometime tonight."

"Who?" her dad said, abandoning the ladder against the side of the house.

"Who indeed?" Irene said. "I want to know who's going to be on the other side of my fence."

"Greta," said Lucy. "Her name's Greta."

"Greta who?" said Irene.

"Greta. . . . She's the sister of a friend. Or of a friend of a friend. I had a roommate in Germany who knew this girl named Bettina who spoke perfect English—"

"You don't know her last name?" her dad said, now looking as concerned as her mom, who was shaking her head so hard, one of her curlers came loose.

"No," Lucy said. "But I'll find out." How, Lucy wondered, were her parents still able to make her feel like a kid who hadn't done her homework?

Irene was pulling the rogue curler from her hair. "You're going to have strangers move into your beautiful house?"

"Beautiful?" Lucy said. "You hate my house."

"That's beside the point," said Irene. "How do you know they won't trash the place?"

"Because we'll be living in their apartment in Berlin. I take care of her home, she takes care of mine. It's like a two-way hostage situation." Lucy stood up, figuring it was high time to tell the kids the plan. "Do y'all want the graduation leftovers?"

"Lucy," Irene said, getting up as well, her fists planted on her hips, "if you're fixing to go through with this terrible idea, you've got a lot to do." And she began counting on her fingers. "You've got to empty your closets, put clean sheets on the beds, stock up on pet food, clean the cat boxes and guinea pig cage, empty your night table drawers and bathroom cabinets, hide your valuables, and—"

"I know all this," Lucy said, although half the things her mother had listed hadn't even registered until now.

"Are they using your cars?" Rex said.

"I guess," said Lucy.

"And vacuum your cars," said Irene. "You need to pick up Alice's allergy meds—"

"Are your passports valid?" her dad said.

"Yes," Lucy said, proud she'd managed to find them.

"That's the most important thing," he said. "Passports and a credit card."

"What are you going to tell your bosses?" said Irene. "You love that job, you've been working so hard to prove yourself to them."

Lucy had hoped she wouldn't ask. She'd given little thought to the content or form of Monday's presentation, or how she was going to keep her bosses from finding out she'd fled the country. "I'm not going to tell them anything. I work remotely anyway," she said, trying not to hyperventilate. "So they won't even know I'm out of town."

"There's a time difference," Irene said, stepping toward her. "A *big* time difference."

"I know that," said Lucy. "How many hours?"

"Eight?" said her father. "Nine?"

"Have you told Mason you're leaving the country?" Irene said.

"Satellite snafu," said Lucy, wishing she could talk to him, wishing he were going with them. "I can't reach him."

"If there's one thing about Mason," Irene said, "he's a very good problem solver. Maybe you should hold off—"

"I'm a good problem solver too," Lucy said. She was sure Mason would admire her gumption. When Mason and Lucy had first met, he was not put off by the fact that she was a single mom living at her parents' house. Rather, he'd invited himself over for dinner, bringing flowers for her mom and a Lego set for Jack. Six months later he proposed at the Mansion and offered to adopt Jack in the same breath. She'd said yes to both.

"All right then," said Irene. "Let's start on the house. Rex, the gutters will have to wait."

Her dad picked up the ladder and carried it back to the garage.

"Are you really sure this is what you want to do?" Irene said.

"This isn't about me," Lucy said. "This is for Jack."

But whether her excitement was coming more from a need to flee Dallas for Jack's sake or from her own desire to go back to Berlin, she couldn't say.

It was okay, she decided, if it was both.

Two hours later, Lucy wheeled her suitcase out of her bedroom. They were late, and everyone else was waiting in the car. The house was quiet for the first time all day.

She quickly reread the email she'd drafted to Greta in German, proud she'd been able to retrieve so many words after all these years:

Leber Greta, it began. *Mein zwiebeln, Sonne, und mich fruenen uns Berlin fahren und leben in dein wohnung. Ich hoffe all gehts gut fur du und das Vieh hier in Dallas. Wir haben sex Schlafzimmer, so es gibt viel spaß fur du und dein Mann hier. Wenn du Frage habe über mein Haus, mein Autos, mein Putzfrau (bezahlt schon bei mich), oder meine Nackt bärin, sag es mir. Fröhliche Haus-svappung! Tschuss!*

She was worried she was forgetting something. After two sleepless nights, she was not thinking very clearly and had almost poured cat litter in Piglet's guinea pig cage.

Her father honked the horn in the driveway.

Lucy hit send.

She did one fast, final walk-through. She hadn't done all she should to get the house ready for the Germans, but she hoped it was good enough. Piglet was hiding in his little plastic shelter, so she couldn't say goodbye to him. On the floor by the front door, she found Zoe's stuffed rabbit, Fred, left behind as usual; she picked him up and put him in her carry-on bag on top of Mason's phone and wallet, which she'd felt an urge to keep near her. She kissed the dogs and shut the front door. Just before getting in the car, she stopped at the curb and threw a black garbage bag containing every manner of trash from broken pool toys to old cosmetics to expired ketchup—even Jack's cap and gown—in the bin.

PART 2

Did you ever notice that the first piece
of luggage on the carousel
never belongs to anyone?
—Erma Bombeck

Twelve thousand meters above the Atlantic Ocean, Greta woke up, raised her seat, and tapped Otto on the shoulder. "I have to get up," she said over the deep rumble of the plane's engines.

Otto's leg rest was up, his laptop was open on his tray table, and he was typing as though his life depended on it.

"Honestly, Otto," she said, tapping him again. "Can we talk, please?" She took in her husband's stiff posture and furrowed brow. "I was only dropping off our key."

He stopped typing and turned to her. "I didn't even know you knew Mr. Lance, except to pass each other on the stairs. But there you were, laughing and getting drunk on champagne first thing in the morning."

"I know him . . . a little," she said. "And I've never understood why you have such a low opinion of him. He's a perfectly nice man."

"I don't like him," he said, frowning like a grumpy child.

"I know, which is why I didn't mention I've had a few conversations with him."

Otto stared off blankly into the aisle. "I haven't in many years seen you to be having so much fun," he said.

That was possibly true. Otto hadn't brought out her joyful side in quite some time. Other things did—art and wine, friends and books—but Otto spoke mostly about colleagues who wronged him, tasks that were overdue, and weather that disappointed.

"And what about you?" she said. "You never even smile anymore."

"And why should I smile?" He turned back to his computer. "I learned from the *Arschloch* today that Moritz has published a paper against me."

"What do you mean?"

"He claims I made *falsch* data, that I have committed intellectual *Betrug*." He pointed to the email he was writing. "I now must defend myself."

"Fraud?" said Greta. "*You?*" Poor Otto. Moritz really was a monster.

"I am writing to the editors of the *International Journal of Bone and Joint,* saying I will reproduce the data, and Moritz will be made to take back his libidinous claims."

Greta leaned over to look at his screen. "*Libelous,*" she said.

Otto hit backspace on his keyboard and retyped the word.

"I'm sorry that your place of work has become a battleground," she said.

He stopped typing. "The *Stimmung* there is *immer negativ,* and my colleagues themselves are destroying my . . . *Seele?*" he said.

"Soul," she said. "Some time away will be good for you."

"This letter needs to be *perfekt.*"

"I'm sure it will be." Greta leaned in and kissed his cheek. "I have to get up," she said, "but when I get back, can we at least try to enjoy the flight?"

She unbuckled her seat belt and stepped over him, wishing he would reach out and touch her as she passed. Instead he hugged his laptop to his chest to make sure she didn't bump it as she reached the aisle.

She moved through the darkened cabin, past rows of business-class passengers who were working, watching movies, or sleeping. She passed the bulkhead and stepped into the area where the Lufthansa flight attendants were preparing the second meal. Sidling through an open bathroom door, she slid the latch to the right, and as the light flicked on, she was shocked at the sight of her pale face. They'd had so much rain in Berlin all spring, Greta could barely remember what it felt like to walk around without an umbrella. She and Otto would benefit from sunshine, the one thing she was certain Dallas had in abundance. Adam had promised good food as well. Cowboys and lifeguards. She marveled at the thought of getting a tan while reading a steamy novel by Lucy Holt's swimming pool.

When she returned to their row, Otto had put his laptop away. Greta climbed over him and landed heavily in her seat.

"I look haggard," she said. "What a shock."

"Not at all," Otto said, "but I am feeling *sehr alt.*"

Greta had never thought of Otto as old. But the fifteen-year age gap between them was becoming more apparent. His face was aging well, but his joints were not. He was energetic enough to get up at the crack of dawn for surgery, but after work, he no longer had the desire to do anything at all. She couldn't even remember the last time they'd gone to a movie together or had dinner with friends.

"If it makes you feel any better," she said, "Bettina was just saying how young you're acting, whisking us off to Texas."

"How was your night with Bettina?"

"We had martinis, and then she went home with a stranger."

Otto frowned. "I do not think Bettina should be having gender traffic with strange men."

His direct translations so often failed. She did not correct him. In fact, she wished she hadn't mentioned Bettina's sex life at all; it was one thing for *her* to judge her sister, but she did not want Otto judging her. "She's an adult," she said. "She knows what she's doing."

She looped her arm through his and put her head on his shoulder. "This morning I was thinking about the fun we used to have, driving around in the old Beetle, kissing and—"

"We should get rid of it," Otto said plainly, just as if he were telling her to throw out moldy cheese from the refrigerator.

Greta raised her head, feeling like she'd been slapped. "No," she said, "how can you say that?"

"Or we should give it to Emmi."

"Emmi can't drive."

"Eventually she will. We never drive it anyway, and it's too old. Why are you holding on so . . . *fest*? You're very sentimental these days."

"That car," she said, a wave of nostalgia welling up inside her, "is very important. It's a reminder of something we—"

"I don't need a reminder," Otto said, patting her knee. "You're right here with me, at the start of a new time for us," he said.

And then a flight attendant walked up as if on cue, handing them each a glass of champagne and offering her congratulations.

"What's this?" Greta said.

"You said we should enjoy the flight." Otto looked up at her. "And it's our anniversary."

Greta was taken aback. "It isn't," she said.

"It is. Twenty-two years ago we met on a Lufthansa *Flugzeug* from London to Frankfurt. And here we are, traveling again together, but in the opposite direction."

"Otto," she said, her face flushing. She hadn't remembered. "That's very sweet. Thank you."

"I am *optimistisch* about what is coming," he said. "I googled the internet last night while you were out, and I learned that Texans are *freundlich* and self-assured."

"All of them?" Greta said.

Otto smiled; it had been so long since she'd seen him try, she found herself staring at the upturned corners of his mouth.

"Yes, all of them," he said. "So here's to thirty million new friends," he added, and lifted his glass. "Or maybe thirty new friends. Or even three would be nice."

Greta thought that was very well put. She raised her glass as well, looking him in the eye. But just as she was about to take a sip, the pilot made an announcement about turbulence ahead, and the flight attendant rushed by, whisking away their full glasses of champagne.

The first leg of the trip was behind them. When the wheels finally hit the ground in Newark, the passengers broke out in applause. The plane taxied to the gate, and Lucy, grateful they'd survived, helped her girls gather their things, wondering how Zoe had managed to spread out so completely on this short leg of their long journey. Her barrettes, pens, book, and headphones were under the seats, and she almost left her iPad behind in the seat pocket.

After two sleepless nights, Lucy had thought she might pass out after the plane took off from DFW. She should have known better. The twins had been delighted one moment to be on a plane and bored the next. And toward the end of the flight, somewhere over Virginia, they'd hit turbulence, and Alice had gotten scared. She'd cried and clung to Lucy's arm every time the plane rattled and jolted. When the crew stopped service due to the storm and strapped themselves into their jump seats, Lucy had turned to Jack across the aisle to give a weak smile.

He'd leaned toward her.

"Tell Alice not to worry," he'd said. "Planes are engineered to withstand high winds and even lightning strikes. Our chances of dying are slim."

Lucy had not passed his message on.

The plane parked at the gate, and Lucy wrangled the girls, their bags, and her tote down the aisle. Jack had gone ahead with her roll-aboard and was waiting for them in the terminal, leaning against a wall with his head tipped down toward his phone. Lucy looked around for a sign telling them where to go.

"The AirTrain's that way," Jack said, pointing down the concourse, "but our flight's been delayed two hours."

"Oh," said Lucy. On the one hand, it was a relief to know they weren't in a mad rush to make their connection, but on the other hand, she was itching to get on with it.

"Do we *have* to take another plane?" said Alice.

"Unless you want to swim," said Jack.

"I'm hungry," said Zoe.

This trip was not supposed to be punitive. If anything, they needed to heal from the trauma of the last forty-eight hours. "I've got an idea," Lucy said. She needed to work during the next flight and be able to function when they landed, and that would not be easy after a night in coach. The kids followed her to a customer service counter where she cashed in every mile she had and paid a small fortune to upgrade them all to business class. By the time the transaction was complete, the storm had gotten worse, delaying their flight another hour. But with their new boarding passes in hand, Lucy felt calmer.

The smell of French fries wafted through the air, and they spotted a restaurant a few yards down the concourse. There was certainly no hurry to switch terminals.

They got a table by the window where they could see the storm raging and dozens of planes grounded at their gates, their red lights blinking.

"Our flight might get canceled," Jack said.

"Don't even say that," said Lucy.

Zoe was turned backward in her chair so she could watch the

trucks and workers out on the wet tarmac, while Alice was playing a game on Lucy's phone.

"I'm starving," Jack said, staring at his menu, looking slightly dazed, "but I'm not hungry."

Lucy understood; she too had had a stomachache for two days. But already, Dallas was receding into the past and their morning of packing up and clearing out seemed like eons ago. She was glad to be gone. And while Jack hadn't said so, she was sure he was too.

"I'm sorry I forgot to tell you," Lucy said, "Rosie came by this morning. She said to tell you she's your best friend, no matter what, and she'd love to hear from you."

He nodded, keeping his eyes on the list of burgers.

"Why don't you send her a text?"

He shook his head.

"She was very upset," Lucy said. "She just wants to know you're not mad at her."

"Don't be mad at Rosie," Zoe said, turning around to face the right way. "She's the nicest."

Alice sat up straight and gasped, staring at Lucy's phone. "Guess what about Mia Yamamoto."

"Who?" said Zoe.

"The botanist," said Alice, her voice high-pitched and anguished.

Alice was obsessed with the who's who of the ARC 6 biosphere; she had a picture of the Alpha Red Canyon team on her bulletin board and knew all kinds of trivia about the personal life of each participant, like Mia, the Japanese botanist who baked pastries in her free time, and Veronique, the French microbiologist who fixed up old car engines. Alice had calculated all their ages in Martian Sols.

"What about her?" Jack said.

"She's gone," she said, looking crushed. "She went home."

"No, she didn't," Lucy said. "Where'd you see that?"

"The NASA website," said Alice, showing her the phone.

"Impossible," Lucy said, reaching for her phone. "No one can *leave.*"

Alice shrugged. "Don't shoot the messenger."

Lucy skimmed the article, thinking Alice must have misunderstood. But she had not. Mia, it said, had left the biosphere for personal reasons. Lucy felt her heart racing. Sandra had just preached to her about the integrity of the project, the necessity of mimicking an actual Mars expedition, of being cut off from the outside world, and yet Mia had opened the faux air lock and walked out? What was that, if not a total breach of everything the mission stood for? And wouldn't Mason leave too if he had any idea what was going on with Jack? Mason was not a quitter, but in a crisis, he would choose his family over the project without hesitation; Lucy was sure of it.

There were a few new articles about Alpha Red Canyon that popped up on Google. She found a style blog that gave a thumbs-up on the official uniforms they were wearing, complimenting the practicality, the modern, sporty cut, and the color combinations—tans and muted greens—of the uniforms. More surprising, there was a link to a profile in *Time* magazine about Yağmur and Veronique. Lucy scrolled through the article in which the brilliant Turkish doctor was asked about her role as chief medical officer and her background as a physician. There was a picture of her at her home in Turkey with the strange musical instrument Mason had mentioned in his email. And the young, French microbiologist Veronique was asked about her recent breakup with a lawyer named Dwayne Randall, a well-known legal expert who often appeared on cable news. And then there was one more picture in the article that made Lucy's breath catch in her chest. It was a group photo from their first day, and there was Mason, *her* Mason, looking relaxed and handsome in a fitted T-shirt with the ARC 6 logo. Mason and five women, five young, smart, and attractive women. He was wearing the new glasses she'd helped him pick out the week before he left and a pair of silly yellow socks she'd given him to wear with his regulation Crocs. He was leaning back comfortably, a DustBunny drone sitting on the table beside him. He looked content and well rested.

Lucy, meanwhile, had chewed her fingernails down to nothing and was pretty sure her hair was falling out from stress.

"Look," she said, turning her phone, "it's Dad."

Alice reached for the phone, knocking a water glass over with her elbow. They reached for their napkins and grabbed the sticky, laminated menus. The waiter came, but before they could place their orders, Zoe jumped to her feet, looking stricken.

"Fred!" she shrieked. "Where's Fred?"

Fricking Fred. Zoe lost her stuffed rabbit so frequently they were all used to this particular brand of panic and started looking under the table and around their chairs.

The waiter walked away.

"Did you leave him on the plane?" Lucy said.

"I don't know," Zoe said, her voice high-pitched.

Lucy picked up Zoe's backpack, rummaged through it, and then looked through her own tote. "We've got plenty of time," she said, trying to assuage Zoe's growing worry. "Jack, watch the girls. Don't go anywhere. I'll go back to the gate."

"I want to come," Zoe said.

"Fine," said Lucy, taking her hand.

Lucy and Zoe retraced their steps back to the gate. They had to wait in line until Lucy could talk to the agent behind the counter. She showed her boarding pass and begged for someone to search all around the seats they'd been in. The man was understanding and asked them to wait while he used his walkie-talkie to tell whoever was cleaning the plane to look for the stuffed animal.

Lucy turned around to scan the gate area, in case Zoe had dropped Fred as they were walking through the terminal. Haggard travelers were camped out, some lying down on the floor, using their duffel bags as pillows. Lucy had picked a hell of a day to flee town. Through the constant stream of announcements about flight delays and cancellations, she tried to imagine how she would console Zoe if Fred was actually lost this time.

The agent was frowning; they'd searched the plane, he said, but a stuffed rabbit was nowhere to be found. And when Lucy looked down to break the terrible news, she was horrified to find that Zoe was missing as well.

Greta felt ill when they arrived in Newark. During the descent, the plane had lurched and rocked and dropped, making her doubt they were going to survive the landing at all. She was almost relieved to learn their flight to Dallas was delayed two hours as she couldn't bear the idea of boarding again without a chance to have her feet on the ground.

She and Otto made their way through an endless line at immigration and finally got to the baggage claim, where their suitcases never appeared. They stood there, watching the empty carousel go around and around, until they gave up and went to file a missing luggage report with the airline.

"We'll send your suitcases on to Dallas," the employee said, "if they're found."

"*If?*" said Greta.

"I meant when," he said.

With nothing but their carry-ons, they took the AirTrain to transfer to the domestic terminal. Through the windows of the tram, Greta watched the rain spattering the runways and the wind howling. For this kind of weather, they may as well have stayed in Berlin.

⚷

They walked through the crowded terminal, stopping at a Starbucks not far from the gate.

Otto ordered a coffee, but club soda was all Greta's stomach could handle. Motion sickness ran in her family, and she knew from experience it would be another hour at least before it faded.

With their drinks in hand, they found seats not too far from the gate to sit out the storm.

Otto took the top off his cup and blew on it. He leaned forward to take a sip, and then jerked away, splashing coffee on his pants. "*Scheiße*," he said. "Too hot." He got a Kleenex from his pocket and pressed it to his crotch. "*Wasser*. I need *Wasser*." He held his hand out.

"Did you burn yourself?" Greta asked, passing her water bottle.

"Yes. And oh, look, I have made a *Katastrophe* of my pants."

Greta watched as Otto poured club soda on himself and dabbed at the coffee stain with the tissue. He was making it worse. "Better to leave it alone," she said.

He studied the splotch. "How embarrassing," he said, and shrugged at her. "I will now have to sit in this chair for the rest of my life."

Greta's stomach was still roiling. "In that case, could you watch my bag? I need to walk this off."

"Where else can I go?" he said.

She paced up and down the terminal, grateful she'd worn comfortable shoes to travel, and then went into a shop to buy candy to get the sour taste out of her mouth. She also bought copies of *Time*, *People*, and *The New Yorker* to get caught up on American politics and culture.

She checked the monitor on her way back and returned to the gate. Otto had finished his coffee and was looking absently out the window.

"Feeling better?" he said.

"A little, yes. But our flight's delayed another hour."

"You will not believe it," he said, "but my pants are even getting worse." He stood up. The dark spot had spread.

"Maybe get paper towels from the bathroom?" she said. She handed him *The New Yorker*, which he held over his crotch as he walked away, still limping slightly from his stubbed toe earlier that day.

Travel, Greta thought, is not for the faint of heart—unless one got to travel like the Schultz family. For her very first meeting, the family had flown her on a private plane with a wood-paneled interior and leather bucket seats. The pilot and flight attendant introduced themselves to her, and then they jetted to an island in the North Sea, where Sebastian Schultz himself, founder of the biggest energy conglomerate in the EU, had greeted her at the door of his Sylt estate. He led her into a dining room where the doors opened to the ocean, and the whole family, dressed in cool linen pants and loose white tops, was gathered around a long, bleached-wood table, fans twirling overhead. Greta was told to sit at one end of the table, and Sebastian took his seat at the other, and he laid out the family's mission: to collect art to donate to the city of Berlin as a way of building their reputation as philanthropists and connoisseurs. Like the software mogul Hasso Plattner, who had donated his collection of French Impressionist art to a museum in Potsdam—including a record-setting $110 million Monet haystack—Sebastian wanted to become a benefactor, but for the city of Berlin.

As the staff circled the table, refilling glasses of sparkling water, lemonade, and rosé, Greta asked for a few specifics—for example: Were they, like Plattner, interested in French Impressionism? Or were they thinking of something else, German Expressionism maybe? Or contemporary art? What, she asked, was their vision? The family members looked at one another, each waiting for someone else to begin. Finally, Sebastian's wife said she loved a little Renoir still life of pomegranates she'd seen in a friend's breakfast room. His brother said he found Richter impressive, mostly because he was nine years older than he and still alive. Sebastian's sister expressed bewilderment over the popularity of Lucian Freud, objecting to the "fleshiness" of his nudes. Her husband said seascapes always made him feel small and a little depressed, but landscapes were very grounding. Sebastian's eldest nephew suggested they consider Warhol and Picasso, noting how erotic some of them were, waggling his eyebrows at Greta. A college-aged grandchild asked whether Kehinde Wiley could be commissioned to do their portraits.

And then Vanessa—who had recommended Greta to her grandfather after their chance encounter at the café—chimed in to say they should seek out newer talent, support up-and-coming artists not yet in the mainstream. She asked the family to consider focusing on contemporary art that *moved* them, rather than on names, usually of dead white men, that had already garnered a stamp of capitalist approval. Down with the patriarchy! Enough with the old masters! Her speech got a brief round of half-hearted applause that made her smile.

Sebastian cleared his throat then, almost aggressively.

Greta looked up from the notes she was taking and glanced at him; Sebastian Schultz was clearly not moved by anything his granddaughter had said.

The sea air blew in through the open doors, ruffling the petals of the white roses in their vases. Behind Sebastian was a spectacular view of sand dunes and the ocean beyond. He crossed his arms and looked at Vanessa, a slow shake of his gray head. The purpose of building a collection, he said, as though he were addressing an unwieldy group of kindergartners, was to show the world that they were serious people. As such, the art collection should convey a very particular image, one of certainty and substance. This project, he said, was not about whims; it was not about fads and was certainly not about feminism. It was about the family's identity in the public eye.

In the silence that followed, Greta asked for their budget; certainty and substance weren't cheap. Sebastian slid a piece of paper to his sister, who passed it to her husband, who passed it to their son, and so on, all the way down the table to Greta, and she pretended not to be shocked when she saw the sum. This was a curator's dream.

But within a week, the squabbling began. Vanessa copied Greta on an email to the family, suggesting they at least consider some female painters and sculptors, and an in-law replied, accusing her of reverse sexism. A second in-law chimed in, insisting they buy only German artists, while a third said that reeked of nationalism and would make them all look like Nazis. Sebastian's unmarried brother replied, saying the in-laws should stay out of the conversation altogether as they weren't actually family, which set off a firestorm on both sides.

Finally, Sebastian sent an email, saying he'd made a mistake letting so many *verdammte* cooks in the kitchen. He and Greta would work alone to build a collection of European masterpieces. What he wanted—and it was his money, he reminded them—was a Vermeer. And he would damn well get one regardless of what anyone else had to say about it.

Greta's job was part negotiator, part family therapist, and part bearer of bad news; for example, given the scarcity and demand, Sebastian Schultz was never going to get a Vermeer. They discussed other artists he admired, Renoir, Kirchner, Degas. And just as Greta was beginning to envision the collection as a whole, she did the impossible and found Sebastian Schultz a Vermeer. She would never forget the look on his face when she told him.

Now she was losing the chance to build something out of that extraordinary opportunity. She was being exiled to Texas, where, yes, she would perhaps get a tan, but she would become irrelevant in the art world.

Otto came back and sat down in the seat beside his briefcase. "I used the hand dryer," he said, "but I look anyway like a man with *Inkontinenz*. Are you eating candy? May I have some?"

"You don't eat sweets," she said.

"*Normalerweise*," he said, "but it looks good."

She reached over their bags and handed him a Hershey's Kiss. "You might not like it," she said. "It's not as good as Lindt or Milka. The texture is waxier."

"You hold very strong opinions about chocolate."

"*Selbstverständlich*," she said. "I'm German."

Otto carefully removed the foil wrapper and bit the Kiss in half. "You're right," he said, chewing, "but still, mmm."

She looked over at him in surprise. "What's gotten into you, Otto?"

"What do you mean?"

"Champagne and chocolate?"

"Why not?" he said. He leaned back and looked at the travelers milling around.

Greta got her phone and connected to the airport Wi-Fi. "Oh my," she said, "Lucy wrote to me. In German."

"I didn't know she speaks German," Otto said.

Greta could barely make it through the first sentence. "She doesn't."

"What does she say?" Otto asked.

"I have no idea," said Greta. Lucy had made an effort of sorts, but a painful one. "She hopes everything goes well with the livestock."

"What is 'livestock'?" said Otto.

"Cattle," said Greta.

Otto turned to her and smiled. "There are cows?"

"Liver . . . ?" said Greta, starting over and trying to parse Lucy's incomprehensible sentences. "She's bringing onions to our apartment."

"Why?" said Otto.

"How should I know? Something about a cleaning lady and sex and a naked bear?" She handed Otto her phone, her stomach starting to hurt again. It seemed all too fitting that Bettina had steered her into a mess of some kind. "I am not taking care of cows," said Greta pointedly. "Or goats or any other kind of farm animal."

"I have *Allergien*," said Otto, putting on his reading glasses, "to most animals. I hope this is a misunderstanding."

Greta was furious with herself for committing so hastily, and after a night of drinking! Why hadn't she asked more questions? It was not like her to rush into a big decision. "I should have packed away all the china," she said, hating the thought of this woman swooping in to take over her things. "I should have replaced every plate in the kitchen with melamine from Ikea. I don't want this woman driving our car or using my new cooktop. Unlike her, I don't have a cleaning lady, and she'll ruin all of my—"

"Greta," said Otto calmly, handing back her phone, "you go too far. Send to me this message, and I will be the one to respond with a few *Regeln*."

"Fine," she said, forwarding the message to him, "but be polite. I don't care if she likes us, but the fate of our apartment is in her hands."

"*Naturlich*," he said. "I will be friendly, just like a Texan."

"And tell her to ring Adam's bell to get the keys. He's expecting her."

Greta put her phone down when she noticed, not far from her feet, a stuffed bunny rabbit; she picked it up off the floor and brushed some lint off its fur. It was well worn and floppy, like the stuffed dog Emmi had as a child. Greta adjusted the bunny's ears and looked around the gate area, in case the owner of the rabbit was nearby. Then she propped him up on the arm of her chair.

Flipping through the pages of *Time* magazine, she landed on an article about a town in the southern part of Texas called Marfa, which was some kind of contemporary art hub, attracting visitors from all over the country. Greta dog-eared the page. Then she skimmed a profile on an attractive doctor who'd moved to the United States from Istanbul to work for NASA; Yağmur, the article said, missed Turkish food and her mother.

Greta looked out the window to where their plane was parked and waiting. Behind it, the storm still raged, rain pelting the runway. It felt like a bad omen. In the distance she could see the Manhattan skyline, just out of reach. Otto was focused on his phone as he typed out his response to Lucy Holt. His mood—despite his stained pants and lost luggage, accusations of intellectual fraud and endless travel delays—seemed to be improving the longer they were away from home. She could not say the same about hers.

And then something happened to brighten the day. A little girl, maybe seven years old, ran to her with her hands outstretched.

Greta smiled and held up the rabbit. "Is this yours?"

The girl nodded.

"What's her name?"

"*His* name," the girl said. "That's Fred."

Greta smiled and held the rabbit up to her ear. "Fred says he's very happy to see you. He's been worried." She looked Fred in the eye and shook his paw. "It was nice to meet you, Fred. I wish you a very nice voyage." And she handed him to the girl, who was beaming. "Where's your mommy?" Greta asked.

The girl turned to look as a woman rushed over, breathless and harried. She was petite, wearing cropped jeans and sneakers. She squatted down and hugged her daughter. "You scared the living day-lights out of me," she said with a slight southern drawl. "Never *ever* run off like that again."

"Sorry," the girl said, holding up the rabbit. "She found Fred."

The woman exhaled with relief. "Oh my goodness," she said, "thank you so much. You saved the day."

"It was nothing," said Greta.

The woman nodded her head at Greta and took the girl's hand before the two of them walked away.

It did not seem all that long ago that Greta would clasp Emmi's hand as they made their way through a crowd, afraid of losing her. She watched now as the mother leaned over, whispered something, and kissed the top of the little girl's head. The girl looked back at Greta and waved.

Greta sat back, pleased to have played a part. "Did you see that, Otto?" she said.

"See what?"

"A happy ending." She reached across their bags and put a hand on Otto's shoulder, half hoping that more problems could be so pleas-antly resolved as that one had.

Business class was a luxury to be sure, but as soon as they entered the cabin, Lucy realized she had not thought through the concept of pods. While the plane was taking off and landing, she wouldn't be able to talk to or even see her kids. Jack was in heaven with his fully reclinable seat, but the girls were looking small and lost in theirs. Lucy did her best to get them settled, showing them how to use their in-seat monitors and reminding them not to watch anything that wasn't rated G. Zoe held on to Fred as Lucy helped her with her headphones and started a movie. She gave Alice a kiss, reminding her not to get up, even if she felt scared again, even if the plane jostled around. Lucy took her own seat at the window and then got up one more time to double-check the girls' seat belts. Finally, a flight attendant made her sit and buckle her own. And then, as the plane took off, she closed her eyes and thought of Mason, who was becoming farther and farther away. There was certainly no turning back now.

She looked out her window as they flew over New York City, shocked that she had gone through with this plan, that they were actually on the way to Berlin! She had so many wonderful memories of her year there, of the patient woman who taught German classes, of reading *Buddenbrooks*—in English, of course—on a bench in the Tiergarten, of drinking *Sekt* with friends at KaDeWe, the big department store, in the early afternoon. She could picture her apartment and her bedroom with the big square pillows and the down comforter. She could see Bjørn's face, his strong jaw and ocean-blue eyes.

Living in a house directly next to her parents was not where Lucy had imagined she'd end up. She'd been very independent when she'd left Texas for college, deciding to spend her junior year abroad. She loved everything about Europe and dreamed of a life overseas after graduation. She flew home to Dallas before her final year at Vanderbilt; if her parents saw how changed she was, they didn't mention it. Maybe they noticed the superficial details, like the three new holes in her left earlobe, the Dunhills they found in the car, and the airy, Bohemian clothes she'd taken to wearing. But they didn't realize she'd decided to live overseas. She would find a job in London or Copenhagen or maybe even return to Berlin and become fluent in German. No matter what, she would be free to travel and would decide for herself where she wanted to settle.

As she was packing to go back to college, it dawned on her that she'd missed a period, or possibly two. She took a test and waited, without feeling especially worried; she was on the pill and was pretty darn good about taking it regularly, most of the time.

"How good?" her mom said to that, and after Lucy confessed that the test had been positive and that the test she'd taken after that one had been positive as well. They were in the living room, and Irene was pacing the periphery while Lucy's dad was sitting in a chintz armchair in the corner, rocking slightly and holding on to his head as though his palms had been superglued to his scalp.

"I mean, do you take it every single day, without fail," Irene asked, "as per the instructions?"

"I may have missed a day or two at some point," Lucy said, biting her fingernails, "but then I just take a couple together to make up for it." She had her bare feet tucked under her on the couch, and she turned to look at her dad. He'd closed his eyes, and Lucy had a feeling she'd said the wrong thing.

Irene stopped pacing and stood directly in front of her with her fists on her hips. "That's not how it works," Irene said. "And stop chewing your nails." She looked down at Lucy, shaking her head. "I can't tell what's going on under that getup you're wearing," Irene said.

Lucy had on a long skirt with a loose blouse she'd bought at a flea market in Berlin. It was the kind of outfit she imagined an eighteenth-century poet might wear to write by candlelight.

"So," her mom said, like a challenge, "why don't you tell me how pregnant you think you are."

Lucy wished she could tell her mother it was none of her business. Instead, she squinted at the ceiling, doing her best to think her way through her calendar, recalling the past few months. "I'm, like, barely even . . . at all."

"Can you be more specific?" Irene said, the words barely making it past her clenched teeth.

"Let's see—I took that trip to Spain"—*the tapas and the museums! the medieval towns and the beaches!*—"and a big group of us took the train together back to Berlin, and it was then, more or less."

"On a *train*?" said Irene.

"More or less," said Lucy.

"Oh Lord," said Irene. She turned to Lucy's dad. "Rex Henley, say something!"

Her dad opened his eyes and dropped his hands. "Lucy's on the *pill*?"

Irene sighed. "Yes, Rex, Lucy's on the pill. Can you keep up, please?"

"Well . . . who's the father?" he asked.

Now, that was a fair question. And Lucy had an answer because she knew exactly who it was, and she really liked him.

"Yes, I'd like to know that too," Irene said. "Is this a boy you know from college?"

"Not exactly," Lucy said. "His name's Bjørn."

"*Bee Yorn?*"

"Bjørn," Lucy repeated, pronouncing it carefully.

"Bjørn who?"

"Bjøøøøørn . . . Well, he's a friend of a friend. Of a friend."

Her dad stood up, looking as flustered as he had when he'd walked in on Lucy and her seventh-grade friends playing a kissing game. "You don't know his last name?"

"Not off the top of my head," Lucy said. "I can find out." But the truth was she had no idea whether she could. She would have to call the girl she'd roomed with in Berlin and have her friend Bettina ask her boyfriend to ask his classmate from Wesleyan to get the name of his Australian friend who introduced them all to the cutest blond boy Lucy had ever seen, who was traveling back with them to Berlin. Lucy had had the best sex of her life, twice on the overnight train and several times at her apartment. "He was spending the semester studying existential philosophy in . . . Valencia maybe? But he's from Denmark."

Rex bent over, hands on his knees, breathing like he'd just crossed the finish line after a marathon. "This is a bad dream," he said, "and we're going to wake up any second now . . ."

"Her trip to Spain was in April," her mom said, turning her back on Lucy. "She's already"—and she counted on her fingers—"halfway there. So buckle up, y'all, because this is happening. I'm going to make an appointment with an OB right away, and Lucy's going to track down that boy."

Lucy did not return to Vanderbilt. She stayed home with her parents and nursed her baby in the middle of the night in her childhood room with the floral wallpaper and the canopy bed.

Jet-setting around the world had been a girl's fantasy, one that got replaced by the reality of diapers and playgrounds. But she'd be lying if she said she hadn't wondered what her life might be like instead if things hadn't gone the way they did. *What if . . . ?* What if she hadn't fallen for that Danish boy who loved Haribo Fizzy Colas and American sitcoms, who read Aristotle's *Poetics* on the train and scribbled notes in the margins?

But she had fallen for him, and she'd gotten pregnant. Lucy's dream of moving overseas evaporated. And yet here she was, flying past Newfoundland and out over the Atlantic on her way to Europe.

As soon as the plane hit its cruising altitude, far above the storm, she got up to check on the girls. Alice was watching *The Little Mermaid* with headphones.

"You okay?" Lucy said.

She nodded. "This is a much better plane," she said loudly over the sound of the engines.

Lucy looked at her screen. "Did you know that Ariel," Lucy said, "is a Disney addition to the fairy tale? Hans Christian Andersen didn't give the mermaid a name."

"What?" said Alice, sliding her headphones off her ears.

"Never mind," said Lucy.

Across from her, Zoe was sound asleep with her bunny in her arms. Lucy said a silent thank-you to the fellow traveler in Newark who'd saved the day. Then she reclined Zoe's seat and covered her and Fred with a blanket.

Jack was sitting a couple of seats in front of her, watching the flight map as though he needed proof that he was getting farther and farther from home.

"You okay?" she said.

"Yeah, but I wish Dad was coming with us."

"Me too," she said.

The flight attendant was coming down the aisle with the drink cart, so Lucy went back to her seat. She got her laptop out and started by calculating the actual time difference between Berlin and LA. Her workday would begin at six in the evening and would not be over until two in the morning; *that* was going to suck. Was it even possible to be in one place while pretending to be somewhere else?

The flight attendant offered a glass of champagne. Lucy declined.

She found the file on Laurel Hotels and reviewed the mock-ups she'd made of the guest rooms, hallways, and lobby, excited to think this would all be brought into being. Over the next several weeks, she would source the furnishings and flooring, pick the tiles and fabrics, select the art and the decorative objects. She'd gotten quite a few messages of congratulations from members of the team, most of whom worked in the LA office. She'd never had such kind, responsive, and capable coworkers before and always felt lucky, even if she only saw them on a screen.

As she worked, in that nowhere-land between one continent and another, Lucy lost track of time and created something she couldn't wait to show to Bryn, Harper, and the others.

She looked out the window at the black sky, thinking of the Little Mermaid and how a price had been exacted for her trading in one life for another. Would there be a price to pay for this deal she'd made with Greta? All Lucy wanted was a safe haven. And for the first time since the shit had hit the family fan, she felt something akin to hope.

PART 3

I don't believe there is anything on earth
that you can't learn in Berlin—
except the German language.
　　　—Mark Twain

If I owned both Hell and Texas,
I'd live in Hell and rent out Texas.
　　—General Philip Henry Sheridan

To: ALL
From: Harper and Bryn

Hello, team!

As you know, we have signed a contract with Laurel Hotels. Congratulations, Lucy!

Everyone will need to bring his/her/their best to this collaboration for us to meet Laurel's ambitious timeframe goals.

Please be prompt to all meetings. Come prepared! Cameras on!

Schedule for MONDAY.

9:00 a.m. PST: In-house organizational meeting for Laurel Hotels project

1:00 p.m. PST: In-house creative team meeting

2:30 p.m. PST: In-house logistics team meeting

4:00 p.m. PST: Introductory meeting with team from Laurel Hotels

5:00 p.m. PST: Full in-house team wrap-up

This project is the right challenge for us at the right moment in our company's history. Let's do this!

Sincerely,
Bryn and Harper

◉ DALLAS

....

Twenty-two hours after leaving Berlin, Greta and Otto arrived in Texas. Their Uber pulled up in front of a gray concrete structure that, at first glance, looked a bit like an East German office building. Or a prison. But to Greta, it didn't matter that it was odd-looking or even ugly; staying in Lucy Holt's house had to be better than checking in to a Holiday Inn on the side of a highway.

Greta felt around in the dark for the handles of her tote bag and then stepped out into air so hot and thick, it didn't seem breathable. Insects buzzed in the trees overhead. She looked up and down the street. Even in the dark, she could tell that Lucy's house was an ugly duckling in an otherwise very attractive neighborhood.

Otto was standing beside her with his briefcase. "Here is not a ranch with cows," said Otto, sounding almost disappointed.

"No, *Gott sei Dank,*" she said.

The Uber drove off, and they approached the entrance, lights flicking on by motion sensor as they walked down the sloped path. Under porthole windows by the front door, Greta ran her fingers through the soil of the flowerpot, in search of a plastic rock Lucy had promised was there. Dirt lodged under her nails. Otto stepped around her and jiggled the door handle.

"Found it," said Greta. Inside the fake rock was not a key but a little transponder gadget. She spotted a pad by the door and held the device to it. She heard a click, brushed the dirt off her hands, and pushed the heavy door open.

There was an instant shift as they went from the humid outdoors into the air-conditioned quiet of the house. The entry had steel beams cutting across the pitched ceiling, and beyond it, the room opened up like a cathedral. There was a sleek, suspended staircase on one side with a round light fixture hanging over it like a full moon. The house was a glimpse into the future.

And then—to Greta's shock—two dogs came bounding toward them out of nowhere.

Greta's heart leapt and she shrieked as the animals circled and barked at them, either in enthusiastic greeting or angry alarm; Greta couldn't tell which. One was short and stocky. He looked vicious but quickly bumped against Greta's legs, licked her hand, and sat down on her foot. The other one was fluffy and yapped without interruption, while jumping on Greta with sharp little claws.

"No," she said firmly, "sit." The dog rolled over on his back and kicked.

Otto had retreated through the open doorway and was standing outside on the doormat, looking petrified. "*Vorsicht*, Greta," he said, waving her back outside. "Move away at once."

A gray-haired man rushed into the entry then. "The Germans!" he said. "You finally made it. You must be Greta," he said. He put out a weathered hand to her and then relieved her of her tote bag. "I'm Lucy's dad."

"Hello," Otto called, waving from outside the doorway. "It is nice to meet you, Mr. . . . ?"

"Henley. But you can call me Rex," he said with a smile. "Come on in. The dogs are friendly. They're just excited to meet you."

"Whose dogs . . . ?" Greta said.

"They live here," Rex said.

Lucy had not mentioned dogs.

Greta stepped out of her shoes, and Otto, who had never related to pets or responded to them or understood what they had to offer, came inside, tentatively stepping over the threshold. He took off his loafers and lined his pair next to hers by the front door as the dogs sniffed him.

Rex smiled, looking at their socked feet. "Look at you, making yourselves at home." Mr. Henley, Greta noted, was wearing tennis shoes inside the house. "Can I help you with your bags?"

"Unfortunately not," Greta said. "The airline lost our luggage."

Seemingly out of nowhere, a woman spoke: "The front door is open."

Greta looked around to see who else was there.

"That's the captain," said Mr. Henley. He stepped around them, closing the door behind them.

"The captain?" said Otto.

"It's a smart house," Mr. Henley said. "Voice-activated. You can control the lights, the temperature. Just tell her what y'all need, and she'll take care of it."

Otto looked amazed. "We need our suitcases," he said to the ceiling.

"I don't think that's quite in her purview. Hey, Captain," Mr. Henley said to the ceiling. "Play 'Goodbye Earl.'"

"Playing 'Goodbye Earl,'" the voice said.

Music came out of the ceiling. Greta got goose bumps.

"I'm no expert in technology," said Mr. Henley, tapping his foot along with the music, "not like Mason, but I'll try to show you how everything works tomorrow."

"Mason?" Greta said.

"Lucy's husband."

Lucy had not mentioned a husband. "He went to Germany with her?"

"No," said Rex. "We like to say Mason is on Mars, but he's really doing a six-month stretch out west in New Mexico. He's at Alpha Red Canyon."

Otto tipped his head in confusion, but Greta understood Rex's meaning right away, and she felt the hair on the back of her neck stand up. Lucy had gone to live in Germany while her husband was serving time in jail. But for what crime?

Rex led them into the kitchen, giving each dog a treat from a jar on the counter.

Never had Greta seen a kitchen like this. There was an industrial-size refrigerator with double doors. The gas range had six burners, and the island's vast, stainless steel surface made Greta think of an aircraft carrier. Everything here was scaled for preparing meals at a busy restaurant, not feeding a family. What a cook this Lucy must be!

The singers belted out their song through the overhead speakers as Rex pointed out the enormous back window where the trees were lit up in the darkness. "We live right over there, in a little house on the other side of that fence, so just holler if y'all need anything. Lucy left a few things for you in the fridge, a whole lot of boiled shrimp mostly, long story, and I can point you to the closest grocery store in the morning."

Shrimp seemed an odd thing to leave for houseguests. Greta had completely cleaned out her refrigerator before leaving, wiping down the shelves with a nontoxic cleaner.

"Or I'd be happy to take you to Costco sometime if you want to stock up," Rex said.

"What is that?" Otto said.

"Costco? Oh you'll love it," Rex said.

He pointed to the corner where a cage was perched on a low table. "Now let me introduce you to this little guy."

Greta was speechless.

"This here's Piglet. He's dumb as a brick, but gentle," Mr. Henley said. "I'll show you how to change his cedar chips tomorrow."

"What is it?" Greta said, walking over to look in the cage.

"A guinea pig."

A rodent in the kitchen? How unhygienic! Rex opened the cage and took out a small, tan and white *Meerschweinchen*. Greta glanced at Otto, wondering whether he too was counting animals in his head.

And then—almost as if this entire arrangement were some kind of practical joke—a cat walked into the room and jumped on the island.

Otto sneezed.

"A cat too?" said Greta.

"That's right, and there's two more around here somewhere," Rex said, patting Piglet's head. "One of them can be a little mean, but we've never figured out which was which, other than the hard way. Best to keep them all inside anyway, what with the cars and the coyotes."

Coyotes? Greta swallowed hard, cursing Lucy, Otto, and Bettina in her head. *Six pets?* Lucy had clearly gotten the better deal in this swap: a tidy, well-appointed apartment in Berlin with zero responsibilities.

The house, she noticed, didn't smell *bad* exactly, but it smelled busy, like an unholy combination of laundry detergent, grilled meat, and dirty shoe insoles.

"You want to hold him?" Rex said, offering up Piglet, who was staring at her blankly.

"No, thank you," Greta said.

"This home is quite large," Otto said, his hands on his hips as he admired the spacious kitchen. "What must it cost to run a house this size?"

Greta squeezed her eyes shut. "Really, Otto," she said, "we shouldn't ask Mr. Henley about—"

"Rex," he said, correcting her, putting Piglet back in his cage. "And my son-in-law would be proud to tell you this place has a carbon footprint of next to nothing. Passive, he calls it. Geothermal heating and cooling, solar panels running the power, a compost system, and the whole thing's insulated using technology from the international space station. It's ugly as sin if you ask my wife, but it's efficient. Can I get y'all anything?" Mr. Henley said. "How about a beer, Otto?"

He opened a drawer in the side of the island, and Greta saw rows and rows of canned and bottled drinks.

"No, thank you," said Otto. "I think I only need to sleep. It was a quite long day."

Rex patted the dogs on the head. "They've been out already," he said, "so they're ready for bed too. Hey, Captain, unlock the back door."

There was a click, and Rex opened it and stepped outside.

Otto shook his head in sleepy amazement.

"Why do you say 'Captain'?" Greta asked. It seemed silly to name what was essentially a computer.

"Because from our house," Rex said, smiling, "this place looks like a Carnival cruise ship. Good night, then." He tipped an imaginary hat, closed the door behind him, and walked away.

"How do you turn off the music?" Greta called after Rex, but he did not hear her. He crossed the slate patio and faded into the darkness at the far side of the yard. He hadn't told her the names of the dogs or where she and Otto were supposed to sleep. Greta wished she were back at home and could climb into her own bed.

The lead singer was screaming quite loudly now about packing a lunch and going to a lake. "Turn off the music," Greta said to the house. But the song kept playing.

Greta turned around to find Otto had disappeared. Only the cat was there, perched on the counter, staring at her, lashing its tail.

She backed out of the kitchen and into a living room that was larger than their entire apartment in Berlin. The house was contemporary, but it wasn't cold. It looked lived-in, like someone had jumped on the couches and run races across the floors. There were shelves filled with board games and puzzles and books. Greta could not imagine the kind of woman who lived here.

And then she noticed a stain on the living room rug, coffee possibly or something much worse and dog-related, and she stopped to look at it. Would Lucy remember that that mark was already there, before Greta and Otto had arrived on the scene? She got her phone, took a picture of the spot, and then created a folder in her photos she called "Damages." She added a picture of the side of the sofa that had been shredded by a cat.

"*Schau mal, Greta*," Otto called from the next room. "You won't believe size of the *Fernseher*."

She found him with the dogs in a cozy den, staring at a huge TV that floated on the wall above a fireplace.

"It's as if we've been living in *das neunzehnte Jahrhundert*, and now we come to this house, and we see what is actually possible." He turned to her, looking amazed. "To watch *Fußball* on such a big *Bildschirm*? I will never want to go home."

Greta smiled to think Otto could be made this happy over a television. They did not own one in Berlin.

"But I am not so much happy about the animals," he said as one of the dogs licked his socks. "I feel a deception was committed."

The song came to an end then, much to Greta's relief. There was a nice, quiet pause, but then it started up again from the beginning. "How do we make it stop?" she said. She cleared her throat and commanded, "Turn off the music." Nothing happened.

"Excuse me to the captain," said Otto. "*Halt* the music."

"Maybe we won't be able to hear it from the bedroom," she said.

They went up the stairs together, the dogs following behind.

"This is a bad situation," Greta said, a hand on the cool steel railing, her legs weary. "Did you hear what Mr. Henley said about Lucy's husband?"

"I didn't understand," Otto said. "He's in Mexico?"

"*New* Mexico," Greta said, "in jail."

"Jail? How do you know?"

"He's doing 'a six-month stretch out west.'" Greta said. "He's in prison."

"This is the home of a *Gauner*?"

"Apparently," she said. "And the wife of the criminal will be living in our apartment."

Greta looked in the first room off the landing, which was surely

Lucy and her husband's: it had a king-size bed and a large corner window. The music was coming from a speaker directly above the bed.

"No more music, please," Greta said, louder this time.

"I wish I had my sleep-suit," said Otto, unbuckling his belt.

"We'll have to do without," she said.

"But I'm cold." He dropped his pants on the floor and climbed into bed in his underwear. "The house is overly climatized."

"Let's hope our suitcases come tomorrow," Greta said.

Otto sighed and mumbled, "This house feels to me more like a spaceship than a cruise ship." He sneezed twice and fell asleep.

Greta stepped out of her slacks and blouse, folding them on a chair in the corner of the room. She went in to use the large, bright bathroom, wishing she had a toothbrush, and then climbed into bed in her bra and underwear. She could not remember the last time she and Otto had been in bed together with so few clothes on. The sheets were very soft. She rolled on her side and realized she hadn't turned off the light in the bathroom.

"Yes, excuse me?" she said to the house. "Could you turn off the bathroom light?" Nothing happened. "Please? And stop the song," she said. The music played on as the dogs paced restlessly around the room. This was not very relaxing.

Greta wondered how Lucy was faring in Berlin, what she would think of the apartment with its old-fashioned light switches and antique furniture. Would she find it too dated, too small, too . . .

And she felt herself dozing off, with the bathroom light on and a pillow over her head.

⚬━

At two in the morning, Greta woke with a jolt, disoriented and afraid. Over the song about Mary Anne and Wanda, she heard noises, kids' voices and knocking on glass. Otto was snoring, and a cat was asleep at the foot of the bed. The dogs had already run down the stairs and were barking at the front door. Greta wrapped herself in a bath towel, tiptoed downstairs, and looked out the window. The lights were on outside, all along the front walkway, but she couldn't see anyone, no people, no coyotes. So what had she heard?

The woman was singing about "Tennessee ham and strawberry jam" with a thick southern twang as Greta followed the dogs through the kitchen and family room, where they started scratching at a set of double doors. She opened them, and . . . *Oh*, she thought. So *this* was the master bedroom. She looked up at the vaulted ceiling and then walked up to the wide, upholstered bed. A framed mirror covered most of one wall of the bedroom; Greta looked past her own reflection and out to the backyard and pool, both lit up in the night. This was lovelier than any luxury hotel room she'd ever seen. And best of all, the music was not playing here.

As the dogs jumped onto armchairs in the corner of the room, Greta pulled back the covers and climbed into Lucy's bed. She would not miss the sound of Otto snoring or the woman yelling goodbye to Earl.

BERLIN

It was a gray day in Berlin when the pilot landed the Boeing 767 with barely so much as a bump.

As they taxied to the gate, four hours later than scheduled, Lucy looked out at the drizzle and realized she'd forgotten to pack raincoats. Other than the sneakers on her feet, she'd forgotten shoes. She'd forgotten toothpaste and Tylenol.

She turned on her phone and checked the time. Having worked for six hours uninterrupted, she was prepared for her meeting, even if she was sick with exhaustion. She had until six in the evening to set up a quiet place to work so her bosses and the team in LA would have no reason to suspect that she had fled the country at the outset of their company's most important project. She hoped Greta had good Wi-Fi.

She checked her email and saw she'd gotten a message, not from Greta as she was expecting, but from Greta's husband, Otto. Lucy skimmed it, frowning in confusion. He was asking about cows and onions and naked bears. The letter made absolutely no sense.

She got to the end, where he listed some rules and instructions:

When you arrive at our apartment, kling the bell of the man living in apartment 3, Herr Lance. He is an American with very bad character, and I cannot recommend him. However, he is having for you the keys to enter.

Please remove the shoes when you are being indoors. We have an old VW, but driving it is vorbidden. Our car is quite old and it is with *Schaltknüppel*—what you call "schtick stiff," and anyway it is always best to use public transportation.

As you are interested in the German language, I must say to you how important it is to use "*Sie*"/the formal address (not "*Du*"/the informal) when speaking to people you do not know. Otherwise, you are offending by being overly personal, which I warn you is a very bad idea in Germany. That is to say, you should be calling my wife Frau von Bosse and me Herr Professor Doctor von Bosse until we come to an understanding that we will use our first names. This is an important feature of our culture.

With friendly Greetings,
Herr Professor Doctor Otto von Bosse
(und Frau Greta von Bosse)

PS We do not need the services of your housekeeper, as my wife will do all the cleaning.

Lucy shook her head. What appalling people! Did they actually expect her to address them by their last names? And who turns down a prepaid, once-a-week housekeeper! *Fine*, she thought. These people can spend their whole summer cleaning cat hair off the couches.

The girls had slept on the flight and were lively, chattering to each other as they walked through the modern terminal. Lucy had not slept at all and was looking around, bleary-eyed and confused. The airport was unfamiliar to her, so unfamiliar that for a moment she wondered whether they'd flown to the wrong city.

"We're in Berlin, right?"

Jack looked at her as if she'd lost her mind.

"It's just that I thought I'd remember *something* about being here," she said.

They retrieved their bags and went outside to get in the first of a long row of cream-colored Mercedes taxicabs. It was a gloomy day, with heavy clouds hanging over them like a dropped ceiling. Lucy took the front seat and showed the driver her phone with Greta's address on the screen. "*Savignyplatz?*" the man said. "*Ein sehr schickes Viertel.*"

Lucy did not understand a word. Maybe her German wasn't as good as she'd hoped. She looked back at the kids and reminded them to buckle their seat belts.

Nothing out the cab windows looked familiar either. Lucy knew it had been a long time, but she'd assumed some intersection or landmark that might ring a bell.

"*Ich bin . . .*" she said to the driver, but she couldn't think of the word. "I don't remember the *Flughafen* looking so . . . *neue.*"

"Ah," the driver said. "It's a new airport, Brandenburg. Perhaps you are remembering Tegel?"

Lucy wondered what else in Berlin had changed since she'd been here. But as soon as the driver exited the highway, she began to recognize things in this bustling, sprawling, Manhattan-scale metropolis, a city where historic buildings from the 1800s sat directly next to modern ones and the Spree wove its way through parks and past museums. She felt her heart quicken to be back.

"There's a Five Guys," Jack said, pointing to the left.

"And a Starbucks," said Alice.

Lucy understood the allure of the familiar. "Wait, I remember this street," she said, itching to get out of the cab and explore. "Kufooster-damn?" she said to the driver. "Is that right?"

He laughed. "Kur-fürsten-damm," he said slowly.

Lucy repeated it back. "And the zoo is near here, right?" she said.

"*Ja, genau,*" the driver said as he turned at a big train station into a quaint neighborhood. The street was lined with beautiful old apartment buildings, with shops and restaurants at ground level. It was drizzling, but Lucy could imagine having lunch at a sidewalk café in the sunshine or picnicking in the park they drove by. She felt so happy to be away from the stress in Dallas, she wanted to roll down the car window and shout. No one knew them here. They were free from judgment and hostility, from slashed tires and evil eyes.

The driver turned again, this time onto a narrow cobblestone road, and pulled over beside a row of parked bicycles. Lucy paid the driver, while Jack piled the suitcases onto the wet sidewalk. She looked up at the stone facade of the building that would be theirs for the summer; it had balconies with flower boxes, reliefs of angels carved into pillars, tall windows, many flung open wide. It was charming beyond belief.

They rolled their bags up to a worn wooden door and crowded under the stoop to stay dry. She checked the email from Herr Doctor Von La-Dee-Dah and rang the buzzer with the name "Lance" next to it. She saw Greta's buzzer above it and pressed it as well for good measure. There was no answer at either. She waited for what seemed like a polite amount of time and buzzed again, pressing harder and longer this time. She jiggled the door handle.

"Lance," said Zoe, standing on tiptoe to see the buzzers, "like Lancelot?"

"A man of bad character," Lucy mumbled.

"He's bad?" Alice said.

"I'm sure he's perfectly nice," said Lucy, checking her phone. "But where is he?"

"We're late," Jack said. "We were supposed to be here hours ago."

They pressed their faces up to the glass window beside the door. The foyer was the most European-looking thing Lucy had ever seen. It had a twelve-foot-high plaster ceiling with decorative medallions, each with a wrought iron light fixture suspended over the checkerboard marble floor. There was marble on the walls as well, halfway up to the ceiling. On the far side was a curved staircase with a dark wood handrail, an ornate iron baluster, and stained glass windows on the first landing. There was a door that went out the back to a courtyard, possibly a place the girls could play . . . if only they could get in.

"Why are we sharing a house with other people?" Alice said.

"It's not a house," said Lucy. "It's an apartment building."

Zoe left the stoop and sat on her suitcase, straddling it like a horse, getting damp from the drizzle. Jack was scrolling on his phone.

Lucy's hope of getting a nap and shower before work was dwindling; she needed to be clearheaded and settled, and that wasn't going to happen standing on a rainy sidewalk in the middle of the city. "Well," Lucy said, "let's get some food and come back in an hour."

"What about our stuff?" Alice said.

Lucy looked at the pile of suitcases. So much baggage. "We're going to have to bring it along," she said, wiping a strand of hair off her forehead. "Does anyone have paper? I'll leave the guy a note."

Zoe opened her backpack and gave Lucy a piece of yellow construction paper and a pink marker that smelled like bubble gum.

Standing under the stoop, Lucy wrote Adam a message, asking him to call. She scribbled her phone number under her name and slipped the folded paper halfway through his mail slot.

They put their backpacks on and rolled their suitcases down the bumpy sidewalk and around the corner onto Schlüterstraße. The first restaurant they found was an Italian place called Mondo Pazzo where they were greeted with *Buongiorno* instead of *Guten Tag*, which Lucy found disorienting. It wasn't what Lucy had in mind—she'd imagined schnitzel and spätzle—but it would do. The waiter walked them past the wet outdoor seating area and into the dining room, ushering them to a table in the back with a red and white checkered cloth. He helped Jack pile the suitcases along the wall beside them, and they all ordered plates of spaghetti.

The food came—comforting and delicious—and still the neighbor didn't call. Lucy stalled after the plates were cleared, ordering tiramisu and gelato, but the girls began to get restless. Lucy thought she might fall asleep right there at the table and ordered an espresso. What were they even doing here? She cursed Greta in her head.

Another half hour went by, and Lucy gave up. She waved to the waiter to get the check, having made up her mind to find a hotel for the night. She was googling "hotels near me" when her phone pinged. For a split second she imagined it was Mason: *Stay where you are, babe! I'm coming to get you!*

But it was a text from an unknown number:

Adam here. Back @ apartment now w keys. Have 2 go soon. Where r u?

The man texted like a barbarian. She took a deep breath and texted back: We will be there in 3 minutes!!! PLEASE do NOT leave!!

She did not regret the caps or the exclamation points.

It was still raining. They walked back the way they'd come, and when they turned the corner, they saw a man standing in front of the apartment building under a big black umbrella, looking up and down the street for them. When he spotted them—they were hard to miss, after all—he waved.

"Lucy? You finally made it," he said.

"Mr. Lance," she said, an edge to her voice. "Nice to meet you."

His hair was mussed in a way that looked like he'd either spent a lot of time on it or none at all. "Adam, please," he said. "Any friend of Greta's . . ." He held his umbrella over her head. "I didn't expect so many of you."

"These are my kids," Lucy said. "Jack, Zoe, and Alice."

"Hey, guys," he said. The guy had a terrific smile. "Rough trip?"

"We were delayed in Newark," said Lucy, "for four hours."

"Yeah, I figured when you didn't show up this morning," he said with a lift of his broad shoulders.

"So you're the American neighbor," she said.

"Expat," he said. "I've been here about six months already, on my own."

Divorced, Lucy thought. The "on my own" was so telling.

Zoe tapped her arm. "Can we go inside now?" she said.

"You guys are apartment four," Adam said, "which is actually the fifth floor." And he pointed up to a beautiful balcony. He handed

Lucy two keys, one of which she thought had to be a toy. Or a joke. It was heavy and worn, and it looked like it unlocked the gates of a fourteenth-century fortress. Or a prison. It had a deep red ribbon tied around a brass loop.

"Yeah, I know," Adam said as she gawked at it. "Greta's partial to antiques. Her apartment has the original door and lock because, you know, *authenticity*. It's just so . . . her. And I mean that in the best possible way." He handed her another key. "Here's the key to the outside door."

"Great," Lucy said. "Thanks."

"She asked me to remind you not to wear your shoes inside. They just had the floors redone."

"Yeah, I got an email with some rules," Lucy said, feeling like she could be open with him, one American to another. "They seem a little . . . uptight?"

"Otto, for sure," said Adam. "But Greta's a real sweetheart."

"He actually reprimanded me for calling them by their first names."

"Classic Otto," he said, and shook his head with a laugh; he was not a bad-looking guy. "Sorry to run, but I've got to get back to the studio." He looked at their luggage. "Can you guys manage all this? I hate to rush off—"

"We're fine," said Lucy, putting her heavy tote over her shoulder.

"It's five flights up," he said, and pointed up again, "just above mine."

"Got it," said Lucy.

"You've got my number," he said. "Text if you need anything." He waved and walked quickly away.

Lucy took the normal key, slipped it in the lock, and opened the door.

She and the kids wrestled their luggage into the entry. As soon as they were inside, Lucy began to feel hopeful; they had some kind of home base now, and there was just enough time for a rest and a quick shower before work.

Jack had already started up the stairs.

Lucy looked around the entry. "Where's the elevator?"

"There isn't one," said Jack.

"Wait— *What?*" Five flights and no elevator? Lucy dropped the handle of her suitcase and picked it up using both hands.

Zoe sat down on the second step, trying to drag her bag off the floor.

"Leave it," said Lucy. "We'll come back for it."

They started up the creaking wood stairs, one flight and then another. Each flight was split into two, with a wide landing in between. On the second one, Lucy put her suitcase down to rest, looking out the window at the wet, leafy courtyard. There were a couple of cars parked around the periphery, a classic VW bug among them, yellow with a convertible top, probably the car Herr Doktor Van Bossy Pants had forbidden her to drive.

They finally reached the top floor, where Jack was leaning against the wall with his eyes closed.

Lucy put the large, brass key in the lock and turned it. She opened the door.

"Lovely," she said, stepping into the foyer. There was a coat rack in the corner, a velvet-covered antique bench, and a demilune table with a porcelain vase on it. The floors were laid in a herringbone pattern with a gorgeous honey-colored finish. "Now I get it," she said, and stepped out of her sneakers.

The girls pulled off their shoes as well and wandered into the apartment.

"I'll bring up the other suitcases," Jack said, and he walked back out to the stairwell.

"Thank you!" Lucy called after him.

There was a door on their left that led to an office, cramped but with a tall window that faced the street. There was a couch and an antique desk, complete with a fountain pen and inkwell. Perfect; this is where Lucy would work every night. She put her tote bag on the desk chair.

The other doorway off the foyer opened to the kitchen, which was surprisingly modern given the age of the building. A shiny glass cooktop disappeared into a stretch of black granite, and the refrigerator—absurdly small—had a sleek, cream-lacquered front that matched the cabinets. On the counter there was an envelope with Lucy's name written in thick cursive.

Through the kitchen, she went into the dining room, which had a round table with carved legs and a heavy base, encircled by straight-back antique chairs upholstered in black horsehair.

There were French doors opening to a living room with stiff sofas that Lucy would have to cover up with sheets to make sure the kids didn't ruin them. Ornately framed oil paintings hung on the walls and silk curtains pooled onto the floor. Every surface had some decorative piece of porcelain or fragile crystal. Everything looked museum-worthy, precious, and breakable. Lucy thought of those perfectly preserved rooms in a palace, viewed from the other side of a red velvet rope. This was a truly terrible place for eight-year-olds.

She went down the hallway and found a bathroom with a small floating vanity, a nicely tiled shower, and a bidet.

She followed the sound of the girls' voices and found them across the hall in a room where Zoe was jumping on a big bed, a comforter tossed on the floor.

"No roughhousing," Lucy said. "We have to treat this house gently."

Jack came in the room and dropped the girls' suitcases on the floor.

"Careful," Lucy said. "And take off your shoes."

"Fine," Jack said, sighing with annoyance and stepping on the backs of his heels to take off his Vans. "Happy now?"

"Look, I don't make the rules here," Lucy said. "We're all going to have to act like we're living in the Dallas Museum of Art, okay?"

"We don't take our shoes off at the museum," Alice said.

"We're going to have to be so careful," Lucy said, "and no going out on the balcony unless I'm with you. And no touching . . . anything."

Lucy went back to the hall and looked in the next room, which was likely Greta and Otto's bedroom. It had a hard, tightly made bed, an armoire in a nook against one wall, and . . .

"Wait," Lucy said, incredulous. "No, we're all sharing *one* bathroom?"

Jack came up behind her. "I don't get it," he said. "Where am I supposed to sleep?"

"Oh no," she said. "No, no, no, no." She walked back down the hall, hoping some additional room had gone unnoticed. But there were only two bedrooms, meaning Jack would be sleeping on the couch in the little office, the office Lucy had planned to take over for work. Back in the kitchen, she opened the envelope to find a long, detailed letter from Greta, written on expensive stationery. Flipping through the pages, Lucy learned that the trash had to be separated into six separate recycling receptacles, the dryer came with a complicated instruction manual that involved emptying a water tank, and the apartment did not have air-conditioning.

There was a crashing sound from the bedroom, and Lucy ran down the hall to find Zoe holding the pieces of an antique plate, broken seashells and porcelain shards scattered around her bare feet.

"Uh-oh," said Alice.

Zoe burst into tears.

DALLAS

Greta opened her eyes, looked up at the cathedral ceiling, and remembered where she was. She felt hemmed in somehow and sat up to find that the dogs had abandoned their armchairs and were asleep on what should have been Otto's side of the bed. And Otto? She hoped he wasn't wandering through the neighborhood in search of his missing wife.

She got out of bed, wrapped the bath towel around herself, tucking one corner into her cleavage to make a strapless dress of sorts, and left the five-star bedroom with the dogs at her heels. There was no sign of Otto in the kitchen, but the song about Earl was still playing.

The house was even more impressive in daylight. One of the kitchen walls was covered in a thick, gray, felt-like material and had children's art thumbtacked onto it. Lucy had not mentioned children, and Greta wondered how many she had and where they were. Summer camp perhaps. There were also sketches of robots, sophisticated ones with annotations and mathematical formulas in the margins. Greta looked out the window in the direction that Mr. Henley had walked last night, past the patio where several large round tables were set up in the grass, signs of a large backyard party. A rectangular swimming pool sparkled in the sunlight, a pink flamingo raft floating in the middle and a fountain pouring water off a ledge at the far end. Greta felt a little guilty then; maybe Lucy had gotten the worse end of this deal after all.

Greta's apartment, however, did not come with the task of caring for multiple pets. The dogs were looking at her expectantly. One cat was on the counter, pacing back and forth and mewing, and the guinea pig squeaked from his cage.

She needed caffeine. There was a built-in Miele coffee maker in the wall, and she found an oversize mug that said "Boss Mom." She put it on the shelf and pushed the button for a cappuccino.

While the machine whirred and ground the coffee beans, she waited, listening, and finally came to understand that Wanda and Mary Anne had murdered that no good Earl.

Greta adjusted her towel and walked through the house with her cappuccino. In the dining room there were several framed black-and-white photographs of landscapes, all set in small towns, in fields, and on ranches. There were horses and cows, fence posts and barbed wire, all impressive compositions. She checked the signature and did a double take: Lucy's father was the photographer. Greta was fascinated; she wouldn't have thought the man holding the guinea pig last night had an artistic side.

The dining room table had a deep scratch in the surface and the cane seat of one of the chairs was broken. Greta would snap a picture later for her "Damages" folder that she planned to send to Lucy for their records.

The dogs began barking at her, so she went back to the kitchen, unlocked the door, and stepped out onto the patio. The flagstones were warm and rough on the soles of her feet. She walked past the party tables to the edge of the pool and dipped her toes in the turquoise water. It was so peaceful here; the only sound was birdsong and the splashing of the fountain, none of the city noise—garbage trucks and ambulances—she was accustomed to.

From here, the house, all concrete, sharp angles, and glass, showed itself to be exactly as Rex had described: a thoroughly modern, oddly shaped cruise ship.

Something brushed up against Greta's foot, and she jumped back as a cat rolled on the grass beside her. "*Oh Gott*, oh no," Greta said. She didn't dare pick him up. Instead she backed up toward the house, calling, "*Komm, Kätzchen.*" The cat ignored her, so she tried again in English, making her voice high-pitched. "Come, kitty, come here," she said, but the cat ran in the opposite direction toward a little gate in the fence and ducked under a bush. It was her first day there, and a cat had already escaped on her watch. She rushed to the door and pulled it closed to prevent another from getting out. When she turned back to the pool, she saw that the short-haired dog was taking a swim—was that even allowed?—snapping at the water like a croc-odile, while the other was eating grass. And there was yet another cat under one of the tables, crouched low to the ground, its tail thrashing. This was very, very bad.

She would have to find treats inside, something she could use to lure them all in. Greta went back to the house, only to find that the door handle wouldn't budge. She cleared her throat and spoke loudly to the doorknob: "Open the door, please." Nothing happened. She knocked on the door, calling, "Otto!" There was no sound in the house, no movement. She looked at the windows of the upper story, knowing she could not possibly be heard through the space-rated insulation.

There was nothing to do but wait.

She sat on a lounge chair by the pool and put her feet up, wishing she had clothes on. Wishing she had her phone so she could call Otto. Wishing she hadn't blundered so badly on her first morning.

Time passed, who knew how long. Greta had finished her coffee and was starting to sweat. Mosquitos bit her ankles and the nape of her neck, and she needed to go to the bathroom. A leaf blower was roaring from somewhere nearby. The dogs were asking to go inside, and the cats were nowhere to be seen.

She got up and knocked loudly on the kitchen door again. The third cat—striped like the others—was watching her resentfully from the kitchen counter.

There was a sound behind her, and she turned to see the gate open. A woman walked into the yard. She was wearing a smart-looking sheath dress with bright gold jewelry and pink lipstick. Her hair was in curlers. Both dogs, one dripping wet, ran over to meet her.

"Oh, no you don't," the woman said to the dogs. "Sit!" The dogs sat.

Greta tightened her towel and crossed her arms to cover her chest.

"Well, hello there!" the woman called out with a warm smile. "Look at you, enjoying the pool already."

Greta preferred this interpretation of her outfit to the more accurate one. "Good morning," she said.

"I'm Lucy's mom, Irene." And she opened her arms and hugged Greta as though they'd known each other for years, as though they were family.

Greta knew most Americans were huggers, but her mother was not, so hugging strangers was not something she was accustomed to. Irene gave one final squeeze and let her go.

"I heard from Rex y'all got in real late last night, so I figured you'd probably sleep in, but here you are, up and at 'em."

Greta was up all right, and she was mortified to be practically naked. She smiled at Irene, who had the look of a woman who held strong opinions and got regular Botox treatments.

Irene handed Greta a tote bag. "Rex says the airline lost y'all's luggage. We thought you might need some things to tide you over."

"Thank you," said Greta, looking in the bag to see folded T-shirts and travel toothbrushes.

"Now first things first," she said. "A company is coming by at ten to pick up all these tables and chairs Lucy rented. They'll carry them right out the side gate."

"Was there a party?" Greta said.

"Not exactly," said Irene, dropping her smile. "It's a long story."

"Speaking of long stories," Greta said, "I'm afraid I've had a mishap." Her cheeks felt hot, and she wondered whether she'd already gotten sunburned. "I came outside to see the pool, and I'm sorry to say, two of the cats escaped before I could stop them. And then, I locked myself out of the house, and I don't even have my phone to call my husband, who has never slept this late in his life." She forced a smile, feeling incredibly stupid.

Irene looked confused. "Why's your English so darn good?"

This was not what Greta had expected her to say. "My mother's American. She's from New York."

"Is that right?" said Irene. "I mean, I hear a slight accent, but . . ." And then she raised a finger. "First rule of Dallas: cats and air-conditioning stay inside."

"Yes, I'm so sorry, Mrs. Henley," said Greta, adjusting her towel.

"Irene," Irene said, and she turned to survey the yard. "Don't you worry. We'll wrangle 'em."

"Thank you," said Greta, stepping away from the dog who was licking her bare knee. "What are the names of the dogs?"

"The big one's Tank," said Irene, pointing to where he was rolling in the grass. "And this here's Bunny. They're both rescues." She patted the pale, fluffy dog on her head.

"Why Bunny?" said Greta.

"Zoe is obsessed with rabbits."

"Who's Zoe?"

"My granddaughter, of course. Lucy has eight-year-old twins. And a teenage son. Didn't she tell you? They're all living in your house."

"Apartment," said Greta. Lucy definitely needed to work on her German; in her email, she must have meant "twins," not "onions." The idea of Thing 1 and Thing 2 running loose in her beautiful home made Greta feel sick. She should have hidden the Anna Katharina Block painting and the Kirchner woodcut in a closet. She should have packed up the Lalique and the Nymphenburg. "We rushed into this arrangement, and didn't ask each other any of the right questions," Greta said, scratching at a mosquito bite behind her ear. "Or any questions at all, really. I knew nothing about pets. And my apartment is quite small."

"Well, desperate times, I guess," Irene said, taking Bunny by the collar. "At least you both got where you needed to go."

Greta supposed that was true. "If you have a spare key, I'd like to get dressed."

"You don't need a key," Irene said.

They walked to the door, and Irene showed her how to enter into the keypad the six-digit code, which Greta committed to memory. It was a relief to be back in the cool of the house, but she didn't feel like she could go upstairs without helping Irene find the cats she'd let out.

Irene got a can of tuna and took it outside to the middle of the yard, popping it open and setting it down in the grass. She waited until the two cats came slinking over to her and grabbed the first one, bringing him inside. Greta was too scared to pick up the other. So Irene went back out for the second, who hissed and clawed her ankle when she put him on the kitchen floor. Greta was horrified. "Are you okay?" she said, certain that cat scratch fever was a real thing.

"Barely broke the skin," Irene said, wetting a paper towel to wipe the blood off her leg. Then she washed her hands, brushed the cat hair off her dress, and looked up at the ceiling. "'Goodbye Earl'?" she said. "First thing on a Monday? You must be in a mood."

"I don't know how to turn it off," Greta said.

"Hey, Captain," Irene said, "turn off that music."

The music stopped.

"Thank you," Greta said, exhaling with relief. "She would not listen to me."

"You've always got to start with 'Hey, Captain' to get her attention."

Greta was desperate now to go put her clothes on, but Irene didn't leave. Instead, she went to the built-in Miele and helped herself to a cup of coffee. "Hey, Captain, what's the temperature outside?" she said.

"The temperature is ninety-six degrees," said the captain.

"Already?" Irene said.

Bunny vomited a pile of grass and drool on the kitchen floor. Irene acted as though this was a regular occurrence. She got a paper towel and wiped it up. "Time to feed the cats. I'll explain all of this to you when I get home from work tonight," she said.

Greta was impressed; Irene had to be close to seventy. "Where do you work?"

"I run the front desk of a large dental practice," Irene said. "I deal with people all day long, scheduling appointments for everything from cavities to braces to dentures. I handle insurance claims and have to keep all the supplies stocked. Same job for thirty years. I'm not like Lucy. I don't like change. Last time I left Dallas was five years ago."

"Where did you go?"

"Switzerland," she said. "Rex had a bee in his bonnet about seeing alpine cows. Very pretty place, great cheese, but lord, I hate to fly. I was so happy to get back home. We still live in the same house Lucy grew up in."

Greta felt a pang of guilt that she wasn't helping her own mother pack boxes. "My mother is about to move from the house I grew up in," Greta said. "My father died a few months ago."

"I'm so sorry," Irene said. "Do you have children, Greta?"

"A daughter," Greta said. "Emmi. She's at the university in Freiburg, so we haven't seen her much this year. But she's coming here to visit us soon." Not soon enough, of course, and Emmi probably couldn't stay as long as Greta wanted. But she would take whatever she could get.

Irene's smile faded a bit. "I'm sorry she won't get to meet my grandson," she said. "He's college age too." She reached up and touched her curlers.

Greta could not bear to be in her state of undress for another minute. She took the bag Irene had given her and said goodbye, excusing herself as she left the kitchen.

"I'll still be here," Irene called after her.

For how long? Greta wanted to ask. As Greta was passing by the front door, she noticed that one of her shoes was missing. She wondered whether she'd accidentally left it outside the previous night while the dogs were making such a fuss over their arrival. She opened the door to check, but her shoe was not on the mat. Instead, Greta spotted what appeared to be the excrement of several dogs, along with a ball of paper. She unwrapped it from around a stone and read the words: *Asshole loser!*

Greta shut the door firmly and locked it. Then she went back to the kitchen, where Irene was pouring dog food into two bowls. "One of my shoes is missing, there's a large pile of feces on the doormat, and I found this note." She held out the paper.

Irene set the bag of dog food on the counter and took the paper. Greta watched her go pale.

"Those little sons of bitches," Irene said, wadding it up in her hand.

"Who?"

Irene looked up. "Just some neighborhood brats," she said with a smile. "It's nothing really, a little prank."

"A *prank?*"

"You know how kids can be," Irene said with a shrug. She put the bowls of dog food on the floor and watched as they dug in. "I'll get Rex, and he'll clean the mess up off the porch."

"Yes, but . . ." Greta wasn't sure exactly what to ask but felt she should know who had sent such an aggressive message. "Who—Why . . . ?"

"It won't happen again," Irene said. "Or on second thought, it probably will." She sighed. "Lucy's son ruffled a few feathers around here, which is why they left town in a hurry. It's not what people think, but it didn't look good."

"What didn't look good?"

"It's nothing for you to worry about," Irene said, sweetly but with resolve. "And it's not my story to tell. My grandson's a good boy who did a very dumb thing, and I'll leave it at that."

Greta nodded, but she felt very skeptical of these people. In her experience, good people didn't behave in such a way that led to angry notes, dog poop, exile to Berlin, and six months in a New Mexico prison.

"As for the missing shoe," said Irene, "I would check the dog beds. I'm sorry to say it's probably a goner."

Greta had no suitcase, no shoes, and no desire to spend another minute on this cruise ship. If only she could disembark.

BERLIN

The Wi-Fi was absolutely terrible. On her second night of meetings, Lucy blurred her background, hoping to mask the mayhem going on in the tiny apartment behind her, but that didn't stop Harper from leaning in and saying, "What's going on over there, Lucy? You're really pulling focus today."

It was midnight in Berlin and the girls were still up. "Sorry, my office is . . . being painted," she said.

"Oh?" said Harper, sounding very suspicious. "Is that why your energy's so off today?" And then she froze.

Lucy booted and rebooted the Wi-Fi three times. Alice and Zoe were arguing in the next room, so Lucy muted herself whenever she could during the consequential discussions they were having about construction schedules, materials, furniture, and communication flow.

She begged the girls to go to bed—and she could hear Jack trying to make them, promising candy the next day if they would sleep—but jet lag won out, even over bribery.

At almost two in the morning, Zoe pinched her finger in the bathroom door and wailed. Lucy turned off her camera and muted herself to go comfort her, and when she returned to the meeting, she'd missed some crucial point a man on the Laurel team had made about branding. He had to repeat himself for her, and Harper and Bryn made their annoyance glaringly obvious.

This project required her full concentration, and she could not concentrate. She wanted to shine, to make her coworkers as happy to have her on board as she was to be there, but so far, her performance was a disaster.

After logging off at three in the morning, she settled on two facts: she had to get the girls on German time and she needed a better place to work.

⚬—

Later that morning, she turned off her alarm, rolled over, and looked around Greta's room. Across from the hard bed was an old, crackled painting of a floral arrangement. It was pretty but dark—almost funereal with its black background and drooping blooms. Lucy studied the faded pink petals and the butterfly hovering just above a red poppy, feeling pretty sure she and Greta wouldn't like each other. Greta had actually emailed an itemized list of damaged items she'd found in Lucy's house that she didn't want to be held responsible for, attaching pictures of her dinged-up floors and stained carpets as evidence. Lucy had written back, saying, "The way I see it, a house should be lived in and enjoyed. Please don't worry about such things."

Greta had answered: "While I appreciate the sentiment, I hope we both agree to treat each other's valuables with the utmost respect."

Zoe had already broken one antique plate, and Lucy couldn't make any promises that there wouldn't be another accident or two. She didn't answer.

She missed Mason with her whole body. Leaving Dallas hadn't dampened the longing or distracted her from his absence; rather, she felt all the more unsettled to be so far away from him, and the lack of communication felt a million times worse now that she was in a foreign country. She could not bring herself to write him again until she had better news to report. Instead, she had imaginary conversations with him, conjuring his opinions on the cheesy painting on the wall, the hard mattress, the bidet.

She got dressed and went to the kitchen to make coffee in the

French press, a device she'd had to google to learn how to use. While it brewed or steeped or did whatever it had to do, she stood in the working Wi-Fi zone and checked her phone. There was a message from her mother: Tank ate Greta's shoe. She locked herself in the backyard wearing nothing but a towel. Even half-naked, she's got style . . . practically regal.

Regal? That hurt; Lucy's mom would never describe Lucy as regal. Cute maybe. Impulsive certainly. She adjusted her posture and started to answer her mom but thought better of it; it was the middle of the night in Dallas, and her mother always left her ringer on.

She'd gotten an Instagram message from Greta's sister, Bettina, saying she planned to stop by sometime to say hello. And there was a long email from Harper to ALL, outlining problems that urgently needed solving and asking team members to bring their A game. Lucy wanted to—did she ever—but her C game was the best she'd managed so far.

She went back to the kitchen and pressed the plunger on the coffeepot. The only cups in the cabinet were Nymphenburg porcelain, and Lucy took a careful sip from a gold-rimmed cup, placing it back in its saucer gently, feeling like a dowager countess.

Jack came out of the little office where they'd removed the back cushions from the couch and made up a bed with sheets and pillows. Lucy had not apologized for the sleeping arrangements, even though Jack was taller than the couch was long. This apartment was far from ideal, but she had done the best she could to get them out of Dallas as quickly as possible. Some sacrifices would have to be made this summer. She only hoped her job wasn't one of them.

"*Guten Morgen,*" she said, trying to sound cheerful.

"Hey," he said. He was wearing boxers and a T-shirt, and his hair was a mess. Like Lucy, he was not and had never been a morning person. He got out the small container of milk and box of cereal she'd bought the day before; both were almost empty.

"*Wie geht es dir heute?*" she said.

"Huh?"

"It means how are you today? *Wie geht es*—"

"Can we actually . . . not?" he said, rubbing his eyes.

"Speak German?" Lucy said in surprise. "Don't you want to learn the language while we're here?"

"Not really," he said. "It's not like we're going to be here forever."

That remained to be seen. Lucy had no idea when it would be safe to go home.

"Well, we're here now," she said, leaning her elbows on the counter, "for however long, and we should pick up a few words. It might even be useful to you down the road."

"What for?" he said.

"I don't know," she said, "but it could be." She took a sip of her coffee. It was good actually, better than what she made at home. "Can you help me brainstorm? I need some good ideas on how to keep the girls quiet while I'm working."

He didn't answer.

"Jack?"

"I don't know what you expect me to do," he said. "I can't lock them in their room. They get in fights and act bratty and—"

"I'm not blaming you," Lucy said. "I'm just—"

"Of course you are," he said, looking through the kitchen cabinets. "It's my fault we're even here, and believe me, I feel guilty enough about all of this." He ran a hand through his messy hair. "I sent an email to MIT last night."

Lucy set her cup down. "You did?"

"I got myself into this mess," he said, "and I have to fix it."

"Well, what did you write? Like exactly?" Lucy had put thought into such a letter, believing there were several land mines that should be avoided, certain phrases—"dollar values" and "popular girls." He needed to take responsibility while simultaneously rejecting the school's version of events. She had assumed they would write several drafts to get the tone just right.

"I just explained what happened," he said.

"Explained it how?"

Jack got a bowl, shallow and thin-rimmed, and a spoon that Lucy suspected was sterling silver. "I just gave my side of the story. I know it's a long shot," he said, "but do you think they'll listen?"

Lucy didn't have the faintest idea but it seemed unlikely. "Maybe?" she said.

"I know you wanted to help me write it, but I felt like the email should come from me," he said. He poured the cereal and put the box down. "I'm sorry you can't work here. I'm sorry I ruined Dallas for all of us."

"You didn't ruin Dallas," she said.

"I did." He leveled his gaze at her. "And I can't go back there, probably ever."

"Of course you can—"

"I can't," he said, firmly enough that it startled her. "But you, Zoe, and Alice are going to have to."

It was hard to imagine driving up to the elementary school and facing the other Rockwell parents. But it was possible the story would fizzle out over the course of the summer and people would eventually forget all about it.

"Let's not get ahead of ourselves," she said. "We're out of the fray now, and we happen to be in this great city. Let's settle in and make the best of it."

Jack poured the milk and then put the carton away in the tiny refrigerator.

"I'll get Zoe and Alice up this morning," she said, "and we'll do something really fun and wear the girls out so at least they'll go to sleep at a normal hour."

There was a loud knock on the door then, and Jack picked up his cereal bowl and went off to his room.

As Lucy went to see who was there, she couldn't help but notice the absence of exuberant barking that her brain associated with the appearance of a visitor.

She opened the door to Adam, who greeted her with a bouquet of flowers. "Welcome to Berlin," he said. He was in a T-shirt and jeans, and either he or the flowers smelled amazing.

"Adam," she said, "that's so nice."

"I want to apologize for being rushed when you got here the other day," he said. "I feel like a jerk for not helping you with the bags."

"Too many stairs," she said, "but we managed."

She stepped back to let him in. Adam closed the door behind him, took off his shoes, and followed her into the apartment. Lucy went to the kitchen to look for a vase.

"I thought I'd check in," he said, "to see how you guys are doing."

From the kitchen, she could see him looking around the dining room with curiosity.

"This is exactly how I imagined it," he said. "Wow."

"Haven't you been here before?" she asked.

"No," he said. "Greta has been to my place a few times, but they've never had me over."

Lucy wasn't really surprised to hear that, given Herr Whatever's mention of Adam and his bad character. But Adam was coming across like a decent enough guy so far. "That's not very nice," Lucy said. She found an etched vase in a cabinet and filled it with water.

"It's not her fault," he said. "Otto's not all that friendly, and Greta has been really wrapped up in her job. You know she's a big-deal art collector?"

"I didn't, but that makes perfect sense. Do you want coffee?"

"Sure, thanks."

Lucy got another gold-rimmed cup and saucer out. "Can I ask," she said, "how important is it to speak German here?"

He was leaning in to look at a still life on the dining room wall beside the silk curtains. "Don't bother. Pretty much everyone speaks English."

Maybe Jack was right and they didn't need to bother, but Lucy thought it would be a missed opportunity for them all.

"Why?" he said. "Do you speak German?"

"I thought I did," said Lucy glumly, "but I couldn't even understand the woman at the grocery store yesterday."

Adam came into the kitchen, and she offered him milk and sugar.

"I can't get myself to take lessons," he said, "but I probably should. I'm having a hard time fitting in here. I think it's because I tend to blurt out whatever's on my mind, and some of the Germans I've met seem shocked by me. Not Greta though," he added quickly. "She's half-American, and you can definitely tell."

Lucy cut open the paper wrapping from the flowers and began putting them in the vase one stem at a time, brightly colored tulips, tea roses, and peonies, a far more cheerful sight than the depressing depiction in Greta's bedroom. "Her apartment's beautiful and all," Lucy said, "but it's a bad match for us. It's too small, and the Wi-Fi's awful."

"Why are you guys here," Adam said, leaning against the kitchen counter, "if you don't mind my asking?"

"We had to leave town in a big, fat hurry, and I sort of rushed into this whole house swap thing."

Adam squinted at her. "Are you a fugitive?"

"I mean, we're not *not* fugitives," she said. "Let's just say we had our reasons for blowing town."

"Interesting," he said, "but I won't pry, at least not until I get to know you better." He was holding the coffee cup by its tiny handle, the saucer perched in his other hand. The sight made Lucy miss her mugs from home.

"The problem is," she said, "I have to work on California time, which really sucks."

"Shit," he said, "how are you going to keep that up?"

"I have no idea," she said, adding the last rose to the vase. "My daughters are making it impossible to appear even the least bit professional on Zoom. I need a twenty-four-hour WeWork. Do you think that exists around here?"

"I have no idea," he said, and raised his coffee cup to her. "But I'll tell you what: you can use my place."

"Excuse me?" Lucy said, looking up from the flowers.

"Oh," he said, "was that weird?"

"I mean, I appreciate hospitality as much as the next guy," she said, "but you definitely sound like a serial killer."

"No, really," he said, "my schedule's upside down too, and I'm usually out all night anyway, so you can use my place if you want. I have a spare room with a desk."

"Out all night" seemed like some kind of red flag, but the words "spare room" and "desk" were music to her ears. Lucy was so tempted to say yes, at least for a few days. "Am I going to end up in your freezer?"

Adam scoffed. "Have you *seen* the size of German freezers?"

"Good point." Greta and Otto's could barely hold two ice cube trays and a box of popsicles.

"But there is a catch," Adam said, taking the last sip of his coffee and setting the cup down on the saucer. "I'm going out of town next month, and I don't have anyone to water my plants or feed my fish."

"You have a *fish*?" A fish was not the pet she would have guessed for a good-looking, forty-something-year-old man. "A fish is better than a snake," she said, "but it's still a little suspect."

"I'm lonely," he said, with a little shrug. "And a fish is better to come home to than no one at all. Pathetic, I know."

"Are you divorced?" Lucy said. "Sorry, I also have a tendency to blurt things out."

He didn't look offended that she'd asked. "I'm almost divorced," he said, leaning his elbows on the counter. "We've been separated for a while."

"I'm sorry," Lucy said, throwing the paper wrapping from the flowers in the trash. "What happened?"

"A lot of things. We got married right out of college," Adam said, "and we're 'incompatible' now, or at least that's what my wife tells me. Like I really want kids, and she doesn't."

"And why," she said suspiciously, "are you usually out all night?"

"Working," he said. "I signed this German band after I heard them play at a venue in Brooklyn. They ended up getting a big record deal, and next thing I knew, I was moving to Berlin as their producer. Now I have to scout new talent pretty much every night so the label won't regret hiring me."

"And you bought a fish to keep you company," she said. "Are you in Berlin to stay?"

"I guess?" he said. "Anyway, my offer's sincere: If you need a quiet place to work, I'll give you a key. And in exchange, I'm hoping you'll take care of my fish while I'm away."

Lucy was more than willing. She was ecstatic over this proposition.

"What's his name?"

"Fish."

She tipped her head. "Groundbreaking," she said. "And how long will you be gone?" she said.

"About two weeks. Maybe three. I'm going to New York to finalize the divorce, and I have to move all my stuff out of our apartment and storage unit." He gave her a sad smile. "And I have to say goodbye to our dog."

"Ouch, sorry," she said. "What if I accidentally kill your plants?"

"You won't. They're indestructible."

"What if I kill Fish?"

"I'll get over it."

"How's your Wi-Fi?" she said.

"Outstanding."

Lucy picked up the vase of flowers and walked it over to the coffee table in the living room. She imagined the girls knocking it over, water spilling on the antique Persian. She moved it over to the dining room table. There she worried a rogue petal might stain the polished wood. She carried the vase back to the kitchen and set it on the counter. "Thank you, Adam," she said. "I accept."

⚷

Lucy and the kids spent the day walking all around their new neighborhood. Lucy's one task of the day was to check out a nearby pool, where she signed the girls up for lessons. They had schnitzel and fries for lunch—a total hit for all four of them, which almost never happened—and then stopped at a playground. When they finally returned to the apartment, Lucy had an hour before work, and all she wanted to do was crawl into bed and go to sleep. She called her mother instead.

"How's my 'regal' tenant?"

"She got off to a rough start," Irene said, "but her English is better than mine. She and Otto are not what you'd call animal people."

"Are the pets okay?"

"They're fine. I'll keep an eye on them. How are things there?"

"To be determined," said Lucy. "You were right as usual: I rushed into this whole thing without thinking any of it through."

"You fled like a bat out of hell—"

"I already said you were right," Lucy said. "You don't have to rub it in."

"You didn't let me finish," her mom said. "I was about to say, you did the right thing, getting Jack out of here. You showed real strength. And it's not like things are getting any better around here yet. So bravo to you."

"Is it bad?"

"Nothing you need to worry about."

"Do the Germans know about Jack?"

"I don't plan to tell them," her mom said, "but they might hear things. You know how people talk."

Lucy did know, and she hated it. She sat down on the slipper chair in the corner of the bedroom. "Greta seems bitchy," Lucy said. "She sent me a bunch of pictures to show all the stains and scratches on everything from the rugs to the cars. She even took a picture of Tank's chewed-up dog toy, like doesn't she get that that's the whole point of a dog toy? Does she actually think I'm going to send her a bill after this?" She rubbed a smudge on the tabletop next to her. "Is she going to send *me* a bill?"

"I don't know, but maybe you should offer to buy her a new pair of shoes. Tank really went to town on hers." \

"Fine," Lucy said. "But she sounds kind of awful."

"Mmmm," said Irene. "I think I like her. I'm going to take her on a little tour of Dallas tomorrow."

"You definitely don't have to do that."

"I want to," she said. "And Jack's friend Drew came by the office yesterday. He lost his retainers for the eighth time and needed new impressions made."

"Isn't that confidential patient—"

"And he told me Jack won't take his calls or answer any of his messages. He looked like he was going to cry right there in the waiting room."

"Well, retainers are very expensive," Lucy said.

"That wasn't my point."

"I know," Lucy said, "but Jack's not up to talking to his friends right now."

"Just remind him, this wasn't Drew's fault. He pretty much broke my heart, saying how much he misses Jack."

"Poor Drew," Lucy said. "But then again, Drew's heading to Harvard in the fall, so he'll be just fine."

"Now who's being bitchy," Irene said. "Things aren't easy for Drew, and you know it. He can barely make eye contact with me and he's known me since he was eight."

"You're right," Lucy said. "I'll talk to Jack." She could hear the girls laughing in their room. "You want to say hi to Zoe and Alice while I put my face on?"

"I've only got five minutes before I have to leave for work myself," she said, "but sure."

Lucy gave her phone to the girls and then put on a blue blouse, eyeliner, and mascara. She brushed her hair and got her laptop, ready to walk down one flight of stairs to her new office.

She hadn't told her mother about the arrangement with Adam because she wasn't sure how she could explain it without having to answer a million questions about who this stranger was and whether she was making good, thoughtful choices.

She probably wasn't. She often didn't. But she was doing the best she could. As she put on a little lip gloss, she hoped maybe Greta might blunder at some point—break a window or set off the fire alarm. It would make Lucy feel a whole lot better to know Greta had flaws too.

To: Greta von Bosse
From: Benjamin Binstock

Dear Frau von Bosse,

    Greetings! I have been following the exciting news about the long-lost Vermeer you purchased at auction for the Schultz Foundation's Collection with great enthusiasm. As soon as *Girl with a Red Turban* could be viewed by the public, I flew to Berlin to see it for myself. It is magnificent! I offer my congratulations to you and the Schultz family—and to the National Gallery for the privilege of welcoming this exquisite painting into its collection.

    However, I have a theory about the painting that I would love to discuss with you. Could we meet sometime? Or talk on the phone? A few years ago I wrote a book called *Vermeer's Family Secrets*. If you have read it, you will know where I am going with this! Please let me know when we can have a conversation about *Girl with a Red Turban* and the genius who actually painted it.

Sincerely,
Benjamin Binstock

The thing about the Vermeer was that it was expensive. It was very, very expensive because not only was it a Vermeer, it was an outstanding Vermeer. *Girl with a Red Turban* was possibly the most remarkable work Johannes Vermeer ever painted. It brought to mind *Girl with a Red Hat*, but technically, it was far superior, a perfect example of Vermeer's mastery of depicting light as it falls across the model's face and onto the folds of gold fabric that drape on her shoulders. The girl's riveted gaze, her slightly open lips, and her coy smile convey a confidence and amusement that almost challenge the viewer. Or mock her. And his use of perspective in depicting the room behind her—the open doorway and the shadows on the wall—was sublime.

Before going to auction, the painting had gone through all manner of examination, and x-radiographs had indicated there had once been a male figure standing in the background in front of a crooked painting, both of which Vermeer had removed. In Greta's mind, this mystery—the unknown man, the art askew—only heightened the sense of intrigue in the composition.

The authenticated *Girl with a Red Turban* had surfaced at the best possible moment, just before she'd made the first acquisition, and Greta had been almost as pleased by the fortuitous timing as she was by the painting itself. Sebastian Schultz instructed her to outbid everyone—collectors from the United States, the UK, and China. The extravagance of the purchase meant that while the rest of the collection would still be impressive, it would be somewhat less so, as they now lacked the funds to acquire, say, a Richter or a van Gogh. A few family members grumbled that too much had been invested in that one treasure. But once they saw the Vermeer up close, they were, for the most part, thrilled. Sebastian's sister had called Greta a miracle worker.

And now some art historian was questioning the painting's authenticity, which Greta could not help but take as an attack on her credibility. Raising doubts about a work wasn't unheard of, of course, but Greta wasn't happy about it, given the significance of this particular acquisition and the boost it had given her reputation.

She woke up to the jarring email and read it again over coffee. Benjamin Binstock had not listed any affiliation under his signature—no university or museum—so Greta sat at the kitchen counter and googled him. He had been on the faculty at Columbia and Cooper Union, and he'd been a fellow at the American Academy in Berlin. He was a Vermeer scholar whose book outlined a bold theory: Binstock believed that Johannes Vermeer's daughter Maria had painted several works attributed to her father, such as *Portrait of a Young Woman*, hanging in the Metropolitan Museum in New York, and the contested *Girl with a Flute* at the National Gallery of Art in DC. Clearly, he now included *Girl with a Red Turban* on his list of paintings he thought were Maria's.

Greta felt obliged to inform Herr Schultz about the email, given that he'd paid €60 million for the painting in question. She forwarded Binstock's message, saying that she thought it best to ignore it but that she would follow his instructions on whether to respond.

She hit send. And then, out of a niggling curiosity, she ordered Binstock's book on Amazon.

Otto came downstairs before work, carrying a pair of jeans.

"Otto," Greta said, "whose pants are those?"

"I found them upstairs in a *Schrank*," he said, holding them up to himself. "Do you think *der Sträfling* would mind if I try them on?"

"Mason is not a *prisoner*," Greta said. She'd googled Lucy's hus-

band and found out that the "six-month stretch out west" Rex had
mentioned referred to Mason's participation in a NASA biosphere
project where he was bringing his skills as a solar expert and systems
engineer to a simulated Mars environment. She had told Otto, but he
still called Mason the convict or the jailbird or *der Gefangener*.

"And no, you shouldn't try on his pants."

Greta's suitcase had arrived a few days before. She had taken it
in hand and guided it through the house and into Lucy's room, as if
she were welcoming an old friend to town. She felt grateful for each
of her garments as she unfolded them and hung them up in the bedroom closet.

But Otto's suitcase was lost for good, and he desperately needed
clothes.

"I'll go shopping for you today," she said.

"*Danke*," he said. "My new colleagues are very relaxed, and I
would like to fit in. Could you buy me some pants *wie so*"—he held
up the jeans—"instead of my usual *Hose*? And some sport shoes?"

"You're going to wear sneakers to work?"

"New Balance," he said. "It's what they are all wearing. I would
like to be feeling more comfortable." Otto was smiling.

"I take it you like these doctors."

"*Oh, ja*," he said. "They are super cool. I find it wonderful here."

Greta was also finding life in Dallas pleasant enough, for the
most part. She'd taken a few trips to the grocery store in the dinged-up
Prius and found it easy to drive on Dallas's wide streets and to park
in the expansive lots. But she could not get used to the temperature
extremes, going from the oppressive heat of the outdoors to the icy
cold of the dairy aisles and back out into the heat.

That day she went to NorthPark on Irene's recommendation, and
Greta walked around the mall in awe, not only because of the scale
of the place and the number and variety of stores it held, but also
because of the art—world-class art! Henry Moore, Frank Stella, and
Katharina Grosse. Roy Lichtenstein and Jim Dine. It was a museum

inside a mall, a merging of consumerism and culture that delighted Greta's American side and horrified the German in her.

She bought Otto two pairs of Levi's, three button-down shirts, and a pair of New Balance sneakers.

⚷

The following Saturday, Rex let himself in the back door and invited Otto and Greta on a tour around downtown Dallas to give them a bit of the city's history. Greta opted to stay home as she'd already gone on a nice drive with Irene that included a stop to see the original downtown Neiman Marcus and a walk through the Nasher Sculpture Center garden. Greta wanted to focus her day on Emmi's arrival. She was going to shop for her favorite foods and pick up flowers for her bedroom. She had only a little over a week to spend with her daughter and wanted the visit to be perfect. "But you should go," she told Otto.

Otto nodded enthusiastically, getting up from his breakfast. "Yes, I would like that very much."

As Greta watched the men walk outside and across the yard, she wondered whether Rex and Irene really were this nice, or Lucy was asking her parents to keep an eye on her and Otto, which was completely ridiculous. Greta was taking excellent care of the house— better than Lucy herself maybe—which meant she was spending a lot of her time cleaning, too much of her time.

That morning she put a pile of dog towels in the dryer, emptied and then loaded the dishwasher, and put clean sheets on the beds. Using a combination of vinegar and dish soap, she managed to re-move a stain, spaghetti sauce by the look of it, from one of Lucy's carpets. She would leave this campsite better than she found it.

After she finished the day's housework, she took a seat on the massive sectional sofa in the den and called her mother, who greeted her with a "Hello, hello" in a voice lighter and higher than it had been in years. "I'm in my new apartment."

"How was the move?" Greta said. "I feel terrible I'm not there to help."

"No need," Lillian said. "Tobias is so capable. He managed everything perfectly and told the movers exactly what to do and how to do it, and not a single thing was broken."

Tobias's name was dropped in every conversation with her mother these days.

"Was it hard to say goodbye to the house?"

"A bit, yes," Lillian said. "I woke up very disoriented in my new room."

"But do you like the apartment?"

"It's awesome," she said, sounding more Emmi's age than her own. "So much less to manage. And I can walk to everything."

Greta missed walking. All she did in Dallas was drive from one parking lot to the next. Few of the streets even had sidewalks, so when she took the dogs out, they all walked down the side of the road, right along the curb. "Lucky you found a building with an elevator," Greta said. "And I love that you're only ten minutes away from us."

"If you come back," Lillian said casually.

"Of course we're coming back," said Greta, getting up at the sound of the dryer beeping. "Why wouldn't we?"

"It might be hard to leave the US once you've spent a little time there. Are you enjoying yourselves?"

"It's fine," said Greta. "I'm very excited for Emmi to get here."

"She'll love it," Lillian said. "There are so many things that are better there. Like ice water in restaurants."

Greta disagreed. Ice water made her teeth hurt.

"And free refills on coffee," her mother went on. "Jaywalking. Jif peanut butter. Drive-throughs. Bounty paper towels. Small talk. Carcinogenic artificial sweeteners. Strip malls. Excedrin PM. . . ."

Greta's German father had met Lillian in New York and proposed only three months later. The newlyweds moved to a suburb of Berlin, even though Lillian didn't speak a single word of German and didn't know anyone there. It can't have been easy, and even now she used the wrong articles and pronouns from time to time and sounded very much like a foreigner. But her German was good, and after twenty-five years, she was fully embedded in German culture and in her social life. And yet she still had moments when she would itemize for Greta and Bettina all the things that were better in her homeland.

"Why don't you come visit us?" Greta said. "I'd love the company, especially after Emmi leaves—"

"I can't," Lillian said. "Tobias is cooking up other plans for me."

"Plans?" Greta said, slightly alarmed. "What plans is Tobias cooking up? Now that you've moved, you don't really need him anymore, do you?"

"Oh, I do," said Lillian. "He's a godsend. There isn't a single thing that man can't do. He got my television working and my internet hooked up in no time. Remember those Bauhaus sconces? He's hanging them on either side of my bed as we speak."

Greta was glad to hear the sconces hadn't been sold along with the house, but she wasn't enjoying the image of Tobias in her mother's bedroom. "I'm glad he's helping, but—"

"And he set up all my bills on autopay."

At that, Greta put her mother on speaker and texted Bettina: Urgent—We need to look into Tobias.

"He's so handy," her mother was saying.

"Mom, why don't you pack a bag and come to Dallas?" Greta said. "We have loads of extra space and more ice water than you'll know what to do with."

She could hear her mother talking to someone in the background. And then she laughed. "Mom?"

"Sorry," Lillian said. "There's still a lot to do to settle in here."

"Has Bettina come over to see your apartment?"

"She's very busy," her mother said. "Tobias needs me, Greta. Must run." And she hung up.

Greta immediately got her laptop, went to the kitchen island,

and googled Tobias to see whether there was anything newsworthy about him, any stories about arrests or drug use or what exactly he'd done to get kicked out of his father's company. The search proved useless because his name was too common. She was about to call Bettina when her phone pinged with a message from Adam:

Hey you. Just wondering how you are. Hope this finds you at a pool checking out hot lifeguard ;) All great with Lucy. She's at my place every day for wifi and quiet. I'm going to NYC for 2 weeks in July. Don't suppose you're planning to visit your daughter there? If yes, wine? Dinner?

Greta read the message again. What was Lucy doing in Adam's apartment? Greta's Wi-Fi was perfectly adequate, especially if you stood in the hall close to the router by the laundry machines.

Hi Adam, she replied. I'm sorry Lucy is a bother. How are her children? Not loud, I hope.

She stared at her phone, waiting for him to respond.

No, no—Love the kids! And Lucy is great. So much fun! & no worries—shoes off at all times haha.

Fun? That was annoying. And how would he know that Lucy's shoes were always off? She stared at her phone, horrified to realize that she was jealous. *Ridiculous,* she thought. But there was something about that word "fun," the same word Bettina had used to describe Lucy.

The doorbell rang, which sent the dogs into crazed fits of barking. Greta approached the door cautiously, worried it might be the vandals who had struck two more times since she'd arrived, once with shaving cream on the walkway and another time with toilet paper in the trees.

But this was no vandal. A beautiful woman, wearing a long, floral dress with sandals, was standing on the porch. She had windblown hair, graying at the roots, and a lot of silver jewelry.

"Oh," she said, with a look of disappointment, "you're not Lucy."

"No," said Greta. "She's not here." The dogs were trying to get out to greet the visitor, nudging Greta's legs with their noses, so Greta stepped outside and closed the door behind her.

"I'm Sylvie," the woman said, and then she held out a rose-colored envelope. "Could you give this to Lucy for me? I just moved in next door, and I told her I'd be having a ladies' get-together once I got settled in."

Greta had seen a moving truck parked on the street the day before and a troop of sweaty men carting boxes and furniture up the walkway into the pillared Colonial next door.

"I know most people do evites these days," Sylvie said, "but I'm old-school."

"I'm sorry," Greta said, handing the envelope back, "but Lucy's gone for the whole summer."

Sylvie looked crestfallen. "Oh, what a shame. She didn't mention she was going away."

"It was last-minute," Greta said. "She exchanged homes with me, sort of on an impulse."

Sylvie looked down at the envelope in her hand. "Seems like a lot of people aren't around." She gave a sad little shrug. "I guess it's the heat. Everyone escapes to Telluride or Nantucket."

"I'm Greta," Greta said, wondering whether the friendly thing to do, the Texan thing, would be to invite the new neighbor into the air-conditioning for a glass of ice water.

"What a pretty name," Sylvie said. She perked up then and offered the envelope again. "Well, if *you'd* like to come, you'd be very welcome. I hope that's not too level-jumpy. It's just, I'm finding that not everyone knows what to make of a woman starting over again at my age." She tried to laugh.

Greta reached out and accepted the invitation. *Be fun*, she thought. "Thank you, Sylvie."

"You'll come?" Sylvie looked thrilled. "I'll have some tidbits and wine. Very casual."

"Sounds perfect."

"Great. Can I ask," Sylvie said, "what the impulse was?—I mean, why did y'all swap homes?"

"My husband's working at Southwestern for a year. He's a foot surgeon. And Lucy . . ." She had no idea why Lucy had been in such a rush to leave town. "Well, I don't know."

Sylvie leaned in and lowered her voice. "Did her leaving have anything to do with the 'pranks'?" She made air quotes with her thin fingers.

"Prank" was exactly the word Irene had used. "You know about that?" Greta said. She had tried, more than once, to ask Irene for information, but Irene was guarding the family secrets.

"When I stopped by here a while back," Sylvie said, "I felt so bad for Lucy. Someone had slashed her car tires and egged the front door. And then later I met this woman down the street who said—" She suddenly stopped herself, waving her hand, her turquoise rings flashing. "No," she said, "no, I'll stop right there—I don't want to be a gossip."

"Actually," Greta said, "it would help to know what you've heard. I've never met the Holts, and they're living in my apartment." Greta had googled Jack but found only that he was a National Merit Scholar, winner of some robotics competition, and a member of a local climbing gym. His Instagram was private.

"Well," said Sylvie, looking reluctant to share, "I don't have any reason to believe this is true, but I met this lady who lives on the corner." She pointed down the street. "And when I told her which house I'd bought, she said to be very careful because the teenage son in the house next door to mine was involved in some kind of . . . sex trafficking ring."

"No," said Greta, her hand flying to her chest. "*Sex trafficking?*"

Sylvie took a step closer. "She said he was kicked out of school and sent to one of those behavioral rehab camps in Idaho, so that no one would press charges, seeing as he's eighteen and all and would be tried as an adult. But the woman I talked to got all this thirdhand, and

I don't believe everything I hear anyway. I sure wouldn't want anyone talking bad about my kids."

"Neither would I," said Greta. "And some of that can't be true. The son is living with his mother in my apartment in Germany."

"You see?" said Sylvie. "That's exactly why I should never spread rumors. Shame on me! He's probably a perfectly nice young man."

But Greta wondered whether the truth might be somewhere in the middle. And what would she tell Otto and Emmi about this? Maybe nothing. Emmi would be appalled to sleep in the home of an alleged sex trafficker, even if the rumors were unverified.

"Did you say Germany?" Sylvie said. "I knew I heard an accent. You're a long way from home. How do you like Dallas?"

Greta knew this woman probably didn't care; as her mother often reminded her, Americans, unlike Germans, had an irrepressible love of small talk. But she decided to indulge her.

"It's very nice," she said. "My daughter is coming to visit tomorrow, and I can't wait to see her. She's studying law in college—the system is different in Germany because you specialize in professional education earlier. She's going to New York this summer to intern at a law firm."

Sylvie smiled, warmth and kindness in her eyes. "Well, you must be so proud of her."

"Do you have children?" Greta said.

"Two," said Sylvie, "all grown up. Such is life." She blinked and added, "I was thinking this fall I might take one of those walking or biking tours in Europe. Backroads or Butterfield and Robinson. I've got the time. I just need a friend to go with me, but every last one of them is either married or doesn't like to travel."

"You could go on your own," said Greta.

"Yes, I guess I could," Sylvie said, sounding reluctant.

Sylvie seemed nice, and the American side of Greta wanted to ask her a string of personal questions, starting with what happened to her marriage. But her German side prevailed, and she kept her curiosity to herself.

"Anyway, I'm so happy you'll come to my little shindig," Sylvie said, "seeing as we're both new here. I don't know that it will be very well attended, but . . ."

"Thank you for inviting me," said Greta, holding up the envelope. "I'll definitely be there."

"I better get back to unpacking," Sylvie said. And she walked away down the front path, her skirt flowing behind her, her sandals making slapping sounds on the flagstones.

Greta went inside and put the pink invitation under a magnet on the refrigerator. If some other neighbors attended this party, she might find out what kind of people the Holts really were.

***

Otto came in through the back door after his outing with Rex, carrying shopping bags in one hand and a small Texas flag in the other. She could tell in a glance that he was in high spirits.

"I have learned today so much interesting informations," he said as the dogs circled him, "about the Kennedy assassination, and Bonnie and Clyde, oil wells, the neon Pegasus, Big Tex, and the frozen margarita machine! We should take a long drive tomorrow to see the *Landschaft* outside of the city limits."

Greta noted his slightly mischievous smile and asked, "How many frozen margaritas did you have?"

"Only one," said Otto, his cheeks flushed, "but it was quite strong. And after our tour, Rex has showed me Costco, a most unbelievable, very large store." He held his arms out. "There is everything you can think of, Greta. They sell potatoes and car tires and computers and refrigerators and *Lachsfilet*. I am not believing my eyes."

Greta pointed to his shopping bags. "So did you buy salmon or car tires?"

"No, this is from a different shop named Cavender's. *Warte mal.* Go to nowhere. I want to show you."

He took his bags and went upstairs. To her disappointment, Otto had never made the move to the downstairs bedroom to be with her, saying he preferred the higher floor and didn't want to sleep with the dogs on the bed. Greta hadn't pushed. She liked having her own space. Not only did Otto snore, but he got up to use the bathroom several times at night, and Greta had a hard time falling back to sleep. And yet—it made her sad. She did not want Emmi arriving to find her parents sleeping in separate rooms. Tonight, they would move his things downstairs.

While she waited for him to return, she checked her email and saw that Sebastian Schultz had already replied with two pithy sentences in German, telling her that he'd spoken to the curator at the museum in Berlin, who dismissed Binstock's email as "*völliger Blödsinn.*" He instructed her not to reply to Binstock or to any requests for comment from the press on such baseless theories.

Greta thought "utter nonsense" was a little strong, but she was relieved. She answered, saying she understood and would ignore any inquiries on the subject.

Then she texted Emmi:

So excited to see you, Schatz! Please don't be late for your flight.

Emmi texted back:

Me? I'm never late haha

She sent a picture of herself then with Karl and Monika, sitting outside at a café. Emmi looked very happy but also tired. She was such a hard worker, and Greta zoomed in on the dark circles under her eyes, hoping the visit to Dallas would give her daughter a chance to catch up on sleep. Emmi had always been a mature, sensible girl, born with a strong sense of right and wrong, and she was quick to become outraged in the face of injustice. Studying law was the perfect fit for her.

Greta could hear Otto whistling. He entered the kitchen, and Greta gasped at the sight of him.

"I will wear this to pick up Emmi at the airport tomorrow," he said. "What do you think?"

Otto was . . . she could not say whether it was the red embroidered shirt, the tall cowboy hat, the big, rectangular belt buckle, or the pointy boots that shocked her most.

"Who . . . are you?" she said.

"Look at this," he said, smiling as he opened and closed a shirt button. "Rex says they're called 'pearl snaps.' *Genuine* pearl snaps!"

"*Mein Gott,*" said Greta.

"Nice, or? I am fitting in here like a fish in water." He turned this way and that so Greta could admire him. Otto, as it turned out, was the fun one.

She remembered again what Adam had said about a grizzled cowboy. That he would seduce her under the stars. Well, here he was. At least she and Otto would share a bed again tonight, and maybe that would lead to something more. She could only hope.

MESSAGE TRANSMITTED FROM MARS VIA NASA DEEP
SPACE NETWORK

To: Lucy Holt
Dallas, Texas

Hi Love,

How are things with you and the kids? I'm sure you are
all appreciating the shift to summer vacation: fun days of
swimming and sunshine and no school. What's everyone
up to? Wondering if you heard back from the Laurel Hotel
people about your plans for them, if Jack's job is going well,
if the girls had fun at the end-of-year sleepover. I'm missing
you all so much.

We have received NO messages, and I'll be honest—it's
tough. The psych group is clearly testing the impact of
communication failures. I guess this approach makes sense
since they need to create the experience of total isolation
so they can monitor the psychological stress of long-haul
missions, but man, it's hard :(

Mia left—which was strange. We weren't told in advance,
nor do we know if she was asked to leave or couldn't take
the pressure or what. We woke up for our 6:00 a.m. duties,
and she was gone. We had a meeting to divvy up her chores,
and the only good thing to come out of it is the rest of us
have been allocated her water rations.

My DustBunny squad is on duty and so far, so good.
I can't tell you how gratifying it is to see them cleaning
Martian dust off the solar panels, just like they do at
home. The bristle heads are working perfectly, and their
maneuverability is exceptional. I am very proud of them.

Nextersol, we will have a simulated dust storm, so they'll really be put to the test. There are so many factors at play, wind speed and weight distribution and suction strength. It's possible they could get blown right off the face of the planet, which would lead to severely reduced power in the long term. Wish us luck!

Not to be a total asshole, but Yağmur is getting on my nerves. She is a skilled yaybahar player to be sure, but the instrument is so large, it takes up most of our limited recreational space, and I wonder if I should bring up this "elephant" in the room. Nightly concerts and discussions are a little much now that we know each other, and to be honest—you know me—I need a bit of silence. I may have caught Veronique rolling her eyes while Yağmur droned on last night and am thinking I may raise the topic with her privately to see if we feel the same way.

I have time alone in the fitness room each day where I've been doing some pretty basic exercises, jumping jacks and lunges, and I'm enjoying those moments to myself and finding them restorative. Oh Lucy, I would love a good, hot shower. The towels here suck. I couldn't stop thinking today about our bathroom, and I had the strongest sense memory of the penny tiles under my feet, and the smell of that body wash you always buy, and the rush of water on my head . . . and you. It was a lovely thought but painful to know we're going to be apart for so long. I don't think I realized how hard this is going to be. Sometimes it feels like I'm in a prison. It's a privilege to be here, and yet I'm ticking off the Sols on a piece of paper.

I hope NASA "fixes" the UHF antenna so I can hear from you and get some family news. I was thinking: Jack will need a very good winter coat for Boston. Maybe go to

REI and have a look? I wish I could help get him ready for college.

Love you,
Mason
Science Officer, MARS (Alpha Red Canyon 5)

BERLIN

Adam's office had a plain Ikea desk, a perfectly neutral background for Zoom, and high-speed Wi-Fi. Lucy would occasionally hear the pitter-patter of her girls' feet overhead, reassuring her that everyone was okay upstairs. And by nine or ten at night, it was quiet, and she would know that Jack had gotten his sisters to bed. They had agreed not to tell the twins that Mommy's office was directly downstairs; otherwise, Zoe and Alice would have found a hundred reasons to knock on the door.

After three weeks in Berlin, Bryn and Harper seemed to have absolutely no idea that Lucy had left the country, nor that she was consumed with family matters. They were impressed by the ideas Lucy had presented to keep the design consistent across all six hotels while working with the architectural idiosyncrasies of each individual building. And just that day, Lucy had presented a new Danish furniture company she'd found called Bang that made bed frames that fit the vision for the rooms perfectly; the team loved it. She was coming across, thanks to this work oasis, as focused and organized, which was a kind of miracle given that she was sleeping five hours a night if she was lucky.

It was Friday, and because they were ahead of schedule, Bryn and Harper suggested the team log off at lunch, which was only ten o'clock at night for Lucy. With relief, she closed her laptop and emerged from the office to the sound of jazz music playing in the living room.

"Honey, I'm home," she joked. She hadn't seen much of Adam, as he was usually either out or asleep when she came in and out of his apartment.

Adam was not alone. There was an enormous dog lying on his sofa and a woman browsing through his collection of records. She turned as Lucy came in.

"*Bettina?*"

"Lucy," Bettina said, lighting up at the sight of her. She breezed across the room and kissed Lucy on both cheeks. "Look at you."

Lucy was not much to look at in her gray sweatpants and the slippers she'd bought at KaDeWe on Kurfürstendamm because of Greta's shoes-off policy. She was also wearing a gray silk blouse and lipstick, a glaring mismatch between top and bottom.

"Look at *you*," said Lucy. "You look exactly the same. But I mean, *exactly*." Bettina had flawless skin and long, wavy hair that went past her shoulders. She was a knockout in skinny jeans and high heels. She was just as Lucy remembered her. "What are you doing here? It's so late."

Bettina checked her watch and shrugged. "I stopped by to say hi, and your son told me where I could find you."

Adam was standing awkwardly, looking at Bettina with great interest—how could he not? "Greta's sister!" he said with delight. "She just appeared."

"Do you two know each other already?" Lucy asked.

"No," Adam and Bettina said at the same time.

"We knew *of* each other," said Bettina as she sat down on the couch.

"I knew of you. You knew of *me*?" Adam said.

"Greta may have mentioned you."

"And who's this?" Lucy said, indicating the dog beside her.

"Til," Bettina said, "named after Til Schweiger."

"Who?" said Lucy.

"*Who?*" said Bettina. "Only Germany's most famous actor."

"*Inglourious Basterds*," said Adam.

"*Atomic Blonde*," said Bettina, "and like every German movie ever made."

Lucy kneeled to pet the dog.

"Drink?" Adam said.

"Sure," Lucy said, seeing the whiskey in Bettina's hand, "unless you want to go up to Greta's."

"I'd rather stay here," Bettina said, "if Adam doesn't mind."

"I don't mind at all," he said.

"Good," Bettina said, "because Greta would kill me for bringing Til, and I'll feel guilty wearing shoes in her apartment, and I'm not taking these off." She pointed a toe to show them off. "They make the outfit."

"In that case," Lucy said, "I'll have whatever y'all're having."

The goldfish was swimming in little circles in his bowl on top of the chrome deco bar cart where Adam turned to fix Lucy a drink. He'd filled an ice bucket and put out a bowl of nuts. He seemed to enjoy hosting.

"The truth is," Bettina said, "I promised Greta I'd check on the apartment to make sure you aren't trashing the place. She's mad I waited so long to get here."

Lucy smiled tightly. Greta seemed to think Lucy had no sense of responsibility whatsoever. Sure, Lucy had asked her parents to keep an eye on things in Dallas, but only because she worried about her actual living creatures.

"Surprise inspections aren't really my thing anyway," Bettina said, "and her apartment—or what I could see of it over your son's shoulder—looked perfectly fine to me."

Adam handed Lucy her drink, turned the music down a bit, and sat across from them on a low chair.

"We're doing our best," Lucy said, patting the big dog's head. "I moved most of Greta's more fragile things to a high shelf in the linen closet for safekeeping."

"Smart," said Bettina. "What do you think of that painting in her bedroom?"

"The flowers?" The painting had grown on Lucy; she'd noticed over time the depth of it and the level of detail. "It's very dramatic."

"I think it's ghastly," said Bettina. "But it's from the seventeenth century—and painted by a German woman actually, Anna somebody—and would you believe Greta bought it when she was twenty-three years old. I thought she was out of her mind at the time. Now I'm in awe."

"That's so Greta," said Adam.

Bettina turned to look at him.

"She's a connoisseur," Adam said. "She appreciates beauty and things that are well made. It's because of her that I go to antique stores and flea markets now, looking for treasures."

"Well, it's not very relaxing to live with kids in an apartment full of treasures," Lucy said. "We already destroyed one thing, irreparably. Do you happen to know where I can buy antique Meissen? We broke this medium-size plate, pink flowers with a gold rim?"

"That sounds like my grandmother's china," Bettina said, her eyebrows raised.

"Oh my God," said Lucy, a hand flying to her head. "We broke an heirloom?"

"Accidents happen," Bettina said. "She'll get over it."

But her expression made Lucy think Greta would not, in fact, get over it. "Shit," she said. "Don't tell her, okay? I'll confess as soon as I find a way to make it up to her."

"I never tattle," said Bettina with a perfectly executed wink.

Lucy took off her slippers and sat cross-legged on the couch. At least Adam's living room, unlike Greta's, was comfortable. "So what have you been up to," she asked Bettina, "in the last . . . almost twenty years? Married? Kids? Job?"

"No. Hell no. And I love my job. Let's see," she said, looking up at the ceiling briefly and tallying on her fingers. "After college I traveled all over India, China, Thailand, and Japan—just like we used to talk about—and then I moved to New York for a couple of years."

"Oh, I'm from New York," Adam said, looking happily surprised to have something in common with her. "In fact, I'm going back there soon. To Brooklyn. Where did you live?"

"Soho," Bettina said. "I went to grad school and came back to Berlin to get a job in graphic design. I'm freelance, so I can set my own hours, and it's a constantly evolving field. Keeps me on my toes."

"Same with the music industry," Adam said, nodding along. He seemed to be hanging on her every word.

And they were both single—or, in Adam's case, a couple of weeks away from being single—and Lucy felt it would take very little for these two to get together. It seemed to be happening all by itself.

"And what became of *you* after that year in Berlin?" Bettina said.

"This and that," Lucy said. She wondered whether Bettina would find the truth boring. She turned to Adam. "I spent my junior year here."

"Lucy was *wild*," Bettina said.

"I was?" It was hard to remember her former life after years of being a mom, a wife, a carpooler in a minivan, and a pet owner.

Bettina was laughing. "I could barely keep up with you."

"The clubs," said Lucy wistfully, remembering how much she used to love the electronic music, the louder the better, how her ears would ring when she walked out at six in the morning. How she could get almost any guy to buy her a drink just by looking at him. "We would stay out all night," Lucy said. "You were the one who took me to that club, Kater . . . ?"

"Kater Holzig! Yes, and Berghain."

Lucy felt a pang of nostalgia. "It's hard to imagine having that kind of energy anymore, isn't it?"

"Not really," said Bettina. "I still go to clubs."

"I do too," Adam said, "but for me it's work, and I'm often the oldest guy in the room."

Bettina tipped her head back and finished her drink. "I refuse to see turning forty—not that I'm even close yet—as some kind of death sentence."

"I'm almost forty," said Lucy, thinking Bettina couldn't be too far behind her. "My mother always says the forties are the best. You look good, you feel good, and, more or less, you have your shit together."

"I don't have my shit together," Adam said, putting his hand out as an invitation to refill Bettina's empty glass, "and I'm forty-four."

"You don't look it." Bettina offered her glass. "Let's go to a club tonight, for old times' sake. What do you say?"

"Sure," Adam said, accepting the challenge.

Adam went to the bar and Bettina sat back, stretching an arm across Til's back. His tail thumped on the couch cushions.

"Sorry to be a party pooper," Lucy said, "but I'm going to bed. My twins will be up at the crack of dawn, asking me what's for breakfast."

"Twins," said Bettina. "I can't imagine. I met your son. Very tall and blond and well-mannered. He introduced himself and shook my hand like a real gentleman."

Lucy wondered what, if anything, Bettina might be piecing together. It was possible she didn't remember Bjørn at all.

"I can't believe you and Greta never met each other that year," Bettina said. "I used to ask her to go out with us, but she was already married to Otto and no fun anymore." She absently patted her dog, focusing on the wall above Lucy's head. "She must have gotten pregnant sometime around then."

Adam brought her a refill and she sat up, turning back to Lucy. "Remind me, who was that guy you were dating? We met him on that epic trip we took to Italy."

"Spain," said Lucy. So Bettina remembered after all.

"Right, Spain. We met up with some friends, and he was with them. . . . Wasn't he on his way home to Norway?"

"Denmark," said Lucy.

"Yeah, Søren? Or Jørgen?"

Lucy took a big sip of her drink. "Bjørn," she said.

"Bjørn," Bettina all but shouted, "right!" She clapped her hands together, making Til lift his big head and look around the room.

Lucy almost shushed her, sensing Jack's presence in the apartment directly above them.

"He was *hot*," Bettina said, turning to Adam. "Lucy bagged the best-looking guy in Europe. I was so jealous. Whatever became of him anyway?"

"Wellll," Lucy said. She could have told them Bjørn's entire biography and curriculum vitae, that he'd gotten a PhD at the University of Copenhagen, married a brilliant cardiologist named Astrid, and had two daughters with her. The first pregnancy had been complicated, and they almost lost the baby. His mother died of cancer when he was in his twenties. He was a professor of philosophy now, affiliated with the University of Copenhagen's Kierkegaard Research Centre, and they lived in a suburb called Charlottenlund and had a view of the ocean. He commuted to work by train and recently climbed the Matterhorn. "I really have no idea," Lucy said. "We didn't stay in touch."

"Classic college fling," said Bettina.

Bettina seemed to be studying her, and Lucy shifted to find a more comfortable position.

"I had one of those too," said Adam, offering the bowl of nuts. "Believe me, it's better when they don't get serious."

"It's better when *no* relationship gets serious," said Bettina. "I've found that I've never needed to saddle myself with a *partner*, you know?" She held her arms out wide when she said "partner," as if the expectation was to make room for something absurdly unwieldy, like a rhinoceros or an RV. "Did you?"

"Saddle myself?" Lucy said. "Yes, I did. My husband's away on an extended work trip."

"So to speak," said Adam.

"Not 'so to speak,'" Lucy said, turning to him in surprise. "Have you been googling Mason?"

"I was curious," he said with a shrug. He refilled Lucy's glass then too. Lucy was not a whiskey drinker, and it was hitting her pretty hard.

"Well, now *I'm* curious," said Bettina. "Is 'work trip' a euphemism for . . . rehab?"

"'Work trip' is a euphemism for Mars," said Lucy, proud to talk about Mason, "which is a euphemism for a biosphere in New Mexico."

"Wait, I've heard about this," said Bettina. "In fact . . ." She reached for her phone and started scrolling. "I listened to this podcast yesterday— Is he part of that international team, the one that's all women, except for him?"

"Yes," said Lucy. "ARC Six. Or no, ARC Five now."

"ARC Four," Bettina said. "An Israeli engineer just left."

"Are you serious?" Lucy said, sitting up. She got her phone out too and did a quick Google search; Aviva had left the biosphere for unspecified reasons. "My God," she said. "I don't even know what this is going to mean. Maybe he'll come home early."

"Sean Carroll did a whole episode on them," Bettina said, "and apparently the goal is to keep the thing going with almost no communication. They're testing psychological resilience for these upcoming long-haul missions. But hang on," she said, holding up a finger, "getting back to Bjørn for a sec."

Lucy did not want to get back to Bjørn.

"It's all coming back to me," Bettina said, narrowing her eyes at Lucy. "He was super smart. And he had to go home for some reason. Exams or something."

"He was trying to get into a PhD program," Lucy said. The accuracy of Bettina's memory was getting very uncomfortable, and she couldn't figure out how to get her off the topic.

"And did he," Bettina said, "get in?"

"He did," said Lucy. "And he was very happy about it."

"And that was it? It was over between you?"

"Yup," said Lucy, holding up her hands to show there was nothing more to it. "That was pretty much it, more or less."

"Huh," said Bettina. "I kind of figured . . . I mean we were only kids, but I remember thinking you two had a real connection. I was sure you would find a way to make it work."

"Yeah, no," said Lucy, feeling queasy. "We didn't. Puppy love, that's all it was." But in truth it was so much more. Or it was for Lucy anyway. She'd been so happy during those bright, intoxicating days, getting to know him, falling in love.

"And now you've got three kids," Bettina said. "How old are they?"

Lucy's phone rang, and Greta's name appeared on the screen. Lucy had never been more grateful for an interruption. "Look," she said, "it's your sister!" She answered the call and put Greta on speaker, hoping this would put an end to Bettina's interrogation.

"Hello!" said Lucy, getting to her feet. "You'll never believe who I'm with."

"Hi, Greta," Bettina said.

"Hey, you," Adam called out. "Wish you were here."

"We're having a late-night, impromptu party," Lucy said, holding her phone out. "I think I've had too much to drink already."

"But don't worry," said Bettina, winking at Lucy, "I walked through your apartment, and it looks totally perfect."

"How's Texas?" Adam said eagerly.

They all waited through a moment of quiet, and then Greta said, "I thought I might be calling too late, but apparently I'm interrupting the *fun*."

Lucy wished she could start over what was their very first conversation, regretting how flip she'd sounded, how irresponsible. She took Greta off speaker and left the room, leaving Bettina and Adam with the jazz music, the dog, and the whiskey.

"Greta? Can you hear me?" Lucy said, closing the office door and sitting back at the desk where she spent her evenings. It was covered with her pens and notebooks, pads and papers.

"Perfectly," said Greta. Her voice was clipped and tense, with only the faintest accent.

"Is everything going okay?" said Lucy.

"Everything's fine," Greta said, "but there's cat hair on all the furniture, and I'm having a hard time understanding how to use the vacuum cleaner. Your mother says it's a whole house system, but I don't understand what that means."

"I wasn't expecting you to have to vacuum," Lucy said, organizing the mess on her desk. "I have a cleaning lady who comes on Fridays, so I figured she would do it."

"A cleaning lady?"

"Yeah," said Lucy. "A *Putzfrau*?"

"No, I know what a cleaning lady is," Greta said, sounding miffed, "but there is no cleaning lady."

"That's because Otto wrote to me," Lucy said carefully, "and he said to tell her not to come." There was a pregnant pause. "Hello?"

"Can you tell me *specifically* what Otto said," Greta asked. "I'd like his exact words."

Lucy put Greta on speaker again and searched her email. "To be honest," she said, "I was pretty surprised because I said I already paid for her for the whole summer, and it's a lot of house, you know?— Okay, here it is: he said—and I quote—'We do not need the services of your housekeeper, as my wife will do all the cleaning.' I mean . . . ," Lucy said, and laughed. "Personally, I'd divorce my husband for less. No, I'm only kidding," Lucy added. "Sort of. But anyway, I figured you two were on the same page."

"Lucy," Greta said formally, "may I rehire your housekeeper, please?"

"Sorry," said Lucy. "When I called to tell her y'all didn't want her to come, she said she was going to spend Fridays with her grand-kids."

"I see," Greta said, and exhaled heavily. "Well, this is 'a lot of house,' as you say, and the pets shed hair all over the place, and my husband is going through two or sometimes three towels a day, and I would have appreciated the help."

"*Husbands*, don't get me started," Lucy joked. "It's not like mine's any use these days." She heard Tank barking in the background, and it made her heart hurt. She wondered what room Greta was in, the kitchen? her bedroom? "I sure miss the dogs," she said. "But at least I get to hang out with Adam's fish."

She heard Greta clear her throat. "Adam has a fish?"

"Yeah, poor guy," said Lucy. "Adam, I mean. I think his trip to New York is making the whole thing feel very final, especially since his wife is getting custody of the dog."

"His *wife*?"

"I mean, soon-to-be ex-wife," Lucy said, "you know, and hence the fish, if you ask me."

She expected Greta to say something kind or supportive, but there was silence.

"He'll be okay," Lucy said. "He just needs time to process."

"Right," said Greta. "How nice he has you to confide in. Sorry, Lucy. I have to go." And the line went abruptly dead. Lucy looked at her phone, wondering whether the call had dropped or Greta had hung up on her. She had no idea what she could have said to offend her.

She went back into the living room to find Adam and Bettina putting on their jackets, and Til walking in circles with his leash dragging on the floor.

"How's Greta?" Adam said.

"A little tense," she said. "She's annoyed with Otto."

"She actually said that?" Bettina said, her eyebrows raised.

"Not exactly," said Lucy. "But it was kind of obvious. Anyone would be, in her situation." Lucy was prepared to explain what had happened with the cleaning lady, but Bettina was slamming down the rest of her drink while Adam was going around the room, turning off lights. "You're coming with us, right?" he said.

"Where?" Lucy said.

"We're dropping Til at my place," Bettina said, "and then we're checking out a band in Neukölln."

"No, no, no," said Lucy. She could not wait to climb into Greta's bed, stiff as it was, and pass out. "Absolutely not. But you guys have fun."

"Please," said Bettina, "you have to come."

"Impossible," said Lucy, and she hugged her. "But let's do this again soon."

Lucy said goodbye to them in the stairwell and walked the one flight up, feeling unsettled. She couldn't put her finger on which thing was troubling her most, whether it was the shrinking number of biosphere participants or the whiskey or Greta's abrupt hang-up or the idea that Bettina had made all her distant memories of Bjørn feel less like figments of her imagination and more like actual events in her past. Bettina had seen them together. She was a witness.

She opened the door of the apartment to find Jack making himself a sandwich.

"Hey, how was the evening?" she said.

"Really fun. We went to the Legoland Discovery Centre."

"Your sisters are lucky to have you," she said. "How much do I owe you?"

"The tickets were twenty euros each."

Lucy got her wallet and gave him a hundred euros. "And you are officially off duty, sir, until Monday afternoon." She saluted him.

"Cool," he said. He looked at her and nodded, trying hard to smile.

Lucy's breath caught as she took in the earnestness of his expression, the angle of his jaw, the clear blue of his eyes, knowing that a single glimpse of this young man, who was only a few years younger than Bjørn had been at the time, had surely been enough to make Bettina know everything.

DALLAS

As soon as Emmi woke up, she checked her phone. There was a voicemail from Monika, an email from her law professor who was bringing her along to New York, and a sad selfie from her boyfriend, Karl, with the words "*Vermisst du mich?*" She yawned. No, she didn't miss him; she'd only been gone four days. Karl had been clingy before she left, saying she was probably going to fall for some rich American law associate in New York. Emmi understood his insecurity, considering the summer he was facing. Karl would be serving bratwurst and beers to tourists in Alexanderplatz, working for the same creepy manager at the same restaurant where he'd waited tables in high school. Now wasn't the time to hurt the guy's feelings. She texted back that she missed him too.

"Hey, Captain," Emmi said, "open the shades."

And up they went, stacking themselves up into tiny folds and letting all the sunlight in the room.

Her bed was wide and low with soft navy sheets. The room she'd picked was at the far end of the hall. The walls were a soft gray, and there was a large black-and-white photograph over the bed—a field with hay bales and horses—taken by the father of the woman who owned this house. Emmi had posted a picture of it on Instagram. The bookshelves held the same hardbound, well-worn sets of *The Lord of the Rings* and *Harry Potter* that she had left in her childhood bedroom in Berlin. There were also textbooks on coding with Python and how-to guides on climbing. The room had very little else in it, but it felt like a guy's room. Emmi had opened the night table drawers the morning after she'd arrived, hoping to find out more about the person who lived here, but they were empty. The surface of the desk was scratched, stained, and completely bare, although in the bottom drawer she'd found an old ticket stub to a Goo Goo Dolls concert.

Emmi got up and stretched her arms over her head, pulling off her T-shirt without even bothering to close the door. There was no need since she had the entire upper floor to herself. For the first time in her life, privacy was not an issue. Space was not an issue.

She put on shorts, a sports bra, and a tank top and went to brush her teeth and splash water on her face. The bathroom had a long countertop with nothing but *her* things on it, her makeup, her lotion, and her ponytail holders. On the hook behind the door, her bikini was hanging to dry. She opened a cabinet and took out one of a half dozen folded white towels to dry her face and then put sunblock on her burned nose and shoulders. Emmi had never had her own bathroom before.

With a pair of socks stuffed in her running shoes, she went downstairs, following the sound of her mom's voice, and found both her parents in the kitchen. Her mom, still in her bathrobe and slippers, was trying to dry Tank, who was dripping water all over the floor. Her father was leaning against the counter, wearing nothing but a towel around his waist.

Her father was acting very strange. He'd come to the airport cosplaying a backup dancer from *Cowboy Carter* and taken them to a restaurant called Haywire he'd heard about at work. Her dad, who did not think people should eat anything with their hands, not even French fries, had picked up the Cadillac Burger he'd ordered and taken a bite, ketchup and grease running down his chin, looking happier than she'd ever seen him.

"*Halt, Hund!*" her mom was saying, trying to throw a striped towel over Tank. He wiggled out from under it and came over to greet Emmi.

"I don't think he speaks German," Emmi said, leaning over to pat him. She had always begged her parents for a dog, and now—for this short time—they had not one but two, plus three cats and a guinea pig. Last night both dogs and a cat had come upstairs and spent half the night on her bed.

Her mother looked exasperated and sat down on a barstool. "Otto, you'll have to wash a load of towels today," she said. "Since you canceled the housekeeper, you need to help me with the laundry. I honestly can't believe you said *I* would do all the cleaning."

"Seriously, Dad," said Emmi. She had heard this story twice already and fully disapproved. "Not cool."

"I only thought," her dad said, "that you would not want a stranger in the house. And I did not know at the time how large it would be, nor how much animals there are."

"But you specifically said that *I* would do the cleaning," her mom said. "Me." She was holding a pair of sharp scissors in her hand and used them to slice open a box from Amazon.

"Because you are not at the moment working," he said with a shrug, "and I am."

"Stop, Dad. You're only making it worse," Emmi said. Even though both her parents worked, they adhered to an outdated division of labor, meaning her mother did most of the shopping, cooking, and cleaning, and all the laundry. The older Emmi got, the more it bothered her.

"Then let me say this," he said. "I am sorry, and I will do more to help in the household. For example, I can join Costco and take over the shopping." He was eating a slice of watermelon, and every few seconds he would turn and spit a seed into the sink.

"What's Costco?" Emmi said.

"Oh you would be so amazed," he said, wiping his chin. "They are selling *ganz alles* there. Anything you can think of and always in very large sizes. I can buy *Toilettenpapier* to last a year."

Emmi was having a hard time picturing her dad pushing a grocery cart.

"Your father has been skinny-dipping again this morning," her mom said.

"Eww," Emmi said, "gross."

"What does it mean?" he said. "Skinny . . . ?"

"She means you were naked in the pool," Emmi said.

He turned to her mother. "I do not skinny-swim," he said. "Every morning *after* I swim, I am removing my bathing pants. Then I leave them outside to dry in the sun."

"I didn't even know you liked to swim," Emmi said.

"I never have the chance," her dad said, tightening the damp towel around his waist. "It is one of my favorite things about here, a private pool in the backyard. I enjoy very much to swim lanes."

"Laps," Emmi said. "Don't you prefer the ocean to a pool?"

"I do," her mother said.

"I don't," said her dad, seeming to surprise himself with his answer.

Emmi was not used to seeing her parents disagree about anything. But she hadn't spent much time with them in the last year, and they seemed more at odds now. Also she knew her dad had been sleeping upstairs before she'd arrived for this visit; in one of the upstairs bedrooms, she'd found his socks on the floor by the bed and his razor next to the sink.

Her mother pulled a shiny black art book out of the box and ran her hand over the cover. She took it to the island and sat down, opening it to the first page.

The dogs were still circling Emmi, and Tank took one of her Nikes in his mouth.

"No, Tank," Emmi said. "Drop it."

"Frau Holt did not do a good job training her dogs," her dad said.

Her mother looked up from the book. "Do you know what she told me?" she said. "She says that Adam is married."

"Who?" asked Emmi.

"Herr Lance," her father said, frowning, "our Berlin neighbor."

"The music producer?" Emmi said. "I met him once."

"He does not act married," her dad said.

"Lucy says he's getting a divorce," her mom said. "I think it's odd he never mentioned a wife."

"I thought you two had become friends," her dad said.

"Obviously not," her mom said. "If we were friends, I would have known he was married."

"I told you he has a bad character," her dad said. "I have seen him having women over to his apartment. He's a playboy."

"I suppose he is," said her mother. "I'm sorry I ever defended him."

And just like that they were aligned again.

Her mom turned back to her book as her father washed his hands and dried them on a dish towel that he left balled up on the counter. "I must get ready for work," he said. "Let me know if you would like to make a *Rundgang* of the hospital. We can have a nice lunch at the faculty club."

"No tour today," her mom said. "I'm taking Emmi to buy some new clothes for her internship."

"Of course," he said. He kissed the top of Emmi's head and walked out of the room.

Emmi went over to check on the guinea pig as Mrs. Henley came breezing through the back door, calling out her usual "Yoo-hoo!" and putting a cookie tin on the counter next to one of the cats. "I baked y'all a batch of snickerdoodles," she said. "They're heavy on the butter and cinnamon and absolutely perfect with a cup of coffee."

Emmi liked the Henleys. Today Mrs. Henley was wearing pink and white checked capri pants, a pink polo shirt, and Tory Burch sandals that showed off her shiny painted toenails. Her hair was curled and stiff, moving as if it were all one piece. Emmi closed the guinea pig's cage and helped herself to a cookie from the tin. "Thank you," she said.

"Wash your hands," said her mother, who was convinced Piglet was carrying germs.

Without warning, Mrs. Henley reached out and wrapped Emmi in a tight hug. Over her shoulder, Emmi held the cookie and shot her mom a look of confusion. Her mom shrugged.

"I'm really missing my grandkids today," Mrs. Henley said, patting Emmi on the back. She smelled like hair spray. She loosened her grip and then held Emmi by the shoulders. "I wish Jack were here to show you whatever it is young people like to do around here. But the two of you are like teenage ships passing in the night."

"Is he in Berlin the whole summer?" Emmi asked.

"Looking after the twins while his mom works. He's a terrific big brother."

"My best friend is in Berlin. Maybe Monika could meet him and show him around?"

"I doubt Monika has the time for that, Emmi," her mother said, closing her book, "and didn't you say she's going to the beach anyway?"

"Not for another week or so," Emmi said. She could not understand why her mother suddenly gave a shit about Monika's schedule. "I'll ask her. She's very nice, Mrs. Henley. I'm sure she would be happy to take Jack on a tour."

"I insist you call me Irene," Mrs. Henley said. She finally let go of Emmi's shoulders. "And when you need it, the key to Jack's car is on the hook by the garage door. It's got brand-new tires."

"I can't drive," she said.

Irene looked as shocked as if Emmi had just said she couldn't read.

"You can't get your license in Germany until you're eighteen," Emmi said, "and I haven't had time in the past year because of school. There's no need to drive in Germany anyway."

"I've been driving Jack's car," her mom said, "and Otto is driving the minivan."

"Why in tarnation won't you use Mason's car? I wouldn't be caught dead driving that Prius," Irene said. "For goodness' sake, take the Tesla. Just don't forget to charge it."

"Otto doesn't think it's right to drive his new car."

"Mason wouldn't mind one bit. He's not the kind of person to care about that sort of thing. Anyway, you two have a good day. And let me know if you want to come for dinner some night this week." Irene walked out of the house, blowing a kiss through the door after she closed it.

"She's so nice," Emmi said. "Don't you like her?"

"I like her very much," her mom said, "though I'm not used to people showing up unannounced all the time."

But Emmi loved the back door opening and closing. She wished she had grandparents stopping over with cookies. Her own grandmother wouldn't even give them a key to her beach house.

"I don't think Monika should meet Jack," her mom said.

"Why not?"

"It's better not to complicate this arrangement. And we don't know enough about him."

Emmi hated it when her mother acted like she knew best. The way Emmi saw it: Monika and this guy Jack might hit it off. Maybe they'd even have a summer fling. "I'm going for a run," she said.

"You missed your chance," her mom said, getting up and washing the watermelon seeds down the drain. "It's too hot now."

"I'll be fine." Emmi had been living on her own for a whole year, making all of her own choices, and yet her mother could not stop telling her what to do and when to do it.

The dogs followed her to the front door, where she pulled on her shoes and tied them. She opened the Strava app on her phone and headed out. It was hot, yes, but Emmi was in good shape, and after a quick stretch of her quads, she took off down the street. With Dua Lipa's "New Rules" blasting through her AirPods, she picked up her pace; this would be her summer anthem.

At the end of the block, she turned down a long road that seemed to have no end. There was little shade, and the longer she ran, the more she realized that this heat was unlike anything she'd ever felt before. It was heavy and pressed down on her. She wished she'd brought water. After a few more blocks, her skin started to feel weird, prickly almost, and yet for some reason she was getting goose bumps. She kept running until she reached a neighborhood that had even larger properties with gates in front of them. Some had tall hedges hiding villas that were set back far from the road. Some had fountains. One had a lake. She stopped and took a picture of a house that looked like it was modeled after Versailles. Then she turned around to retrace her steps.

No, Emmi wasn't feeling right. She slowed to a walk, trying to catch her breath as her cheeks burned and the pavement went wobbly under her feet. She checked the map on her phone, sorry to find that she was still several blocks from the house. She stopped, put her hands on her knees, and before she even registered what was happening, she threw up right next to a driveway. She straightened back up and tried to breathe slowly, her vision kaleidoscoping. She wiped her mouth on her shirt and took out her earbuds, looking up and down the street, having completely lost her sense of direction.

A white Jeep swerved and pulled up right beside her, a girl behind the wheel. *Barbie?* Emmi thought.

"Hey," the girl called over Chappell Roan blaring from her car speakers, "you okay?"

Emmi didn't answer, and the girl turned the music down.

"You need me to call nine-one-one or something?" she said.

Emmi's head was spinning. "I'm okay," she said, putting a hand out to balance herself on a mailbox.

"Here," the girl said, and she held a plastic bottle out the window.

"I'm okay, really." But then Emmi's knees gave out, causing her body to drop down onto the hot asphalt. It burned her bare legs.

Next thing she knew the girl was kneeling beside her, a hand on Emmi's back, holding something to her lips. "Fuck my life," she was saying, "drink this, okay?"

Whatever it was, it was ice-cold, sweet, and fizzy. "Thank you,"

Emmi said, taking a bigger gulp this time. Much to her embarrassment, she burped. "*Oh Gott*, sorry. I don't know what's wrong with me."

"Heat stroke," said the girl. Her long, blond hair was pulled up in a high ponytail, and her jean shorts frayed at the edges. She had thin, gold bracelets on her wrist and a T-shirt that said *Tulane*.

Emmi tried to stand up, hoping she wouldn't pass out.

The girl had left her car running. "It's hot as balls today, and heat like this will kill you, like, *literally*. You're not from here, are you?"

"No," said Emmi.

"I figured. I mean, 'nless you're literally batshit, no one from here would go running outside on a day like this."

Literally what? Emmi prided herself on being bilingual, so it was a shock that she could not parse the girl's sentences.

"Like straight up tripping or whatever." She was chewing gum, and her breath was fruity. "So where are you from anyway?"

"Germany," Emmi said. "I'm only visiting—"

"You don't look so good," the girl said, handing her the drink. And then she exhaled loudly. "Tell you what, I'm going to do something nutty and give a complete stranger a ride home."

She barely looked old enough to drive.

"I don't want to trouble you," Emmi said.

"Yeah well, I'm not normally the Good Samaritan type, but some kid dropped dead yesterday at a football practice out in Richardson, and I'd rather not be responsible if you croak. Seriously, hop in. You don't strike me as sketch."

Sketch?

"I'm Cynthia, by the way, and swear to God"—she held a palm up, her ringed fingers pressed together—"I'm not a kidnapper."

"I'm Emmi." On shaky legs, she walked around the hood of the Jeep and climbed up into the passenger seat. Cynthia got behind the wheel and picked up a massive pink Stanley cup and sipped something through a fat straw. Emmi gave her the name of the street, and Cynthia stepped on the gas hard, making a U-turn and hitting the curb of the neighbor's driveway. "Oops," she said.

Emmi held on to the edge of her seat. The car was littered with trash: fast-food wrappers, Starbucks cups, and wadded-up packs of cigarettes. As Cynthia took a hard right turn, an empty bottle of te-quila rolled into Emmi's feet.

"So how far did you go anyway?" Cynthia asked.

Emmi checked Strava. "About six miles?"

Cynthia looked at Emmi then like she was . . . *literally batshit?* "Gurrl," said Cynthia, "just, like, *no.* You gotta go where there's AC: a spin class, row house, Pilates." Cynthia sped up into a turn, causing Emmi's shoulder to hit the car door.

"It's up there," Emmi said, feeling sweat trickling down her back, "on the left, the modern one."

Cynthia—with no warning whatsoever—slammed on the brakes. "Fucking shit-fuck," she said.

Emmi looked at her, alarmed, and took her hands from the dash-board, where she'd planted them to keep her face from hitting the windshield.

Cynthia turned in her seat and faced her. "Oh my God—how do you know him?"

"Who?"

"The *asshole*," said Cynthia. "Jack Holt."

"I— Who?"

"The guy who lives in that house."

"I've never met him," Emmi said. "I only . . ." She was stam-mering, and her accent, almost nonexistent normally, was becoming pronounced. "My parents, they're just staying there."

Cynthia was glaring at her as if she were a criminal. "Look, you need to know something about the boy who lives there." She pointed at the house. "He's *the worst.*"

"The worst . . . what?" Emmi said.

"Like, the worst person in the world," Cynthia said. "He ranked the girls in our class, including me, and gave us dollar values."

"Values?" said Emmi, trying to keep up.

"Like we're objects or some shit, things to be bought."

"How terrible," said Emmi.

"I basically had a menty b over the whole thing."

Minty bee? Emmi shook her head.

"Between you and me," Cynthia said, "I thought Jack was a friend. Like, I actually thought I knew him, but then he just sticks a price tag on me, I guess to humiliate me?"

"That's horrible," Emmi said. "How could he do such a thing?"

"Just be careful around him, okay?" Cynthia was deeply upset. A tear caught on her fake eyelashes. "If you want my advice," she said, "stay away from him."

"Yes, definitely," said Emmi. "His whole family is gone." She decided not to say where the family was exactly, that this hated, hateful boy was living in their apartment in Berlin. "I won't ever meet him. I'm going to New York next week."

Cynthia relaxed her shoulders then and smiled wistfully. "Oh, New York's amazing. I'm jelly."

"You're—"

"So where'd he fuck off to anyway?"

Emmi swallowed. "He's in Germany for the summer."

Cynthia looked crushed. "He gets a trip to *Europe*? After what he did?" She rested her forearms on the steering wheel, staring at his house. "He got kicked out, but school was already over and I bet his college takes him anyway. Dudes get away with *everything*. I know this sounds babyish, but he really hurt my feelings."

Emmi liked this girl. She was possibly the most American American she had ever met. "Maybe we can hurt his feelings back," she said. If there was one thing Emmi hated, it was a misogynist.

"What do you mean?" Cynthia said.

"Let me see if I can think of some way to . . . um, teach him a lesson while he's in Berlin."

"Really?" Cynthia put up a hand and high-fived her. "OMG, I *love* this for us. But you don't mean like beat him up or anything?"

"No," Emmi said, "no, of course not. I mean maybe my friends can embarrass him somehow, let him know he can't disrespect women and then run away."

"Amazing. But he can't know it was me," Cynthia said.

"Of course not," Emmi said.

"Awesome." She picked up her phone. "Gimme your deets."

Deets?

"BT dubs," Cynthia said, "my parents are going out of town this weekend, and I'm having a party. It'll be chill if you want to come hang."

"Yes?" said Emmi, touched by Cynthia's openness. "I'd like that."

"And you're okay now? You're not gonna, like, die?"

"I'm okay, and thank you for the ride." She gave Cynthia her Tik-Tok and Instagram and got out of the car. After she watched the jeep drive away, Emmi looked down at the bottle in her hand—Dr Pepper and Cynthia had saved her life. Still feeling strange and a little dizzy, she made her way toward the door. The dogs were at the window, wagging their tails at the sight of her. How could that *Arschloch* Jack have such sweet dogs? And such nice grandparents? And such a cool house? Life was not fair.

And why, why, why did her mother always have to be right about everything, all the time? *Yes*, it was too hot to run. And *true*, Monika should not be told to give Jack Holt a fun time in Berlin.

But with Monika's help, she was sure they could think of an excellent way to punish him.

BERLIN

Before anyone else in the family was up, Jack showered, put Clearasil on his nose and chin, and brushed his teeth. By the time he came out of the bathroom, fully dressed, his sisters were waiting in the hall to use the only toilet.

"You took too long," Alice said.

"At least you get to sleep in a real bed," he said.

Zoe dashed in and shut the door.

"But we're *sharing* a bed," Alice said. "And Zoe kicks me in her sleep."

"Sorry," Zoe said from inside the bathroom. "I can't help it."

Their mom came out of her room in her pajamas, blinking her puffy eyes, looking absolutely wrecked. She barely slept anymore, between her days with them and her long nights at work. He knew she was worried about him, and she didn't even have their dad to help out. "Morning," she said, her voice cracking. "Where are you off to?"

"Don't know," he said. "I'm just going to walk around. I may end up at a climbing gym."

"Great," she said. "Have fun." And then she put her palms together. "Leave your ringer on though? So I don't worry?"

He had given his mom enough reason to stress out recently; he wouldn't add to it.

With a raincoat, his climbing shoes, a Nalgene bottle, and a granola bar in his backpack, he closed the door to the apartment and got his earbuds from his pocket. As he headed downstairs, he ran into Adam on the next landing just outside his door.

"Busted," Adam said, holding his hands up. "I missed my curfew."

Jack was impressed. He'd pulled all-nighters before to study, but he'd never in his life partied until the next morning. And this guy was middle-aged. "Was it fun?"

"Not really," Adam said, "but I think I finally found them."

"Found who?"

"The band that's going to get me some respect around here."

"Yeah? What kind of music?" Jack said.

"Indie rock revival," Adam said. "Think, like, the Strokes meets the Pixies."

Jack was relieved to know who Adam was talking about.

"And they're the whole package; they've got stage presence, a kind of cool, unique sound. Their songs need some work, but at least they're trying to write their own shit. They've got potential." He nodded a chin at Jack's phone. "Who are you listening to?"

Jack showed him his phone.

"Peggy Gou? Very cool."

It may have been pathetic, but after receiving such scorn and wrath from his classmates, it felt nice to get approval.

"So are you in high school or college . . . ?"

Jack looked down at his shoes. "Neither really," he said. What a terrible question to have to answer. "I'm supposed to start college in the fall, but it's kind of up in the air for me."

"Don't do it," Adam said flatly. "You know what I got out of college? A boatload of debt, an unpaid internship in Jersey City, and a wife who wants nothing to do with me. College is a waste of time and money."

Jack smiled. His parents would for sure disagree, but he loved the idea of alternatives.

"But don't listen to me," Adam said. "What's your . . . thing?"

"Math," said Jack. "Science. But I'm not so sure anymore."

"Whoa. In that case," said Adam, "I stand corrected."

"Not necessarily," said Jack, and he shrugged, as though MIT meant nothing to him, as though he hadn't killed himself for six years to get accepted, as though there were paths out there that did not include a bachelor of science.

"I'll see you around, yeah?" Adam said, opening his door. "Maybe you want to go hear a band some night?"

"Sure," said Jack, "that would be awesome."

Adam had no reason to be nice to him. Adam had no reason to be nice to his family, letting his mom work in his apartment, dropping off stuff from the bakery every once in a while. It felt good to know that some people on this planet really were kind and caring; not _everyone_ faked it, not _everyone_ turned on you.

Jack had always considered himself a pretty good guy at heart, so to have been tagged as one of the world's absolute worst ones felt unbelievably shitty.

⌐⊣

There was a point to this outing. In Dallas Jack had a car, which meant he could go where he wanted, when he wanted—within the bounds of reason, of course—all by himself. But here in Berlin he felt like a child again. He hadn't done a single thing on his own since they'd arrived. And spending every single day with his mom and his sisters was causing him to regress. He was cranky all the time, and his mother fussed over him. The couch in the office had a high back and arms, so it felt like he was sleeping in a crib. Last night, he'd had growing pains, a misery he thought was in the past, and had to get a Tylenol from his mom. When he'd finally fallen back asleep, he'd had a nightmare, not a teen nightmare of forgetting to study for an exam, but a kid nightmare involving a cartoonish monster. He needed to start acting his age again, so he'd made a plan to spend the day on his own like a normal person.

It rained in Berlin all the fucking time. He stopped to put on his raincoat, wishing he felt better, more like himself. Ever since the day he got in trouble, Jack had felt this hard little knot of agony that had taken root in his stomach, and there was no making it go away. He was going to have to live with it, possibly forever.

Sometimes eating helped. He stopped at a bakery and waited in line, watching the woman in front of him to see what and how she ordered. And when it was his turn, he paused his music and pointed, saying a few words in German because—he would never tell his mom—he'd been doing Duolingo when no one was watching. He got a salted pretzel and a coffee. When he handed over the money, the woman behind the counter made an angry face.

"*Haben Sie 'was kleiner?*"

"Sorry?"

She sighed. "Smaller bills, please."

"Sorry," Jack said again, looking through his wallet and feeling his face turn red as the man behind him grumbled with impatience.

The woman was shaking her head, holding the bill up to the light as if he were paying with counterfeit cash. Jack reached in his pocket and found six euros in coins. He handed them to her, and she handed him back the hundred bill and gave him his change. This one interaction—his confusion and her hostility—wore him out. He took his pretzel and coffee and walked out, trying to shake off the feeling of not belonging.

The night before, he'd studied the map and found a trek that would take him through the big park in the middle of Berlin all the way to the Brandenburger Tor. From there, he would head to Checkpoint Charlie and to a climbing gym he'd found online called Urban Apes. It would be the first time he'd gone bouldering since the whole fiasco, and he looked forward to it, to starting fresh with a new chalk bag, judging difficulty levels, and following the colored holds. He'd never had a bad interaction with a fellow climber at a gym.

He turned off the playlist he was listening to because Billie Eilish was bumming him out, reminding him of his friends; for as long as he'd known them, he'd never gone this long without talking to Drew, Rosie, or Sam, and he missed them even more than he missed his dogs, which was really saying something. But he'd shut them out, too angry and ashamed and miserable to talk. He felt a kind of homesickness for them. He felt it for his dad too.

The only good thing about his dad being completely off the grid was not having to see the disappointment on his face. His dad wouldn't even be mad, would never lose his temper like Sam's dad did all the time, or give him the silent treatment like Rosie's mom, or make him feel any worse than he already did. Jack could not remember his life before his dad was in it.

And he never would have guessed that the football-size robot Jack had helped develop would break up their family, especially since his dad built it for *them*, had invented the thing to clean dirt off the solar panels of their very own roof. NASA wanted the drone's technology, but what they ended up taking was the inventor himself, the systems engineer who built the hardware and wrote the software, who knew how to troubleshoot and make repairs, and who could adapt the thing to work under pretty much any conditions. Jack's dad was a genius, everyone knew that. What Jack hadn't known was that he would be willing to ditch them all for six months.

And now his dad had started doing these workouts in the biosphere that were being livestreamed, and some fitness buff was posting clips of them on TikTok, and they were getting a weird amount of attention. It would have been super cringey if they weren't popular, but the comments about his dad were all heart-eye, muscle-arm, and fire emojis, which was embarrassing in its own way.

He was passing a pond in the middle of the Tiergarten that made him think of Turtle Creek, where Sam lived. He threw his empty coffee cup in a trash can, retied his shoelaces, and switched to a more upbeat playlist, but the first song, Miley Cyrus's "Flowers," reminded him too much of Cynthia. Only Rosie knew how much time he'd spent with her, and the only reason he'd told Rosie was because he'd needed her for an alibi.

"SAT tutoring?" Rosie had asked. "Dude, is she at least *paying* you?"

"Gross, no," said Jack. "She just needs a little help. It's not a big deal."

"Do her parents know?"

"No," he said.

"So . . . why's it a secret?"

Jack had shrugged like it was perfectly reasonable, although he didn't really get it either. "I guess it's because Cynthia's scores went down after they hired that lady who costs, like, twenty thousand dollars. She doesn't want them or anyone to know she's getting even more help and—"

"Yeah, but . . ."

Jack waited for Rosie's brutal take on this situation; she had a chip on her shoulder about the snotty, popular kids at Rockwell, and Rosie never held back her opinion on anything.

"Isn't Cynthia basically a total bitch?" she said. "She's never given any of us the time of day."

Cynthia wasn't a bitch, and Jack decided right then that he would use his time with her not only to raise her scores but also to get her to know what a good person Rosie was, to get Cynthia to like all his friends. He would talk them up to her.

"We've been neighbors forever," he said, "before middle school made everyone cliquey. She's nice, actually. You'll see."

"Has she ever invited you to a single party?" Rosie said. "No. Or showed up at your house to hang out? Or stopped to talk to you in the hall at school?" Rosie was shaking her head. "I don't know," she said, "it feels to me like she's using you."

That stung. But despite Rosie's warnings, he went to Cynthia's anyway, sneaking through the back gate. She was nice to him, and she would bring snacks to the pool house, where they would sit on the couch together with SAT books and scratch paper, working their way through math problems. He would calm her down when she got upset over a wrong answer. One day she cried and called herself stupid; he couldn't bear for her to think that. Cynthia's scores had skyrocketed from 1150 to 1340, but she never talked to Jack in the hallway at school, and she never befriended Rosie, and she did not, in fact, invite Jack and his friends to her house for the huge party she threw the weekend before graduation. Jack had seen the cars parked up and down her street. He'd gone straight to Rosie's house and told her she'd been right about everything.

"Like I said, the girl's an irredeemable bitch," Rosie said that night, just minutes before he made the decision to scrape the web for data and write the code that got him expelled. He'd been filled with bitterness.

Rosie squinted at him. "You didn't, like, have a *thing* for her, did you?" Rosie said.

"God, no," he said, and then, to get her off the fucking topic, he threw in the name of another classmate, "but Nell is kind of perfect."

"*Nell?* Duh. Nell's a goddess. *I* like Nell. God, that's a relief," she said. "I feel better about your taste in girls."

❀—⚡

Jack had made it to the end of the lush, tree-lined park and now stood smack in front of the Brandenburg Gate. He walked around the crowded, cobblestone plaza with all the other tourists who were milling around and taking selfies. He had read the Wikipedia page to know a bit about what it was and where the wall had once been, sep- arating East Berlin from West, and then he took a picture as well—a good one in which the Goddess of Victory and the four horses stood out against a dramatic, cloud-filled sky. He had no one to send it to.

He turned and walked down a broad boulevard called Unter den

Linden and down a few side streets until he reached a landmark he'd seen online called the Gendarmenmarkt. It pretty much blew Jack's mind, this wide-open square, flanked by two huge cathedrals with a concert hall in the middle. The sun came through the clouds for a moment, and he took a seat on the steps, watching people walk across the plaza. There were big groups of kids, carefree and relaxed, joking around with one another, unburdened by the knot of agony that Jack carried around with him everywhere he went. They were on their phones, taking countless pictures of themselves and each other, and Jack imagined what they would post on Instagram. Group selfies in front of the Schiller statue in front of him: *Some old dead dude #summer #collegebound #travel #friendsforlife.*

Jack watched the happy students—juniors in high school, he guessed—and hated them.

The knot tightened.

He hadn't thought he was hurting anyone because he hadn't meant for anyone other than his friends to see the list. He'd only wanted to prove mathematically—in jest and in fact—that while he might be worthless, Cynthia and her friends were heartless, terrible people. But he had not included any guys in the data, so while he had sworn and even believed that there was no misogynist intent behind his math, Principal Neal hadn't believed him, because on some level maybe there was.

Introspection sucked. Jack shook his head, trying to push his shame away and appreciate the sights around him. He stood up and to his great surprise, he got a notification on Instagram. This was almost impossible, as he'd made his account private and removed all followers who hadn't already blocked him, making an exception only for family members. All that was left on his page, after he'd deleted almost all of his posts, was one picture of Tank and Bunny, one of the Boston skyline taken from the MIT campus, and an image of his family that his grandmother had taken for her annual Christmas card.

He opened Instagram and saw he'd gotten a follow request from a girl he didn't know. Her name was Monika, and her profile said she was from Berlin. Her posts featured groups of friends, outdoor parties, and dance clubs. She had a nose ring, pink hair in one picture and purple in another, and she seemed in every way too cool for the likes of him. She was either a bot or the request was a mistake. He ignored it.

But his phone pinged a second time with another girl from Germany asking to follow him. He clicked on her profile. Emmi was a college student in Freiburg with a great smile, and she had recently posted several stories: sunlight reflecting off pool water, a plastic bottle of Dr Pepper, and—as Jack leaned into his phone in surprise—a picture of Tank and Bunny sitting in her lap. It felt like an episode of *Black Mirror*. Her most recent post was a picture that showed the photograph his grandfather took that was hanging over Jack's bed.

He quickly texted his mom: Who's the girl staying at our house?

She answered right away: Emmi. Your grandmother says she's nice. Having a good day?

He sent a thumbs-up.

And before he let himself overthink it, he accepted both Emmi's and Monika's requests and then followed them back.

Seconds later he got a message from the girl with pink or purple hair:

Hallo! I hear from Emmi you are visiting Berlin for the summer. Meet for coffee? Wednesday afternoon?

This, he thought, was why his mother had whisked them away from Dallas, removing him from the scandal, away from people who thought terrible things about him. That's so nice!!!!! he wrote back. Where and what time?

There was a pause during which he realized he'd looked psychotically eager using that many exclamation points. But Monika replied:

1900 Café (Charlottenburg) Wednesday 5:30

Okay, he wrote, see you there. Thanks, Monika! Looking forward to it.

He would have to bring his little sisters along, but that didn't seem like an entirely bad idea. He would be less nervous with them there. He was glad his skin had cleared up a little.

The knot in his stomach eased ever so slightly as he got up and walked the periphery of the Gendarmenmarkt. He imagined sitting in a café with someone his age. It would be cool to hang out with someone who knew nothing about his stupid list, who knew nothing about him at all. It was what he needed. New people, new experiences. A fresh start.

Jack took a few more pictures of the cathedrals to his left and right, and then he checked his map to see how far he was from the gym. Once he got his bearings, he adjusted his backpack straps and started walking, marveling—as he often did, and as his father always encouraged him to do—at the power of human ingenuity. A social app had helped his mother find them refuge in a foreign country and had just connected him to two people he'd never met before. Another app was guiding him to a gym in a neighborhood where he'd never been as another counted his steps along the way. Spotify allowed him to listen to whatever music didn't totally fuck his mood.

Jack could not say what made him stop in his tracks to read the sign on the building he was passing, but the words caught his eye, the name Søren Kierkegaard practically jumping off the wall. Kierkegaard, the plaque said, had once lived in this very place. Jack looked up at the building and then back at the sign. There was a quotation: "Subjectivity is truth—subjectivity is untruth." That statement made no sense—how could subjectivity be both truth and untruth?—and yet he was interested. He turned the words over in his mind as he headed south toward Checkpoint Charlie. There was his subjective truth about what had happened, and then there was Cynthia's truth. Hers wasn't true, but then maybe neither was his. Jack typed the phrase into his notes app to google later. Although, he thought, if there was anyone who could explain the quotation to him, it was Bjørn.

His parents had told him that his biological father was out there somewhere, ready to hear from him if the time ever came. All he had to do was tell his mom, and she would arrange a meeting or a phone call. But they'd stopped bringing Bjørn up years ago because Jack had never shown any interest in him. Jack had a family, he had a father. He never had a gap in his life that needed to be filled. But now he was facing a void. He did not have a plan, or a solution, or any understanding of his failings or of his strengths—if he even had any. He had no clarity, nowhere to go once this trip to Berlin was over, no clue what to do with his life. He was in the midst of a kind of existential crisis that philosophy was built for. And his biological father, according to everything he'd read about him, was someone who could help him think it through.

As for his own father, he might as well be on Mars.

In the little office where Jack slept, there was a desk with an old-school fountain pen, a jar of ink, a box of thick, cream-colored stationery, and an envelope filled with stamps. Jack liked the idea of writing a formal introduction to his philosopher father, handwritten in a loopy script. Jack's handwriting was abysmal, so he would have to practice if he had any hope of his words being legible. And what words would he choose to make a first impression?

New York Times International Edition
Arts and Culture

Renegade art historian Benjamin Binstock has made a claim on the *SmartArt* podcast that the recently discovered *Girl with a Red Turban*—auctioned at Sotheby's after being discovered in a Swiss vault—is not a Johannes Vermeer. While acknowledging that the painting's canvas was cut from the same bolt of cloth and primed with the same grounding as Vermeer's *Lacemaker* (1669–1670) and that every expert believes it to be authentic, Binstock has stated that *Girl with a Red Turban* was painted by another artist in the studio, possibly after Vermeer's death. If he can prove his theory, it would mean that the Schultz Foundation spent €60 million on a painting created by Vermeer's eldest daughter, Maria.

In 2009, Binstock made a similar claim about other Vermeer paintings in his provocative book, *Vermeer's Family Secrets*. The National Gallery in Berlin, home of the new acquisition, has not commented, nor has Greta von Bosse, curator of the Schultz Foundation's art collection.

Binstock told the podcast's host: "The Schultz family should be proud to have bought *Girl with a Red Turban,* an extraordinary work of genius. Nothing has changed regarding the painting's unique visual qualities, which are the basis of the work's value, historical significance, and exalted status. As Nietzsche said, 'We have learned to love all the things that we now love.' The Schultz family loved the painting when they thought Johannes Vermeer painted it. Why not learn to love it now, given the intriguing possibilities of its creator?"

DALLAS

Vermeer's Family Secrets had arrived. After Otto and Emmi went off to bed that night, Greta—thinking she might read a chapter or two—got comfortable on the couch in the den. She could not put the book down. Throughout the night, the dogs wandered in and out of the room to check on her, confused by her absence from the bedroom. At around midnight, Emmi came in as well.

"You're still up?" she said.

"Only a few more minutes," Greta said. "I swear, I'm going to bed soon."

"You should really get some sleep," Emmi said, "or you'll be cranky tomorrow."

It seemed their roles had reversed.

Eventually Greta fell asleep on the couch, the book open on her chest, Bunny at her feet.

⚷

Otto woke her up early the next morning before he left for surgery. She sat up and ran her fingers through her tangled hair.

"You never came to bed," he said, offering her a cup of coffee. "*Willst du jetzt Kaffee?* Or would you rather sleep a few more hours and have it later?"

"No, I think I'll get up," she said, "and take the dogs for a walk before it gets too hot out." She stretched her back and then showed him the book. "I was reading about Vermeer's life and family and his studio, and I have to say, this Binstock makes a convincing argument. He's really got me thinking." She blew into her coffee mug.

"Argument for what?" said Otto. "Is this the nonsense about his daughter?"

Greta looked up at him, frowning. "How do you know it's nonsense?"

"I don't," said Otto. "But you said Herr Schultz and everyone at the National Gallery called it nonsense. *Haarsträubende Theorie*, you said. Or was it *völliger Blödsinn*?"

Otto was right, of course. Greta put the book down. "The *Berliner Zeitung* has asked me for a comment. I got an email from the newspaper's art editor."

"And what will you do?" Otto said, looking alarmed.

"I'll ignore him, of course," said Greta, "as instructed. I'm not allowed to comment."

"That's for the best," said Otto. "Why cause a problem when there doesn't have to be one? Now, what fun plans do you make with Emmi today?" he said.

"We're going to the Dallas Museum of Art," she said. "And then we could meet you for lunch, if you want."

"*Gerne*," said Otto. "One o'clock?"

He leaned over and kissed her on the top of her head. And then he donned a Rangers baseball cap, tossed his minivan keys in the air, and caught them. "Another day of sunshine," he said, and walked out of the room.

❧

Greta took Bunny and Tank for a walk through the neighborhood. It was beautiful out, lush and green, thanks to the sprinkler jets spraying water across the grass in every yard up and down the street. As they circled the block to go back home, a woman from the house on the corner wished her a good morning as she was picking her news-paper up off the walkway. Strangers greeting her on the street was not something Greta was accustomed to, but she waved back, wondering whether this might be the neighbor Sylvie had mentioned, the one who had spread the terrible rumor about Jack.

Emmi had also heard a rumor from a girl she met in the neigh-borhood. And while Cynthia's version of the story was bad, at least it wasn't as bad as sex trafficking. Emmi had been absolutely appalled nevertheless.

"That Jack is such an *Arschloch*," she'd said. "I can't believe he's actually living in our apartment."

"I think the best thing we can do is forget we ever heard any-thing," Greta had said. "Just because we're living in each other's houses doesn't mean we have to get involved or wrapped up with these people."

Emmi had accused her of being complacent in the face of sexism, not just in this situation, she'd said, but in her everyday life.

And, in a way, she probably was.

⸻

Emmi still wasn't awake. Greta dropped the mail onto the growing pile on the kitchen counter and then filled the dog bowls with water. She opened her laptop, searching for whatever she could find on Binstock and Vermeer. There were articles in *The Atlantic*, and on ArtNet News and NPR. The arguments being made were very credible, and Greta couldn't understand why they hadn't gotten more attention from mu-seums and art historians. What would be the harm in contemplating a theory? Of course, she knew the answer in her case: How would it look if she'd guided the Schultz family to spend a fortune on a Ver-meer, only to ask them to consider that maybe it wasn't one after all?

She went outside to get the bathing trunks and towel Otto had left hanging over a lounge chair that morning. And there was Mickey, using his net to scoop the leaves out of the pool. This man was not Adam's depiction of a pool boy. Rather, he was middle-aged and heavily bearded, and he wore baggy gray gym shorts. And she was not playing her part in Adam's fantasy either, reading a steamy novel while he piled the leaves into a messy clump on the flagstones. She wanted to text Adam to tell him all this, but she was too angry and hurt. He'd known Lucy for only a few weeks and had completely opened up to her, while he'd kept the most important details about himself secret from Greta. Adam was not a friend.

Greta went back inside and was starting a load of laundry when Emmi came in, holding an oversize coffee mug in one hand and a green Stanley water bottle they'd bought the day before in the other. "Tell me you're not washing Dad's clothes," Emmi said.

"Good morning to you too," Greta said, adding a scoop of detergent to the machine. "Your father is working very hard these days, and he doesn't have time for this kind of thing."

Emmi frowned. "He can wash his own towels," she said. "I know you'll say it's none of my business, but your marriage is based on an outdated paradigm. My professor says that women with children spend twice the amount of time doing household chores as men with children. It's entrenched from childhood, and we have to reject this traditional model. By doing Dad's laundry, you're reinforcing a societal problem and setting a bad example."

Greta turned from the washing machine to face her. "Your professor said I'm setting a bad example?"

"She didn't say you specifically." Emmi sighed and drank from the water bottle. It was enormous and had a handle and a drinking spout, and Greta didn't know what was wrong with drinking from a proper cup. "I'm just bringing to your attention," Emmi said, "an example of the deeply ingrained sexism in our culture. Any step that brings about equality is worth taking. You should make Dad do his share of the household work and then you'll be part of the solution."

"And otherwise, I'm part of the problem?"

"No, I'm not saying that exactly," Emmi said. "I just think we should all do what we can to make things fair. Should I get ready to go?"

And she walked off with her two drinks.

⚊⊶

Greta went back to the kitchen and sat down at her laptop again. She did not like to think of herself as doing anything that undermined women. Yes, she and Otto lived by an outdated paradigm, but she certainly thought of herself as a good role model, as a woman who had always balanced work and motherhood, who certainly thought women were equal to men, maybe even better, who wanted every opportunity for her daughter.

She thought of Maria Vermeer, knowing exactly what Emmi would want her to do. She opened her email and wrote to Sebastian Schultz again, simply floating the idea of a meeting with Benjamin Binstock, perhaps over Zoom, just to hear him out. And then they could decide for themselves whether it was believable that Maria Vermeer might have been the one to create such an exquisite painting. If she did paint it, Greta wrote, shouldn't she get the credit?

By the time she was out of the shower, she'd already gotten her reply, not from Herr Schultz but from his lawyer. It was a short message, saying she was not to contact Binstock under any circumstances, and she was never to speak about this subject in any public forum. Doing so, it said, was verboten and would be considered a violation of their trust in her. Greta understood very clearly that the smartest, most sensible—the only—thing to do would be to drop the subject entirely.

⚊⊶

Greta and Emmi went to the Dallas Museum of Art late that morning to see a contemporary art exhibit called *He Said/She Said* that fittingly questioned "the myth of the sole male genius."

They walked from room to room together, stopping to look at the pieces that caught their attention, just as they had when Emmi was too young to go to museums.

"Mom," said Emmi, grabbing her by the elbow. "If this isn't a sign, I don't know what is."

"A sign?" Greta said. When Emmi got on a soapbox, she could be relentless.

"Yes, that your generation tolerates casual and even blatant misogyny in a way mine never will. We don't stand for men treating us like shit."

"I don't know that I need another lecture—"

"I'm just saying— Look!" And she turned Greta by her arms, making her face the artwork head-on.

It was called *Pergusa* by Olivia Erlanger and featured an actual Maytag washing machine with a large mermaid tail coming out of it.

"This piece is literally telling you to stop doing a man's laundry," Emmi said.

"Or maybe it's saying"—Greta tilted her head and studied the work—"that it's tough to be a fish out of water?"

"Mom," said Emmi, giving her a withering look.

"Your father is not just a *man*," Greta said patiently. "And while I appreciate your strong opinions, you should know that relationships are a little more complicated than you realize at this point in your life, and not everything can always be exactly fair. What I hope is that you'll find a partner someday, if that's what you want, and the two of you will figure out what works for you, and that might mean you both have to compromise at times, but you do it because you love each other."

Emmi suddenly hugged her. "I love you, *Mami*," she said. "I just want you to be happy. You're the best mom in the world."

Hot and then cold. Needy and independent. Emmi was tough to navigate these days, and as Greta hugged her daughter back, it occurred to her for the first time that maybe it was for the best they weren't spending the entire summer together. And that idea made her want to cry.

8—

They left the museum and got back in the Prius to go meet Otto for lunch. Greta turned the air-conditioning on high and then headed in the direction of UT Southwestern.

"I'm sorry we're leaving you alone tomorrow night," Greta said as she pulled out onto the street. "Your father can't turn down an invitation to the Judsons' house."

"No, it's fine. I've got plans anyway. Hey, what's that?" she said, pointing out the window.

"The Meyerson Symphony," Greta said. "Wait, what plans?"

"I got invited to a party," Emmi said casually.

"Whose party?"

"That girl I met when I was out running," Emmi said. "The one who told me about Jack Holt." She huffed out a breath. "It makes me sick to think that guy's living in our apartment. And that we're actually driving around in his car. It's so creepy."

Greta was not sure why she felt a need to defend a boy she'd never met, but something, and maybe it was her fondness for Irene and Rex, led her to speak up. "Let's hold off on judging him so harshly," she said, "since we don't really know what happened."

Emmi shrugged. "Cynthia wasn't making the story up," she said. "I could tell."

"I know," Greta said, "but a story can have a lot of different versions, depending on who's telling it. I think it's best to have all the facts and make our own decisions, don't you? You're a budding lawyer after all."

And as she made this careful speech, she knew she wasn't going to be able to let go of the Vermeer question until she got a few facts herself. No one in the establishment would ever take seriously the idea that Vermeer's twenty-two-year-old daughter was capable of painting something so masterful, unless Greta somehow forced them to. Why wasn't it possible that a young woman could hone her craft and outperform her father? The whole topic made Greta deeply uncomfortable, especially since she'd just taken Emmi to see an exhibit that demonstrated the importance of acknowledging women in the male-dominated canon.

Greta's phone rang and she handed it to Emmi to answer when she saw Bettina's name on the screen.

"Hey, there," Greta said. "I'm in the car—"

"Did you know Mom's taking a trip to New York?" Bettina said.

"No, she never—"

"She was going on and on about American peanut butter, and how much she misses Broadway theater, you know," Bettina said, "one of her pro-America rants. And then she just called to say she's flying to JFK."

"But I invited her to come to Dallas," Greta said.

"That may be," said Bettina, "but she's going to New York instead, and she's bringing Tobias with her."

Greta gripped the steering wheel. "She's what?"

"I know," Bettina said. "And I admit it's getting weird now."

"Please, Bettina, can't you do something?" Greta said. "Why don't you call Tobias and ask him directly what's going on?"

"Tobias tried to call me actually," Bettina said, "but I didn't pick up. You know I slept with him in college, right?"

Greta did not know, nor was she surprised. "Emmi's in the car, just so you know."

"Oooh, hi, sweetie," Bettina said, sounding very delighted and not the least embarrassed.

"Hi, Tante Bettina," said Emmi. "Who did you sleep with in college?"

"Right," said Bettina. "I had a short-lived thing with this guy Tobias, and he thought it meant something, and he wrote this super embarrassing poem . . . I really don't want to reignite anything. How do you like Dallas, Em?"

"It's cool," said Emmi. "There're two dogs at the house where we're staying, almost as cute as Til."

Bettina laughed. "I'm glad you said *almost*."

"Have you gone to see Mom's new place?" Greta said. "I think you should talk to her face-to-face."

"She keeps putting me off," Bettina said, "saying she's too busy."

"She says *you're* too busy." Bettina, Greta thought, could not be counted on for anything. "You didn't even check on our apartment, did you?"

"I went there," Bettina said defensively. "But how could I *demand* an inspection of the premises? You have nothing to worry about anyway. Lucy's not a partier like she used to be. She's all grown up."

Greta was relieved to hear it. "What's she like?"

"She's still cute and has that southern twang. And Adam! Why didn't you tell me you've got such a good-looking neighbor? What a nice guy."

"Is he the man who moved in downstairs?" said Emmi.

"Yes, and he's married," Greta said flatly. "And I didn't think he was your type anyway."

"He's getting divorced," said Bettina, "and he's definitely not my type. He might be Lucy's though. They're spending a lot of time together."

Greta put on her blinker and got in the right lane. "They've gotten close, huh?" she said, imagining Adam and Lucy sitting on his balcony, laughing and drinking wine. "You don't think they're, you know . . . ?"

"Fucking?" Bettina said bluntly.

"*Bitte*, Bettina—"

"I'm still here," said Emmi.

"Shit, sorry," said Bettina. "But yeah, probably? Lucy's very at home in his apartment."

Greta was appalled. She couldn't stand the idea of Lucy and

Adam together. "I don't want to know all these unsavory things about that family," she said.

"You're right," said Bettina. "It's none of our business. We don't know what kind of arrangement Lucy and her husband have. They're spending six months apart? I certainly couldn't go six months without having sex."

Emmi was laughing.

"I met Lucy's son, Jack," Bettina said.

And at that, Emmi stopped laughing.

"And I'll just say he looks an awful lot like Lucy's hot Viking I told you about. *And* he's eighteen years old, so you do the math."

"None of our business, though," said Greta, "right?"

"Touché," said Bettina.

"Was he a jerk?" Emmi said.

"Was who a jerk?" said Bettina.

"Jack," said Emmi.

"Oh, no, he was super polite. A real gentleman. I've got to go. *Bis später*, you two. Have fun." And she hung up.

"A *gentleman*?" said Emmi. "I seriously doubt that. More like a master bullshitter."

Greta was tired of talking about and hearing about the Holts. She stopped at a red light by the campus. "At least your grand-mother will take you out for a nice dinner in New York," said Greta. The light changed, and she turned to go to the spot where Otto said to meet him. And there he was, waiting outside one of the university hospital buildings, waving. He took them on a grand tour around the impressive, sprawling campus. Greta was proud of Otto, and as they walked toward the Faculty Club, she could see how proud he was of himself. As he told them about this building and pointed out that facility, Greta thought how lucky she was that she and Otto had respect for each other and were faithful. They had his-tory. They had love. They had Emmi. It would be greedy to expect more than that.

⊸

The next morning, while Emmi slept in, Lillian called.

"You'll never guess where I am," Lillian said.

"New York City," said Greta, putting her coffee down on the kitchen island and closing the Vermeer book. She'd spent hours poring over every colorplate and cross-checking Binstock's claims with other sources. "Bettina already told me. What prompted this trip?"

"Tobias," she said. "He made me realize I've been homesick. A couple of weeks in New York is exactly what I need."

"You could have come to see me," Greta said. "You still can—"

"Tobias already got us tickets to everything in town. You know, your father never liked New York. But Tobias was so excited to come."

Her relationship—was it a crush?—on this much, much younger man was making Greta uncomfortable. "Where are you staying?" she said.

"The Pierre," Lillian said, "right across from Central Park. It's got old New York glamour. You know Elizabeth Taylor stayed here. I wish you could see it. We have the most beautiful view."

"The same view?" Greta said, sitting up taller. Surely they weren't— "I mean, from the same—"

"We'd love to have dinner with Emmi when she gets here," her mother said. The casual use of "we" was alarming.

"I tell you," Lillian went on, "I've never met anyone quite like Tobias. He never tires. He has more energy than anyone I've ever met."

Cocaine, thought Greta. *Ritalin and Red Bull?*

"And he's a born traveler. You'd think he knows New York better than I do, the finest restaurants . . ."

"Mom, this is really awkward, but I have to ask: Are you . . . ?" And she waited, hoping her mother would catch her meaning, and hoping at the same time that she wouldn't.

"Oh, goodness, no," her mother said, and laughed. "Can you even imagine such a thing?"

Greta exhaled loudly with relief. "*Gott sei Dank*, phew," she said. "I was worried—"

"*I* could never afford this hotel or first-class plane tickets. No, no, Tobias upgraded me with his miles, and he's paying for the hotel. He has a friend who got him some kind of deal."

Her mother hadn't caught her meaning after all. Greta was relieved Lillian wasn't footing the bill for this extravagant trip for two, but she was all the more mystified about this relationship.

"But . . . why?"

"Tobias has friends in high places. Everyone seems to love him."

"No, but why is he . . ."

"Spending time with me? I suppose he likes my company," she said. "Is that so hard to believe?"

It wasn't. Her mother was, in fact, very good company. But Greta couldn't shake the feeling that Tobias was up to no good and would somehow break her mother's heart.

"It's just that he's so young," Greta said.

"But he's an old soul," Lillian said. "Must run. We have dinner reservations." And she hung up abruptly as usual.

Greta checked the time. Normally, she would let Emmi sleep, but today she decided to wake her up. They both had parties to go to that night, and Greta had booked appointments for them to get their nails and hair done. Their time together was running out, and Greta wanted to make the most of every minute.

BERLIN

Grocery shopping in Germany wasn't for sissies. The first time Lucy went to buy enough food to feed her family of four, she went by herself, having forgotten she was expected to bag her own groceries at a speed that was completely unrealistic given the breakneck pace at which the checkout clerk flung the milk, plums, and bread down the conveyor belt. Lucy couldn't keep up. Another shopper, standing way too close behind her, made an exasperated grunt because it took Lucy too long to pull out her debit card. And then, when she was all done, she had to walk half a mile home and up five flights of stairs carrying the heavy bags. She took Motrin the next day for her aching shoulders.

She knew better now and brought the kids along to help. The three of them stood at the ready that day, bags in hand, taking turns grabbing ice cream containers and onions and boxes of pasta as the items barreled toward them. Zoe got overly excited and missed her bag completely, tossing a glass jar of applesauce on the floor. It shattered, of course, Zoe cried, and they left the store in complete disgrace.

But for once it wasn't raining when they headed out to the street, and Zoe pulled herself together more quickly than usual after Alice offered her a fistful of gummy bears. When they stopped to wait for the light to change at busy Ku'Damm, Lucy put her bags down and unzipped her sweatshirt.

"Bleibtreu," said Lucy. The light turned green, and she picked up her bags again. "Isn't that the loveliest name for a street?"

"Not really," said Jack.

"But do you know what it means?" Lucy said. "Stay true. Or stay faithful. I think it's pretty."

And the street itself was very pretty indeed. This neighborhood was nothing like the area where Lucy had lived in college. The housing complex in Kreuzberg had been gritty and loud, surrounded by dive bars and nightclubs, perfect for college students. But this area, Charlottenburg, suited Lucy better now. It was clean and quiet, and there were flower shops and cafés, boutiques and wine bars. It was perfect, and she wished Mason were there to enjoy it with her.

As they passed a playground, Zoe asked whether they could stop for a few minutes.

Lucy's arms were already aching, so she was happy to take a break. They went through the gate, set their bags down, and the girls ran off to play. She and Jack sat together on a bench. And just at that moment, the sun came out.

"No way," said Jack, and he looked up at the bit of blue sky.

"Shocker," said Lucy. She too tilted her face upward.

Jack's mood had shifted a bit in the last few days, and there was something about him—the tiniest uptick in, was it *cheer*?—that made her hope he might be healing.

"You know that girl Emmi?" he said. "She connected me to a friend of hers here. We're going to meet at a café."

"*Ausgezeichnet*," Lucy said. "Your grandmother says Emmi's really nice."

Lucy was not imagining things; Jack *was* a little more cheerful. And Lucy was grateful to Emmi—and maybe even to Greta—for having had anything to do with that.

"I guess there are worse places we could have ended up this summer," she said.

"Kierkegaard fled Copenhagen in 1841," Jack said, "and guess where he went?"

The words "Kierkegaard" and "Copenhagen" made Lucy look over at him in surprise. "I don't have any idea," she said. "Where?"

"Here. Berlin," he said. "Isn't that crazy?"

"Damn," Lucy said. "And I thought we were being original."

"Nope, Berlin is *the* place to go if you're running from scandal."

Lucy smiled; she could not have felt more gratified to see this touch of humor.

"I knew we did the right thing," she said.

"It was weird," he said. "I was walking around the other day and happened to pass the building where Kierkegaard lived when he was here. It has this quotation on a sign about subjectivity being truth and untruth."

Why, she wondered, was he still talking about Kierkegaard? "What does that mean?" Lucy said.

"I think it means there can be more than one version of the same story," he said, "but it's probably way more complicated than that. I'm no philosopher, but there's probably some deeper meaning."

Philosopher? Lucy did not like where this conversation was going. "Is something on your mind, Jack?" she said.

He picked a chestnut up off the ground and tossed it in his hand. "Actually, yeah," he said. "I wrote a letter to Bjørn."

Lucy felt the blood drain from her face. "You . . . ? When?"

"Today," he said. "I already mailed it this morning."

"Wait . . ." She tried to swallow and found she couldn't. "You didn't want to talk about it first?"

He shrugged. "It's no big deal."

But it was. Jack had no way of knowing that, but this was a very big deal, a huge problem, in fact. Lucy's head was spinning as she tried to come up with some way to control the damage.

"I looked up his institute," he said, "and I thought, why not just send a letter to introduce myself?"

"But . . . ," Lucy said. Her heart was pounding. "I mean, why now?"

"I want to meet him," he said. "I never did before, but it just seems like the right time now." He turned to look at her. "What is that word you say? Aus-get-psyched-ed?"

"*Ausgezeichnet,*" she said flatly.

"Excellent, right? Wait, you're not mad, are you? You always said I could contact him, that he'd be happy to hear from me."

"Mad? Why would I be mad?" And she wasn't mad. She was panicked. "But you know what?" she said. "I just realized we have to go." She called the girls, with no small degree of urgency, and they came running.

"What's wrong?" Jack said, getting to his feet as well. "Are you feeling okay?"

"Yeah, great," Lucy said. "I feel great."

"Why are we leaving?" Alice said.

"I just . . . I forgot we bought ice cream," Lucy said.

They picked up all the bags and went through the playground gate. All the optimism Lucy had felt had vanished, and she wondered how she was going to handle yet another catastrophe while her husband was, for all intents and purposes, on Mars. It wasn't Jack's fault, of course. It wasn't entirely hers either. But Bjørn had absolutely no idea he had a son.

DALLAS

Greta sat in the passenger seat as Otto drove down Preston Road in Lucy's minivan (with its Rockwell School bumper sticker and little stick figures of the whole family, including the pets, going across the length of the back windshield) to Dr. Judson's house. Otto was wearing a navy suit Greta had bought for him at Neiman Marcus with a crisp white shirt and tie, and he looked every bit the dignified doctor. Greta had on the same Prada slingbacks she'd worn to the party at the Schultz Foundation and was happy to have another formal occasion to wear them.

"Maybe we should have taken Mason's Tesla tonight," she said.

"I could never," Otto said for the umpteenth time.

Greta looked out the window as they passed the strip mall she'd been to earlier in the day with Emmi; it had a cupcake shop, a bookstore, and a nail salon. "I finally get to meet this Dr. Judson," she said.

"You'll like Troy. And I'm sure many of my colleagues will be there."

Greta imagined a long, candlelit table and hoped she would have interesting people sitting beside her.

"You're finally calling him Troy?"

"Oh yes. Troy is very . . . chill," said Otto.

"*Chill?*"

"He is the best colleague I am ever having."

Greta tightened the ribbon on the box of truffles in her lap, a gift to show her gratitude to the people who had welcomed Otto so warmly.

"I have to warn you though," he said, "these doctors are . . . I really don't have the word for it. They are making a lot of jokes."

"That must be refreshing," Greta said. "Or are you in culture shock?"

"I like it," he said, "but it's hard understanding them sometimes. They make wordplay and cultural humor. And they speak very, very fast." He leaned forward to look out the window. "Is this the house?"

Greta checked the address on Otto's phone. "Yes, I think so." It was a grand, symmetrical brick mansion set back from the street. There were two oak trees on opposite sides of the front yard with white and violet pansies planted in beds around them. The grass was vivid green.

Otto pulled into the wide circular drive, and a man in black pants and a vest waved them forward.

"Is that Dr. Judson?" Greta asked.

"No," said Otto. He rolled down the window. "Hello, we are Dr. and Mrs. von Bosse here to see Dr. Judson."

"Right," the young man said, and then he tried to open Otto's door.

"You are parking the car?"

"Yes, sir," said the man. "Just leave it to me."

Otto turned to Greta before getting out. "Valet parking, like a five-star hotel."

"*Wunderbar*," she said. She did not want to walk any farther in her heels than she had to. Holding the box of chocolates, she stepped out of the car into the hot evening air, adjusting the sash of her silk wrap dress and hoping she wouldn't sweat before they got to the air-conditioning. She looped her arm through Otto's, and they walked up to the front porch together. There were oversize planters flanking the columned front porch, each with little American flags circling the rim. Otto rang the bell.

The door opened, and a man threw his arms up when he saw them. "Whoa!" he said, looking positively delighted.

"Good evening, Troy," Otto said.

"Otto! Look at you!" Troy stepped out and clapped Otto on the back. "Wow, I'm sorry I wasn't clear; tonight's just a cookout. Come on in, man!" Troy was wearing beige-colored, ill-fitting cargo shorts and a short-sleeved, seersucker button-down shirt. He had on some kind of boat shoes without socks. "And you," he said, turning to Greta, "must be Greta."

Greta tried to smile and extended her hand just as Troy leaned in for a hug.

"Great to meet you," he said. "Gosh, you two look ready for dinner at the White House. Where's your daughter?"

"Was she invited?" said Greta, flashing a look at Otto. "I had no idea."

Given a choice, Emmi would have probably chosen Cynthia's party over this one anyway, but Greta was annoyed Otto hadn't known to include her.

"Come on in," Troy said. "I'll introduce you around."

Otto placed a hand on Greta's back as they walked into the house. Greta was flushed, wondering how Otto could have misunderstood the dress code so completely.

Troy led them through the foyer, with its baroque gold-framed mirror, dark blue floral wallpaper, and curved center staircase. Four small children in bathing suits ran past them, yelling on their way up the stairs. In the family room, a woman in white jeans and a sleeveless red top was cheering at a huge television screen on the back wall: "Let's go, Seager!" A bunch of people whooped.

"The Rangers are doing great this season," Troy said. "You follow baseball?"

Greta and Otto shook their heads.

"Kristy," Troy called, "come over here and meet Otto."

A young woman with blond hair came over to them. She was wearing a short denim skirt and white sandals to match her white toenails. "Finally," she said, hugging him, "I get a face to go with the name. Troy has not shut up about you."

"And this is his wife, Greta," Troy said.

Greta handed Kristy the box of chocolates. "Thank you for having us," she said.

"Aren't you sweet," she said. Then she looked down at Greta's feet. "Well, bless your heart. You want to borrow some flip-flops, hon?"

"No, thank you," Greta said, trying to stand casually in her high heels.

"Let me know if you change your mind," Kristy said.

Troy pointed to the bar. "Make yourselves at home, you two," he said. "And head on out back when you're hungry."

They went outside, and Greta felt sweat trickle down her back as she and Otto went through the buffet line. There was loud music playing, and kids were running around the yard, sword-fighting with pool noodles. With their plates in hand, they joined a group of people at one of the many tables covered with Stars and Stripes cloths.

"I think we can be more comfortable," Otto said in her ear before taking off his suit jacket and hanging it over the back of a chair, taking off his tie, unbuttoning the top button of his shirt, and rolling up his sleeves. Now he almost fit right in.

But Greta was wearing silk and pantyhose, and there wasn't a damn thing she could do about it.

She was introduced to a handsome cosmetic surgeon and his young wife, Lisa. Lisa was wearing a sarong and a bikini top. She had a toddler squirming in her lap who was eating fistfuls of French fries. Next to Otto was his colleague Betsy and her husband, Bob, a smug-looking car dealer who was staring into his beer.

Greta looked at her plate of food, realizing she had no silverware. She glanced around the table and noticed that no one else was using any. She spread her napkin across her lap.

The plastic surgeon said something that Greta couldn't quite hear over the pop music. She looked up to find that he was talking to her.

"I'm sorry?" said Greta.

"What do you do?" he repeated.

"Oh, I help people build art collections."

"How interesting," Lisa said.

"I used to work at an auction house," Greta said, "but I'm shifting gears to work with private clients or organizations."

"See, that's the thing about women," Lisa said, bouncing the baby on her knee. "We reinvent ourselves. I'm going back to work, just as soon as this little guy is out of diapers." She removed a chunk of her hair from her toddler's sticky hands.

"Have you tried the bread?" Otto said, passing Greta the basket.

"Those are *buttermilk* biscuits, Boss," said Betsy. "Aren't they just sinful?"

"Mmm," he said. Otto was living his best life.

"Boss?" said Greta.

"That's our nickname for him in the department," Betsy said. "Dr. von *Bosse*."

Otto having a nickname was almost unimaginable. Greta couldn't wait to tell Emmi.

"What kind of art do you buy?" Lisa said.

Greta took a sip of wine before answering. "That depends on the client," she said, giving up on the food. The ribs were too messy to eat, the corn too difficult. "I'd like to think I could work with anyone, on any budget. It's up to me to figure out what people like."

"I hear you've got Rex Henley living practically in your backyard," Betsy said. "Rex is kind of a celebrity around here."

"Yes," Greta said, "his photographs are hanging in the Holts' house. He's very good."

As soon as she said the name "Holt," Greta noticed a shift, a glance between Lisa and her husband, a change in Bob's posture.

"Rex has a book out about the changing landscape of Texas," Betsy said. "It was written up in *The New York Times*."

"He's such a nice man," said Greta. "He and Irene have been wonderful to us."

"Do you know the Holts?" Lisa asked.

"We're staying in their house," Greta said, glancing around the table. "But we've never actually met them."

"We made a home exchange," said Otto. "It is win-win."

"That's quite a family," Bob said. "A husband who ditches his wife and kids to pretend he's on Mars and a son who's a sexual predator."

There were murmurs around the table. Greta squeezed her napkin.

"I can only imagine how Betsy would react," Bob said, "if I came home and told her I was going to shack up with five young women in the middle of New Mexico."

"I admit," Betsy said with a tight smile, "it wouldn't go over well. But Mason's a scientist and this is NASA after all, so in his case—"

"Look, I'll just come out and say it," Bob said, a mean glint in his eye, "if my daughter's name had been on Jack's list, I would have gone over there and pummeled that little shithead with brass knuckles."

Greta put her wineglass down, shocked by his violent rhetoric. Who talked about a teenager that way?

"Lord have mercy," Betsy said. "You can't punch a kid, *Bob*. And anyway, Jack Holt got expelled from Rockwell, so I'd say he was punished enough."

Otto looked up from the rib he was devouring. "Our daughter heard about the list from a girl in the neighborhood. Is it true then?"

Greta was aghast; Otto never seemed to understand when to keep family conversations private.

"It's true all right," Bob said. "He's a bad egg."

"You don't *know* that," Betsy said sternly. "Can we be Christian about this, please?"

Bob shook his head. "If I have anything to say in the matter, that whole family will get run out of town. I don't know why you insist on giving them the benefit of the doubt."

"Innocent until proven guilty," Betsy said. "That's why." She leaned toward her husband, and Greta watched as she whispered something in his ear.

Bob glared at her and stood up. "I think I'll get something a little stronger. Anyone want a little tequila?"

No one answered, and he skulked off. The toddler in Lisa's lap reached his little hand onto his mom's plate, put his palm flat in the barbecue sauce, and then smeared it all over the skirt of Greta's dress.

"Oh, I'm so sorry!" Lisa said. She handed her son over to her husband and grabbed a napkin, getting to her feet. "No, your beautiful dress!"

"It's fine," Greta said. "It's my own fault for wearing silk to a pool party." She laughed as though she found the situation funny, which she did not.

Lisa dipped her napkin in water and handed it to Greta.

"Thank you," Greta said, standing up as well, "but I'll go fix myself up." She walked away from the table, hoping sweat hadn't darkened the back of her dress. She made her way inside, past the baseball enthusiasts, to the ladies' room. In the bathroom, she leaned against the gold velvet-flocked wallpaper and closed her eyes, hating everything about this party. Then she looked in the mirror to assess the damage. She wiped the thick red sauce off her skirt as best she could. And then—*why not?*—she stepped out of her shoes, lifted up the skirt of her dress, and pulled off her sheer stockings, stuffing them in her handbag. She used a tissue to fix her running eyeliner and to dab the sweat from her hairline and décolletage. She reapplied her lipstick.

She wanted to kill Otto.

Stepping her bare feet back into her shoes, she took a deep breath and opened the bathroom door, walking right into Bob, his glass filled almost to the top with tequila.

"If it makes you feel any better," he said conspiratorially, "I hate this party too."

"Not at all," said Greta, stepping away from him. "I just wish I'd known—"

"If it were up to me," he said, "and I got a chance to take out a woman like you, with a sexy accent and wearing a dress like *that*?" His eyes scanned her from her shoes all the way up to her cleavage, "we'd be drinking Dom and eating raw oysters at the Mansion. You're too gorgeous for this shit."

His breath was boozy. Greta took a step back.

"Instead," he said, "I guess we'll have to make the best of things. I'll be admiring you from afar." He winked and walked away.

Greta wished she'd told him off. Emmi probably would have.

⚯

The people at the table had swapped out in the brief time Greta had been gone, and someone else was sitting in her chair. No one, not even Otto, moved to make room for her. She wished Emmi were there with her.

Greta wandered across the yard, the heels of her shoes sinking into the grass. She walked toward what she thought was a tennis court, but as she got closer she could see it was smaller, and the players were using paddles rather than rackets. *Pickleball!* She smiled, sorry she couldn't send a picture of this scene to Adam.

⚯

It was still light out when they left. Otto hummed as he drove, tapping his fingers on the steering wheel.

Greta had taken off her shoes and was rubbing the balls of her feet. "I was dressed for a night at the opera," she said, "not the circus."

"I'm sorry about that," Otto said. "But Troy and Kristy are very good hosts, *oder?*"

"They certainly have a high tolerance for mayhem," Greta said. "I had a hard time hearing anyone over the music, the children were running wild, and there was no silverware."

"There was no need for silverware."

Greta turned to him. "You *hate* eating with your hands."

"I am in Rome," he said, looking at himself in the rearview mirror, "doing as the Romans."

Greta's stomach grumbled. She felt sorry for herself.

"It would be nice for us to make a party, yes?" said Otto. "In a few weeks? We could use the Holts' grill."

"We don't know how to grill," Greta said.

"I will learn," said Otto. "We could host a Bavarian *Biergarten* party. *Oktoberfest* in *Sommer*. Sausages and *Kartoffelsalat*. Fun, yes?"

Otto did not cook and had never shown any interest in cooking. He had never wanted to invite his colleagues over to their apartment. Greta felt she was losing control of her life.

"It is a nice life to be made here," he said. "Don't you agree?"

She supposed it was, for some people.

⊖⊣

Emmi had texted that she had just left for her party when they got back from theirs.

Greta got out of her stained dress, took a quick shower, and put on a nightgown. Then she climbed into bed, getting as close to Otto as she could, draping one arm across his body to get his attention. It seemed only fair that something good should come out of this otherwise miserable night. She'd shaved her legs after all.

He held her hand but was otherwise still.

"Otto?"

"*Ja?*"

"I'm glad we're sleeping in the same bed again."

Otto sighed. "I have *Bauchschmerzen*," he said. "I think I ate too much."

Greta had barely eaten anything. She rolled away from him, frustrated, and stared up at the ceiling in the dark, missing the noises her apartment made at night, the radiators knocking and the floors creaking.

On the night table, her phone lit up, and she reached over to see she'd gotten a message from Adam.

> Hey G! Just saying hi again. Haven't heard from u ☹ I'm heading to NYC soon but want you to know yr apt is in great hands. Lucy is awesome. Hope you're having fun in TX.

Greta hated how bitter she felt. Was he sleeping with Lucy? Bettina had certainly thought so. *Poor Mason*, she thought, locked up in his biosphere, having no idea.

Greta ignored Adam's text.

She wished she could sleep, but she was too agitated. She had plenty of reasons to be awake and restless. Emmi was at a party with kids she didn't know and was leaving Dallas in only two days. Her mother was gallivanting around New York City with a crush on a bad boy. And then there was the issue of the Vermeer. If only she could know for sure, if only she could do a bit of digging herself.

What she needed, what she really wanted . . .

She nudged Otto. "*Schläfst du schon?*"

"I'm awake," he said groggily.

"I was thinking," she said, "I'd really like to go to New York with Emmi."

He rubbed his face. "Hmmm."

She sat up. "I could help her get settled, Otto. And while I'm there, I'll check on my mom. Win-win," she added. "Maybe you'd like to go with me?"

"I can't go anywhere," he said, "but I think it's *eine gute Idee*. You should go."

"It will be expensive," she said.

"Yes, of course," he said, and yawned, "New York is always *teuer*. But we can manage. And you will have big fun."

The idea of a trip to New York was giving Greta butterflies, and she felt too energized to sleep. She kissed Otto on the cheek, got out of bed, and went to the kitchen to get her laptop, hoping there was still an open seat on Emmi's flight.

DALLAS

*Emmi was standing outside Cynthia's house, trying to find the cour-*age to walk into the party all by herself, wishing Monika was there to go with her. They'd FaceTimed yesterday, and Emmi was not surprised that within a few minutes, they'd come up with a perfect plan to humiliate Jack Holt. Jack could run to Germany, but no way could he hide.

Emmi would not, she decided, tell her mother about their scheme, knowing she would disapprove of any involvement.

From across the street, Emmi studied the mansion, intimidated by the sight of fifteen or more cars parked along the curb in both directions. She'd walked the two blocks from the Holts' house in a short dress and sandals, her hair blown out and nails done, thanks to her mom, so she wasn't going to turn around and go back. Instead she forced herself to walk up to the door and ring the bell. No one answered. She followed the sounds—of pop music and splashing—to the back gate, which someone had propped open with a brick.

The backyard was crowded and loud, and Emmi almost skulked away. But then she spotted Cynthia getting out of the pool in a pink bikini, her long hair dripping water on the ground.

"Hey," Cynthia said when Emmi walked over. "You made it."

"Hi," Emmi said, feeling shy and unsure of what to do with her hands.

A guy walked by and handed Cynthia a bottle of vodka, his flip-flops slapping on the wet concrete. Cynthia kept her attention on Emmi.

"You look adorbs," Cynthia said.

"Thanks."

"Warning, everyone's pretty shit-faced already, so you've got some catching up to do. We got a keg." Cynthia took a striped towel from a lounge chair and wrapped it around her waist. She looked at Emmi with hope in her eyes. "Any update on Operation You-Know-Who?"

"My friend Monika and I have an excellent plan for him. I'll text you tomorrow night to tell you how it goes." Emmi looked down at the pool, where a couple was making out in the deep end.

"That's Madison," said Cynthia. "She's my bestie, you'll totally love her. And Austin. They're, like, practically engaged. It's disgusting. Come on, I'll introduce you around." She led Emmi into the crowded pool house.

Someone put a red cup of beer in her hand, and she struggled to catch names over the music. There were two Ashleys, a Harper, a Courtney, and a Winnie. A Steve, a Trevor, and a Hunter. Emmi could not keep them straight. Everyone was beautiful.

"Some of the guys here are idiots," Cynthia said in her ear, "but I can steer you toward the decent ones if you're interested in hooking up."

"I have a boyfriend," Emmi said, an apology in her tone she hadn't intended.

A girl in jean shorts staggered up to them and leaned on Cynthia. "I love you, Cyn," she said.

Cynthia looked at Emmi over the drunk girl's shoulder and rolled her eyes.

"I love you too." She patted her on the back. "Are you gonna puke?"

"For sure," the girl said, sounding thrilled about it. "Yeah."

"Fuck my life," Cynthia said, and then yelled, "Coming through." She put an arm around the girl and guided her through the pool house, clearing people out of the way.

Emmi was on her own. She watched the beer pong for a while,

one arm wrapped around her own waist. Four girls were working on the choreography for some kind of dance but kept laughing too hard to get through it. A group of guys watched and egged them on. Emmi took a sip of her beer and went outside where it was quieter.

She was considering slipping back out the gate when she noticed a group sitting around a table on the far side of the pool. There was an empty chair. She bravely walked over and introduced herself. The girls, she learned, were Allie, a red-haired girl who appeared to be very drunk, Nell, and Becca. Emmi repeated each name, pointing to make sure she got it right. The boy was Sam. He was wearing a straw fedora, and he seemed very different from the guys playing beer pong inside.

"Nice to meet you all," Emmi said as she sat down.

"I love your bracelet," Becca said.

Emmi put her hand to it, touching the little Tiffany charms her grandmother had given her. "Thank you."

"And your dress," said Becca. "Is that Free People?"

"No," Emmi said. "It's from Germany."

"Hollldd on a minute," Allie blurted out, adjusting her bikini top, which was dangerously close to falling off. "Are you that girl from Paris Cynthia told me about?"

"I don't think so, no," said Emmi.

"Yes, you are," Allie said, wagging a finger at her. "You're that French girl."

"I'm from Germany," Emmi said.

"See," Allie said to the group. "I knew it!" She took a shot of tequila, slammed the little glass on the table, and shuddered. "I heard all about you," she said.

"France and Germany aren't the same thing," Nell said. She leaned in and moved the tequila bottle out of Allie's reach.

"Practically," said Allie.

"Acchhh zo, ze *Fraulein* eeez from *Deutschland, ja?*" said the boy Sam with an exaggerated accent.

Emmi turned to see him smiling at her slyly.

"Nossing to say? Verrrry interesting. Vee haf vays of making you talk."

"Sorry, what?" And then Emmi understood: he was making fun of her. "Wait," she said, "is that what you think Germans sound like?"

"Pretty much," Sam said. "I'm working on my German accent. I'm playing Dr. Einstein in *Arsenic and Old Lace* this summer."

"Is it a play?" Emmi said.

"It's an American classic," said Sam, like he couldn't believe she'd never heard of it.

"I got a lead role," said Becca.

Becca was a show-off. She had one hand on her collarbone, the other on Sam's knee. "You should come see us," she said. "It's going to be hilarious."

"But it's dark humor," said Sam, nodding wisely, "if you're into that."

"No, hang on, y'all." Allie was shaking her head, clearly struggling to place Emmi. "She's the girl who's staying in Jack Holt's house."

Sam looked up at her from under the brim of his fedora.

Did these kids hate Jack too? Because Emmi certainly didn't want to be associated with him. "I don't know Jack," she said quickly. "But yes, my parents are staying in his family's house."

"Really?" Sam asked. "Why?"

"My dad is working here, so he and my mom—"

"Where are the Holts?" he said.

Emmi did not want to say. "They're away, at least until the end of the summer."

Sam nodded, narrowing his eyes. "What a coward. I knew he'd taken off."

"Wouldn't you run away if you were him?" Becca said.

"What's the deal, Sam?" Nell said, sitting forward in her chair and facing him. Nell didn't have the same Instagram look of Cynthia and so many of the girls at the party, with the long, thick lashes, arched eyebrows, injected lips, and impossibly white teeth. Nell seemed more mature somehow, and Emmi liked her style, her barely buttoned, sheer cotton shirt and wide, high-waisted jeans. Her fingers were curled around a vape pen. "Isn't Jack, like, your best friend?"

"No," Sam said.

"You aren't in touch with him?" Nell said.

"Why would I be?" Sam said. "The guy's a loser."

Emmi hated that word. It was a bully's word. She took a sip of her beer and looked away.

"*Loser?*" Nell said. "Seriously? What happened? The four of you were inseparable."

Sam shifted in his chair.

"Drew's such a sweet guy," Nell went on. "Rosie's brilliant, and Jack—"

"Drew's got zero rizz, and Rosie's basic," Becca said. "Girl needs a makeover."

Emmi had always thought her English was pretty decent, but her lack of comprehension around people her own age made her feel like a beginner.

Nell ignored Becca. "I figured you were upset Jack got expelled," she said.

Sam's face had turned red. Emmi saw him swallow.

"Upset?" Becca said with a laugh. "Sam's the one who showed me the list. And I showed it to Cynthia, and her mom went absolutely ballistic—"

"You?" Nell said to Sam. "You're the one who got Jack in trouble?"

"He thought I should know what that asshole was saying about me and all of us," Becca said. She leaned over and kissed Sam. "He's my hero."

Nell rolled her eyes. "I don't buy it," she said. "Jack was my lab partner in bio all junior year, and he was always so decent to me. No one becomes an asshole overnight."

Emmi was intrigued; Jack had a defender in this girl.

"It's pretty simple actually," said Sam. "Jack is bitter because he's never had a girlfriend."

Nell was shaking her head. "He never came across like an angry guy. He was always nice."

"Maybe you should date him then," Sam said.

"I'm not saying I want to *date* him," Nell said. "It's just confusing to hear you talk bad about him."

"According to Jack's list," Becca said, "I'm worth a small Mercedes while you're worth, like, a Starbucks Frappuccino. You're the one who should be the most pissed off at him."

"And yet I'm the one telling you," Nell said, her voice strong, "Jack liked me. We got along."

"The only good thing about Jack Holt," Becca said, "is that he's the reason Sam and I got together."

"You're wrong about him," Nell said. "Everybody is. I even went to the principal, the disciplinary committee, and my teachers, and I told them I thought Jack should get a chance to show and explain the math he did. I assumed you stood up for him too." No one at the table said anything.

"You're seriously wrecking my vibe, Nell," said Allie. "No more talking about that asshole. Shots! Let's do shots."

Emmi turned as three shirtless guys wrestled a fourth, who was fully clothed, into the pool.

Nell got up from the table and walked away. Emmi watched her cross the lawn and go out through the gate.

Like anywhere else, there were mean kids mixed together with the nice ones. In Berlin Emmi was pretty sure she knew who was who. Here she wasn't entirely sure. But she could make a good guess.

She got up then as well and followed Nell out of the yard.

⚊⚊

Half an hour later, Nell dropped Emmi off in front of the house. Before she even went inside, Emmi tried calling Monika to tell her to slow the plan down, or maybe even cancel it altogether before they punished a boy who maybe wasn't such a bad guy after all. Monika didn't pick up.

The dogs—Jack's dogs—ran to meet her at the door. She loved being welcomed by them, being visited at night, being greeted every time she walked into a room. They followed her to the kitchen, where she got them treats from a glass jar on the counter. She looked up and happened to spot her mother outside, pacing by the pool, a lit cigarette between her fingers. Emmi's mom did not smoke.

She backed away from the window, wondering whether she'd gone too far in pointing out her dad's accidental sexism and feeling like things she knew nothing about were afoot in the family. She went upstairs to her room—possibly Jack's room—and tried calling Monika again and again, unsure of whose version of the story she should believe.

BERLIN

As usual, it had rained all day. Jack held his sisters' hands as they walked down wet sidewalks past a playground in the direction of the train tracks that crossed the south side of Savignyplatz.

Zoe tugged on his hand. "Can we stop?"

"Not right now," Jack said. "I don't want to be late."

"Who are we meeting?" Alice said.

"Her name's Monika."

"Is she your girlfriend?" Zoe said.

"No," Jack said, "and don't say anything dumb like that in front of her."

"Does she speak English?" Alice said.

"I assume so," said Jack. "Pretty much everyone speaks English here. Sometimes they speak English better than we do."

Zoe squeezed his hand. "Why?"

"I don't know," Jack said. "Our education system is flawed."

"Is that why my grades are so bad?" said Zoe.

"*Yo hablo español*," said Alice.

"I don't," said Zoe.

"Listen," Jack said, stopping in his tracks, "just promise me, you'll just be nice, and you'll let me talk to this girl, and you won't say anything to embarrass me."

"Like what?" said Zoe.

"Like . . . anything. We want to make a good impression on her because she's friends with Emmi, and Emmi's parents are taking care of our pets. So we want Monika to tell her we're normal people."

"We're not normal people?" said Alice.

"We are," he said, and started walking again. "And we want Monika to see that." Jack was feeling very anxious, aware as always of the knot in his stomach.

He'd tried reading Kierkegaard's *The Concept of Anxiety* but found it impenetrable. He was bad at many things, but studying—reading and understanding—was not usually one of them, so when his attempts to make sense of Kierkegaard's philosophical writings failed, Jack was all the more intrigued. He'd had almost no practice in reading philosophy, and deciphering this shit turned out to be really hard. He'd googled the Kierkegaard Research Centre and clicked on the "Staff" page to find Bjørn. There was a picture of him at the top of the page; they looked eerily alike. He tried to read some of Bjørn's writing on Kierkegaard, stuff about "existence spheres" and how Kierkegaard said these spheres—aesthetic, ethical, and religious—gave life value and lead one to "becoming a self." Jack reread the pages multiple times, feeling like his head would explode.

A biosphere, he thought, was a lot easier to understand than an existence sphere. But he hoped Bjørn would answer his letter. He was really looking forward to meeting the guy.

⊶

Jack and his sisters turned the corner onto Knesebeckstraße and crossed the street. Sitting outside the café was the coolest-looking girl Jack had ever seen. She was wearing a long white skirt with clunky biker boots and a tank top with a skull and crossbones. Her hair was long and untamed and had a streak of blue on one side.

"Hey," he said, still gripping the girls' hands. "Monika?"

She pulled off her sunglasses and looked up from her phone. "Jack?"

"Yeah, hi. Thanks for meeting me."

She looked at the girls in surprise. "And who are you?"

"I'm Alice," his sister said, kicking the sidewalk with her sandal.

"Nice to meet you, Alice," Monika said. "And?" she said, turning to Zoe.

"Zoe," Zoe said.

"Are you *Zwilling*? Twins?"

They nodded at her with eyes wide, clearly awed by her and feeling shy. He felt exactly the same way.

"I hope it's okay they came along," he said.

"Of course," she said. "No problem." She spoke English with a heavy accent and a lot of confidence.

Jack took a chair across from her. On the table was a half-finished fruit and cheese plate, a slice of cake with one bite taken out of it, and an empty plate that had the remnants of a salad. There was also an empty champagne glass and a cappuccino that appeared to have just been served.

"Am I . . . late?" he said. It looked like she had ordered almost everything on the menu and had been there for quite some time.

"No," she said, sitting back in her chair.

Zoe leaned on him shyly, and Alice sat carefully in the chair beside him.

Monika tapped her fingers on the table, not impatiently, more like she was assessing him and finding him lacking. Her nails were painted black. She took a sip of her cappuccino and dabbed her upper lip with a napkin.

"What do you think of Berlin?" she said.

"It's great," he said. "It's good to be away from Dallas."

"Why is that?" she said, cocking her head and watching him closely.

He wished he hadn't said that. "The weather?" he said. "Dallas is very hot in the summer."

"So what are you doing while you're here?" she asked. "Do you have a job?"

Jack pointed to the girls. "They're it. I'm babysitting in the evenings while my mom works." He both hoped and feared Monika was about to invite him to something. "I'm free on weekends."

"So all day you do . . . what?" Monika said. "Are you studying?"

"I was," Jack said. It was starting to feel like an interview, which was super confusing. "I'm between high school and college, so I'm on a break. But I guess you—"

"You must be bored," she said. "I have to stay busy all the time. Otherwise, I go . . . *verrückt*? Umm, out of my mind." She spun her finger in circles by her ear.

Jack felt he was failing a test. "Same," he said. "I wish I had more to do this summer. Too much free time is never a good idea."

"Are you looking for something?" she said, her face brightening.

"Yeah," he said, "I guess."

"Because an idea is just coming into my mind," Monika said, tapping her temple. "Do you want to do something good? Volunteer maybe?"

"Sure," he said. And he did.

"Can we order food?" said Alice impatiently.

"Yeah," Jack said. "We'll get menus as soon as someone comes."

"I have a friend at an organization called Alle Tage," Monika said. "They do very important work. Do you speak any German?"

"I don't." He found himself focusing on the small, silver stud in her left nostril.

"*Aber ich spreche schon ein bisschen*," said Zoe.

Jack looked at her in surprise. "Excuse me?"

Zoe shrugged, like she hadn't just done something completely mind-blowing. "The kids at the pool won't talk to us in English," she said.

Alice turned to Monika. "*Warum hast du blaue Haare?*"

Jack was stunned. All he'd learned so far was a handful of words, *bitte* and *danke*, *ja* and *nein*, *rechts* and *links*. He would have to up his game to keep up with his sisters.

Monika smiled and touched a hand to the blue streak. "Because I like it. And it's my body, my hair, my life, so I get to do whatever I want."

"Did you have to ask your mom?" Alice said.

"No," said Monika, "and when you're my age, you'll also get to do whatever you want without asking permission."

Jack tried to picture his sisters as teenagers, blue streaks in their hair; it was impossible to imagine, and he kind of hated the idea.

Monika's phone rang with a jangly tune. Jack glanced at it just long enough to see a girl's picture on the screen and the name "Emmi."

She silenced the call.

"*Ich muss auf die Toilette*," Zoe said.

Even Jack could understand that. "Okay," he said, "but go together." Alice got up reluctantly and the two went inside the café.

Monika's phone rang again, and again it was Emmi. This time she not only silenced it but turned it over.

"Can you start tomorrow?" she said.

"Sure," Jack said, thinking it would be fun to spend a few hours with her, serving meals at a shelter or whatever they were going to do. He hoped it wasn't out of his skill set.

"You'll need to learn a few German words, although some are basically the same in English. *Brauchen* means need. So when you go to a location, you ask, *Brauchen Sie Binden?* Go on."

"Brau-ken Sie . . . Binden?" Jack said.

"*Genau*," said Monika. "The *ch* is soft. *Brauchen*."

Jack repeated after her, feeling silly; he didn't even know what he was saying.

"*Sehr gut*," she said. She was smiling.

He nodded, feeling like he'd finally passed a test. "Where do I meet you?"

"I won't be there," she said.

"Oh," said Jack, trying to mask his disappointment. "So . . . who am I meeting then?"

Before she could answer, a guy came up from behind her and put his hands over Monika's eyes. She pulled them away, laughing. He leaned over, and Jack could swear he was about to kiss her when she said something quickly to him. Jack tried to parse a phrase or even a word, but Duolingo had not prepared him for this fast exchange, most of which was spoken with Monika's face turned away.

The guy looked at Jack then but did not say hello and did not offer his hand.

"Sorry, we have to run," Monika said, getting her keys and phone off the table. "We're leaving town tomorrow."

"Ah," said Jack, disappointed their meeting was ending so soon and so abruptly. It felt good to talk to someone his age.

While Monika got her jacket from the back of her chair, the guy stood there, feet apart and arms crossed, like a stocky bodyguard. Or a bulldog.

"Are you going on vacation?" Jack said.

"Work," said Monika. "We got jobs in Heiligenhafen."

"Where's that?"

"It's this town on the Baltic Sea. Very pretty."

"Sounds cool," said Jack.

Zoe and Alice came back to the table, eyeing the newcomer.

"I'll put you in touch with my friend Nathalie who organizes the volunteers," Monika said, "and she'll tell you what you need to know." She stood up next to the guy who was shorter than she was by a few inches. She turned to the girls.

"*Tschüss,*" she said. "*Viel Spaß in Berlin.*"

"*Tschüss,*" the girls said.

"And good luck," she said to Jack, smiling at him for the first time. "I really think this is the right thing for a guy like you."

They walked away and once they got halfway down the block, the guy stepped closer to her and Monika slipped a hand into his back pocket, turned her head, and kissed him.

"A guy like me?" he said. He turned to Alice and Zoe. "What does that mean?"

The waitress came out then, for the first time since they'd arrived, and handed Jack a bill for €47.50.

"*Wir schliessen bald,*" the waitress said.

"Sorry?"

"They're closing," said Alice.

He looked down the sidewalk and saw a flash of Monika's blue hair before she turned the corner and disappeared.

⚡

In spite of getting stiffed with the bill, Jack went the next morning to the meeting spot: a crowded landmark—the Siegessäule—in the middle of the Tiergarten. He stood at the base of a column, topped by a winged goddess, when he spotted a group of people gathering with a sign that said *Alle Tage*. He noticed that, much like his dad on so-called Mars, he was the only boy there. Monika's friend Nathalie, who was petite and had blond hair with a spiky crew cut, arrived and as soon as she spotted Jack, she introduced him to the group and then spoke German at length. They were all looking at him. Jack, never one to think anything was about him, had the paranoid feeling that he was being discussed. Nathalie even pointed at him. One girl shook her head at him, her lips pressed together in disgust. Nathalie then pulled a T-shirt from her satchel, holding it up so everyone could see: it had emblazoned, on the front and on the back, a crudely drawn but anatomically detailed vulva. They all laughed.

Jack felt a pang of humiliation. He looked around the circle of girls, who were smirking openly now, and felt the knot in his stomach tighten. This was an ambush. Emmi must have heard all about the scandal from someone in Dallas—it could have been anyone really—and wanted to teach him a lesson.

Nathalie held the shirt out to him. "If you want to help us, we need to know you are an ally. You agree that there should be no shame in female anatomy?—*Keine Scham*," she said, "so you'll wear this." Her accent was strong but she spoke quickly.

The other girls stood by and waited. Jack felt he had no choice in the matter and pulled the shirt over the one he was wearing.

"Do you know what our organization does?" she said.

Jack shook his head.

"Alle Tage donates menstrual products to help people who are experiencing period poverty." She paused, watching him. "It's a very important issue and has everything to do with society's lack of respect for people identifying as women. If men got periods, there would be free tampons in every bathroom."

"Right," Jack said, although he'd never given the issue much thought.

"Without tampons and pads, girls miss school, women miss work. So," she said, "you are handing out menstrual products with us, yes?"

"Sure," Jack said under her watchful glare. "I mean, yes."

"Because we know all about you," she said, "and how you are treating the girls at your school. *Hör zu*, if you're actually here to help, good. It may help make up for the harm you caused. But if you're only an *Arschloch* who disrespects women, you should fuck off now and leave."

Jack looked down at the T-shirt. This was like some version of *The Scarlet Letter*, a public reckoning of his mistake. He accepted her challenge. He would show up, he would pass out tampons all summer to make amends.

"No, I'll help," he said.

"And don't think you're going to find a girlfriend here. No one is interested in you."

Her bluntness was almost a relief; the rules were clear. And he was surprised to find the knot in his stomach ease slightly.

Late that afternoon, he pulled the T-shirt off and took the subway back to Savignyplatz.

His mom and sisters weren't home. Jack went into the office, collapsed on the couch, and held a pillow over his face. Then he sat up and went to Emmi's Instagram profile. Her most recent post was strange to see: Emmi, sitting on *his* couch in *his* family room with *his* dogs. Bunny in her lap, Tank licking her face. This stranger was living his life. She was pretty. From her posts, he could see she was well liked and involved, not that Instagram was the best source of information for learning the truth about people, but that was Jack's impression nevertheless. There were pictures of her with friends, Monika among them, and a throwback post of her and Monika from many years earlier: preteens on a beach posing with their arms outstretched. And then he got to a group picture that made him pause. Right next to Emmi was that short guy who'd shown up at the café, Monika's boyfriend. He was tagged, so Jack clicked his profile and found out his name was Karl and he also lived in Freiburg.

He decided—with no expectation of a reply—to send Emmi a message.

Hey Emmi, Just want to say thanks. I met Monika and her boyfriend, and she put me in touch with an organization here—it feels very good to contribute to a cause that helps women, especially since I screwed up so bad in Dallas.

There was a knock on the apartment door. Jack sent the message and got up to find Adam on the landing.

"Got plans tonight?" he said.

"Babysitting," he said.

"You know the Telescreens?"

"Yeah."

Adam held up two tickets. "I'd love the company."

"Really?" Jack said. This invitation was a reward he did not deserve. But he also felt a rekindling of something he'd lost, the feeling of something to look forward to.

"Yes, really. Tell your mom to give you the night off," Adam said. He squinted at Jack, a look of concern in his eyes. "Everything okay?"

"Not exactly," said Jack, "but I'm trying to fix it."

"Come down at like ten or so, and we'll Uber to the venue. You can tell me what's bugging you if you want. Or not. Whatever."

"Thanks," Jack said.

He thought it might be good to have a guy to talk to; his dad certainly wasn't around.

⊶

His mom agreed to work upstairs after the girls went to bed, so later that night, Jack brushed his teeth, combed his hair, and put on his Telescreens T-shirt. He looked down and immediately took it off again; wearing a Telescreens T-shirt to a Telescreens concert was almost as dumb as wearing a vagina T-shirt to pass out tampons.

Just before he was leaving, he got a reply from Emmi:

What boyfriend?

That was all, and her question felt like a test he was sure he was going to fail.

Sorry, I meant Karl.

Dots came up immediately.

What makes you think Karl is Monika's boyfriend?

Jack was stumped. How could he *not* think the guy was her boyfriend? He bit his lip, trying to figure out what to say. He tried to sound as neutral as possible.

Did not mean to label them. It just seemed like they were together?

Together . . . how?

He didn't want to seem creepy, like by mentioning the way Monika had put her hand in the guy's back pocket and kissed him after they walked away. He decided to stick to facts.

Like she said they were going to some beach town together. And they seemed kinda close.

He tried to remember the name of the town, but he couldn't.

Emmi never responded anyway. And Jack now had something new to worry about; had he actually managed to offend even further a girl he had never met?

BERLIN

Lucy was spending another evening in Adam's apartment trying to work up the courage to call Bjørn, imagining his reaction to what would surely be the biggest shock of his life.

Of course, she had tried to tell him at the time. On four separate occasions, she'd called, and each time she'd found the truth impossible to tell. When she'd first learned she was pregnant (and was secretly imagining he might ask her to move to Denmark), he told her he'd just been accepted into the PhD program of his dreams and could not wait to throw himself headfirst into the serious study of philosophy. He would become a professor, as he'd always wanted. Unbeknownst to her parents, Lucy had congratulated him and ended the call without telling him she was twenty-four weeks pregnant. The next time she tried, he told her his mother was dying of cancer. A year after that, she called again, and he announced he was engaged to be married. Each time she tried to tell him, he shared news that silenced her. And then she tried once more, just before she met Mason, and his response that time made her rip out the page of her address book with his name on it and throw it in the trash.

Standing in front of the window in Adam's living room, Lucy called in sick to work. As guilty as this lie made her feel, she knew it would be impossible to concentrate on the project, and not only because of her panic about Bjørn. The lack of sleep was killing her. It was a miracle her bosses didn't suspect she was out of the country and in a wildly different time zone. She'd had one nerve-racking moment when they raised an issue with a Midwestern factory that put in a very low bid for cloth wall coverings. They discussed whether Lucy should lay eyes on the material, in case it looked as cheap as it actually was. But Lucy had quickly convinced them that swatches would be adequate to assess the quality and sheen of the fabric, and to her relief, they'd agreed to spare the expense of a trip.

Her laptop was open on the coffee table with a blank email draft. All she'd entered so far was an address she'd found for Bjørn on his website. She was running out of time, but how to begin? She poured herself a glass of wine from a bottle on Adam's bar cart, sat down, and began to type: *Dear Bjørn, It has been about fifteen years since we last spoke, and I know you don't want to hear from me. However,*

She got up again and looked out Adam's window at the balconies and turrets of the ivy-covered building across the street. A woman was walking down the sidewalk with three dogs on leashes.

Lucy looked up at the clouds and tried to complete the email. *I know you don't want to hear from me. However . . .*

There was no stopping Jack's letter from being delivered. So what choice did she have? *However, my son wants to see you because . . .*

Her phone rang, and she was surprised to see Greta's name. They hadn't spoken since the night Lucy got tipsy with Adam and Bettina, and Greta had basically hung up on her.

"Hello, Lucy," she said, her tone as cool as the AI voice in the house. "How are you?"

Lucy could picture her counterpart sitting stiffly at her kitchen island, drinking coffee out of her mug, living some parallel version of her life. Maybe Greta could be the one to call Bjørn to break the news in that calm, even voice. "Honestly, I'm not doing all that great," Lucy said before she could think to censor herself.

"Is something wrong?"

"Not really." Lucy didn't think she should share anything personal with the likes of Greta. "Did my mom ever show you how to work the vacuum? I'm sorry again about the confusion with the cleaning lady."

"It wasn't the worst thing to happen," Greta said. "Otto is helping with a bit of housework now. He's even doing laundry."

"Oh, good," Lucy said, though in truth she found this admission shocking. Had he not done laundry before? "And how are the pets?"

"The dogs have grown on me," Greta said, "and they're the reason I'm calling. I'm going to New York for a few days, and your parents say they can help Otto with the pets until I get back. I hope that's okay."

Lucy was going to owe her parents a big, fat thank-you gift when she got back. "If it's okay with them," she said.

"And if you don't mind me asking," Greta said, "your mother told me you might know of a hotel in New York that isn't insanely expensive."

"Well, yes and no," Lucy said, walking over to refill her wineglass. "It's more along the lines of an Airbnb. It's a property my company renovated in the Meatpacking District. But you might not like it."

"Why? What's wrong with it?" Greta said.

"It's not a normal hotel. There's no front desk. And there's no room service or amenities or anything."

Greta didn't say anything, and Lucy figured she was too snobby for such a super-hip, offbeat spot. "It's in a brownstone that used to be a brothel, so picture a lot of red velvet and satin. It's all very sexy."

"Is it . . . dirty?"

"That depends on what you mean by dirty," Lucy said, sitting on the couch. "I'll send you a link so you can judge for yourself." She put Greta on speaker and found the website. "Whatever you decide, I hope you have a good trip."

"We'll see," Greta said. "I'm going to find out if my mother is having an affair with a man who's ten years younger than me."

Lucy put down her wineglass, shocked Greta would share such a thing. "That sounds complicated. And awkward."

"At least I get to escape Dallas for a few days."

"You mean escape the heat? Or do you not like Dallas?"

"I like many things about it," said Greta. "Your house, for example. The museums. But I'll be lonely after Emmi leaves. Otto has so many new friends at work, but your parents are the only people I've befriended so far. And I met one person I actually hate."

"Really?" Lucy was in no mood to defend anyone in Dallas. "Who?"

"I shouldn't say."

"Please," Lucy said, wondering whether it was someone she knew. "You can tell me."

Greta sighed. "Just between us, there's a doctor named Betsy Harper who works with Otto, and her husband is awful."

Betsy and Bob. Lucy knew them, of course; Dallas could be very small. "Their daughter goes to my kids' school—she's a couple of years older than my girls. Bob has a reputation for being a womanizer."

"I'm not surprised to hear that," said Greta.

Lucy remembered Bob cruising past her house in his Mercedes the day after the house was egged. Just the thought of Rockwell parents made her feel tense. She stood back up. "Look, I know you've heard things about my son," she said. "And I want you to know, he's not what people say he is."

Greta was quiet for a moment. "Some people like to hold on to the worst version of a story," she said, "but I find it hard to believe Irene and Rex would have a grandson who disrespects people."

Lucy looked at her screen, shocked. Maybe Greta wasn't all bad. "I guess you know Adam will be in New York too," she said.

Again Greta paused before answering. "He texted something about a trip," said Greta. "Seems you two have gotten . . . close."

"Oh yeah, Adam's terrific," Lucy said. "Are y'all going to see each other there?"

"I don't think so," Greta said flatly.

Lucy was sure Adam would be disappointed to hear it. "He might need a friend," she said, "given what he's going through."

"I don't know anything about what Adam's going through," Greta said, an edge to her voice. "He never even told me he was married, so I wouldn't exactly say we're friends."

"Really?" Lucy tried to recall the conversation in which Adam had said he was getting divorced. "He just kind of blurted it out, I think," she said. "Or maybe I pried? I can't really remember."

"Either way, he feels like he can talk to you," Greta said. "I guess I lack that American openness."

"Just so you know," Lucy said, "Adam says the nicest things—"

"I have too much going on to see him anyway. Otherwise, I would ask him to bring you your mail. It's really piling up, and some of it might be important."

She listened while Greta rattled off the senders: a letter from the Dallas Theater Center, a program for the Dallas Symphony in the fall, a few bills Lucy would need to pay online. "And there's an envelope here from the Rockwell School."

"Oh," Lucy said. She could picture the school's blue logo on the envelope. Maybe this was one of their pleas for donations or something to do with the girls' homeroom assignments. "Would you mind opening it?"

"Are you sure?" Greta said.

"Yes, I'm sure." Lucy could hear the tear of the envelope, the crinkle of paper.

"Let's see. 'Dear Mr. and Mrs. Holt,'" Greta read. "'While the unpleasant events that transpired in the spring were deeply regrettable in myriad ways, there seem to be growing implications from Jack's actions, beyond his unavoidable expulsion.'" Her voice slowed and quieted, but she kept going. "'It has come to our attention that several Rockwell parents have formed a task force with the mission of removing your family from the Rockwell community. These parents say their strong feelings stem from the misogynist nature of—'" Greta stopped reading. "Maybe I should just take a picture of the letter and text it—"

"No," Lucy said. Her heart was beating so fast, she felt sick. "Keep going."

She heard Greta take a breath. "'. . . the misogynist nature of Jack's actions. We have no choice but to hear and respect their concerns. As your generous donation funded the construction of our science pavilion, we would like to show our gratitude to you by facilitating any efforts you make to transfer Zoe and Alice to a different school. Please know, we are not refusing your daughters' entry for the coming school year. However, we feel it would be best for everyone if you were to withdraw them voluntarily and give them a fresh start somewhere they will be more welcome. Sincerely, Kevin Neal.'"

Lucy couldn't speak, could hardly breathe.

"Lucy?" Greta said. "Are you there?"

Lucy wasn't sure which part of the letter was most shocking. There was the matter of Kevin throwing her girls to the curb, which was absolutely unfathomable and cruel. Lucy and Mason had served as class parents, volunteered for countless school duties, and hosted fundraising events. Jack had been a student at Rockwell since kindergarten. Not to mention the fact that the girls were entirely innocent in this situation, and yet the administration was unwilling to stand by them in the face of building pressure from a parent mob.

But even with the principal's appalling words ringing in her ears, Lucy had gotten stuck on a different part of the letter. She sat down. "Read that line again, the one about the donation."

Greta cleared her throat. "'As your generous donation funded the construction of our science—'"

"Yeah, that's what I thought you said." Everyone at the school knew an anonymous donor had swooped in and written a check to build Rockwell's enviable science center, but no one knew who it was, including Lucy. But it could not have been Mason. She and Mason had only been together for about six months at that point, so it was inconceivable that he would have . . .

Lucy was reeling. Her girls were being taken out of the only school they'd ever known as a penalty for their brother's actions. And if Jack found out about this, his guilt would consume him.

"Greta, I would really appreciate it if you—"

"It goes without saying. I'll keep it to myself. I'm really sorry."

"Thank you," Lucy said. She was pacing the living room. She would not send her girls where they weren't wanted.

"What should I do with the letter?" Greta said.

"Throw it out."

Lucy heard the sound of paper ripping. And then they were both quiet.

"Thank you for sending the link to the hotel," Greta said.

It occurred to Lucy that, she too should be making travel plans. Because the only real solution to her Bjørn problem would be to get to him in Copenhagen before Jack's letter did. This secret, kept far too long, should be shared face-to-face. "I'm . . . actually going away too," she said, trying out the idea. "How far away is Copenhagen?"

"Not far," said Greta. "It's about an hour flight."

She would somehow have to turn this into a work trip. And she needed to go by herself; that was the bigger issue.

"You consider Berlin safe, right?"

"It's like any city," Greta said. "I wouldn't want Emmi taking the U-Bahn in the middle of the night, but in general, yes, it's very safe."

"I thought so." If, God forbid, there was an emergency—and there wouldn't be—she could get back fast.

"I wonder if you could do me a favor?" Lucy said. "There's a box with my name on it in the garage. I know this is a pain, but there's an envelope in it that I need. Do you think you have time to find it and FedEx it to me today? I can text the details—"

"Sure. FedEx it to my apartment?"

"No," Lucy said, "directly to Copenhagen. I'll get a hotel and let you know the address."

"I'll find it now," she said.

"Thank you. And please," Lucy said, "don't read the letter or mention any of this to my parents, especially that I'm leaving town. My mom tends to worry and—"

"I understand," Greta said. "This whole conversation is between us."

"Thank you, Greta. Have a good trip to New York."

"*Gute Reise*," said Greta.

Lucy hung up and turned around to find Adam standing in the doorway.

"You're home," she said.

"Greta's going to New York?"

"A last-minute trip," Lucy said awkwardly. "Something to do with her mother."

Adam saw the bottle of wine on the coffee table. "Ah," he said, "I see we're drinking at ten in the morning California time. Perfect."

"I owe you a bottle of pinot," she said.

Adam poured some wine for himself. "Work problems?" he said.

Lucy scoffed at how much more serious her problems were compared to what was going on with the hotel renovation. "Personal problems," she said, closing her laptop on the coffee table. "Are you dreading your— What's the opposite of a honeymoon? A divorce-cation?"

"It'll suck," he said. "So how is Greta anyway? She's not responding to my texts."

"Her daughter's visiting," Lucy said. "She sounded busy."

Adam nodded, looking as though he would like to believe her.

She'd gotten a different impression of Greta during their call and wasn't sure what to make of it. "What's Greta like anyway?" she said.

Adam pressed his lips together as though she had given him a very serious task. "Greta," he said, concentrating. "She's smart and intimidating at first. She's got excellent posture, like her neck is so . . . She's objectively beautiful. But she's someone you can talk to once you get to know her, and she has a terrific laugh. She dresses sort of classic, but it always turns out sexy, even though I don't think that's what she's going for. And she's just really warm and kind. . . ."

Before Lucy's eyes, Adam had turned to complete mush.

Lucy was tempted to come right out and ask him what was going on, but she didn't want to scare him off. "Cool, cool," she said. "Her sister's a lot of fun, don't you think? I was thinking the other night you and Bettina might make a cute couple."

He pointed to himself and then shook his head. "No, no, Bettina seems great, but . . . no."

"Why not? Are you still hung up on your wife?" Lucy knew all too well how easy it was to get hung up.

"Oh, God, no. That ship has sunk. I need to sort myself out before I get into another relationship. And anyway, between you and me," he said, and clasped his hands between his knees, "I'm kind of into someone else. But don't ask me who."

"Who?" she said. "Let me guess: A backup singer in a band?"

"No," he said, "I'm not a total cliché."

"As long as it's not me," Lucy joked, "because I'm really happy with our WeWork situationship."

"No, no," Adam said with a laugh. "I promise I won't make this weird." He sat back. "I've been dying to ask: How do you feel about your husband and this whole Mars thing?"

Adam was changing the subject. "What do you mean *feel*?" Lucy said.

"I listened to that podcast Bettina mentioned the other night," he said, "and then I kind of went down a Mason rabbit hole. Does it bother you at all? That he's gone for so long? And that people are becoming obsessed with him and those livestream workouts he's doing?"

"I think 'obsessed' is a little strong." Lucy too had been surprised at the attention Mason was getting on social media, although the girls were thrilled by it.

"And do the jokes bother you? That he's living with a 'harem'?"

"*Harem?*" Lucy said. "What have you been reading?"

"I saw this cartoon of him and the other scientists where a couple of them are pregnant, and the drones are running around them like toddlers, like they're their children. It's just one big happy polygamist family on a hippie compound."

"Right," she said. "They've got it all wrong." In truth the media jokes and insinuations were starting to get to her. Mason and Veronique had been featured on NASA's Instagram page together, giving a video tour of the outpost, making the whole "communication failure" a complete farce. Veronique, with her gorgeous French accent, had made Mason laugh. He'd looked comfortable with her.

"If Mason isn't what's bothering you," Adam said, "why don't you tell me why you seem so twitchy?"

Her phone pinged and she looked down to see that Greta had given Lucy's link a thumbs-up. She could not imagine what Greta would think of that hotel. She and Mason had spent two anniversaries there—thanks again to her parents—and had loved every minute, but Greta seemed too conservative to appreciate anything slightly raunchy.

Her phone pinged again: Greta had texted a link in return, for a hotel in Copenhagen. A very nice place, she'd written.

"I'm taking a little trip," Lucy said, looking up from her phone, "and I'm hoping it's okay with you if Jack feeds your fish while I'm away."

"I think he can handle it," Adam said. "Are you going for business or pleasure?"

"Business," she said quickly. "Strictly business."

⸙

The kids were eating pizza in the dining room when she got back to the apartment.

"You're early," Jack said as Lucy went straight to the sideboard and got them all coasters for their glasses.

"It was a strange day," she said, putting a trivet under the greasy pizza box. "How are you guys?"

"Did you hear," Zoe said with her mouth full, "the biosphere got a delivery yesterday."

An image popped into Lucy's head of a pizza delivery boy knocking on a corrugated metal door in the desert. Lucy laughed. "They can't get a delivery," she said. "There are no deliveries on Mars."

But she realized Zoe was being completely serious. "What kind of delivery?"

"Flowers," said Zoe.

"*Flowers?*" said Lucy.

"Veronique got flowers," Alice said. "It was her birthday."

Lucy was certain they were mistaken. "No," she said. "Veronique did not get flowers. They can't get anything from outside the biosphere because they're on Mars, and no one, not even Amazon delivers on Mars. Where did you read that?"

"It's all over the internet," said Jack. "Look it up, hashtag flowergate. No one knows how they got them in."

"How *who* got them in?"

"Mom," said Alice impatiently, "they don't know."

"This is ridiculous," said Lucy. "I can't even get a message to Mason in an emergency, but Veronique gets flowers?"

"What emergency?" said Zoe.

"Any hypothetical emergency," Lucy said, utterly flustered.

"There was a breach," said Alice. "They're investigating."

"Are you having pizza?" said Jack.

"No, thanks," she said. "So here's the thing. I have to go on a little trip."

Alice looked up. Zoe knocked her water over.

"I'm not going far," said Lucy, jumping up to get paper towels from the kitchen. "And I won't be gone long. But I have to go see this factory that makes bed frames."

"Who's staying with us?" Alice said, her eyes wide.

"Jack," said Lucy, coming back and wiping the table.

Jack sat up straight. "Me? Really?"

"Of course," said Lucy. "You're responsible, you're mature. Why not?"

"Sure," he said, nodding confidently. "I can handle it."

The girls looked worried.

"I trust you completely," Lucy said.

"Where are you going?" Jack said.

Lucy forced a smile. "Oslo," she said, coming as geographically close to the truth as she could think to get without actually telling them where she was going.

She had called Bryn and Harper from Adam's office, saying she felt uneasy about the factory that was making the bed frames and she needed to see the workmanship for herself.

"You're willing to go all the way to *Copenhagen*?" Bryn had said.

"Well, sure," Lucy said. "I mean, absolutely. We can't trust swatches in this case. I should go see how they're made."

"I thought you were out sick today," said Harper, with that suspicious tone she often used.

"I am," said Lucy, and she coughed. "But I'm just . . . concerned about these bed frames."

"You're a team player, Lucy," Bryn had said.

The praise made her feel bad; the team had nothing to do with it.

She examined the tabletop; either the water or the heat of the pizza box had left a foggy smudge that looked permanent. Greta had made a list of damaged items she wasn't responsible for, while Lucy was going to have to make a list of ones she *was*: a Meissen plate, an antique dining table, a scratch on the entry floor. She wondered how much more she would owe Greta before they swapped places again and went home. After the letter she'd gotten from Rockwell, Lucy wondered whether going home would even be possible.

MESSAGE TRANSMITTED FROM MARS VIA NASA DEEP
SPACE NETWORK

Hey Lucy,

As you've maybe heard . . . or maybe not? ~~ARC 6~~ ~~ARC 5~~
ARC 4 appears to be in every way a complete shitshow. I feel
like a character in a space-themed Agatha Christie novel.

We have had drama. Veronique's ex-boyfriend (that legal
expert on cable news all the time, Dwayne) hiked through
the desert, slipped past security, and put a bouquet of red
roses in our kitchen with a birthday card—all while we were
sound asleep in our (miserably uncomfortable) cots. I guess
he thought we would all keep this breach of protocol to
ourselves, but Veronique felt a duty to report the incident, and
the bouquet was tossed out the hatch. Dwayne was offended
by the rejection and then got it in his thick head that there is
something "going on" between Veronique and *me*, which is
just absurd. He broke into the biosphere *for a second time*
and attacked me with harsh language and some ineffective
martial arts moves. I somehow wrestled him to the floor and
held him down until security came and took him away.

As if that wasn't bad enough, one of the officers who
came inside had Covid and Aviva later tested positive.
So she's gone now, leaving me with Yağmur, Anjali, and
Veronique. The whole vibe is fucked. It doesn't help that
the food sucks, the socks you gave me have a hole in the
toe, and Anjali has started whistling a cappella show tunes.
Off-key. Loudly. All the time. I smile when she does this. I am
trying to smile, alone and with the crew, because I believe it
will trick my brain into thinking I'm happy, and it may have an
infectious quality, whereby we will all feel companionable,
even though we're sick to death of each other.

Other news:

1. Dwayne is getting disbarred because he broke into what is a secure federal facility, a crime that will be prosecuted as a misdemeanor under Title 18 U.S.C.1752. Ha.

2. We told Yağmur it's enough already with the yaybahar taking up all our rec space; she took it very badly, but . . .

3. As a result of said extra space, I learned how to do a handstand. Exercise is saving me.

4. Four of the DustBunnies needed serious repair, and we don't have any more parts. I got creative and found I could replace the bristles of the drone cleaning pads with the filling from a few dozen (of the excessive number of) maxi pads NASA supplied. They'll require more frequent replacement but are in working order. Phew.

God, I'm homesick for you. I was thinking last night about the first time I ever saw you, sitting right behind me at Meyerson for that winter night of Russian romance music (Stravinsky, Rachmaninoff, and Tchaikovsky), and you were so mad because you couldn't see the orchestra over my big head. If I hadn't heard you sigh—the way you do whenever you're feeling fed up—I would not have turned around in the intermission, would not have offered to swap my seat for yours, would not have asked you out for dinner after the symphony was over. I feel so sad when I think we might never have met. How empty my life would be. The very thought of it— I get choked up. All because you sighed. . . .

Loving you,
Mason
ARC 4, New Mexico

PART 4

A road to a friend's house is never long.

—Danish Proverb

NEW YORK

Greta and Emmi emerged from the Midtown Tunnel into a bright, beautiful Manhattan afternoon. If there was any gloominess to the day, it was coming from Emmi, whose mood had suddenly and inexplicably turned sour the day before. She had barely spoken a word all day, sleeping, or pretending to sleep, throughout the flight. She was now angled away from Greta, chin in her hand, staring out the window.

"Are you going to tell me what's wrong?" Greta asked once again as their cab lurched down Second Avenue.

"It's nothing," Emmi said, crossing her arms. "I'm just nervous about my internship."

Greta did not believe her. "Are you mad I came along? Because I'm not going to get in your way—"

"It's nothing to do with you," Emmi said. "I don't want to talk about it."

Greta dropped it.

Their cab made two stops, the first in the East Village, where Emmi had found a sublet through a friend of a friend. From the street, the building appeared to be in disrepair, making Greta worry about rats, roaches, and—because of the broken light over the front door— muggers. She hugged Emmi goodbye on the sidewalk, reminding her of their dinner plans with her grandmother that evening, and got back in the cab to cross town.

It felt strange to be neither in Dallas nor in Berlin, and Greta wondered whether Lucy would find it strange too, to be taking a trip within a trip. That morning Greta had unearthed the letter Lucy asked for. It was buried in a box marked *Private*. The flap on the envelope was unsealed and the envelope itself, with its Danish stamp, looked worn, as though it had been opened dozens of times before, and yet Greta kept her promise and did not read it. Instead, she slid the letter into a cardboard FedEx mailer and handed it to the clerk, curious to know Lucy's secret.

Her hotel was on Little West Twelfth in the Meatpacking District, although "hotel," as Lucy had warned, was not quite the right name for it. There was no sign, only the number of the building above the door. Greta used a code to let herself into the brownstone, a former brothel that, according to the website, had been renovated in a manner that stayed true to the building's scandalous past. She pushed the door open and wheeled her suitcase inside, feeling like she was trespassing in a private home. The entry was lit by an Art Deco chandelier and paneled in rich mahogany. Through a beaded curtain, Greta could see the parlor with its soft velvet couches and red-tasseled table lamps. On the far side of the room was a bar stocked with glasses and bottles of "hooch," arranged in neat rows with hand-scrawled, hokey labels: *Bathtub Gin* and *Bootleg Whiskey*.

According to the text message she'd received, her room was on the third floor, and after walking up the carpeted stairway, lined with black-and-white photographs of women in varying states of undress, she found a door with her room number. She entered another code and pushed open the door to . . . a boudoir. Attached to a medallion in the middle of the ceiling, sheer red fabric draped over a wrought iron bed, the literal centerpiece of the room. Greta put her purse down on a chaise lounge, upholstered in black velvet. On the wall beside her hung framed copies of Picasso's drawings of couples engaged in sexual acts. The tall windows facing the street were adorned with heavy brocade drapes, and in the corner, a gold-framed mirror was tilted against the wall, reflecting the bed back at itself. *Be aroused*, the room seemed to shout. Greta was not so easily manipulated.

There was no luggage rack. There was no ironing board. The lighting was dim.

She unpacked her bag, hanging her clothes on an open rod. Her tailored blouses and slacks didn't belong here; this room called for satin robes and silk negligees. She brought her toiletry bag into the bathroom and perched it on the edge of the pedestal sink. The walls were covered in dark bronze subway tiles, and there was a black claw-footed bathtub, big enough for two.

Instead of a minibar, there was a QR code. The management offered free delivery from four restaurants, a liquor store, and a place called the Pleasure Chest. Curious, Greta clicked on the link, and when she realized it was a store for sex toys and other unmentionables, she immediately closed it again.

No, as Lucy had suspected, this hotel did not suit her.

She took Benjamin Binstock's glossy book to the chaise and flipped it open to the colorplates. There were five Vermeers on display at the Metropolitan Museum of Art, two of which the author claimed were painted by the oldest daughter, Maria. No one, not even Sebastian Schultz, could stop her from going to see the paintings while she was here, from doing a little investigating for herself. What was the harm in looking?

She sat on the chaise and called Otto.

"You arrived?" he said. "*Wunderbar*. How is Emmi?"

"Still grumpy. I don't know what's upset her."

"I'm sure it's only nerves," he said. "Send me a picture from tonight. I want to see the three generations of women together in New York."

"Good idea," she said. "I'll ask my mother's young boyfriend to take it."

Otto laughed. "You are getting some funny ideas in your head these days," he said, "about your mother, about those paintings. You aren't one to get caught up in *Verschwörungen*."

"These aren't conspiracies," said Greta. "They're possibilities. They're questions."

"As long as you are keeping a *klaren Kopf*," he said.

"Don't I always?" But it was true that her head was not as clear as it should be. Although she'd stayed silent, ignoring the art editor from the newspaper who'd contacted her again, the Vermeer predicament was making her forgetful. "Could you do me a favor, Otto? I never told that woman next door—Sylvie—that I'm missing her party. Could you knock on her door? And tell her I'm very sorry to miss it."

"Yes, I will tell her. And I'm sorry I couldn't come along with you in New York."

"Me too," she said. But she looked at the bed taking center stage in the room, inviting and hedonistic with its satin sheets and plush covers, and was glad Otto wasn't there to see it. To be rejected in this setting would be too painful to bear.

8—

Greta met Emmi in Union Square, a halfway point between her hotel and the East Village, and they took a cab uptown to meet Greta's mother. Emmi sat, staring glumly out the window, answering questions about her sublet and her new roommates without any detail or enthusiasm.

Greta was done keeping quiet. They were in bumper-to-bumper traffic on Madison Avenue, which was the perfect opportunity to make her daughter talk. "Since you're stuck here with me for forty-something blocks," she said, "why don't you tell me what's wrong."

"It's nothing," Emmi said.

"It's not nothing," Greta said, "and you'll feel better if you get it off your chest."

"I don't want to make a thing out of it," Emmi said, "and it's probably *Quatsch* anyway."

"So tell me," Greta said.

Emmi turned to face her, looking more angry than sad. "I heard from someone in Berlin that Monika and Karl are together. Like *together*."

"That's absurd," Greta said. "Monika would never— Who told you that?"

"Someone who saw them and immediately assumed they were a couple because they were so 'close.'"

"Maybe it just looked that way. They've been friends for years."

"But you know how Monika is going back to Heiligenhafen? Apparently, they're going to the beach together."

Greta clenched her teeth at the idea that Monika and Karl would betray her daughter. But the last thing she wanted to do was feed the fire. "Let's take a deep breath. I'm sure there's been a misunderstanding," Greta said. "You know rumors can take on a life of their own."

"I know," said Emmi, sounding frustrated, "and I don't want to think the worst." She looked out the window as the cab inched along. "So how do I find out for sure? I'm thousands of miles away—"

"You have to give them the chance to explain," Greta said. "Be direct and ask for the truth."

"Right," said Emmi, a serious expression taking over her lovely face. "I should confront them."

"Of course," said Greta, "and then you can put this idea out of your mind because frankly, you've got more important things to focus on this summer."

Emmi nodded and then turned to her. "I'm sorry I won't have much time to see you while you're here," she said.

"Oh, don't worry about me," said Greta. "I've got things to do here myself. I just want to know that you're okay."

But Emmi had turned her attention to the passing buildings out the window, a slightly tortured look on her face.

⚷

When the cab pulled up in front of the Pierre, Greta paid, and she and Emmi stepped out into the warm summer evening. Before they got to the door of the hotel, Greta spotted Tobias walking toward the hotel from down the street. She hadn't seen him in at least ten years and was surprised to find he'd graduated from the grunge look he'd sported in his twenties. He was dressed in khakis and a navy blazer, his damp hair parted on the side and neatly combed.

She and Emmi waited until he saw them.

"Greta," he said, smiling at the sight of her and setting down a Bergdorf Goodman shopping bag. "*Schön dich zu sehen!* You look gorgeous, as always." He kissed her on both cheeks.

Tobias's English was spoken with a posh British accent, since he'd gone to some boarding school in the UK when he was quite young, the first of many places his parents sent him to get him in line.

"And you must be Lillian's favorite granddaughter," he said, turning to shake Emmi's hand. "I think I met you once when you were a baby."

He had, Greta remembered, at an outdoor party at his parents' villa. He'd presumably had too much to drink or said the wrong thing to the wrong person, because she remembered his mother pulling him away from a group of guests and marching him inside the house.

In the intervening years, Tobias had become dashing, and Greta could see why her mother was smitten. "So," he said, "shall we go up?"

"That's okay," Greta said. "We can wait for her in the lobby."

"No, it's fine. She'll want you to see our room."

Our room. Greta glanced at Emmi to see whether she'd caught that too, but her daughter was preoccupied by her phone. Greta tried to breathe as Tobias walked them down the marble hall to the elevators, and as they rode up to the fourteenth floor, she could only hope that there were two beds in the room.

"What are you doing these days?" Greta said to break the awkward silence. "Last I heard, you were working for your parents."

"Yes," he said, shaking his head, "that ended badly. My parents and I are estranged, unfortunately. For the time being," he added. "I always hold out hope for a reconciliation."

"I'm sorry to hear that," Greta said as they stepped off the elevator. She had the feeling another guardrail had just come off; not even his parents were keeping tabs on their wayward son.

He walked them down the hall and flashed a key card, opening the door into an elegant living room that was painted a buttery yellow and had large windows overlooking the park. As racy and sensual as her hotel room was downtown, this place was the opposite, proper and staid. Greta was deeply relieved it was a suite; at least she would be spared the embarrassment of seeing their possibly unmade bed.

Emmi went over to take in the view of Central Park, as Greta cast her eyes around for a sign of her mother.

"I'll go check on Lillian," Tobias said, putting his shopping bag on an armchair before walking out of the room.

Everything about this situation was setting off alarm bells; what if Tobias was an actual con man?

Emmi sat with Greta on the couch. "My apartment sucks compared to this," she said.

"Then it's good you have to be at work all the time," Greta said.

Tobias came back into the room, saying, "Lillian's getting out of the bath. *Meine Güte*, I can't tell you how glad I am to see you, Greta. I have so many memories of our families spending time together when we were kids. Your parents were the nicest people I knew."

Greta ignored this attempt at connecting. She decided she would have to get answers, even with her daughter sitting right beside her. "*Hör zu*, Tobias, Bettina and I would like to know—"

"How is Bettina?" he said, taking a seat across from them on the edge of a Queen Anne chair. "Did she ever tell you I used to be madly in love with her? I hope I wasn't too embarrassing, but I'm pretty sure I wrote her some terrible poetry."

Lillian breezed into the room then wearing a bathrobe and slippers, her hair wrapped in a towel. "Hello," she called out. "So sorry I'm not presentable yet. I don't know what's gotten into me."

Greta got up to greet her mother. She had color in her cheeks and was smiling widely. Lillian was not a hugger, but she held Greta's shoulders and gave them a squeeze. Then she reached out to Emmi, holding her hand and admiring the bracelet on her wrist, touching its little charms. "You're wearing my graduation present," she said.

"Always," Emmi said.

"I want to hear all about the new job," Lillian said.

"It's just an internship with a law professor," Emmi said modestly. "I start tomorrow."

"I was telling Tobias earlier," Lillian said, still holding Emmi's hand, "that I was about your age when I met your grandfather here in New York. He was in town for work, and next thing I knew I was moving to Germany with him and having babies and building a whole life in another country. This very summer you could fall in love with someone from . . . Japan, and next thing you know, you'll be moving to Yokohama and speaking Japanese."

"Too far away," Greta said.

But Emmi was smiling. "Or he'll move somewhere for me," she said.

"Either way," Lillian said. "It goes to show you never know whose path you might cross and what change will come of it."

"I made a reservation at the restaurant downstairs," Tobias said.

"He hates to nudge me," her mother said, finally letting go of Emmi, "but I'm late for everything these days. I'll go get dressed."

"No rush at all," Tobias said. "In fact, I have a little present for you." With childlike enthusiasm, he picked up the bag from Bergdorf's and handed it to Lillian.

Greta was bewildered as she watched her mother tighten the sash on her terry-cloth robe before taking the bag and sitting on a chair.

"Tobias, you shouldn't have," Lillian said. "He spoils me."

"No, it's just a little something to get you in the mood," he said, and perched on the arm of her chair.

Greta could not begin to understand what was happening. She and Emmi sat back down as Lillian opened the bag and unwrapped tissue from a royal-blue, beaded . . . nightgown?

"How beautiful," her mother said, holding the garment to her body.

"Mom," Greta said, "*what* is—"

"A caftan! I've never had one. I'll be the most elegant passenger on the boat."

"Boat?" said Emmi.

"What boat?" said Greta.

"Haven't you told them?" Lillian said.

"I thought you should," said Tobias.

Lillian turned to them. "Just last night," she said, "Tobias got a call from a friend—or a client really—who asked if he wanted to sail his yacht from Ensenada to Vancouver. And Tobias invited me to come along."

Greta felt as though all the rules of the universe were being broken. This made no sense. "You're going on a boat with who? From where to where?"

"She's a sixty-foot Oyster," said Tobias, excitement in his eyes. "There will be six of us on board—five guests and a crew member—sailing for a month or so from Baja to British Columbia. We fly out tomorrow morning."

"I'm sorry," Greta said, "but this is— Did you say *client*? What exactly do you do, Tobias?"

"Nothing really," he said. "I sell dinghies."

"Oh, don't be modest," Lillian said, "we've talked about this. You have every reason to present yourself with confidence. Tobias is not only a capable captain, he has a very successful company that makes sleek, inflatable boats that all the big yachts need to get to land."

"My parents still think I'll go bankrupt any moment," he said, "but we're doing okay actually. In fact, we just made a sale to your former boss, Herr Schultz."

"He has a yacht?" Greta said.

"And a dinghy to go with it," said Tobias. "It's a niche business, but it turns out a lot of wealthy people need what we sell."

Greta recalled that day years ago on the Wannsee, ten-year-old Tobias flinging himself overboard. She tried to imagine her widowed mother boarding a boat the next day with this reckless man and his pals. In Mexico. There could be hurricanes. Or pirates. Her mother was over seventy. "Honestly," Greta said, "I think this is a *terrible* idea—"

"*Mom*," said Emmi, exasperation and embarrassment in her voice, "she wants to go. I think it's cool."

"It sounds very dangerous to me," said Greta.

"Not at all," said Tobias, and he put a hand to his heart. "It's going to be a spectacular voyage."

That did not make Greta feel better.

"Oyster," he said, "is a top-of-the-line British yachts builder that makes the most luxurious, well-crafted, safest boats in the world—"

"You could literally be describing the *Titanic* right now," Greta said. She took a deep breath and sat up straight. "I'm sorry, but I have to ask. Are you two . . . ?" She pointed at her mother and then at Tobias and back again.

"Are we . . . what?" her mother said.

"You know," said Greta, who could never be as blunt as her sister.

Tobias and her mother looked at each other. And then they started to laugh.

Emmi covered her face.

"Oh, my goodness, Greta," Lillian said, folding the caftan back in the tissue, "what an imagination you have!"

"*Deine Mutter ist wundershön*," Tobias said, placing a hand on Lillian's shoulder, "but no. I'm just happy to be friends with a woman your mother's age who doesn't think I'm completely worthless."

"Tobias's parents were always so hard on him," Lillian said, frowning. "They still are."

"Well, even so—and I'm sorry for jumping to the wrong conclusion," Greta said, relieved on the one hand, and yet all the more baffled on the other, "why would you want to go off on a boat trip with a bunch of strangers? Come to Dallas with me instead. You can wear your new caftan by the swimming pool."

"Of course I'll visit you," her mother said, "but I don't want to miss the chance to cruise up the coast of California. I plan to do a lot of traveling in the coming years, which is precisely why I sold the house. And I may as well tell you, while I'm at it: I've decided to sell the beach cottage as well."

Emmi let out a gasp.

"I know you're very attached to the house and to the Baltic," Lillian said quickly, "but I don't want the responsibility anymore. It's time to let it go." She motioned her hands then as if she were shooing away a minor annoyance. "I'm relieved to get that off my chest."

Emmi stood up, looking like she'd been slapped. "Where's the bathroom?" she said.

"Use mine," said Tobias. "Past the entry on the right."

So, this was a two-bedroom suite. Greta wished she'd asked for a tour as soon as they'd come in and saved them all some embarrassment.

Emmi left the room.

"Honestly," Greta said, knowing her daughter would return with swollen eyes, a red nose, and a wadded-up tissue in her fist, "did you have to drop a bomb like that the night before she starts her job?"

"Is there ever a good time to drop a bomb?" her mother said. "That house is in terrible shape, and I don't want to spend my last years on this earth dealing with plumbers and carpenters and roofers. In *German*. I've already called a Realtor."

"Slow down," Greta said, "*bitte*, before you do something so . . . irreversible."

"I agree with Greta," Tobias said, "not that it's any of my business, but I don't see the rush."

It certainly wasn't his business, but Greta was glad Tobias wasn't behind this decision.

"Then I'm sorry to disappoint all three of you," her mother said,

standing up. "But I'm alone now, and I need to move on without bur-
dens holding me down. I don't expect you to understand, but that's
the way it is." She took her caftan and marched out of the room.

Greta and Tobias sat in awkward silence for a few seconds.
"Would you like a glass of wine?" he said.

"Please," she said. She waited while he went to the bar to open a
bottle. "I'm sorry," she finally said, "that I thought you were sleeping
with my mother."

Tobias turned and looked around the room. "I can see how this
all might have been *falsch verstanden*."

"Well, I apologize for misreading the situation. But I still don't
understand this . . . friendship," she said. "You got a nice invitation to
go travel on a yacht with friends. Why bring my mother along?"

"I think she'll enjoy it," he said plainly. "And I like her company."

"Why?" Greta said. "Who's going to be on this boat anyway?"

"Three guys I know, all sailing enthusiasts," he said. "*Keine Sorge*."

But Greta *was* worried. She pictured a frat party, drunk men on
a boat playing childish games, ignoring her mother or endangering
her. "I don't like this plan," Greta said, "and I think you'd have more
fun without her there."

"Maybe our friendship doesn't make sense to you," Tobias said,
pouring the wine, "but I really want her to come. I have the feeling
when I'm with her that good things will happen." He walked over to
her and offered her a glass.

Greta gratefully accepted it and took a sip.

"I don't mean to encroach on your family," he said, "but Lillian's a
breath of fresh air after a lifetime with a mother who always thought
the very worst of me."

Greta wanted to argue, but he'd taken the wind out of her sails.
"Just . . . don't let anything bad happen to her," she said.

"I promise," he said. He glanced toward the doorway. "Do you
think Emmi's okay?"

"I'll go get her," Greta said, getting up. "The news about the beach house is heartbreaking for her."

She walked out to find her, but Emmi was right there in the entry, standing halfway inside an open coat closet.

"What are you doing?" Greta said.

"Nothing," she said, turning around, her face perfectly composed. "Should we go eat?" And she walked past Greta into the living room, light on her feet, hands in her dress pockets.

Greta had come all the way to New York and felt more concerned about her mother, not less, and more concerned about Emmi, not less. *Lose-lose*, she thought. She hoped her trip to the Met tomorrow would give her a win.

COPENHAGEN

- -

Lucy was far outside her comfort zone as she walked through the Copenhagen Airport. This last-minute trip involved too many firsts. It was her first time in Denmark and the first time she'd ever left her kids alone. It was the first time she'd been in a different country from them, and the first time she'd lied about where she was going. It was the first time she'd taken a trip to see a man who didn't even know she was coming.

And it was now the second time she'd traveled to a foreign country without Mason knowing where she was.

She'd texted Jack as soon as her plane landed, and by the time she was in a cab, he'd already texted back a thumbs-up emoji. She would have liked more information, but she knew she was going to have to accept messages from him in whatever form they came and no matter how abbreviated. A sign of life was a sign of life, after all.

The cab dropped her off in front of 71 Nyhavn, the hotel Greta had recommended. Before going inside, Lucy took a picture of the canal and texted it to her. And then she wrote: Hope you're enjoying NYC and the brothel lol.

She rolled her suitcase into the attractive brick building and looked around. It was as if Greta had read her mind: 71 Nyhavn, a two-hundred-year-old renovated shipping warehouse, was the exact style that had inspired the pitch Lucy had delivered to Laurel Hotels. It had beautiful old beams across the ceilings, fresh white walls, and classic, functional furniture. Neutral colors, clean lines. Her room, as functional as it was attractive, was bright and had a view through black-framed windows of boats in the canal and verdigris steeples on the other side.

She was settling in and feeling grateful when Greta texted her back: The hotel you recommended is not my taste, but at least it's cheap.

Lucy stared at her phone. *God*, even if she had her good side, that Greta was such a prig. Yes, Lucy was tired of Bryn and Harper's brothel theme too, but that didn't mean one couldn't appreciate it and enjoy the fun. Greta needed to lighten up.

She started to text her back something snarky, but she stopped herself. Instead, she texted Adam: How's NYC? You holding up okay? In case you need a night on the town, PLEASE get Greta to go with you. She seems SO in need of some laughs.

Adam texted back: I could use some laughs myself. She's in nyc? Where's she staying?

Lucy hesitated a moment, and then she texted him the address of the hotel.

⚷

After unpacking, she sat at the desk with her laptop and opened her email. She looked out the window, composing her thoughts.

Dear Bjørn,

It has been about fifteen years since we last spoke, and I know you don't want to hear from me. However, there's something I need to say. I happen to be in Copenhagen for work and wondered if we could meet for coffee. Are you free in the next day or so? I promise not to take too much of your time, but it's very important.

My best to you and your family,
Lucy (Henley) Holt

She reread the email and hit send, a feeling of dread coming over her as she imagined him receiving it.

She called her mother, knowing she would catch her just as she was heading to work.

"Hang on," her mother said as soon as she answered. There was muffled noise in the background, followed by barking. "All right," she said, "just had to finish cleaning the litter box. Three cats make one hell of a mess."

"I'm so sorry," said Lucy. "Can't Otto do more to help out?"

"Otto's got back-to-back surgeries this morning," Irene said. "I'm happy to take over while Greta's away."

"I wanted to let you know," Lucy said, bracing herself for her mother's reaction, "that I'm away too. I had to take a little work trip."

"What do you mean?" Her mother's voice was suddenly intense. "What trip? Where are you?"

"I'm in Oslo."

"Oslo, as in *Norway*? Why?" There was more rustling, and Lucy could tell she'd been put on speaker.

"Hi, Lucy," her dad called out.

"Hi, Dad," said Lucy. "You're on duty too?"

"Someone has to change Piglet's cedar chips," he said.

"Sorry," Lucy said again. "And thank you."

"So," her mother said, "you were saying you're in Norway?"

"You're in Norway?" her dad said.

"Yeah, I told Bryn and Harper I'd come here to check out this factory that makes bed frames—"

"I wish you'd let us know before you and the kids go flying all over kingdom come," her mother said, her exasperation clear.

"How are the kids?" her dad said.

"They're fine. They're . . . in Berlin," Lucy said. She bit her lower lip and winced in anticipation.

There was a pause. "Lucy," Irene said. "You did not leave those precious children all alone."

"Jack's eighteen," she said, "and perfectly able to—"

"Why are you lying to me?" her mom snapped.

"Excuse me?"

"You're in Denmark," she said.

A foghorn blew in the canal outside the window. "No, I'm not. I'm in—"

"I can track your phone, Lucy, and I can see right here with my own eyes that *you* are in Copenhagen, Denmark."

"You can *track* me?" Lucy said, reeling. "Mom! That is such an invasion—"

"Of course I can track you," Irene said, "just like you can track *your* children."

Lucy got to her feet and stammered, "N— No, I can't track my children. The girls don't even have phones, and Jack's too grown up for that—as am I!"

"Don't change the subject. What are you doing in Copenhagen?"

Lucy huffed in frustration. "Like I said, there are these head-boards—"

"Headboards schmeadboards," Irene said. "Tell me the truth."

"Fine," Lucy said, taking a breath, "Jack has gotten curious about Bjørn recently, and he wrote him a letter. So I decided to come here and talk to Bjørn before Jack makes a plan to meet him. I don't know enough about him or his family, and I don't want to set Jack up for upset or disappointment or confusion, especially after everything he's been through."

There was a pause.

"Makes sense to me," her dad said.

"Yes, it's about time," Irene said. "This is good. Jack *should* know Bjørn. I've been saying that for years. Good."

Lucy breathed a sigh of relief. "Okay then."

"But that does not explain why you lied to me," her mom said. "Why did you say you were in Oslo?"

"I don't want Jack to know I'm here."

"Whyever not?"

"I just . . . don't." There was no way to explain herself without revealing yet another layer of her dishonesty.

"I'm worried sick," Irene said. "How could you leave those kids by themselves in a foreign country? What if, God forbid, there's an accident? They don't even speak the language."

"The girls have picked up a little—"

"What if Alice gets sick? Or Zoe runs off at the playground?"

Lucy felt as defensive as she had the day she'd told her parents she was pregnant. "Everything's going to be fine," she said. "I know what I'm doing."

"Rex, say something."

"Jack's a capable young man," Rex said. "He can take care of his sisters."

"As long as nothing goes wrong," Irene said, "but something always goes wrong."

"She has a point," her dad said.

"When are you going back to Berlin?" Irene said.

"In a couple of days. Three, tops. Or four, depending on work . . . and when I hear from Bjørn."

"Are you saying"—Tank barked then in the background, as if joining in Irene's outrage—"he doesn't even know you're there?"

"I sent an email," Lucy said weakly. "I'm sure he'll answer soon."

Irene exhaled loudly. "You did not think this through, Lucy. You never think things through. I've never known anyone to be as impulsive as you are—"

"Yes, I know," said Lucy, "but I'm doing the best I can."

"Three cats," Irene said. "You adopted three cats and two dogs and then left the country. I've had it." Lucy's mother hated to be late for anything, most of all work, so it was unsurprising when she said "I've got to go."

Then she hung up the phone. Lucy could not remember a time when her mother had hung up on her.

᠊

She spent the afternoon at the headquarters of Bang, half an hour outside the city. The CEO had worked at BoConcept for years and had gone off on her own to design durable leather upholstered bed frames that could be ordered in large quantities. They were expensive, but Lucy loved the look of these beds, and she liked the CEO who walked Lucy through the manufacturing floor. They had a conference call with Lucy's team in LA in the early evening. After conferring with Bryn and Harper, they wrapped the deal by the end of the day. Lucy was so distracted, doing the part of her job she loved best, that she almost forgot the real reason she'd made this trip. Almost.

As soon as she said her goodbyes and got in a cab back to the city, she checked her email and saw that Bjørn had not answered. She sunk into a Hamlet-style angst; he was blowing her off and she had no idea what to do. She preferred to think her email landed in his spam or that he and his family were away on vacation. But the most likely possibility was that he had no intention of responding. How terrible would it be if she showed up at his place of work?

She called Harper as soon as she was back at her hotel.

"Great work today," Bryn said. Harper and Bryn were together because of course they were. "What time do you get back to Dallas?"

"Actually," Lucy said, "I was thinking I might stay here another day or two." She scrambled for a justification to prolong her stay. "The hotel I'm in has these gorgeous milk-painted shutters that would be so perfect for Laurel." As she was talking, she took a picture of them and emailed it. "I was thinking, since I'm here anyway, I could pay a visit to the manufacturer."

"I thought we'd already settled on shades," Harper said.

"I see the image," said Bryn. "Are these decorative or functional?"

Lucy opened and closed the shutters in her room to find that they indeed blocked most of the light. "Both," she said. "They would add a nice detail, don't you think? And they would solve a problem for the buildings that can't accommodate shade brackets above the window frames."

"All right," said Harper, sounding skeptical, "but keep in touch with us."

After they hung up, Lucy texted Jack just to make sure the day had gone well. He sent emojis: a smiley face and a slice of pizza.

She got out of her work clothes, put on jeans and sneakers, and went down to the lobby to get a restaurant recommendation. The desk clerk suggested a place and then handed her a FedEx envelope that had arrived all the way from Dallas. She stared at it a moment before putting it in her purse. She texted Greta: Just want to say thank you—FedEx arrived. I will Venmo you. Sorry the hotel isn't to your liking.

She wandered along the crowded canal, admiring the brightly painted buildings until she found the bistro the hotel recommended. She sat at the bar and ordered salmon and asparagus with a glass of wine. It was so rare for her to spend time by herself, and she appreciated the chance to be alone. In spite of the stress, this was a much-needed break from the constant responsibility of her kids. But as she paid her bill, she saw the envelope tucked in her purse and couldn't help but think how much better she would feel if Mason were with her.

It was still light out when she stepped out of the restaurant into the cool night air. Her phone pinged, and she stopped short when she saw Bjørn's name in her inbox.

Dear Lucy,

What a nice surprise. It would be wonderful to see you after so many years. Can you meet for dinner at Høst, tomorrow night at 7:30?

Fondly,
Bjørn

The email was polite and warm, which was heartening. But Lucy could not begin to imagine what his reaction would be to the news that he'd fathered a child eighteen years ago. Would he be angry? Cold? Would he demand a paternity test? Would he think she wanted something from him? And how would Astrid take the news when he went home and told her? Would they both despise her?

But this wasn't about her anyway. This was about Jack. And for his sake, she would find a way to be levelheaded and diplomatic, to calm whatever conflict arose and to clear the path for her son to meet the man who had banished her from his life.

Otto called just moments after Greta woke up. She sat up in the decadent wrought iron bed, having slept surprisingly well, and stretched.

"Good morning," she said.

"How is New York?"

"Interesting," said Greta. "My mother is not having an affair with Tobias."

"As I told you," he said.

"But she is flying to Mexico, as we speak, to take a trip on a yacht with a group of young men she's never met."

"Lillian is full of surprises," he said. "And you'll never guess where I am going tonight," he said.

"Where?"

"A party! I went to Sylvie's house to cancel for you, and she invited me to come."

"But I thought—"

"Yes," he said, "I will be the only man there. She is making for me an exception."

"I hope you enjoy yourself," said Greta, marveling at how open and social Otto was becoming. "I think she's in need of new friends."

"I only hope the other women won't be disappointed to have me there."

"Bring wine," Greta said. "And offer to help with the dishes."

"*Ja, gute Ideen,*" he said. "How is your hotel?"

Through the draped sheer fabric enveloping the bed, she could see herself in the full-length mirror, her hair tousled, her nightshirt slipping off her shoulder. The room was working its magic on her after all. "It's growing on me," she said. "May I tell you why, *meine Liebe?*"

"No, stop! Bad dog, no!"

Greta heard splashing; Tank had jumped in the pool.

"I have to go, Greta. *Bis später*," he said, and hung up.

Greta sighed. She got up, opened the curtains, and made herself a Nespresso. Settling onto the chaise, she checked her phone. She'd gotten a text from Lucy during the night: Just want to say thank you—FedEx arrived. I will Venmo you. Sorry the hotel isn't to your liking.

Greta chided herself for having said anything negative about the hotel to Lucy. She responded: I apologize, Lucy. The hotel is fine. I don't know why I complained. I'm out of sorts these days—about Emmi, my mother, Otto. Even Adam.

She hit send and almost right away, her phone rang. Lucy was calling.

"I'm sorry," Lucy said, her voice tight.

"*I'm* sorry," Greta said. "I like the hotel. I think when I first got here—"

"No, this is about Adam," Lucy said. "I overstepped; I told him where you're staying."

Greta had not even told Adam she was coming to town, had not answered any of his messages. "I doubt he cares, and I won't see him anyway," she said. "But why did you tell him? I mean, I thought that you and Adam . . ."

"That Adam and I . . . what?" Lucy sounded genuinely curious.

"I heard you're in his apartment all the time," Greta said, putting her coffee cup down, "so I thought maybe . . ."

"What? You thought I was sleeping with him?" Lucy laughed. "Why would you think that?"

It was the second time in two days Greta had asked the same personal question, and she'd been wrong both times. She was acutely embarrassed. "I'm so sorry, Lucy. Adam keeps telling me how much he likes you, and—"

"No, no, no," Lucy said. "Adam doesn't like me, Greta. Adam likes *you*."

⚬—

Greta left her hotel for the third time. The first time she forgot her purse, and the second time her phone. Lucy was wrong, she had to be wrong. Adam wasn't interested in her in that way, nor did it even matter. It was a dead-end topic. She shook her head and walked faster. She would not give such a troubling notion any room to percolate in her mind. She had more important things to think about.

She took the subway uptown, but when she got off at Eighty-Sixth Street, she realized she was on the wrong side of Central Park. Greta had never lived in New York, and it showed. She walked east along the paths, through Central Park and past the Reservoir, until she reached Fifth Avenue and the Metropolitan Museum of Art. She had already bought her ticket online, and with a museum map in hand, she went up the grand stairs and into the European collection in search of Gallery 614, the room that housed the museum's five Vermeers. The first thing she saw as she walked toward the room, past a seventeenth-century blue and white Delft vase, was Vermeer's *Allegory of the Catholic Faith*, centered on the dark blue wall. The paintings directly to the left and right of it, *Study of a Young Woman* and *Young Woman with a Lute,* were the reasons she'd come; Binstock made a very convincing argument that Vermeer's daughter had painted them both. He described the "undeniable weaknesses" of *Study of a Young Woman*—the poorly depicted arm, the incorrectly scaled body and head, the badly rendered folds of fabric—and attributed them not to a lack of skill but to Maria's young age and inexperience. As Greta stood before the painting, she could see why he believed it had not been painted by the same artist who painted *Girl with a Pearl Ear-*

ring, or even *A Maid Asleep*, which was hanging on the same wall. She waited for a couple to step away and then walked over to see the depiction of the girl seated with her head resting on her hand, her chin down, her eyes closed. She read the label on the wall and learned that Vermeer had removed a male figure from the doorframe in the background, just as he had in *Girl with a Red Turban*.

Greta stepped back and closed her eyes, trying to remember the details of the x-radiograph image she'd been shown when *Girl with a Red Turban* was being authenticated: it revealed that Vermeer had removed the figure of a man standing in front of a crooked frame. Even at the time, Greta had wondered why Vermeer would have perched the artwork in the painting on the wall at an angle, when everything else in the room was perfectly aligned. That missing figure and the invisible, tilted rectangle raised questions Greta burned to answer. What if *Girl with a Red Turban* was a self-portrait of the girl, rather than a portrait? What if the figure in the background was Johannes Vermeer himself, standing beside his easel, working in his studio? If that was true, then it was Maria's name that should be on the wall, not her father's.

But to say so, to raise these questions, would be like driving her career and reputation into a brick wall. After a few more minutes, she walked out of the room to go someplace else to think. She headed down the stairs and wandered in the direction of the Robert Lehman Wing, stopping when an eighteenth-century Meissen figurine caught her attention. Called *The Kiss*, this exquisite German piece was no more than twenty centimeters high and featured a couple embracing, the gentleman's arm wrapped around the lady's waist, their lips just shy of touching. The pair, properly dressed as they were, were leaning into each other with palpable desire, her floral skirt swaying, his jacket flung open. It was beautifully made, this fine, porcelain object, and it left Greta feeling very alone and in desperate need of human touch and affection.

She walked out of the museum and sat on the steps, unable to shake the feeling that something—trouble or change—was coming, whether she was ready for it or not. She watched the people milling around the fountain and tried to keep her mind focused on the concrete issues of her day: Was Emmi having a good first day at work? Had her mother landed safely in Ensenada? But she could not stop thinking about the Vermeer, of what the right thing was to do, what Emmi would want her to do.

Scheiß drauf, she thought. She took her phone out and, without allowing herself another moment to be cowardly and change her mind, called Sebastian Schultz.

⊶

When Greta got in a cab to go back to her hotel, she knew she had committed some form of professional suicide. She felt reckless. She didn't regret telling Herr Schultz her new doubts about his prize painting, even after he hung up on her, but oh, how she feared the fallout, knowing she would be mocked, dismissed, attacked, and possibly even sued for placing herself in opposition to the Schultz family and the National Gallery in Berlin.

As the cab headed down the West Side Highway, Emmi texted:

Work is going great but can't have dinner—sorry! :(

That was disappointing. She wanted to tell Emmi everything, that she'd sacrificed her own reputation so a young woman could be credited for her accomplishments, but it would have to wait. A night on her own in New York wasn't a bad thing under normal circumstances, but tonight, it sounded lonely. Greta was practically vibrating with adrenaline.

Her cab turned onto Fourteenth in the direction of her hotel and she got another text, this one from Tobias. He'd sent a picture in which Lillian was posing with him and three other men on the deck of a ship, all holding glasses of champagne. Her mother was wearing the blue caftan and she looked positively radiant.

The cab stopped and when she looked out the window, she saw him and gasped. Adam was sitting on the steps of the brownstone, looking up and down the sidewalk with an expression of hope and expectation.

He was there, he'd shown up for her, and didn't that make him a friend after all?

"I hope it's okay I'm here," he said, walking up to her after she stepped out of the cab. "I haven't heard a word from you."

It was funny seeing Adam here in this gritty spot, so far from home and from their perfect building in Charlottenburg. "I'm sorry about that," she said. She closed the door and stepped away as the cab took off. "I have no excuse really other than I was being childish."

He smiled at her. "I've never known you to be childish."

"Can I ask," she said, putting her purse over her shoulder, "why you never told me you're married?"

Adam dropped his smile. "I'm sorry." His face turned red, and he looked so young to her then, his slightly pained expression, his tousled hair, that she felt matronly and old in comparison. "I guess," he said, "I didn't want you to know I'd failed. You always seem so sure of yourself, so together, and I'm still figuring things out and making mistakes."

"I thought it's because you find me stiff and formal and overly German," she said, noting that she was standing stiffly and formally even as she said it. "Maybe you think I'm too uptight to be under-standing."

"No," he said, "not at all. I think you're— Look, can I take you out for dinner so we can catch up? And, I don't know, toast the end of my marriage?"

"As friends?"

He hesitated. "I've missed you, Greta," he said, his voice catch-ing. "I'm sorry I kept my impending divorce from you. I thought you might think less of me, and I needed you."

"You're not obligated to share your personal life with me," she said, with a casual shrug. "You don't owe me anything."

"I do actually," he said. "If it hadn't been for you, I don't think I could have stood the loneliness of my first winter in Berlin."

"You never showed it," said Greta. "Or maybe I wasn't paying close enough attention."

He leaned toward her, only for a moment, and then righted himself. "Fresh start?" he said.

She nodded. "I'm glad you're here," she said. "I just did something that may ruin my career."

"What happened?"

"Let's just say I had a consequential trip to the Metropolitan Museum of Art."

"I'm sorry I wasn't there," he said. "You're supposed to take me on a museum tour at some point, remember?"

"That's right," she said. "Come on in, and I'll show you Lucy's brothel instead."

He nodded happily. "Onward ho," he said.

Something was coming, she thought again—trouble or change—and all she could do was embrace it.

COPENHAGEN

To keep herself from jumping out of her skin from sheer nerves, Lucy spent the day walking through Copenhagen, starting with Rosenborg Castle and the Botanical Garden. She meandered along the walking streets, stopping at Royal Copenhagen, where she bought Greta a porcelain plate to replace the one Zoe had broken. It wasn't Meissen, but she hoped it would ease the blow when Lucy was forced to fess up to her list of damages.

At the Glypototek museum, she spent far too much time circling Rodin's *The Kiss*. It was so beautiful, this marble sculpture of a couple in a passionate embrace—the woman's arms around the man's neck, his hand on her bare hip—and it filled her with longing for Mason.

She left the museum and made her way back along the canal to her hotel. She showered and dressed for dinner, her hands shaky as she buttoned her blouse, unable to decide whether she should come out with the news about Jack right away or wait until dessert. What if he was nothing like the young man she'd known in college? What if he was hostile and cold? What if she disliked everything about the father of her child?

⚷

When Lucy walked into the restaurant, she looked around the room at all the faces, in search of a man she hadn't seen in almost two decades.

But it was a woman who tapped her on the shoulder. "Lucy?"

She turned to see a tall, striking Nordic woman and recognized her at once from her years of googling Bjørn.

"Astrid," she said.

"Bjørn is running late."

Astrid was just plain stunning in real life, and Lucy felt her face grow suddenly hot from embarrassment. To have this conversation in front of Bjørn's wife would be mortifying. "It's nice to meet you. How did you know it was me?"

"Bjørn has pictures of you," she said, her lips just barely smiling.

Lucy had pictures of Bjørn too. On that fateful day when she'd bought a pregnancy test at Dougherty's in Preston Royal, she'd also dropped off eight rolls of film. Among the snapshots of all the sights she'd seen in Europe were pictures she'd taken of the handsome Dane, all boxed up now in her Dallas garage.

"Our table is ready," Astrid said.

The hostess walked them through the dining room, and Lucy felt some kind of menopause-style hot flash take hold as her nervous system went absolutely haywire; even her hands felt hot. She took her seat in a hard spindle-back chair across from Astrid. What must this woman think of her?

"So," Astrid said, her elbows on the table, her fingers clasped. "I've heard a lot about you."

Lucy was caught off guard. "I doubt that," she said, waving her hand to indicate her complete lack of importance. "Bjørn and I hardly knew each other, and it was a long time ago."

"And yet here we are," Astrid said, looking at her with unflinching candor. "All these years later."

Astrid had a smooth, lovely voice, and Lucy would bet a thousand Danish kroner that she had an excellent bedside manner.

"I was surprised when Bjørn said you'd reached out after all this time," Astrid went on. "We both were."

"Sorry if this is strange," Lucy said. "I'd like to explain—"

But she was saved by the waitress who came to the table to offer menus. Astrid leaned in on her tan, bare forearms. "I'll order a bottle of wine, yes? Would that be okay?"

"Please," Lucy said. As Astrid spoke Danish to the waitress, Lucy wondered whether this dinner was going to get more awkward or less once Bjørn showed up. Her hands were trembling, so she sat on them.

"Now then," Astrid said as the waitress walked off, "tell me about yourself."

"Oh, nothing much to tell," said Lucy. "I live in Texas with my husband and three children. My husband's away at the moment—"

"Yes, I read about him," she said. It seemed Astrid knew as much about Lucy's life as Lucy knew about hers. "It seems you married a brilliant man."

"I did," Lucy said. "As did Bjørn. A brilliant woman, I mean. You." No, Lucy was not at her best. She had not prepared herself for spending the evening with Astrid, although, of course, she should have. She wished she'd explicitly included her.

"Lucy," Astrid said purposefully. "Bjørn and I have different opinions on how to say what needs to be said tonight, so I'm just going to be very open with you before he arrives."

Lucy braced herself, but for what? An accusation that Lucy still had feelings for this woman's husband after so many years? A jealous tirade?

"Jack is Bjørn's child."

Lucy blanched. If this were a play, Astrid had just stolen her most dramatic line and delivered it herself.

"I apologize if I'm wrong," Astrid said, "but I'm not wrong, am I?"

Lucy swallowed. She hoped the wine was coming and fast. "Yes," she said quietly. "I mean no, you're not wrong. Bjørn is his biological father." It felt good to say it out loud, and yet Lucy dreaded Astrid's reaction.

Her expression was inscrutable. "Does Jack think Mason is his father?"

"No, Jack knows about Bjørn," Lucy said. "I told him when he was young."

"And Mason knows?"

"Of course," said Lucy.

"When you learned you were pregnant," she said, "why didn't you tell Bjørn right away?"

"I tried," Lucy said. "I really did, but I could never find a time when the news wouldn't blow up his life."

"So you are here to blow up our lives now?"

Lucy had never met a woman so self-assured, so clear. And why, she wondered, had the waitress failed to bring them water or anything liquid to swallow the sawdust in her mouth? "I have no desire to blow up anything," she said.

"Then why does your mother send us Christmas cards?"

Lucy leaned in. "She what now?"

"Your mother," said Astrid. "She sends us a Christmas card from Dallas every year. And one year, when Jack was perhaps eight or nine, I looked very closely at the picture, and I could see the resemblance."

Why, Lucy wondered, was she even surprised her mother would have taken the liberty to make contact?

"If you suspected Jack might be Bjørn's," Lucy said, "why didn't you ask me?"

"We thought you had your reasons for keeping it a secret all that time, and we didn't think we should impose. Maybe you didn't want your husband to know the truth. But now," Astrid said, "he's away on his Mars expedition, and maybe you're trying to . . . well, I don't exactly know what it is you want."

Lucy put her palms on the table and took a breath. "Let me be clear. I am very, very"—and as she spoke, she realized there were not enough "very"s in the world—"very happily married. I want nothing from you or Bjørn, I need nothing. But Jack would like to meet him, and while it would be nice if we all got along, there's no need for you to see me ever again if that's what you and Bjørn want, and I assume it is. The last thing I aim to do is cause a problem."

Astrid relaxed slightly in her chair, leaning back as the waitress came with the wine. It took forever for her to open the bottle and pour it.

She felt a hand on her shoulder then and looked up. And there he was, her first love, the man who had inadvertently played a pivotal role in her past and present. Bjørn had a few lines around his eyes, but she would have recognized him anywhere. Lucy stood up, unsure of what to do, but Bjørn opened his arms and hugged her. She felt the hurt he'd caused all over again, just as she was overcome with affection for him.

She wiped her eyes on her napkin and sat back down across from Astrid.

"We have everything out in the open," Astrid said, putting a hand on Bjørn's sleeve, "so let's just move forward. Lucy says Jack would like to meet his father."

"It's true then?" he said, sitting beside his wife, looking at Lucy with an eager expression. "But I don't understand. Why didn't you tell me?"

"That's not our concern," Astrid said. "I'd rather hear about Jack."

"I'm only wondering," he said, "why Lucy didn't say something sooner. Eighteen years is a long time—"

"I tried," Lucy said, facing Bjørn with a self-assuredness of her own. "As you know, I called quite a few times."

"Yes, but I wish you had kept trying. You should have tried harder."

She leveled her gaze at him. "I couldn't."

Bjørn cocked his head. "I don't understand. We would have liked to know, yes?" he said, looking to Astrid to back him up.

"The last time I called," Lucy said, "I left a message that you never returned. But then I got your letter and understood very clearly how you felt. It silenced me, which was what you wanted."

"It was a long time ago," he said, shaking his head. "What letter . . . ?"

She took out the letter Greta had unearthed for her and placed it on the table. It was humiliating to present it. She opened the envelope, remembering how she'd felt when it arrived in her parents' mailbox. How excited she'd been to open it, and then how crushed she'd felt upon reading it. She unfolded the paper and read aloud: "'Lucy, Communication from you is not wanted, not now or ever. Stay away from my family and cease all attempts to contact me. What we had was short-lived and is now OVER. I have no feelings for you. I am married and have my own life, and it does not include you. I will say goodbye now, for the last time.'"

Bjørn had gone pale. "I never said such things," he said. "Why would I—"

Lucy turned the letter around so he could see it for himself, typed on his letterhead, signed with a black fountain pen. "I understand why you felt the way you did," Lucy said, "newly married and all. In retrospect, I know I should have written you back anyway and told you about Jack. I owed you that. I wasn't very mature back then."

"But," he said, examining the page, "why— I always liked to hear from you."

And at that, Astrid got up and left the table.

"Shit, I'm sorry," Lucy said, putting a hand to her forehead.

"But— Will you excuse me a moment," he said, and rushed after his wife.

This was a catastrophe. Lucy sat back in her chair, defeated. So much for coming to Copenhagen to smooth things over. She folded the letter and put it back in her purse, wondering whether either one of them would ever come back.

She finished her glass of wine, replaying the conversation in her mind, and Bjørn returned to the table alone.

"I'm so sorry," Lucy said.

"No, forgive me. I'm rather shocked at the moment." Bjørn looked so much like her son, his current expression so similar to Jack's that terrible day in the principal's office when he knew his life was getting upended.

"I only brought the letter," she said, "to explain why I kept something so important from you for so long, and to apologize—"

"It is not *my* letter," he said, turning his palms open on the table. "Astrid wrote it."

It took a moment for Lucy to process this admission, and when she did, she felt oddly calm. Something that had never made any sense to her before was suddenly perfectly explained.

"I am very angry with her right now," he said, red splotches on his pale cheeks. "Such a dishonest, terrible thing she did. I can't imagine how you felt. I don't think I can forgive her for this," he said. "How could she—"

"Actually," Lucy said, taking a deep breath, feeling hope she could do exactly what she'd come to do, "I understand Astrid very well. She thought she needed to protect her marriage from a threat. She wanted me to go away."

"But you didn't deserve that. And you were raising our child."

"Astrid didn't know that," Lucy said. "And anyway, we were young and stupid, weren't we? Don't be mad at her."

"But if she hadn't written that letter, I might have known Jack all these years." He looked at her, and then sat forward. "Tell me about him, please."

Lucy took a deep breath. "Jack is kind and sensitive, and he's so smart," she said. She was tempted to go on, to tell him more, to describe every wonderful quality he had and every challenge he faced, but it didn't feel right. It was not her place. So she left it at that. Jack's relationship with Bjørn would be between them. "He's written a letter to you. I hope you'll consider getting to know him."

"Of course, I'd love that. It's so good to see you, after all this time. Since we're here," he said, turning, perhaps to look for the waitress, "shouldn't we order dinner? I need a moment of calm before I go home to Astrid."

She smiled at him. "No," she said, and shook her head. She had not come here to reconnect with Bjørn. And when she'd told Astrid she didn't want or need anything from them, she'd been wholly honest. "But it was really good to see you." Yes, she could see a version of Jack's face in his, and something in his voice as well. Nature refused to be denied. But there was no denying the role of nurture, either, and Mason had always been Jack's father. From the start, he'd been caring and kind. From the start, he'd noticed Jack's curiosity in the world around him and wanted him to have every opportunity to learn and grow, at his school and beyond. From the start, he'd loved his son.

Oh, what she would have done to have Mason with her. She wished she could— No, she decided then that she was done being apart from him. She would break into the biosphere, not with guns blazing maybe, but with sheer determination to bust him out. She wasn't sure how to do it, but it was time to bring Mason home.

PART 5

Life is not a problem to be solved,
but a reality to be experienced.
—Søren Kierkegaard

We've gotten through. We're still here.
—Willie Nelson

Dear Greta,

I hope it's okay that I tracked down your email address from Troy. I'm the woman you sat next to at the pool party at the Judsons' house—my kid destroyed your dress. I wanted to offer to pay for the dry cleaning, but I couldn't find you again that night. The offer stands!

Would you be interested in helping me find some art to buy? I will be so happy to pay your going rate. But I want to be honest—all I've got are framed museum posters and inspirational wall hangings from Target. I feel like it's time for me to have things that are more grown-up and *real*. I'd be very interested, for example, in buying one of Rex Henley's photographs.

Are you in Dallas permanently? Just FYI, I told my friends about you, and lots of them would love your help. Maybe I could throw a little get-to-know-you party and introduce you around!

Best,
Lisa Larkin

BERLIN

Jack still couldn't believe his mom had left him in charge of his little sisters. His parents had taken trips before, but his grandparents would always come stay with them, and they always took care of everything. This time he was on his own. It felt good. In spite of his massive screwup, his mom still trusted him.

The responsibility made him strict. As soon as his mom left for the airport, he became something of a drill sergeant, keeping the girls in line, getting them up and dressed and out the door. He felt a need to keep them busy. The first day they spent hours at a huge playground in the Tiergarten before he took them to a movie theater to see *Kung Fu Panda 4*. The next day they all went with Nathalie in the van to deliver boxes of tampons and maxi pads to an immigrant shelter in Reinickendorf, and he still managed to get the girls to the Stadtbad Charlottenburg indoor pool for their class on time. While the girls swam, Jack sat in the bleachers and called out encouraging remarks as they flailed around in the water. They'd made friends there and chatted with them after practice in the shallow end.

Jack threw a towel over Zoe's head after she got out of the pool. She stuck her arms out straight in front of her and walked toward him without bending her knees.

"What are you supposed to be," Alice said, "a ghost, a robot, or a zombie?"

Zoe didn't answer. She tried to make scary sounds, which just came out funny. Jack kept a straight face because it was important to take Zoe seriously.

"Maybe she's all three," he said. "A zombie-robot-ghost."

He sent them into the girls' locker room to change and met them on the other side. They came out with their hair combed and their backpacks over their shoulders, looking up at him expectantly. They were both in pretty good moods as they stepped out into the late-afternoon drizzle.

So Jack could not say what made Alice grab Fred away from Zoe, wave him over her head, then drop him in a muddy puddle. It happened so fast, he couldn't stop her.

Zoe screamed, picking Fred up and shaking the filth off him.

"It was an accident," Alice said, burying her face in his leg.

"Was not," Zoe cried.

"Was too."

And then Zoe smacked Alice on the arm and all hell broke loose. Jack stood between the girls, trying to calm them down, begging them to cool it, at least until they got home. People up and down the sidewalk were staring.

"I'll wash him," he said, and "He'll be fine." He made Alice apologize, *even if it wasn't on purpose*, and she did, but he could tell Zoe's mood was going to be pretty much fucked for the rest of the day. They walked down the street in silence, the twins sulking and mad, and Jack decided—between the shit weather and their bad moods—this was enough of an emergency that they would stop for ice cream and candy, even if it ruined their dinner.

Ten minutes later, he was doling out junk food: potato chips, gummy bears, chocolate, and sodas. Jack only hoped the sugar high wouldn't backfire on him at bedtime.

He bit into a handful of M&M's and, out of nowhere, got a wave of nostalgia for Dallas—driving his car down Preston Road, listening to music and drinking a Slurpee from 7-Eleven. He missed the pavement, the stop signs, and the houses in his neighborhood, his backyard, his friends, his grandparents. His pets. He even missed the heat. This sudden longing for home was so strong, it almost stopped him in his tracks, but Zoe pulled on his arm, and they kept walking through the rain to their building.

They climbed the endless stairs, stopping at Adam's apartment to check on the plants and feed the fish. The girls stuck their fingers in the soil to decide whether water was needed and argued over who got to add fish flakes. He let them each put a tiny pinch on the surface of the water.

They locked Adam's door and went up the final flight of stairs. Jack got the clunky key to put it in the lock, only to find that the door was already open. He had locked it behind them; he was absolutely sure he had.

"Maybe Mom's home early," he said, "but stay here, in case." The girls nodded and held hands, their fear of a burglar trumping any lingering anger with each other. He pushed the door open and went inside.

Jack was tall, but he was not in any way equipped to fight anybody. He did not know how to throw a punch. And he realized he didn't even know how to call the police in an emergency; did 911 work in Germany?

He took a step forward and saw a pair of shoes by the door. They were small. White Stan Smiths with a flash of green at the heel. A suitcase was parked beside them. Not his mother's.

Leaving his own shoes on, in case he had to run, he took one more step and heard a sound coming from the kitchen. He quietly pushed the door open and saw a girl leaning over a kitchen drawer.

"Hi?" he said.

The girl spun around and screamed at the top of her lungs.

Jack yelled then too and then put his hands up. "It's okay, it's okay," he said. He recognized her face but could not imagine what she was doing here, even if the apartment was more hers than his. The last picture she'd posted was from Washington Square Park, an ocean away.

"Emmi, right?"

He felt his sisters knock into his legs, clinging to him. Zoe was crying.

"Jack," Emmi said, a hand on her chest, her hair falling across her face. "I'm so sorry. My God, you scared the shit out of me."

"Same," he said. He took a deep breath and then laughed. Emmi laughed too. Zoe was not finding any of this funny.

"Who are you?" Zoe said.

"I'm Emmi. I live here. Or I sort of live here."

"Why did you scream?" Alice said, her hands still clapped over her ears.

"I was really startled," Emmi said. "I didn't mean to scare you. I was hoping to . . . I came to get something, and I thought I'd be in and out before anyone got back. I'm really sorry."

Zoe was still sniffling, and Jack leaned over to hug her. "It's okay," he said. "It's pretty funny actually. We all scared each other."

Zoe took a deep breath. "Do you want ice cream?" she said.

⸺ 🔑 ⸻

Jack got the girls in bed later than usual and read them a quick story, and when he came out afterward, it seemed Emmi had left, and he could not deny his acute disappointment that he hadn't had a chance to talk to her without his sisters around.

But then he spotted the open balcony door and found her sitting outside with a bottle of wine and two glasses. He brushed the rain off the empty chair and sat down, looking out at the street. "It's so nice here," he said. "It's too hot to sit outside in Dallas."

"But I really liked it there," she said. She was braiding her hair, watching him closely. "Your house! I had the whole upstairs to myself. And you have such nice grandparents and so many pets. I really envy you."

Jack choked back a laugh. He was not a person to be envied. "But this apartment and this city. There's history here."

"Your house has five bathrooms and a pool. You definitely win."

He shrugged. "Maybe I like Berlin because it's a refuge."

Emmi picked up the wine bottle. "I don't know if this is my mom's or yours," she said, pouring them each a glass and then handing him one.

Jack took a sip, appreciating the warmth as he swallowed, liking how grown-up this felt.

"When I was in Dallas," Emmi said, "I met some of your friends."

Jack's stomach twisted. *Predator. Loser. Incel.* "I'm generally hated," he said quickly. "I guess you heard all about it."

"I heard," she said. "And I believed the story at first, until I found out that it was more complicated than people said." She leaned forward. "Look, I'm really sorry about Monika and the whole tampon thing."

"No, it's okay," he said, and he meant it. "I'm glad to have something to do while I'm here. And Nathalie's been really decent."

"But that was terrible of me," Emmi said. "I don't even know you, and I just took Cynthia's word for everything."

He felt something akin to panic at the sound of that name. "I don't know how to explain what happened," he said. "Cynthia despises me now. They all do." It hurt so much to say it out loud, and yet it was a relief.

"Not all," Emmi said. "Nell doesn't despise you."

Jack looked up in surprise. "Of course she does."

"She doesn't," Emmi said. "She considers you a friend. Did you know she went to the teachers at your school to defend you?"

Jack felt a lump form in his throat. To hear that someone, anyone, had stood up for him was almost impossible to believe. He looked away to hide his face from her. "Nell's really cool."

"She is," said Emmi. "But I also met Sam. I hate to be the one to tell you this, but that guy is an asshole."

Jack sat back, a sick feeling taking over, a thought he'd been pushing away. "Sam's not— He's socially weird sometimes, but he's a good guy."

"He's not," she said, shaking her head angrily. "He's not a friend to you. Maybe it's not my place to say this, but he said some terrible things."

"Like . . . about me?"

"Yes," she said flatly.

Sam. Jack shook his head, letting the betrayal sink in. "Why would Sam—"

"He's the one who showed the list to Becca," Emmi said, "to get her to like him. He's the kind of guy who puts other people down to make himself look better."

That was so spot-on that Jack just stared at her. Sam had been completely preoccupied with his role in *Our Town*, desperately hoping that Becca might go out with him. He'd started wearing a fedora. And he'd developed a mean streak, teasing Drew for being so quiet, ribbing Jack about his acne.

"I'm glad you told me," Jack said, but he wasn't feeling glad at all. He felt sick. He took a big sip of wine and exhaled slowly.

"I figure I owe you some honesty," she said, "since you told me the truth."

"I did?" he said.

"By accident. You said you saw Monika and Karl together?"

Jack thought back to the day at the café, remembering the way Monika had slid her hand in Karl's back pocket when they walked away. "Yeah," he said.

"Karl is *my* boyfriend. And Monika is my best friend and my roommate."

"Fuuuck," Jack said, feeling his face turn red. "I'm sorry. I shouldn't have said anything." He tried to remember what he'd texted Emmi. "I wasn't even gentle about it—"

"It's okay," she said. "But can you tell me what you saw? Like exactly?"

Jack shook his head. "Like when they were walking away, she kind of kissed him. Sorry," he said, seeing the pain on her face. "Maybe it was just, like, a friendly gesture?"

"Sure," she said sarcastically, "I always make out with guys as a friendly gesture. And what did they say about going to the beach?"

"Just that they had jobs there."

"Where?"

"I don't remember exactly," he said. "Holly-something?"

"Heiligenhafen?"

"Yeah, that sounds right."

She nodded and took a sip of wine. "I was wondering, Jack, if you might help me with something."

Emmi was so pretty, her hair hanging over her shoulders, her eyes bright. In the face of betrayal, she seemed so strong. "Sure. What do you need?"

Emmi pulled her legs up so she was sitting cross-legged. She was at home here, of course she was.

He felt stupid, but he said, "Do you want to stay here tonight? You can sleep in my mom's room—or I mean in your mom's room."

"I hope that's okay," she said. "I didn't exactly think this trip through."

"It's your apartment," he said. "But aren't you supposed to be in New York?"

"Yeah, about that," she said. "Is there any chance your little sisters can keep a secret?"

"God no," Jack said. "Definitely not. Especially Alice. Why?"

"My parents don't know I'm here," Emmi said. "I blew my whole savings on a plane ticket yesterday."

"Why?"

She put her glass down and faced him. "Jack," she said.

"Yeah?"

"Have you ever been to the Baltic?"

⌐⊸

They stayed up until two in the morning talking and scheming and laughing. They finished the bottle of wine and then opened another. She'd asked him how he could tolerate an entire summer sleeping on the couch. She'd reached up and placed her hand on the top of his head. "But you're so tall," she'd said.

As Jack fell asleep, he smiled, knowing she was right down the hall.

⌐⊸

Alice was tapping his foot. "Wake up," she said.

"Ucchhhh." Jack was a lightweight, and the alcohol had utterly wrecked him. "Go watch a movie."

"We're hungry," she said. "And you were drinking wine last night."

Kids, he thought, *are relentless*. He rolled over and blinked his eyes open.

"You're not old enough," she said. Her arms were crossed.

"I am in Germany," he said. "So there."

"Emmi wants to take us to the bakery," Zoe said as she ran into the room. "Do we have permission?"

Emmi! He remembered the plan they'd concocted while drinking glass after glass of red wine. A truly insane plan that would land him in serious hot water if he got caught. His mom would ground him for the rest of his life. He'd never been grounded before.

In the light of day, Emmi would know better than to go forward with it. And if not, he hoped he could talk some sense into her now that they were mostly sober. *Heiligenhafen. Holy Harbor*. A chance to confront Monika and Karl about the truth. "Subjectivity is truth," he'd told her, slurring Kierkegaard's words. "Subjectivity is untruth." He still didn't know what it meant.

"Emmi says we can get any pastries we want," Alice said, "as long as we don't tell Mommy she was here."

"Yeah," he said, noticing the gross taste in his mouth. He needed water. "Emmi's on a top-secret mission, like a spy, okay? We can't tell anyone."

Zoe's hair was tangled. He would help her brush the knots out before she left the house.

"Give me a minute," he said. "I'll go with you guys."

⊶

The four of them sat at the dining room table with boxes of pastries and cookies from the bakery. Jack's head hurt. Emmi, who he was sure had drunk as much wine as he had, looked wide awake and beautiful as she sipped her coffee and talked to his sisters.

"I have a really fun idea," she said, leaning on her elbows. "Do you want to hear it?"

"Yes," Alice said.

Zoe reached into the box for a chocolate croissant.

"I was thinking," Emmi said, "that we could go to the beach today."

Zoe's eyes flew open, and she smiled. But Alice put down her cookie.

"There's no ocean in Berlin," said Alice. "There's a river."

"Yes, but the ocean isn't far away," Emmi said. "We could drive there."

"How far?" said Zoe, who got carsick on longer trips. She was licking chocolate off her fingers.

"Three hours or so," said Emmi. "Four tops. It's very pretty there."

"That's too far," said Alice.

She was right, and the thing to do was to tell Emmi this was a bad idea, that he could not take his sisters away from Berlin without permission, that he could not drive her parents' car without permission. But watching her—this girl who was *from* here after all, and a year older than he was, who seemed to know exactly what she was doing—made Jack think maybe it wasn't such a big deal. How could a day at the beach be wrong? And they would be back before anyone could find out.

Alice was watching him. "Do you want to go to the beach?"

"Sure," he said, like she was asking about the playground a block away, "just for the day."

"Or," Emmi said lightly, "we could spend the night if we want. My grandmother has a cottage there." She held up the key she'd shown Jack the night before, the key she said she'd pinched from her grandmother's purse in New York City.

"I don't know about staying over," Jack said, thinking it would be a whole thing to get the girls to sleep in some strange place.

"We could bring our stuff along, just in case," Emmi said.

She looked at him, and then for no reason, they started laughing.

"What's so funny?" Alice said.

"Can Fred come?" Zoe said.

"Of course," said Jack. "We wouldn't go to the beach without Fred."

"Did Mommy say we can go?" said Alice.

Jack glanced at Emmi. "Definitely," Jack said, lying to his sisters as easily as he might about Santa Claus or the tooth fairy. "Mom loves the beach."

⌐

Half an hour later they were in the courtyard behind the building, piled into a yellow Volkswagen Beetle. The girls were buckled up in the back seat, and Jack was behind the wheel of the coolest car he'd ever seen in his life. Even his dad's car wasn't this awesome or this clean.

"Is this, like, a collector's item?" he said.

"Don't worry about it," said Emmi, riding shotgun as his granddad called it. "The weather is perfect, and we're in no particular hurry."

He looked down, and that's when he saw the manual gearshift. "*Stick?*" he said. "It's *stick shift*? You've got to be kidding me."

"You can't drive it?" Emmi said. She sounded crushed.

"I mean, I *can*," he said. "My grandfather taught me, but I'm terrible at it."

"You should drive," Alice said to Emmi.

"I can't," said Emmi. "I don't have a license. I bet Jack's a great driver though, right?" She patted his shoulder. "You've got this."

"You should know," Alice said, "that Jack is not a great driver."

Jack pushed in the clutch and started the car.

"Why do you say that?" Emmi said.

"He goes too slow," said Zoe, "and he bumps into things."

Jack did not contradict his sisters. And his first act was to stall out with the car in reverse, causing it to lurch backward into a tree. He and Emmi got out to assess the damage. There was a small dent in the bumper.

"I think that was there before," she said.

Jack knew this could not possibly be true.

She looked at him with what seemed like affection, or exhilaration maybe, and then she opened her arms and hugged him. "Thanks for doing this, Jack," she said. "You're a really good guy."

He smiled over her shoulder as he hugged her back. Emmi was great.

When they got back in the car, she turned on the music, put on her sunglasses, and they took off for Germany's northern coast.

MESSAGE TRANSMITTED FROM MARS VIA NASA DEEP
SPACE NETWORK

Hi Lucy,

Anjali left, and I am very close to walking out the door.
I feel like you would give me a pep talk if you were here. But
you're not, so I'll have to remind myself why my presence
matters, why this experiment is worth the pain of being away
from you and the kids. So here goes:

When the time comes for brave men and women to
blast off into space and explore Mars, there must be a
reliable solar energy supply to sustain them, a challenge
given the distance between Mars and the sun. The
DustBunnies have a role in providing future astronauts the
air, water, and food they need to survive so they complete
their missions and return to their loved ones on Earth. If my
DustBunnies fail them, I will have failed them.

I am doing what I can to stay in a good frame of mind,
but it's not easy, especially during my free time. I read and
exercise. I exercise and read. I finished *Because of Winn-
Dixie* (on Alice's recommendation) and *Alone on the Wall*
(on Jack's). I close my eyes a lot because I'm so sick of this
place.

With so few of us here, Yağmur insists that there's
plenty of room for her yaybahar. To my horror, she set it back
up and plays the thing every evening, possibly out of spite. It
is all Veronique and I can do not to murder her.

But I'm not a quitter, am I?

I would sell my soul to hear your voice.

I was thinking today that you would do better here
than me. You would handle the social dynamic with a more
generous spirit and with humor. You're so good for me, you

and the kids, because without you, I'm nothing but the worst parts of myself: stubborn, serious, weighty. You make me light. On Mars, I weigh only seventy-four pounds, so why do I feel so heavy? See!—I keep forgetting where I really am. I wrote a haiku to remind myself and pinned it to the wall by my shitty cot:

> Fake Mars is not Mars
> but it might as well be real.
> New Mexico sucks.

Who knew this experience would be more like *Survivor* than *The Martian*?

Back to work. The DustBunnies send their regards. (I've started talking to them. Is that weird?)

I love you,
Mason
ARC 3, somewhere east of Albuquerque

HEILIGENHAFEN ⚲

It was true that Jack was the world's slowest driver. Emmi understood his caution; he had his little sisters in the back seat, and he was driving an ancient, stick-shift VW that didn't belong to him on roads he didn't know. However, it would be nice to make it to Heiligenhafen at some point during their lifetime.

Jack puttered along in the right lane of the Autobahn, his eyes glued to the road, his head touching the roof of the car, while cars sped past them going 130 kilometers an hour. She was grateful to him, though, no matter how long it took to get there. And the girls were funny and good sports, even though they'd needed bathroom breaks every hour.

Almost five hours into what should have been a three-and-a-half-hour trip, Emmi pointed to an upcoming sign. "This is our exit!" she said. She rolled down the window and leaned out to smell the salt air and then rolled it back up again when Alice said it was too windy in the back seat.

"When was the last time you were here?" Jack said, downshifting, causing the car to jerk.

"Last year." They were passing the last field of wind turbines and hay bales before getting off the highway. "This is the first summer that my family didn't come. I thought an internship in New York was more important."

"And was it?"

"How should I know?" she said. "I haven't started. I called in *krank*."

"*Krank?*" he said.

"*Krank* means sick," she said. "I lied and said I had Covid."

"*Ich bin Autokrank*," said Zoe.

"We're almost there," Emmi said. She pointed to the sign they were passing. "See? Heiligenhafen."

"What does that mean?" Alice said.

"Holy moly," said Zoe.

"Holy *harbor*," said Emmi.

Jack put on the blinker and slowed down even more to take the exit. "I'm pretty much always a rule follower," he said.

"Me too," she said.

"But stealing a car to go watch you have a fight at the beach is turning out to be my favorite activity."

"We *stole* the car?" said Alice.

"What fight?" said Zoe.

"He's joking," said Emmi, "sort of." She felt guilty then; her mother would be so shocked by this outrageous deception. But shouldn't everyone be allowed one grand act of rebellion in their youth? If so, this was hers. All she could do now was hope her parents never found out about it.

The four of them drove into the quaint seaside town, and Emmi was overcome to see the sun on the water and the boats in the harbor. She knew every detail of every building they passed, many of which had dates on them: 1751, 1735. Emmi pointed out the brick town hall, built in the 1800s, originally as the villa of a shipowner. This was midseason, so hordes of tourists were walking around the old part of the fishing village, hiking up to see the brick church, and strolling along the marina.

The market square was teeming with people, and she pointed Jack to a street where she hoped they could park. He hit the curb when he pulled into the space, but when they got out to check the tire, it looked fine.

The girls were happy to be out of the car. They all walked down a cobblestone street until they reached Ton und Text, the only book-store in town.

"Ready?" said Jack.

"I think so," Emmi said.

She was nervous when they walked in, but for no reason; a quick scan of the shop showed that Monika wasn't there. Disappointed and a little relieved, Emmi went to the checkout to ask for her, only to learn it was her day off.

"*Sie arbeitet morgen Nachmittag,*" the man there said.

Bad timing! She did not think they could possibly stay until the next afternoon.

She found Jack in the children's section, sitting on the floor with the girls.

"No luck?" he said, looking up.

She shook her head.

"You could text her and find out where they are today."

"Yeah, later. But for now," she said, "I really want to show you the house."

Emmi could hardly wait to get there. Jack stalled the car twice before she directed him out of the town, across a bridge, and down a long, narrow dirt road that ran parallel to a nature preserve. Every so often, through the bluffs, she could catch a glimpse of the water.

"Okay," she said, seeing the break in the weathered fence, "turn right in there." Jack did, and there, surrounded by wild grasses and sand dunes, was the cottage. It was white with pale blue timber beams, a place to go barefoot and not know what day of the week it was. It made her think of marzipan and lemonade. Emmi started to cry when she saw the "For Sale" sign.

Jack stopped the car, turned off the engine, and put a hand on Emmi's shoulder. "You okay?"

"I'm happy to be here," she said, "but I'm so, so sad." She wiped her eyes on her T-shirt. "I just don't understand how my grandmother could let this place go."

Alice unbuckled her seat belt and leaned forward, patting Emmi on the head. "Don't cry."

"You're right," Emmi said. "I'll stop. Let's go to the beach!"

They got out of the car, and Emmi took in the sight of the place. The lichen and moss were taking over the thatch roof, giving the reeds a greenish hue. Jack was giving the girls their backpacks as Emmi picked up a branch that had fallen across the gravel. She tossed it in the shrubs, imagining how furious her grandmother would be to know she was there. For some reason, she didn't care. This trip felt important.

She unlocked the door. "Sorry if it smells a little musty," she said, stepping inside.

Jack and the girls followed her through the entry, past the steep staircase, and into the living room. Emmi pulled back the linen curtains, and sunlight streamed into the room and across the pale wood floors. She began opening the sets of French doors at the back of the house. The sea breeze filled the room.

"Wow," Jack said, walking out to look at the ocean.

"Why's everything covered up?" Alice said.

"Does it look spooky?" Emmi said. She pulled the sheets off the floral couches and antique tables, waving her arm to dispel the dust motes that had been set aloft.

Alice stood in front of the fireplace, its opening as tall as she was, while Zoe was transfixed by the grandfather clock as it ticked the seconds away.

"Come on, you guys. We can get changed upstairs."

Emmi led them up the staircase and showed them to a room where they could change into bathing suits . . . and maybe sleep if she could get Jack to agree to stay. And then she led him to the room with the best view in the house.

"I'll meet you on the porch?" she said.

Jack had his backpack over his shoulder and pulled the curtains back from the window, his back to the four-poster bed. "Holy moly is right," he said, smiling. "I'm glad we did this, Emmi, even if we get into huge fucking trouble—"

"We won't," she said.

"I definitely will, but this is worth it." He turned and smiled, looking so much more relaxed than he had during the drive. "What's it like here in winter?"

"Even better," she said. "Cold, but we have the beach to our-selves."

"Since we drove all this way," Jack said, "I think we should stay overnight."

"Really?"

"Yeah," he said. "It's not like I can get in any more trouble this year."

They spent the rest of the day on the beach. As she watched the girls playing together in the water, Emmi couldn't help but see herself and Monika in them, remembering summer after summer, the betrayal hitting her even harder than when she'd first found out. And it pained her to think she was losing not only her most treasured friendship but her favorite place as well.

The only consolation was Jack. He was kind and thoughtful. Every time she looked over at him, he was watching her, making sure she was okay.

Emmi suggested they go to a fish restaurant for dinner, given that they were on the Baltic, but Alice made a horrified face and Zoe clasped two hands to her throat and pretended to throw up. They walked instead to a crowded burger place where they could sit out-side, overlooking the boats in the marina.

After they ordered, Emmi sat back and looked around at the

people. This was a tourist trap and not the kind of restaurant she would normally go to with her parents or grandparents. But it was perfect for the girls, who were busy playing tic-tac-toe on the back of a paper place mat.

"You okay?" Jack said.

"Not really," said Emmi. "But I'm glad to be here." And that was when she spotted Monika. Of all the places they could have gone, they happened to be having dinner at the same restaurant. And was she here on a date with Karl? Emmi's eyes scanned the room, looking for him.

But as Monika approached a table not far from theirs, Emmi noticed the apron tied around her waist. Standing in front of a group of tourists, Monika was nodding as they demanded beers, more napkins, and a fork to replace one on the ground. Her hair was pulled back in a messy ponytail, a blue streak hanging loose over her face, and she wiped her forehead with her sleeve. Monika had not one job but two, and she was working her ass off. And then, off to her right, Emmi saw Karl, clearing dishes into a plastic tub.

Jack saw them too and gave Emmi an urgent, questioning look: *Here?* he seemed to say. *Now?* She shook her head. She wasn't going to cause a scene, not in front of all these people, not while her ex-friend and ex-boyfriend were working. Instead Emmi kept her head tilted down, hoping not to be seen.

Without even asking, Jack asked for their food to go, paid the bill, and helped them slip away.

Emmi sat on the back porch with a beer, her bare feet on the coffee table, wondering whether this was the last time she would ever visit the cottage. She was waiting for Jack to put the girls to bed, listening to the waves and watching the seagrass bend in the wind, when her phone pinged with a text from her mother in New York, asking how her day was going, whether the internship was interesting, and what time she would be free for dinner. Emmi felt a wave of guilt as she texted back that everything was great, *danke*, just very, very *stressig*.

So sorry! she wrote. Working late tonight. Keine Zeit für Abendessen :(

Her mom texted back a heart. No worries, I understand! Focus on work!

Emmi felt terrible thinking of her mom having dinner alone in New York, no one to keep her company.

"Hey," Jack said, stepping outside and sitting across from her. "I don't want to keep asking if you're okay, but . . . are you okay?"

"That was so weird," she said.

"You showed restraint," he said. "I was expecting some fireworks. You know, the Real Housewives of Heiligenhafen."

She smiled. "Yeah, I don't know what happened," she said. "I saw them, and I just realized it was over and no amount of shouting or crying was going to change that, and it would just be humiliating. And you know what else is weird? I realized they're kind of perfect together." She felt sick saying it, but it was really true. The three of them had spent so much time together in Freiburg, and Emmi wondered why she hadn't seen it before. "They just needed me to get out of the way."

She leaned forward and passed her beer to him, and he took it, looking a little surprised.

He took a sip. "So what now?" he said. "I mean, what about Karl? Do you still . . ."

Jack pronounced "Karl" with a hard *r*, making her feel like he was talking about some other boy she'd never met.

She picked up her phone and moved to sit beside him on the couch. "I just broke up with him." She showed him the message she'd sent while he was upstairs.

"I'll need you to translate," he said.

"It says it's over, and I don't want to talk about it or be friends."

"Brutal," Jack said, passing the beer back to her. "Are you sure that's what you want?"

"Very sure," she said, putting her phone down. "But I don't know what to do about Monika. Friends are harder to break up with." She leaned back and put her feet up on the coffee table again. "Are you going to write to Sam?"

"I don't know," he said. "He may have ruined my life. How do you write an email about that?"

"Can I ask," she said, gently bumping her leg against his, "why did you make that list?"

He tipped his head down, looking at his hands. "Because I'm an idiot. It was a way of quantifying my shortcomings."

"What do you mean?"

"I created a linear regression model to determine how much money you would have to pay certain girls in our class to get them to invite me out. The math was real, but it was mostly just made-up data about me, like my lack of social skills. The nicer the girl, the less you would have to pay them."

"So that's why Nell was 'worth' so little?"

"Nell was always nice to me."

"And what about Cynthia?"

"I don't think I should talk about Cynthia."

"She must have treated you pretty badly." She took a breath before asking, "Were you guys together?"

He turned to her. "Why would you think that?"

"She said you were friends, but I got the feeling there was more to it."

"I can't talk about it," he said, looking away.

"Why not?"

The wind picked up then, clouds passing low across the sky. She heard laughter coming from the beach.

"You can tell me," she said.

"We weren't, like, official or anything," he said, avoiding her eyes. "We never told anyone."

"Why not?"

Jack looked miserable. He ran a hand through his hair.

"Why not?" she said again.

"Because I was tutoring her, and she didn't want anyone to find out when we . . . you know."

"Okay," Emmi said tentatively, wanting him to trust her, "but what about your friends?"

Jack shook his head.

"You didn't tell them?" she said. "What about her friends?"

He shook his head more emphatically.

"Your family, no? For how long?"

"Seven months," he said, shrugging as though he felt nothing. "Maybe eight?"

Emmi sat up then and faced him. "You two kept your relationship secret for *eight* months?"

"Cynthia didn't want anyone to know," he said, his hands gripping his knees, "and I promised."

"But why?" Emmi could not wrap her head around it. "I don't understand."

He tried to laugh then, but it sounded forced. "She was embarrassed of me," he said. "I'm not cool. I'm awkward, and I don't play football—I mean, why would I want to get concussed? And I don't pretend to be badass or talk like a bro—"

"Nobody likes American football around here anyway," Emmi said, sitting back again, their shoulders touching. "You're a great brother. And you drove me to the very top of Germany, just as a favor. And you're spending your summer delivering tampons all over Berlin. I think you've got a few things going for you."

"Hey," he said. "I've been meaning to ask you. Is Emmi short for something?"

She smiled. "Emily," she said.

He nodded. "I just wanted to know." He sighed and touched a finger to the back of her hand, only for a second. She left her hand where it was, right next to his.

"I wish we didn't have to go back tomorrow," he said.

"Same," she said. And she had so far to go. It was hard to imagine being back in New York. And even harder to imagine returning to Freiburg in the fall. She certainly couldn't go back to the apartment she shared with Monika.

"You know what we should do?" Jack was staring out at the ocean and then he raised his arm and pointed straight out to sea.

She turned to see what he was looking at. "What?" she said. She hoped he wasn't going to suggest a swim in the pitch dark; as much as she loved the ocean, that sounded more terrifying than exhilarating.

It was like he was calculating something in his head, and she wanted to snap him out of it, to bring his thoughts back to where they were, back to her. She leaned into him, moved her hand to the back of his neck, and then she kissed him, knowing she'd wanted to do that ever since the night before, when he was going to sleep on a couch that was way too short for him. Ever since he'd gotten behind the wheel of the VW. Ever since he'd whisked her out of the restaurant and brought her home.

She succeeded in jolting him out of his reverie. He sat forward, wrapped his arm around her waist, and kissed her back.

BERLIN

Lucy was filled with relief when her plane touched down safely in Berlin. Rather than spend another night in Copenhagen, she'd caught the last easyJet flight out, feeling she'd done everything she'd gone to do in Copenhagen and then some. After four days in Denmark, where she'd regained some peace of mind, she was back and couldn't wait to hug her children and tell them they were going to go break Mason out of the biosphere.

When she turned her phone on, she was alarmed to see a staggering number of notifications filling her screen.

She clicked first on a message from Drew's mom:

Lucy! Wow, saw the Good Morning America story on Mason! Where are you anyway??? I really miss you. And Drew REALLY misses Jack.

Good Morning America? Lucy clicked on a link that took her to a video of Mason exercising, his hands outstretched as he windmilled to touch opposite toes. His shoulders were broad and his smile as earnest and appealing as ever, and yet it was crazy to see just how popular he was becoming. She searched the biosphere for news and was shocked to find out that Yağmur had packed up her yaybahar and left. Mason was all alone now with the French microbiologist Veronique. Something about the idea of her husband locked up with just one other woman, a young, smart, French scientist, unsettled Lucy; it was too private, too intimate.

As the plane taxied, she also saw she'd gotten a batshit number of missed calls, voicemails, and text messages from her mother. Twenty-seven of them in all.

Call me

Call me!

Call me, Lucy!!!!!!!!!!

Lucy, I am not kidding around right now. You call me this minute.

Lucy was scared something had happened to her house or to her dogs—or to her father! She called her back right away.

Her mother picked up, sounding breathless. "Where are you?"

"On a plane," Lucy said. "I just landed. What's the matter?"

"The kids are gone. They're not here."

Lucy thought her mother must be having some kind of episode of delirium. She clamped her hand over her free ear as the flight attendant babbled in German about the arrival gate and the baggage carousel. "Mom, we're in Berlin, remember—"

"I know that," she snapped. "*I'm* in Berlin."

Lucy stared at the seat back in front of her, dumbfounded. "Why are you— How—"

"Turkish Airline to Istanbul," Irene said, sounding put out but proud.

"But . . . *why?*" Lucy said, her voice lifting. She turned and smiled apologetically to the woman sitting beside her.

"Caught the connection with one minute to spare," she said, "and we got to Greta and Otto's apartment two hours ago," said Irene.

"*We?*" said Lucy.

"Hi, Lucy," her dad said.

"*Dad?* You guys flew here just because I left town for a couple of days?"

"You bet your sweet bippy," Rex said. "And it's a good thing we came too, because something terrible has happened."

"Mom," Lucy said, trying to sound as calm and measured as she could, "Dad, I'm really glad you're here, I am, but this was a completely unnecessary—"

"They're not here," Irene said again. "I had a bad feeling, like I just knew something was wrong, so we got a key from Otto and caught the first flight out we could get. So here we are and"—her voice caught in her throat—"no kids."

"Jack texted me just this morning," Lucy said calmly, although she too was finding this quite alarming. "He sent a heart emoji."

"Then where are they?" Rex said.

"Probably at dinner or a movie or something."

"At nine thirty at night?"

Lucy checked the time on her phone. "Sure. Maybe?"

"Then why," Irene said tightly, "are all the toothbrushes missing?"

—o—

Lucy got a cab and gave the driver her address. "*So schnell wie möglich, bitte!*" she said. "*Es ist ein Notfall.*" Where these words came from, she did not know. It was the linguistic equivalent of a mother who suddenly displayed extraordinary strength and lifted a car to save her baby.

As they sped down the dark highway, Lucy called Jack again and again, but every call went straight to voicemail. When they'd talked briefly the morning before, he'd seemed hurried but fine. Since then he'd texted twice: All good last night and a heart emoji this morning. She hadn't told him she was coming home early.

The cab pulled up in front of the apartment, and Lucy handed the driver a hundred-euro bill. She did not wait for her change. She got out of the car and bolted up the five flights of stairs. At the sight of her parents, Lucy was overcome with emotion. But before even hugging them, she ran through the apartment, looking for clues. Just as her mother had said, the toothbrushes were missing from the little cup on the bathroom vanity. Fred was also gone, but she couldn't decide whether that was good news or bad.

"Should we call the police?" Irene said, worrying her hands together.

"Wait a minute," Lucy said. "I don't know." She tried calling

Jack again, while she chewed on her thumbnail. Again the call went to voicemail. "There has to be an explanation," Lucy said. "Maybe they're . . . Oh!" she said. "Maybe they're down at Adam's feeding his fish."

"*At whose?*" her dad said. "Doing what?"

Lucy didn't take the time to explain. She went to the entry, walking past her parents' suitcases, and grabbed Adam's key from the table. Since the key was there, she thought, the kids probably weren't, but she went down the stairs anyway, her parents following behind, and opened the door to Adam's apartment. It was quiet. Lucy circled the living room, looking for evidence that they'd been there. There was dirt on the floor by one of the plants, which was slightly reassuring. And Fish was alive. She studied the surface of the water in his bowl and then dropped a few flakes in.

"Lucy," her mother said, "focus!"

"I am," she said. "I'm thinking."

They climbed back upstairs, and her parents followed her into the little office, where Jack's blankets were folded neatly at one end of the couch. His laptop was on the desk, plugged in. Everything looked so normal; surely Jack, Zoe, and Alice would walk in any minute, and how surprised they would be to see their grandparents!

Her phone rang, and Lucy pulled it out of her pocket, hoping it was Jack. But it was Greta's name on the screen.

"Sorry," Lucy said, forgoing any kind of greeting and speaking in a rushed, high-pitched voice. "I can't talk. My kids . . ."

"What's wrong?" Greta said.

"I'm back in Berlin, and they're not here. My kids are gone." Saying it out loud made Lucy feel all the more panicked.

There was a pause and then Greta tried to calm her. "There are a lot of things open late in Berlin—"

"Jack's phone is going to voicemail and I'm trying not to—" She swallowed hard and put Greta on speaker.

"Hi, Greta," her mom said.

"*Irene?*" said Greta. "You're in Germany?"

"I'm here too," Rex said.

"Yeah, so tell us," her mom said, "if we have to call the police—"

"Dial one-one-two," Greta said.

Lucy thought she might throw up. She walked out of the office, leaving her parents to talk to Greta, and went from room to room in search of any kind of answer. In the living room, she noticed that the balcony door was unlocked; that didn't ease her mounting anxiety. She stepped outside to look around, her hands on the railing, and scanned the street in hopes that her kids would come walking down the sidewalk. She felt their absence then like a gut punch.

She went back inside and locked the balcony door, looking around the living room; it was as unlived-in as a museum. She went down the hall, first into the girls' room and then into Greta's. Jack had taken advantage of her absence to sleep in an actual bed. The covers were messed up and a pillow was on the floor. But then a flash of gold caught Lucy's eye. Under the glow of a lamp on the night table was a bracelet Lucy had never seen before.

She picked it up, her fingers touching the array of little charms: a key, a ladybug, a seashell, a tiny suitcase. A woman had slept in her bed. Had Jack invited a girl back to the apartment? Monika? Or the other one . . . Nathalie? This felt so out of the ordinary, so out of character for Jack, that Lucy was utterly stumped. As far as she knew, Jack had never even kissed a girl.

Rex was pacing while Irene talked to Greta. "Yes," she said, "we'll— Wait, hold up." And she stopped talking, staring at the bracelet in Lucy's outstretched fingers. "Greta," she said, "when was the last time you heard from Emmi?"

"Yesterday," Greta said, "here in New York. Why?"

"How many of those charm bracelets does she have?"

"How many?" Greta said, sounding confused. "Only one. My mother gave it to her."

"It's from Tiffany's, isn't it?" Irene asked.

"Yes. Why?"

Lucy checked the clasp of the bracelet. *Tiffany*.

"What would you say," Irene said slowly, "if I told you I'm look-ing at it."

"At Emmi's bracelet?" Greta said. "That's impossible. She was just wearing it. . . ." She paused. "Send me a picture."

Lucy put the bracelet on the dining room table and texted a pic-ture to Greta.

She heard Greta gasp. "I'm calling her," Greta said, and hung up.

"I don't understand," Lucy said, picking the bracelet up again. "Emmi's here? Why wouldn't she tell Greta?"

"Why do teenagers do anything?" Irene said, sounding somewhat calmer. "I blame their unformed frontal lobes."

"Even if she was here," Lucy said, "what's that got to do with my kids?"

"I can't explain it," her mom said, "but I feel better knowing they're together."

"Me too," said Rex.

"Really? Why?"

Lucy's phone rang again.

"Emmi's not answering," Greta said, her voice tense and low. "Do me a favor, Lucy. Go to the laundry room."

Lucy took her phone with her and did as she was told.

"What am I looking for?" Lucy said.

"Look out the window."

Lucy did, scanning the trees in the courtyard behind the building.

"The car," said Greta. "The Volkswagen Beetle. Is it there?"

Lucy pressed her forehead to the glass and looked straight down. The parking spot was empty.

"It's gone," Lucy said.

"*Oh, mein Gott*," Greta said. "I know where they are."

Greta caught the next flight from New York to London and would arrive in Berlin early in the morning. Lucy settled in with her parents for what would surely be the longest night of her life. Jack was a terrible driver, and Lucy hated to think of him on a dark highway—in a tiny VW bug—with his precious sisters in the back seat.

"You should get some sleep," Lucy told her parents.

"As if we could," Rex said.

They were sitting in the living room, and every sound she heard—and Greta's apartment creaked and clanged—made Lucy jump. Irene had put on pajamas, but Lucy didn't want to change in case she had to leave in a hurry for who-knows-what reason.

"I find it impossible to believe," Lucy said, "that some random girl he's never met before could have talked Jack into taking a car without permission to go to some beach."

"I believe it," said Irene. "You haven't met Emmi. If she asked nice, I think Jack would do pretty much anything."

"You really think they're okay?"

"I think Jack is driving twenty miles an hour back from wherever that beach house is, and they're trying to get back here before they expect you to land."

Lucy threw her head back. "I never thought Jack would be so deceitful. I'm his mother!"

"Ha," said Irene. "Talk about the pot calling the kettle black. Who just lied to her mother about her whereabouts?"

"That was different," said Lucy. Although she knew it really wasn't. It seemed children never really ended the push and pull with their parents, even as adults. "If my kids come home safe," Lucy said, "I'll never care about another thing for as long as I live."

Her phone rang, and she reached for it; an unknown number from Copenhagen appeared on the screen. She answered it.

"Lucy?" a man said. "It's Bjørn. I'm sorry to call so late."

Lucy heard voices in the background, the hum of conversation and high-pitched giggling.

"Your children are here," he said, "at my house. They've just arrived."

Lucy jumped to her feet, one hand gripping her head. "Oh my God, what— Are they okay?"

"Yes, they're all fine. Jack and the girls. And their friend Emmi is with them too. They drove from Heiligenhafen, and it took them over six hours to get here, although I can't really imagine how that's even possible. It's only about two hundred kilometers."

Irene was right next to her. "Where are they?" she said. "What happened?"

Lucy held up a finger. "Did you know they were coming? I had no idea—"

"No, it was quite a surprise," Bjørn said happily. "But a wonderful one. Are you still in Copenhagen?"

"No, I took a late flight back to Berlin," she said. "And when they weren't here . . . I've been thinking the absolute worst. I'm so grateful you called."

"Jack's going to call as soon as his phone is charged."

"And— Wait, *why* are they there? And how did Jack find you?"

"He's resourceful," said Bjørn, his voice barely above a whisper. "I hope it's okay if they spend the night with us. Astrid and our girls are making up trundle beds for them."

"Tell Astrid . . ." Lucy didn't want any bad feelings between any of them. "Tell her I said, from one mom to another, thank you," said Lucy.

"Our four girls are getting along nicely. I'll send a picture."

"I'm so glad they're safe," Lucy said.

"We'll talk in the morning after we've all gotten some sleep. Astrid and I could accompany them back to Berlin tomorrow. Emmi says she needs to catch a flight to New York."

"Yes," Lucy said. "Or I could come get them."

"What if we were to meet halfway?" he said. "Astrid and I will bring our girls as well."

"Yes, Bjørn," said Lucy. "I'd love that."

After they hung up, Lucy sent a text to Greta, who was no doubt wide awake on the flight and worrying. Rather than explain the second leg of the kids' trip, she simply wrote: Kids are safe. All okay!

Irene and Rex went to bed in the girls' room, and Lucy went to Greta's, hoping her adrenaline would taper off so she could at least rest for a few hours. She wanted her kids under her roof. She wanted Mason in her bed.

At two in the morning, her phone pinged with a text from Jack:

I'm so sorry, Mom. This was important to me. A + Z are totally fine, don't worry. See you tomorrow. Please don't kill me.

She wanted to give him room to grow, even though that was the hardest thing in the world for a mother to do.

I love you always, she wrote. Come back to me.

To: Jack Holt

We have received notice from Rockwell High School about their decision to expel you at the close of the school year. As you know, we have a policy to refuse admittance to students whose behavior is egregious enough to warrant expulsion.

However, we also received the email you wrote regarding the event that transpired. The committee is, in your case, curious enough to make one request before we make our final determination: Could you please provide the formula that could verify your account of the story? This is not to say that it will positively impact our decision, but any supporting material (the code you wrote, the algorithm you used) would help our committee better understand your specific situation.

You are under no obligation to provide your intellectual property. But please know that without corroborating evidence of your explanation, we will have to deny you admission.

Thank you.
Admissions Committee
Massachusetts Institute of Technology

To: MIT Admissions
From: Jack Holt

$$\hat{Y} = b_0 + alX_1 + \underline{sofs}X_2 + VX_3 + aX_4 + K2NX_5 + CMX_6 + IEX_7 + ttfX_8 + SAX_9$$

Coefficients:

	Estimate	Std. Error	t value	Pr(>|t|)
b0	5.57	1.32	4.22	.043
al	44.4	5.73	7.75	.028
sofs	22.4	3.99	5.61	.003
V	-5.67	2.30	2.53	.212
a	5.03	0.97	5.19	.072
K2N	-16.7	1.12	14.9	.008
CM	2.07	2.89	0.71	.553
IE	-1.12	0.66	1.70	.543
ttf	33.4	4.56	7.32	.002
SA	-4.21	1.22	4.98	.066

Residual standard error: 2460 on 763 degrees of freedom
Multiple R-squared: 0.912, Adjusted R-squared: 0.816

KEY
al = acne level of *x* (value before Accutane)
sofs = *x*'s sense of style
V, s = vehicle driven (by *x*)/average driving speed (of *x* in V)
a = athleticism of *x*
K2N = kind to nerds of *y*
CM = College matriculation, as ranked by *US News and World Report* of *y*
IE = interesting extracurriculars of *y*
ttf = TikTok followers of y
SA = social awkwardness of *x*

x = Jack
y = set [Madison, Nell, Katie, Cynthia, Lilly, Allie, Maggie, Becca, Grace]

BERLIN

To be home! Greta rolled her bag into the arrivals area at the Flughafen, having spent a sleepless night on the plane. The timing and circumstances of this trip were not ideal, but she could not curb her euphoria to be back in Berlin.

She looked around the terminal until she spotted a woman waving at her; a vague memory flashed through her mind, a moment in early June at another airport, in another country. Greta smiled as they walked toward each other.

"Does your daughter have a stuffed rabbit?" she said. "It can't be that— Was that you?"

"You were the one who found Fred in Newark," Lucy said, a look of delight taking over her pretty face. "You were our savior on the trip here."

Greta was growing accustomed to embracing people she'd never met, so when Lucy reached out then and hugged her, Greta hugged her back just as tightly. Over Lucy's shoulder, she took in the shops and German signs around her, the familiar advertisements and kiosks, feeling so happy to be back. "Our kids are okay?" she said.

"They're fine," said Lucy, stepping back and relieving Greta of her bag.

"I'm sorry Emmi dragged them into this," Greta said, still reeling from the shock of it. "I can't believe she did something so—"

"No, *I'm* sorry," Lucy said, locking arms with her. But instead of heading toward the taxis, she turned them in the opposite direction.

"Where are we going?" Greta said.

"It turns out that Jack dragged Emmi into something too," Lucy said. "We're going on a little road trip."

⊶

Once Lucy explained how and why the kids had ended up in Copenhagen, Denmark, of all places, they rented a car and headed to Rostock. Lucy drove the two and a half hours north, chatting the whole way, and Greta had the feeling she'd known her all her life.

"How was your trip to Copenhagen?" she said.

"Complicated," said Lucy with a smile. "And how was New York?"

"Complicated," said Greta. "I made a decision that might destroy my career."

"And how was Adam?"

"It was nice to see him," she said. "He's a good friend."

"Is that all?" said Lucy, glancing at her. "You should see the way he talks about you."

Greta was relieved Adam hadn't said or done anything to cross a line. "He knows me pretty well," Greta said. "And he knows I would never betray Otto."

"No, of course not," said Lucy. "I'm sorry if I muddled things up for you."

"You didn't," said Greta, when, in fact, Greta had never felt more muddled. She'd fought—and won—a battle with desire and was proud of herself for it. It had been so long since Otto had done more than peck her on the cheek, and she couldn't say that Adam didn't spark something in her, even making her fantasize about kissing him. But Greta had to accept that sex was not part of her life anymore. She turned away to look out the window, surprised by the ache in her heart.

⊶

If the Holt reunion was strained—Lucy's patchwork family coming together at a *Treffpunkt* in the historic Neuer Markt—you wouldn't have known it by watching them. Lucy hugged her children before kneeling to meet Bjørn and Astrid's daughters. It was clear to Greta this was the beginning of something for the two families, not the end. And she had a misplaced longing to be part of it all.

Her reunion with Emmi was pricklier.

Emmi approached her sheepishly. "*Es tut mir sehr leid,*" she said.

"You're safe," Greta said, hugging her. "That's the only thing that matters. But why didn't you tell me what you were doing? We could have talked about it. And what about your job?"

"I told them I had Covid," Emmi said. "They're expecting me the day after—"

Greta could not believe her ears. "You lied to a law firm?"

"Yes, but—"

"It's so unlike you, Emmi," Greta said, her exasperation growing. "What made you—"

"You said I needed to confront Monika—"

"I didn't mean *in person*—"

"But then I got there, and I realized I didn't go all the way to Heiligenhafen because of Karl and Monika. I wanted to say goodbye to the house. This was important to me."

Greta hugged her again. "I understand," she said. "And I'm so sorry. It's hard for me too." She wanted, for Emmi's sake, to be positive, to help her look forward instead of backward. "So tell me: Did you manage to enjoy yourself, even though you were sad? At least a little bit?"

"Oh, yes," Emmi said. "Would it be okay if Jack and I drive back in the VW?"

After the betrayal of Monika and Karl, Greta was glad to know Jack was stepping in to be a friend to her. "Of course," she said. "I'm so glad you don't hate him anymore."

"Yeah, no," said Emmi. "I don't hate him at all."

❧

They returned to Savignyplatz in the evening, and as Greta walked into her apartment, the familiar smells and sights made her heart full. Did she notice the scratch on the entry floor, the foggy spot on the dining room table, the missing Meissen in Emmi's bedroom? She did. Did she care? Oh, yes, she did. But she would never mention it. Some things, like friendship, were more important than perfect hardwood floors and antique chairs.

Never had Greta's apartment had as much life in it as it did that night. While Irene and Lucy placed a huge order for Thai takeout, Greta called Bettina and asked her to join them as well. Rex and Jack added the extra leaf to the dining table, and as they all sat down together, Greta marveled that this gathering was taking place. She did not spend her time worrying about the hot containers being passed around or Til wandering under the table or the sticky sauce that dripped in the vicinity of the upholstered chairs. She let it all go, and instead listened to the tales of the kids' unplanned excursion to the beach and beyond, asked the twins about their swim classes and friends, watched with curiosity as Emmi leaned in to whisper something to Jack, and caught Bettina up on their mother's escapades.

After they cleared away the plates, Lucy put a package of cookies in the center of the table and a box stamped with the Royal Copenhagen crown right in front of Greta.

"What's this for?" Greta said.

"It's a little something I bought for you," said Lucy. "It's the least I can do."

Greta opened the box to find a gold-rimmed Flora Danica plate. "Oh, Lucy," she said, admiring the hand-painted flowers, "it's beautiful. You shouldn't have."

"Yes, she should," said Alice, "because Zoe broke your pink plate."

"It was an accident," Zoe said, turning on her sister. "You're such a tattletale."

"It's okay, Zoe," Greta said. "Accidents happen, and this new plate is much prettier."

"Where are we all sleeping tonight?" Emmi said.

"Rex and I checked into a hotel earlier," Irene said. "It's right around the corner."

"And we'll stay downstairs in Adam's apartment," said Greta.

"Are you sure?" said Lucy.

"He said you have a key I can borrow, and I wouldn't dream of putting you out." Greta stood up. "And since we have to be up so early, we should probably go to bed."

Bettina and Til left with Greta and Emmi, and they all hugged goodbye in the stairwell.

Then Greta and Emmi let themselves into Adam's apartment.

It was neat as could be. Greta went over to see the fish.

"I guess I'm sleeping here?" Emmi said, sitting down on the sofa.

"No, you can share the bed with me," Greta said.

"That's okay," Emmi said. "I think I'll sleep better here."

Greta was annoyed, but she found an extra sheet and a blanket and helped Emmi make up the couch.

"Thank you for coming to get me, *Mami*," Emmi said, hugging her suddenly. "I love you."

"I love you too. I'll see you in the morning, *Schatz*," Greta said, knowing it would not be easy to get her up and out the door for their flight. "Do you need anything?"

"I'm fine," Emmi said, lying down and pulling the blanket over her. "Good night."

Greta went back to the bedroom and put on her pajamas. She pulled back the covers of the bed, feeling electrified by the intimacy of sleeping under Adam's sheets, even if he was six thousand kilometers away. She imagined him walking into the room. . . .

She'd kept Adam at a distance, as she should, but when they'd hugged goodbye, chastely and in public, she'd had a very hard time letting him go.

Greta slept deeply that night, comforted by the creaking and clanking of her prewar building.

As soon as she was dressed and ready to go in the morning, Lucy knocked on the door, keys in hand, insisting on driving them to the airport.

Greta could see the exhaustion in Lucy's eyes. "You really don't have to—"

"It's fine," Lucy said. "I have to drop off the rental car anyway."

Emmi came up behind her, makeup on and hair damp, her backpack slung over her shoulder. "Ready?" she said.

"Look at you," said Greta, so pleased there wouldn't be a struggle to get her out the door. "I thought I would have to nudge you."

"God," Emmi said, annoyed. "*Ich kann auf mich selbst aufpassen*," and she rolled her carry-on out the door.

"And to think," Greta said quietly, "she actually needed me yesterday."

Lucy laughed.

Greta checked to make sure she'd left Adam's apartment the way she'd found it, wrote a quick message of thanks on a scrap of paper, and then locked the door, handing Lucy the key.

They were heading down the stairs when Jack caught up to them.

"You're up?" Lucy said, patting his back as he walked by. "Are you coming to the airport with us?"

"Yeah," he said. "Why wouldn't I?"

"Just asking," said Lucy, and she rolled her eyes.

Emmi and Jack got in the back seat, and Greta sat in the front, giving Lucy directions as they headed off to the airport.

Just as they got on the Autobahn, Greta got a text from Tobias: Sorry to have bad news but your mother has severe motion sickness. Dehydration maybe?

"*Scheiße*," Greta said. She counted backward in her head; it was ten o'clock at night in California.

"What's wrong?" Emmi said.

"It's your grandmother," Greta said. "She's sick on the boat."

She started to text him back but then decided to call instead.

"Oh good, Greta," he said. "I hate to worry you."

"Is she okay?"

"*Nein*," he said. "We've only had two days on the boat, but it's not going well. Lillian is *seekrank*."

Greta shook her head. "How seasick is she?"

"She's feeling wretched. Nauseous and shaky. She took Dramamine, and I told her to give it another day, but she wants to disembark as soon as possible."

"Okay," said Greta, "and then what?"

"She says she'll fly home. I can get her to Los Angeles, and I wondered if you could meet her at the marina." A seagull squawked in the background.

"I knew this was a bad idea," Greta said. "Can you put her on?"

"She can't talk right now," he said. "She's currently . . . throwing up."

"Poor thing," said Greta. "Can you take her to a hotel to recover?"

"I can't leave the boat that long," he said. "I was thinking since Dallas isn't that far—"

"I'm nowhere near Dallas," Greta said.

"Oh," he said. "New York?"

"Berlin," she said flatly. "I can't get there for probably . . ." She tried to do the math. "Fifteen hours."

That silenced him a moment, and Greta had no solution to propose either. Even if she called Otto, he wouldn't be able to get there until the next day.

"Maybe she'll get her sea legs after all," he said, weak hope in his voice.

"Unlikely," Greta said. "All I can do is get on a plane and get there as soon as I can. But you can't leave my mom alone in some port."

"Of course not," he said. "She can stay on the boat as long as necessary. Just let me know how soon someone can get here to meet her."

"I'll call you back," she said, and hung up.

She looked out the window at the passing cars, feeling utterly helpless.

"What does your mom need?" Lucy said.

"Dry land," said Greta. "She needs to be picked up at a marina in LA and taken to the airport or a hotel. I don't know. The friend she's with can't leave his boat."

"That sounds complicated," Lucy said.

"She'll just have to stay put until I can get there," said Greta.

As they drove, she looked for connecting flights from Dallas to LAX, wondering how her mother would cope in the intervening hours, if maybe the Dramamine would kick in.

Lucy pulled up in front of the international terminal and put the car in park. She tapped her fingers on the steering wheel and then turned to Greta. "It's not ideal," she said, "but I might have a way to help your mom."

BERLIN

Bryn was the gentler of her two bosses, so she was the one Lucy called from outside the car rental drop-off. While the phone was ringing, she glanced at Jack, who was leaning against the car, texting. Maybe he was writing Drew or Rosie. It seemed the trip to the beach and to Copenhagen had brought him back to life; he looked relaxed and happy.

"Lucy?" Bryn said. "Is this a butt-dial?"

"Hi. And no, I'm actually calling you on purpose. Sorry it's so late."

"Is there a problem?"

"Sort of," Lucy said, biting her fingernail. "I have an odd favor to ask. It's not actually about work."

Bryn didn't answer, so Lucy kept talking, knowing this request was leagues out of the ordinary and that it might even lead to a confession about where she was.

"I was wondering," she said, "if you might be willing to go to Marina Del Rey to pick someone up. She's, well, she's family."

"Sorry, what?"

"Her name's Lillian, and I wouldn't ask something like this under normal circumstances, but she's not feeling well. Nothing contagious, of course," she added quickly. "Just an older lady with a little bout of motion sickness."

"Have you been drinking, Lucy?"

"Fair question," Lucy said. "But in all seriousness, I was hoping you could help me out."

"I mean . . . Why is this necessary?" Bryn said. "Can't she take a cab to wherever she's going?"

"I know it's a huge favor," Lucy said, "but I'd feel better if someone accompanied her. She got seasick on this yacht, and she probably shouldn't be alone."

"Well, this *is* an odd request," Bryn said, and sighed. "But family comes first. Who exactly are we meeting and when?"

"We?" said Lucy.

"I'm still at the office with Harper. We've got that pitch tomorrow."

"Hi, Lucy," Harper called out.

Lucy put a palm to her forehead. She wanted to help Greta in any way she could, but this wasn't going to be easy.

"So how do we find this person?" Bryn said. "And who is she?"

"I'll put you in touch with the captain of the boat she's on." There was no way around the truth. "She's the mother of a very close friend. But the thing is I've never *actually* met her."

"I thought you said she was family," Bryn said.

"On some level, she's family. Or she feels like family, in a way. And I was wondering if you could meet her like . . . now-ish."

"*Tonight?*" Harper said.

"I have a better idea," Bryn said, clearly trying to temper Harper's annoyance. "Why don't you fly to LA first thing in the morning to meet up with this woman, and then you can attend the pitch in person tomorrow and spend a couple of days in the office."

"I can't," Lucy said. "I'm not in Dallas."

"You're not still in Copenhagen?" Harper said.

"I'm in Berlin." It was almost a relief to come clean. "I've been in Berlin all summer. I was afraid to tell you because I worried you might think I was putting in less than a hundred percent. But as you know, I've been working my—"

"Berlin . . . *Germany?*" Bryn said.

"I wondered why your Zoom background changed," said Harper.

"And—that explains why you've looked so exhausted the past weeks. What's the time difference there?"

"I'm not exhausted," Lucy said. "I'm focused, I'm energized—"

"Text us the information about this seasick woman you've never met before," Harper said. "But you should know I'm not happy about this, Lucy. *Any* of it."

Lucy apologized and texted her bosses the number Greta had given her for Tobias, the man who was not, Greta had been happy to report, sleeping with her mother.

She and Jack walked to the S-Bahn.

"Are you getting fired?" Jack said.

"I hope not," said Lucy, but in truth it felt like a possibility.

As much as there was to talk about, Lucy was quiet on the train ride back to Berlin. Sitting beside Jack, she tried to stay awake as she processed the events of the past days.

At some point, the train screeched to a halt, and the conductor made an announcement about a delay.

"Remember when you said I should learn German?" Jack said, interrupting her thoughts.

She glanced over to find him looking at her, his eyes brighter than they'd been since the day he'd gotten kicked out of school.

"I was thinking," he went on, "maybe you were right about that."

"*Ausgezeichnet,*" Lucy said, pleased he'd finally come around. "That's great. What made you change your mind?"

He shrugged. "Bjørn speaks, like, five languages, and it's embarrassing that I can't understand people here."

She smiled, relieved to know he was looking ahead, setting goals. "Are you glad you met Bjørn?"

"Yeah, he's really cool," Jack said. "I like his family." He frowned then and sighed. "But for some reason, I miss Dad even more now."

Lucy nodded. "Me too," she said.

Lucy wanted to show her parents a bit of Berlin since they'd traveled so far. That afternoon they all went to the *Jagdschloss*, a small hunting castle by a lake, a place she remembered fondly from her college days. They walked along the path through the woods until they got to a kiosk, where Rex got in line with the kids to buy ice cream. Lucy and her mom walked to a bench by the edge of the lake and sat down, looking across the water. "You were right as usual about everything," Lucy said. "Mason needs to come home."

Her mom turned to look at her. "Mason is on Mars," she said dryly.

"Mason is in New Mexico," Lucy said. "And I'm thinking it's time to go bust him out."

Her mother crossed her arms. "Where's this coming from?"

"I'm done," Lucy said. "I quit. I can't do this anymore without him."

"Yes, you can," Irene said.

"Well, even if I *can*," she said, "I don't want to. Everything's turned to complete garbage since he left. The kids have no schools, I'm about to get fired, I managed to lose my three children in Europe—"

"You found them again," her mom said, as though that episode hadn't completely shaken them all.

"I miss him so much," Lucy said. "I need him."

Irene sighed. "You're flip-flopping, Lucy," she said. "You're the one who said how important it is to respect his commitment, to understand the importance of what he's doing there."

"I know I did," Lucy said, "but I changed my mind."

Lucy's phone rang: Harper was calling.

"Oh God," Lucy said nervously, "time to get fired."

She sat up straight and answered the phone.

"That was no small favor, Lucy," Harper sniped. Lucy checked her watch; it was seven in the morning in LA. "That poor Lillian was sick as a dog when we picked her up."

"I'm so sorry," said Lucy. "Is she okay?"

"No, she's not okay. She threw up in Bryn's car. We had to drive her to a hospital to get IV fluids. And for reasons I can't even understand myself, I let her spend the night at my place. If she's well enough, we'll take her to catch a seven p.m. flight to Frankfurt tonight, and she'll land in Berlin tomorrow afternoon."

"Her daughter Bettina will pick her up. And thank you, Harper," she said. "I mean that, really, thank you so much."

"This lady better be important to you," Harper said.

She was, although Lucy could not possibly explain why, not even to herself.

Harper cleared her throat. "It was dishonest of you to keep your whereabouts a secret from us," she said. "When do you intend to come back to the States anyway?"

Lucy decided she wouldn't lie anymore. "I don't know."

"I told Bryn we should fire you," Harper said plainly. "But she said you must have had your reasons for leaving like you did. And that it's none of our business that you're only sleeping a few hours a night as long as you're doing your job. So we'll keep you on."

"Thank you," said Lucy.

"For now. But consider your status probationary. This Laurel account is too important to our business for you to be—"

"Yes, I know," said Lucy. "It's important to me too. In fact, Harper, I'd love to talk about the shutters I found in Copenhagen. I was thinking we could—"

"Sure, but before we get to that," Harper said, lowering her voice, "tell me what you know about that good-looking captain who brought Lillian off the yacht."

"Tobias?" Lucy smiled. "I don't know anything about him," she said, "but I'll ask my friend Greta."

People Magazine: Sexiest Man Alive

Unbeknownst to Mason Holt, hot brainiac and lone male on the NASA biosphere project, he has just been named Sexiest Man Alive. With the smoldering smarts of a young Jeff Goldblum, the allure of Stanley Tucci, and the flat-out hunkiness of Patrick Dempsey, Holt has been quietly winning hearts and minds with his adorable band of robotic dusters that are keeping the solar panels squeaky clean on "Mars." Environmentalist, millionaire inventor, philanthropist, and now accidental fitness guru Mason has become an icon. People from all over the globe have been tuning into the biosphere live feed to follow along with Holt's daily routine that brings to mind Jack LaLanne's workouts, with his belted NASA regulation jumpsuit, a folding chair, and a determined smile. With no communication from the outside world, Mason has no idea that Cody Rigsby of Peloton created a series of classes based on his retro exercise rituals, designed to redefine the Dad Bod.

Holt and his biosphere companion, the microbiologist Dr. Veronique Laurent, are the last two remaining members of the Alpha Red Canyon team. Nicknamed "Masonique" by their fans, these two have turned up the heat on this scientific venture by showing that together and alone, they can thrive on a metaphorical desert island.

DALLAS

At high noon, Greta stepped out of the American Airlines terminal at DFW into the sweltering heat. There was Otto, waiting at the curb in Lucy's minivan. He got out of the car, flashing her a bright smile.

"Why, Otto," she said, practically blinded, "what did you do?"

"Very white, *ja*?" he said, running his tongue over his teeth. "Irene made an appointment for me at the dental office where she works. I had Zoom! laser treatment."

"Goodness," she said.

"Now I am all the time smiling."

That would take some getting used to. They hugged quickly and went to put her suitcase in the back of the car.

"And is that a new shirt?" she said, reaching to adjust his collar. "I'm not used to seeing you in red."

"I went to the Gap," he said. "Troy is taking me to his country club tomorrow, so I have bought golf shirts. Do you like it?"

"You look very young," she said. "And slim." All the laps in the pool were starting to make a difference in Otto's shoulders and torso.

He pulled in his stomach and stood up taller. "How was the rest of your trip? I still can't believe our Emmi ran away to the beach. That was very strange."

"She had her reasons," Greta said, not entirely sure that even she had the whole story. As they said their goodbyes in Newark Airport, it felt as if Emmi might have a few more secrets she was keeping.

They got into the car, and Greta buckled her seat belt, looking out the windshield at the beige concrete and the blue sky in front of her.

"And you picked a side in your battle," Otto said. "Herr Schultz must be very angry to know you are making doubts about the Vermeer."

"He is," she said.

"Yet you really believe a young girl made such a painting? Would it not have been better to say nothing about it?"

"Some fights are worth having," she said.

"I disagree. Why wake up a dog that is sleeping?" he said.

She didn't expect Otto to understand. Greta decided to change the subject. "I'm glad I got to meet Lucy. I like her family so much," she said.

"Irene and Rex are *Salz der Erde*," he said. "And your mother is feeling better?"

"Yes, she's flying from LA to Berlin tonight." While she'd waited at her gate at Newark, Lucy had texted a thumbs-up and then asked—at her boss Harper's request—whether Tobias was single, gay or straight, whether he might sail back through LA, might like to have a glass of wine.

"I forgot to tell you," Greta said, "that I got an email from that woman Lisa who sat with us at the Judsons' party. She's married to a plastic surgeon."

"The Larkins," said Otto.

"Yes, she's interested in hiring me."

"*Wunderbar*," said Otto. "That's just what you need here, a project."

"I'll take her to a few art galleries next week and see what we can find," Greta said.

Otto began nodding his head along to the country music playing from the car's speakers. "I have invited Sylvie to the party since she invited me to hers," Otto said.

"Party?" said Greta.

"Yes," he said. "And please no worries because I am doing all the cooking."

"Cooking?" she said. "You never mentioned a party."

"*Doch*," he said. "I told you. I invited Troy and Kristy, Betsy and Bob, plus two other couples from the medical school. They are all coming tonight."

"Otto, no," she said.

"Yes," he said proudly.

"But I've been traveling all day—"

"I am taking care of everything," he said. "I have done all the shopping at Costco, and Sylvie is bringing a dessert."

This was the last way she wanted to spend her evening. "Since when do you throw parties?"

"I finally know people I like. It will be big fun tonight, and you don't have to make any work. You can be my hostess."

She did not want to be his hostess. She would rather crawl into Lucy's bed and go to sleep. She would rather fly back to Berlin.

⊶

When they pulled up to the house, there was a van parked at the curb. A man wearing khakis and a button-down approached them as they got out of the car.

"Excuse me," he said, taking off his dark glasses. "Are you Lucy Holt?"

"No," said Greta. "She's not here."

"We're doing a story on her husband, Mason. Do you know when she'll be back?"

"I'm sorry," Greta said, "I can't help you."

Otto came around the front of the car as the man handed Greta a business card.

"Can you give this to her? Tell her we'd like a comment on what it's like being married to *People*'s Sexiest Man Alive."

Greta took the card and handed it to Otto.

"Mason is becoming famous," he said as the man walked away.

"It must be very hard for Lucy and Mason to be apart so long."

But Otto's mind was elsewhere. He opened the door to the house and the dogs rushed to meet them, wagging their tails and rolling over on their backs. Greta leaned over to pat them, adjusting to the chill of the indoors.

Then she rolled her bag to Lucy's bedroom and left it unopened in the closet.

⚷

Otto was wearing an apron.

Greta watched him from the kitchen window as he poked the steaks and sausages and flipped them, checking a timer on his phone.

When he came back inside, he went to the refrigerator and popped open a can of Coors Light. "Mmmm," he said, "*lecker.*"

"You hate American beer," she said. "You always say it tastes like water."

He swallowed and wiped his upper lip. "It does," he said, "but in this heat, it's very nice." He took a large platter from a cabinet and went back outside.

Greta folded napkins and counted out forks and knives until Otto brought the steaks in and covered them with foil. "I think I got 'em just right," he said.

There was something odd in his inflection. In spite of his grammar and vocabulary, Otto sounded almost . . . Texan.

"Hey, Captain," he said loudly, "turn on Kelly Clarkson."

The music came through the speakers in the ceiling, and Otto hummed along. He opened the refrigerator and took out a bottle of hot sauce for a corn dish he was preparing. Otto did not eat spicy food.

"Did I tell you my good news?" he said.

"I wondered if we were celebrating something."

"Troy and I replicated my study, and the *International Journal of Bone and Joint* has published a retraction of Moritz's paper. I've been . . . *entlastet?*"

"Exonerated."

"And Moritz wrote to apologize to me."

"That's wonderful," she said. "A truce will make returning to Charité so much more pleasant for you." She came up from behind him and put her arms around him.

He patted her hands affectionately. "After dinner, we'll have dessert in the family room so we don't miss the game."

"What game?" she said.

"Baseball," he said. "The Rangers are playing."

⊶

She had to hand it to him; Otto threw a very good party. His Costco steaks were excellent and he'd cooked them to perfection, which was hard for Greta to believe given his lack of experience in the kitchen.

When everyone had finished eating, Greta cleared a stack of plates and put them in the kitchen sink. She opened the back door to let the dogs out, as laughter erupted from the dining room.

"Your husband certainly seems to be enjoying himself," Bob said, setting an empty platter on the counter.

Otto was, in fact, having the time of his life.

Bob came closer. "So this is the famous Holt house," he said, looking around the kitchen. "Goes to show there is such a thing as *too* modern."

"I've come to like it," Greta said. Tank and Bunny came back in, and she closed the door. "It has lovely light."

"You know what else is lovely—" Bob bit his lower lip and raised his eyebrows, making a face that was apparently supposed to convey lust.

"My husband and I feel very lucky," Greta said, abruptly walking away to keep the kitchen island between them, "that we found such a nice family to swap homes."

"*Nice* family?" Bob scoffed. "You're joking, right? Lucy's a terrible mother, and her kid should be in jail—"

"Shut up," Greta said in a tight whisper, pointing a finger in his face. "You don't know them, and you don't know anything about what happened."

"Sweetheart," he said, "lighten up."

"If you say one more disparaging word about Jack, Lucy, or any of the Holts, you'll be sorry."

Bob took a step back and smiled. "Well, well, look at you. You're even sexier when you're mad."

Greta glared at him. "Your daughter is—how old? Nine? Ten? You think she'll never do anything to shock or disappoint you. But she probably will, and I hope the people around you show her more kindness than you've shown to Jack and his family."

"Okay, okay," he said, holding his hands up as though she were holding him at gunpoint.

Sylvie came into the kitchen then with two empty wine bottles, flashing a look of concern as she glanced between them.

Bob gave a curt nod and slinked back to the dining room.

"Hmm," Sylvie said. "I don't want to gossip, but between you and me, I hear that man's a snake."

Sylvie had not brought one dessert. She had brought three: a pecan pie, a peach cobbler, and pineapple upside-down cake. Otto had a serving of each.

Troy clinked his glass and stood up next to Otto, who was sitting at the head of the table looking happier than Greta had ever seen him. "If I could have the floor a moment," Troy said. "Dr. von Bosse here tells me Germans love a speech."

"It's true," said Otto. "We do."

"Well, we published a good study," he said. "So first off, cheers to that." He raised a glass, and Betsy whooped. "You're a great addition to the team, Boss," he said with a hand on Otto's shoulder. "I've been in conversations with the provost the last couple of weeks because we want to bring you on full-time."

Greta's breath caught in her throat as Otto lit up, a gratified, open smile on his face.

"And by that, I mean a permanent position," Troy said, "assuming we can persuade you and Greta to move to Dallas."

Otto looked around the table, his mouth agape. Betsy started clapping her hands. Someone else was whistling.

But before Greta could process what was happening, how her life was changing before her very eyes, she heard a sound directly behind her, a throat clearing followed by a deep voice saying "Excuse me."

The dogs were barking as Greta turned around and saw a man in a jumpsuit who was looking around the dining room in complete and utter bewilderment. She recognized him at once: the inventor, the biosphere inhabitant, the accidental exercise guru. The Sexiest Man Alive.

⚬┳

How does one explain to a person—who has, for all intents and purposes, been living on Mars—why his family is gone and his house is filled with strangers? Greta did her best. While Otto was saying goodbye to his dinner guests, Greta sat down with Mason at the kitchen island and introduced herself, telling him about the Instagram post that led to the house swap and reassuring him that his family was alive and well.

"Are you sure?" he said, patting his dogs absently and looking around as though Lucy would surely walk in at any moment. "I don't understand why they would go to Germany. And for so long."

"You'll have to ask them," Greta said, feeling that Lucy should be the one to catch Mason up on all that he'd missed. "Can I get you a glass of wine? We have leftovers if you're hungry—"

"No thank you," he said. "Is Lucy okay? And the kids?"

"Oh yes, I just saw them, and they're doing well. Maybe . . . you'll fly to Berlin tomorrow and see for yourself?"

"Yes," he said, snapping to attention. "Yes, I'll do that."

Mason was indeed handsome, although Greta was not sure that "sexy" was the word she would use to describe him. But even in this moment of discombobulation, he seemed polite and thoughtful.

He glanced toward the back window and then he got up. "I should go say hello to my in-laws."

"Oh dear," said Greta. "I'm afraid Rex and Irene aren't here either. They went to Germany as well actually."

"They . . . ?" He sat back down again, clearly overwhelmed. "My phone," he said, touching imaginary breast pockets. "My wallet. Do you happen to know where they are?"

Greta did not.

"I need to find them. My closet maybe," he said, standing up again. "I'm sure Lucy put them there." He looked at her, his brow furrowed, his tortoiseshell glasses sliding down his nose. "I mean, may I?"

"Please," Greta said, sweeping her arm to indicate the whole house, "do whatever you need to do. Otto and I will sleep upstairs so you can have your room."

"Right," he said. "I hadn't considered . . . I guess I'm putting you out?"

"Not at all," she said. "I'm really sorry for the confusion."

Otto walked into the kitchen and shook Mason's hand again. "*Willkommen*, Mr. Holt," he said so jovially that Greta wondered whether he'd had too much wine. "We are giving you quite a shock to be here, or?"

"Yes," Mason said. "I can't understand why my family would decide to go to Germany."

"Mason wants to go meet them in Berlin," Greta said quickly, "but he needs his wallet and phone. Have you seen them anywhere?"

"I haven't," Otto said.

"I'll go check in my room," Mason said. "Excuse me." And he walked away.

"What a night," Otto said happily. He seemed oblivious to Mason's distress and to the awkwardness of the situation, while Greta was feeling painfully aware.

"*Wie peinlich*," she said.

"I'm not embarrassed," Otto said. "It is not our fault." And to Greta's surprise, he started scraping plates and loading the dishwasher. "It seems my new colleagues like me very much. I can't describe how good I am feeling."

Greta had been so consumed with Mason's unexpected arrival, she'd forgotten about the job offer. "Otto, do you actually want to move here?" she said.

"*Selbstverständlich*," he said. "I'll need to know more, salary and retirement *und so weiter*, but yes. When I think of returning to Berlin"—he stopped rinsing the glass in his hand and looked up, as if trying to imagine it—"I feel depressed. All I do there is settle for less. Our apartment is small, the weather is gray, my colleagues are not nice."

"But Moritz retracted his opinion," Greta said, willing Otto to come to his senses, dreading that he wouldn't. "Doesn't that change things?"

"Moritz never should have doubted my ethics to begin with."

She couldn't argue with that. "Are you going to ask me how I feel about it?"

He turned off the faucet and dried his hands on a dish towel. "Of course. But what is in Berlin for us? Emmi is no longer there."

"But— But my mother and sister— And our apartment," she said. "Berlin is our home."

"Is it?" he said, and he looked genuinely skeptical.

"Of course." She did not know how he could ask such a question. "Our family and friends, the culture, the parks. I love our life there." And as she said these words, she realized how out of place she'd been feeling ever since they arrived in Dallas.

He nodded and put his hand on her shoulder. "Then we'll go back."

She looked at him then, seeing the melancholy in his eyes. "But I want you to be happy," she said.

"We get to spend a year here," he said, "and that will be enough for me."

But no, Greta thought, it was not enough for him. She would have to be the one to give in.

⚷

She couldn't sleep. As Otto snored, she found the pack of cigarettes Adam had given her and went outside to sit by the pool. She kicked off her slippers and leaned back on a lounge chair, hoping to clear her head but finding herself more and more troubled. Happy for Otto, yes, but heartbroken for herself. Bitter even and deeply homesick. She put her feet up and lit her cigarette, listening to the cicadas screeching overhead.

Her phone rang and her mother's name appeared on the screen.

"Hello from the airport," she said. "We're delayed."

"How are you feeling?" Greta said, relieved to hear Lillian's voice. "Are you okay?"

"Much better. I don't *ever* want to step foot on a boat again," she said. "Your friends Bryn and Harper took excellent care of me."

"They're Lucy's friends actually," Greta said, watching the cigarette burn between her fingers. "I'm glad they were able to help."

"You know, I got a call earlier from my Realtor," she said.

Greta tamped out the cigarette, bracing herself for the news of a buyer.

"It seems that someone broke into my beach house," Lillian said wryly. "At least two of the beds were slept in, but the intruder had the very good manners to close all the curtains, cover the furniture, and lock the door behind her when she left."

Greta felt the heat rush to her cheeks. "I should have told you," she said. "I'm really sorry that Emmi—"

"Stole my key right out of my purse? Went to my cottage without permission? Brought friends along?"

"She was upset," Greta said, "not that that excuses her behavior, but she needed to say goodbye. I'll have her call you to apologize."

"Don't even tell her I know," her mother said with a laugh. "I'd rather my only granddaughter enjoy her time in New York. But you can tell her I've decided to take the house off the market."

"Oh, Mom," Greta said, letting her breath out in a rush, "that's wonderful news. What made you change your mind?"

"Tobias," she said. "He reminded me that even if I want to see the world, I'll need a home where my family can gather. So tell Emmi I said not to worry. And if she wants, we can spend Christmas there, even though I detest winter on the Baltic."

"Thank you, really," Lucy said, "I'm so happy to hear it."

"*Ich liebe dich,*" her mom said, and hung up.

Greta stared at her phone, blinking at this unusual expression of love.

She immediately texted Emmi:

I miss and love you. Good news: your grandmother is keeping the cottage, so rest easy, Schatz.

She was considering going back inside when she heard a door open, and the dogs came running outside. Mason was right behind them, still in his NASA jumpsuit.

"Hi again," he said.

Greta turned and sat up, adjusting her pajama top. "Hello, Mason."

He sat across from her. "Do you think I could borrow your phone to call Lucy?"

"Of course," she said. "No luck finding yours?"

"I found my passport," he said. "But no. I'm desperate to hear her voice."

Greta opened her contacts and called Lucy, handing him the phone.

He put it to his ear. "Straight to voicemail," he said, his shoulders sagging.

Bunny climbed up on Greta's lounge chair, and she scooched over to make room.

"I don't suppose you have Irene's number?" Mason said. "Or Rex's?"

"I don't," said Greta. "They stop by pretty much every day, so . . ."

"Right," he said. "This is awful. I can't even buy a plane ticket."

"Do you need a credit card? You can use mine."

"Could I?" he said, looking hopeful and slightly embarrassed. "I'll pay you back as soon as I—"

"It's the least I can do," she said. She opened Google and began searching for flights. "There's no nonstop to Berlin," she said, "but it looks like you can fly to London tomorrow night."

"No," he said, clasping and unclasping his hands, "I can't wait that long."

It took some searching, but Greta found Mason a seat on a morning flight to Atlanta and an overnight to Amsterdam. From there he could take a shuttle that would get him to Berlin.

"Thank you," he said as she clicked to pay for the ticket.

Greta was happy to imagine a reunion of the Holt family, but when she looked up from her phone, Mason was still wringing his hands.

"They're really okay?" he said. "I have reason to be worried, especially about Jack."

Was this father's intuition or had some bit of news seeped into the biosphere? "They're fine," she said. "Yesterday . . ." Greta paused to think. Had that really been only yesterday that they'd all been in

Rostock? "My daughter was teaching Jack how to say a German tongue twister about *Fischers Fritze fischt frische Fische*—the fisherman fishing fish—and Jack was trying to repeat it, but he couldn't stop laughing. He seemed happy."

Mason did not look convinced. "And Lucy?"

Greta smiled. "She's *eine mitreißende Frau*, we say in German. Captivating. I'm glad our families crossed paths."

"Lucy is the best thing that ever happened to me," he said. "I— I don't know how I survived Mars without her."

Greta pursed her lips together as she heard these words, facing the sad truth that she and Otto had not felt that kind of attachment, that kind of adoration for each other, in years.

"May I ask why you left the biosphere?" she said.

"Because I finally got a message," he said, "for the first time since I arrived. It was a months-old message from my daughter Zoe, and it said 'HELP, Daddy! Jack is going to jail, and Mommy is crying. This is BAD! We need you to come home right this minute.' So I did. Zoe isn't normally one to be dramatic unless there's a good reason, and I knew I couldn't stay there. I need to lay eyes on them for myself," he said, and then he stood up. "I guess I should try to get some sleep. I'll Venmo you for the plane ticket as soon as I get there."

"Good night, Mason. See you in the morning."

He gave a little wave, and the dogs followed him into the house.

Greta considered going inside too, but she needed to think. She put her feet up again and leaned back, watching the trees reflect on the surface of the pool.

Her phone pinged, and she saw that Vanessa Schultz had emailed. She steeled herself for the first angry tirade from the Schultz family.

> Greta! Du Göttin! My grandfather told me about your call
> to him—I knew you were fabulous, but it turns out you are
> a bold, ball-busting woman! A secret apprentice? An art

scandal? A battle against the patriarchy? I love *everything* about this.

I made a call, and the director of the National Gallery has agreed to give us a private viewing of the Vermeer—Johannes or Maria??!—out of its frame. He will not be happy when he discovers why we're there! But if you can convince me, I will work to win him and my grandfather over to your and Maria's side. Let's set a date for as soon as possible.

You must be here for all that unfolds!

Mit freundliche Grüße
Vanessa

PS when can we start working on *my* collection?

Greta spent the rest of the night on the lounge chair, feeling excitement and sadness in turns. She imagined walking up the steps of the museum, smelling the bread at her corner bakery, sitting on her balcony. Knocking on Adam's door. And as the sun came up, she became aware of the birds singing and the fountain splashing, and she knew what she had to do.

She stood up and turned to the house where—in a window upstairs—she spotted Otto, kind, good-hearted Otto, his hands on his hips, smiling at the wide Texas sky.

DALLAS

If Lucy and the kids had been home, Mason would have slept well his first night back. But as it was, he tossed and turned, discovering sometime in the middle of the night that he was not alone in his insomnia; through the bedroom window, he saw Greta—his guest? his tenant?—still sitting out by the pool, sometimes looking down at her phone, mostly staring up at the stars.

Morning finally came. "Hey, Captain," he said, "turn on the lights," and he got up and ready for a day of travel. He shaved and showered and dressed in his regular clothes. He went through his things in the back of the walk-in closet and put socks, boxers, and his favorite T-shirts in his backpack, still searching high and low, every drawer and shelf, for his wallet and phone.

The dogs followed him to the kitchen, where he made a cappuccino, piping hot and so much better than that watery, tepid instant coffee of Alpha Red Canyon. The dogs were asking to go out, so he followed them out the back door, closing it behind him to keep the cats and the AC in. Greta had finally left her lounge chair, but there was Mickey the pool guy, kneeling on the flagstones to check the chlorine levels.

"Hi," Mason said.

Mickey looked up and pushed his headphones off his ears. "Whoa," he said, "you're back."

"I'm back," said Mason. "For now. I'm on my way to meet Lucy and the kids." He looked over his shoulder and saw Tank and Bunny doing their business in the pachysandra. "Everything okay with you, Mickey? Good summer?"

"Sure," Mickey said, smiling broadly. "Can't complain. You either, right? Mr. Sexy!"

"Sorry?" said Mason.

"I admit, I didn't see that coming." Mickey shook his head and shrugged. "But then there's hope for me, right?"

"Sure," Mason said, pushing his glasses up on the bridge of his nose and shrugging back. "Wait, what do you mean—hope for . . . what?"

But Mickey had put his headphones on and turned back to his chemicals.

Did the pool guy find him . . . *sexy*? This was flattering, of course, but certainly out of the blue.

Mason brought the dogs back inside and checked the time. He was about to put his mug in the dishwasher when he heard footsteps on the stairs. He hoped it was Greta, coming to offer him a ride to the airport.

Instead, whoever it was walked through the entry to the garage door, and he could hear a plaintive voice saying quietly, "*Können wir das später besprechen?* You know I can't be late for surgery." It was the German husband, Otto, and he sounded distressed. Mason froze, the mug still in his hand.

"*Später werde ich nicht mehr hier sein.*"

That was Greta. Mason didn't speak German, but he could hear grief and exhaustion in her voice.

"Please," Otto said, "*bitte. Du machst keinen Sinn.*"

Mason had stopped breathing, wondering whether he should alert them to his presence on the other side of the wall. It felt strange to be an intruder in his own home. An eavesdropper, a snoop.

"*Ich liebe dich,*" Greta was saying. "You're happier than I've ever seen you. You've found so much joy. I'm proud of you." Her words seemed harmless, kind even, and yet Otto let out a heartbreaking moan.

"*Ich verstehe gar nichts,*" he said.

"I know," Greta said. "I don't understand either. And I'm sorry, Otto. *Es tut mir sehr leid.*"

Mason didn't move as he heard choking sobs and the rattle of keys. The door to the garage opened and then quietly closed, and a few moments later, the front door did as well. And then the house was utterly still. Mason hadn't understood much of the exchange, but he was pretty sure he'd overheard something shattering.

And also worrisome, his potential ride to the airport had just walked out of the house.

He went to find the Tesla fob, thinking he would just drive himself, but when he went out to the garage, he found the car battery completely dead.

He was heading back in to find the Prius key when the doorbell rang, and the dogs went berserk. Mason followed them to see who was there.

Three young women were standing on the porch. He recognized one, Nell, a longtime classmate of Jack's who had always exuded a mature confidence. Lucy had dubbed her an old soul when she was only a fourth grader.

"Hi, Mr. Holt," she said. "I didn't know you were back."

"Me neither," he said. "I mean, I didn't plan . . . What can I do for you?"

"We're hoping we can get a message to Jack," Nell said.

"Okay," Mason said warily. Tank and Bunny pushed past him, greeting the girls by licking their hands; Mason was not as receptive to these visitors, unsure whether they were friends or foes. Gosh, he wished Lucy were there.

"Just tell Jack that Emmi contacted us," Nell said. "She explained everything."

"Emmi?"

"His lawyer," Nell said, putting her hands in the pockets of her baggy jeans. "Kidding, but the girl can make an argument."

"She sent us Jack's formula," said the girl next to her. She had red hair and definitely looked familiar, but Mason couldn't come up with her name.

"A formula for—"

"The one that got all twisted up and overblown," Nell said. "We just want to talk to him about it."

"About what exactly?" Mason said.

"The list," said the redhead. "We should've been more mindful, instead of listening to Sam. Dude's highly questionable."

"I hate to say I told you so," Nell said to her coolly, "but . . . I did tell you so."

"*Nell*," she said, "we're sorry, okay?"

"Also we think the tampon thing is way cool," the third girl said. She was holding a Starbucks iced coffee and chewing on the straw.

"Tampon thing?" Mason said, thinking this conversation might as well be in German too, given how little he was grasping.

"Totally. So can you let Jack know we came by?" she said. "We're the three cheapest girls on his list— Wait, that came out wrong—"

"And welcome back from Mars," Nell added with a smile. "You slayed."

The girls turned and walked down the path to a parked Bronco, and for a second, Mason considered asking them for a ride to DFW. But no, that was a terrible idea.

There was a woman in the yard next door picking up her newspaper at the curb. "Hi," she called out as she walked back up her path. "You're the astronaut, right? I was at the party when you got home last night."

"Hello," Mason said. In his shock the night before, he hadn't been able to take in the faces of all the strangers sitting around his dining table.

"Welcome home," she said.

"Thank you," he said. He scratched the back of his head. "I'm sorry, but I was wondering if it would be possible . . ." And then he stopped; it was too much to ask. He didn't even know this woman's name. "Never mind," he said.

"Tell me, hon," she said, walking from her property over to his. "What do you need?"

"I'm flying to Germany in a few hours," he said.

"How exciting," she said.

"Yes, I wondered, would you mind calling me an Uber? I don't have my phone."

"Did you leave it on Mars?" she said with a wink.

"In my spaceship actually," he said, though this was no time for jokes. "But I'll Venmo you as soon as—"

"I know where you live," she said, and laughed. "When do you need to leave?"

"Now," he said, practically barking out the word.

"Well then, let's see." She pulled her phone out of her skirt pocket. "It says . . . your driver can be here in four minutes in his black Toyota Camry. I'm Sylvie, by the way."

"Mason," said Mason. "And thank you, Sylvie. Really, I appreciate this so much. I better go grab my stuff."

"Have a good trip," she said.

Mason rushed back into the house, where he noticed that Greta had left a neat stack of mail—mostly bills, along with a thick envelope from a solar energy research group in Norway—on the hall table; he grabbed it all, said goodbye to the dogs, the guinea pig, and a cat who happened to run by, and then he stood outside in the shade of the portico in the wilting Texas heat to wait for his Uber.

A car—a white Suburban, not the promised Camry—came down the street and stopped right in front of the house. The back door opened, and Alice!—his adorable Alice!—climbed out of the car. Mason's breath caught in his chest. She was so tall, and she flashed a grown-up, stern gaze back into the car just as Fred tumbled out and landed face-first onto the street. Zoe, her hair tangled and her smile revealing a missing tooth, leapt out next. She picked

Fred up, brushing the dirt from her hand onto her floral leggings. Irene stepped out behind her, stretching her back with a groan, as Rex came around from the other side of the car and began unloading the suitcases.

Then Jack appeared, looking handsome and well and strong. He thanked the driver before going to help his grandfather with the growing pile of luggage.

Mason felt a swell of love for his family and smiled in wonder as though a flock of endangered birds had landed on his lawn.

The passenger door opened next, and there was Lucy, laughing to herself as she checked to see that nothing had been left behind in the car. She pulled her sweatshirt off over her head, and her hair clip caught on the collar. When she finally untangled herself, she looked up at the house and gasped. Mason ran to her, dropping everything—his backpack, the mail and passport—in the grass as he went. He and Lucy met in the middle of the yard, almost knocking each other over.

"You're here!" she said, touching his face and hands. "But I'm on my way to New Mexico to bring you home."

"I'm on my way to you," he said as the kids came rushing over. "I got a plane ticket and—"

"We spent the night on the floor at JFK," said Alice, his little news reporter tugging on his T-shirt. "Also, we stole a car and left the country and didn't tell Mommy where we were."

"Wait," said Mason, "you did what—"

"Look, Daddy!" Zoe was holding her hands up in his face, waving her fingers. "Emmi put on polish," she said, "and I get to leave it on until it chips."

"How pretty," he said, holding her hand to see, silently vowing never again to be this out of the loop on his family's acquaintances and exploits and jokes and memories. "And very grown-up." His heart ached at the sight of her little sparkly fingernails.

"I'm sorry, Dad," Jack said, looking him squarely in the eye. "I screwed up, and you're going to be really disgusted with me—"

"Never," Mason said, wanting to shield his son, but he did not know from what. "Jack, I would never be anything but proud of you."

Jack had tears in his eyes, and he dropped his head on Mason's shoulder.

Mason too was overcome with emotion. He pulled them all in for a hug, closing his eyes and holding on as tight as he could. But after only a moment, Zoe wriggled away to go see the pets, Rex called for help with the bags, Mason's Uber driver pulled up to the curb in his black Camry, and Alice started picking up all the mail Mason had dropped on the lawn.

"Ummm, Jack," Alice said, looking down at an envelope in her hand. "You got a letter from MIT."

Mason watched as they all stopped whatever they were doing and turned to stare, as though Alice were holding a ticking bomb in her hand.

Jack approached her slowly. "You open it," he said.

"Me?" said Alice, her eyes wide.

Jack nodded, and Alice tore the envelope open. "It says . . . it says your math is pretty good," she said, scanning the letter, "and something about a housing form?"

Jack grabbed the letter, reading it quickly. "So they're taking me?— Even though—" He whooped so loudly that the dogs started barking from inside the house. Jack dropped to his knees on the grass, gripping the paper, looking skyward, and smiling.

Mason watched the moment unfold—Rex tousling the hair on Jack's head, Alice jumping up and down, Irene and Zoe squealing. He held Lucy's hand, looked into her eyes, and kissed her with all the passion and longing of an intergalactic hero who'd blasted through space, traveled *where no man had gone before*, and returned safely with a newfound appreciation for what it means to be home.

Lucy blinked up at him dreamily. "Wow," she said.

"Eww," said Alice.

"Get a room," said Irene.

Lucy leaned in to kiss him again, and for a moment Mason felt like he really was the sexiest man alive. In any case, he was far and away the happiest.

BERLIN

Adam had given himself a stern talking-to when he'd returned to Berlin. This was the start of a new chapter. He had left New York City behind for good, bringing all his earthly possessions with him, and he was officially on his own now. This was it. It was time to settle into Berlin and build a meaningful life.

He had a friend in Greta, so that was a good start. They had, by sheer coincidence, flown back to Berlin on the very same day, running into each other in front of their building as they got out of their respective cabs, Adam with four huge suitcases and duffel bags and Greta with nothing but a handbag, swollen eyes, and a wadded-up tissue in her fist. He was worried about her, but he hadn't pried that morning. Eventually she'd told him, with her usual grace and kindness, that she and Otto were going their separate ways, that she was heartbroken, but no one was to blame, that she would always care about him.

⊶

One Saturday, after they'd been back long enough to settle in, he invited her for dinner. This was not a date. Yes, he was single now, and Greta was too, or was in the process of becoming single, but this was decidedly not the right time for either one of them, especially for her. He knew this. He felt so strongly about it—the importance of setting his all-consuming, heart-pounding crush on Greta to the side—that he'd invited Bettina for dinner as well, just to make sure there was no misunderstanding.

He put on a clean shirt and brushed his teeth, and then went to the kitchen, where he opened a nice bottle of *Spätburgunder* to let it breathe. He set the table for three with the new place mats he'd bought for the occasion and took the pork tenderloin and roasted vegetables and Hasselback potatoes—a meal he'd spent the entire day preparing—out of the oven.

There was a gentle rap on the door, and Greta let herself in.

"Hey, you," he said, finding her in the entry with a box of chocolates in her hand. "Wow, knockout." The words slipped out before he could stop himself. Because Greta was, in fact, a knockout. She was wearing a silk blouse and skirt and shoes that highlighted the curve of her calves. "Sorry," he said. "I only meant it's great to see you. And yeah, you happen to look great too."

He was blushing as he kissed her on the cheek, willing himself to cool it.

"Bettina gave me this blouse," she said, "right off her back actually."

"It suits you," he said. "And I love chocolate, thank you. Come on in." He led her to the kitchen and cleared his throat, saying as casually as he could, "*Was möchtest du trinken? Ein Glas Rotwein?*"

"*Gerne*," she said, and then looked up, astonished. "Adam, you're learning German?"

"Oh, yeah," he said, shrugging it off. "I live in Germany, so . . ."

"That's wonderful," she said. "*Wunderbar.*"

"*Danke*," he said, pouring them each a glass. "It's important, at work especially, but I'm terrible at it."

"*Gar nicht*," she said. "I think you sound lovely."

He was relieved to hear her say that. He'd found a Humboldt University student who agreed to tutor him twice a week and promised he wouldn't let Adam sound stupid or embarrassing. "Then I guess I'll keep at it." They clinked glasses and went out to his balcony, where it was still warm enough to sit. He took a matchbox from the windowsill and lit the candle on the table between them. "How was your day?" he said. Not a scintillating start, but he really did want to know.

"Consequential," she said. "Vanessa Schultz arranged a meeting with her grandfather at the museum. I had my one chance to lay out the theory about the Vermeer to both him and the director."

"Greta!" he said, taking in the excitement that flashed in her eyes. "Amazing. Did they listen?"

She shrugged but looked pleased. "I hope so. I guess I'll find out soon enough."

"For what it's worth," he said, "I think the theory that Vermeer's daughter painted it makes perfect sense, especially given the hidden figure of the man in the painting. When I looked for it, I could see exactly where he would have been, right behind Maria's head."

She turned in surprise. "You went to see the collection?"

"Of course. I've been twice actually. Once while you were in Dallas right after it opened. And I went again last week, so I could understand what you'd said about the background of the Vermeer."

"Thank you, Adam."

"Oh, it was a pleasure. I'd like to go again sometime—with you," he said. "You promised a tour." At the museum, he'd stood in the middle of the room, turning slowly, to study the paintings, one woman on each canvas, from a pregnant Madonna to a naked prostitute. "Your collection . . . ," he said, searching for the right words. "I don't know much about art, but I think it's impressive the way you ask the viewer to consider the role of women and definitions of beauty. And you must be so proud of the centerpiece, the portrait of the girl with the red headscarf."

"Self-portrait," Greta said, an eyebrow raised.

"Yes," he said, "self-portrait."

"Painted by an artist who may never get the credit for it."

The light from his living room was making Greta look radiant, and her hair was so silky he wondered what it would feel like to bury his face in it.

"I'm on a mission now," she said, "and I won't stop until the label beside the painting has Maria's name on it."

"I'll look forward to seeing that," he said, and raised his glass to her.

A dog was barking from a neighboring apartment.

"Have you heard from Lucy?"

"I talked to her earlier today," she said. "She and Mason and the girls might go to Tromsø, Norway, for a few months. There's a research institute there that wants him to adapt his DustBunny drones to deice solar panels."

"So . . . IceBunnies?"

She smiled. "I guess so, yes."

A rowdy group of young people walked by on the street below, laughing and singing, wearing matching red and yellow shirts.

"There's a big soccer game tonight," she said. "Union Berlin is playing FC Bayern." Adam could see that her grief, so evident when she first returned from Dallas, seemed to be lifting.

"Maybe we should go to a game sometime," he said. He would lean into soccer, the same way he was leaning into *Currywurst* and *Weißbier* and everything else Berlin had to offer.

"It's a lot of fun," she said, "but it's hard to get tickets. Bettina and I have gone before."

He glanced toward the kitchen. "Should we give Bettina a call? Find out what's keeping her?"

Greta took a sip of her wine and put the glass down. "Actually," she said, "I forgot to tell you. It turns out Bettina can't make it to-night."

"Oh," he said, "I thought— Is she okay?"

"She's fine," Greta said. "Something came up. I hope you're not too disappointed."

"Not at all. More food for us," he said. Was it possible this was the stupidest remark he'd ever made?

The candlelight flickered, and she was watching him with a look he couldn't read, and then she abruptly stood up. "To be honest, I'm not hungry," she said.

"Oh," he said. "I'm sorry, Greta, are you . . . ?" He couldn't bear to think he'd somehow upset or offended her. He got up as well. "Please don't go. We can just sit here."

"I don't want to sit here," she said. "I want . . ." And she stopped herself. Her hands were trembling.

"What? Tell me," he said, trying to come up with something to say to set her at ease. "What do you want?"

"I need—" She took a step closer, gazing at him with curiosity, with hope. "Are you really asking?"

"Of course," he said. "Anything."

She put her hands on his shoulders and slowly pushed him back into his chair. And—as he caught his breath—she sat on his lap and began kissing him, his face, his neck, his lips. Kissing Greta had been his fantasy ever since he'd first met her, but now, feeling her hair brush his cheek, her breath warm his skin, he was almost too stunned to kiss her back.

"Are you sure?" he said, pulling back to look at her; her eyes were shining, eager. "This? This is what you want?"

But Greta was not interested in talking and so neither was he. She pressed her mouth to his as he pulled her body closer to him, and closer still, until the rest of the world around them—the city, the people, the dog barking, the candle flickering, and the dinner he'd made for her with devotion and pure love—faded away. As far as Adam was concerned, they were the only two people in Berlin.

To: Greta
From: Otto

Liebe Greta,

I am sorry that it has taken me long to write to you. You have been in my thoughts ever since you left Dallas, and I have slowly and quite painfully come to understand that you were right about the need for us to go in separate ways. I miss you very much, but I am happy. And in the words of my favorite country singer Dolly Parton—I wish you joy!

Fall in Dallas is *wunderschön*, and even more so as the temperatures become colder—a high of only eighty-eight degrees yesterday. There is sunshine almost every day. I have never felt better, *körperlich* or *psychologisch*! I furthermore enjoy my job and try to improve my English, and I recently have upgraded to an Executive Membership at Costco.

It goes well for Emmi too, *ja*? We are FaceTiming on Saturdays, and her new apartment looks comfortable. I was worrying that she will be lonely living by herself, but she looks to be very content with school and new friends she is making.

I enjoy the Holts' house while I still can! After Christmas they will return home from Tromsø, Norway, at which time I will move into a smaller house I found quite in the nearby. This is win-win, *oder*? Meanwhile, Irene "pops in" from time to time and brings me her stickerpoodle cookies.

Do you remember Betsy's husband, Bob? I think you did not like him much. He accidentally sent pictures of his *Penis* to a WhatsApp group of Rockwell School parents. Betsy has kicked him out of the house, and he is now living in a Holiday Inn on the freeway.

And do you remember our neighbor Sylvie? Yesterday, she had a very bad *Unfall*! She had climbed a ladder to clean her gutters and she is falling down. After examining her ankle, I was sorry to tell her it was sprained. I am requiring ice and elevation of her foot until she can safely walk on it. As Texans do, I have organized the neighbors to do for her what is called a "casserole brigade."

It is football season! And since I have learned to tell the cats apart, I have named them Zack, Dak, and CeeDee after my three favorite Dallas Cowboys.

How goes it with you, Greta? *Alles okay?*

Fondly,
Otto

PS My suitcase arrived!

EPILOGUE

The family—
that dear octopus from whose tentacles
we never quite escape,
nor, in our inmost hearts, ever quite wish to.
—Dodie Smith, Dear Octopus

Maria Vermeer
Dutch, Delft 1654–1713
Girl with a Red Turban, ca 1676

Oil on canvas

Once thought to have been painted by her father, Johannes Vermeer (1632–1675), this self-portrait is now attributed to Vermeer's eldest daughter, Maria, apprentice in his studio. A young woman gazes directly at the viewer, demanding to be acknowledged. Her fanciful clothing and costume jewelry convey playfulness, while her expression is unnervingly self-assured. X-radiographs reveal that the artist removed a figure from the background: a man, now presumed to be her father, Johannes Vermeer, standing beside his easel. By removing her father from the composition after his death, Maria was able to pass the painting off as her father's work, so her family could sell it to settle their debts to the baker. But indeed, it was Maria, the secret apprentice, who created this masterful painting, one that originally depicted two artists in their studio—father and daughter—and now portrays Maria proudly on her own.

Gift of the Schultz Foundation

HEILIGENHAFEN ⚲

Greta and Lucy are standing together under a string of twinkle lights in the open doorway of the cottage, watching snow fall in the driveway. The wind whips off the sea, making their eyes water.

Lucy is shivering, and she wraps her pashmina over her shoulders.

"I warned you," says Greta. "It gets bitter cold here."

"It might be cold," says Lucy, "but it's perfect."

Alice comes up behind them, her ankle-length dress rustling as she walks. "Why are you guys letting all the cold air in? It's fricking *freezing* in here."

"Sorry," Lucy says, closing the door.

"*Meine Güte,*" Greta says to Alice, "are you even taller than me now?"

"No, I'm cheating," says Alice, and shows off her high heels.

Behind her, a Christmas tree is tucked into the curve of the staircase, lit with real candles. Bunches of holly boughs are wrapped around the banister leading up to the second floor.

Zoe, whose hair has fallen out of whatever updo she had an hour ago, rushes over and grabs Lucy's hand. "Can I have a glass of champagne? Please?"

"Maybe later," says Lucy.

"Bad idea," says Alice, and then she turns around as a young boy races past, dragging a long garland made of green and red construction paper. "Safe," he yells, grabbing onto Zoe's leg.

"Did you finish, Peter?" Alice says.

"*Ich bin fertig*," Peter says, and holds up the garland to show her.

"Awesome," Zoe says, high-fiving him like she does every time Peter performs some trick in the swimming pool during his summer visits. She takes one end of the garland and Alice takes the other, and they try to decide where to hang it.

Adam walks in from the kitchen with a mug of *Glühwein* in his hand and offers Greta a sip. "Lillian says to tell you that she hates the Baltic in winter and the canapés are getting cold."

"She's only pretending to be grumpy," Greta says. "She's thrilled we're here."

She kneels and looks at her son's hands, sticky with glue. "Let's get you washed up," she says, "before you ruin your fancy clothes."

"I've got it," Adam says. He hands her the mug, and he and Peter go off to the kitchen together.

The front door opens, and Mason, wearing a parka and carrying a massive stack of wood, stomps in, accompanied by Bettina's dog, Til, and a flurry of snow.

"My hero," Lucy says. She closes the door, unwinds the scarf from his neck, and kisses him.

"Gross," says Zoe.

"So embarrassing," Alice says, and the twins take Peter's garland and go look for a special place to hang it.

"There's a lot more in the woodshed," Mason says, "so we'll be fine for the night."

"The grandparents will be glad to hear it," Lucy says.

"Especially the Texans," says Greta. "Should I bring them some throw blankets?"

"I'll ask," Mason says, taking the split logs to the living room and crossing paths with Sylvie, who is wearing an embroidered dirndl.

"Gooten abben, y'all," she says. "Itch moose . . . Darn it! Otto wants me to practice my German the whole time I'm here, but it sure is hard."

"It is hard," says Lucy.

"Very tricky," says Greta, "but you're doing great."

"Really?" says Sylvie. She takes a breath and says, "Itch moose Toilettey?"

"*Natürlich*," says Greta. "The bathroom's at the end of the hall."

"Donkey shun, Greta," Sylvie says with renewed confidence.

"*Bitte.*"

Sylvie goes off to find the bathroom just as Zoe and Alice cross back through the entry, this time with Bjørn and Astrid's daughters; they stop to take a group selfie in front of the Christmas tree for Instagram.

There's a raucous burst of laughter from a bedroom upstairs. And then a gust of wind rattles the house, and everything goes dark. There's a collective groan.

"It's all right, everyone stay calm," Tobias calls out. "We're prepared for this." He and Harper walk around the living room, passing out flashlights, lanterns, and emergency candles.

"Tobias is so good in a crisis," Lillian tells anyone who will listen. "What would I do without him?"

Harper casts a glance around the room for Bettina, hoping she can share a smirk.

Lucy and Greta are still in the entry, waiting, their faces lit, first by the candles on the tree, and then by a beam of light that shines through the windows.

Til starts barking as a car pulls into the drive.

"Finally," says Greta, and she clasps Lucy's hands.

"In our wildest dreams," Lucy whispers, "could we ever have imagined—"

"No," Greta says, "which makes all of this even better."

Lucy nods. "They're here!" she shouts, her voice carrying through the darkened house.

The dear friends and family come together from every corner. Bjørn and Astrid follow Otto, who is guiding Irene and Rex through the living room, in hopes of avoiding any trips, falls, or sprained ankles. The twenty-somethings—from Dallas, Berlin, and beyond—feel their way down the stairs, gripping the banister. Bettina slips in through the French doors, having shared a cigarette with the cellist, who quickly rejoins his string quartet, warms his hands, and opens up his score.

⎯

Out in the courtyard, the old VW Beetle comes to a stop.

"Why's it so dark?" Jack says as he turns off the car.

"The power always goes out in a storm," Emmi says. "But it'll be okay." She leans over and kisses him. "Ready?"

"Ready," he says, touching his forehead to hers.

They step out of the car. Emmi holds the skirt of her wedding dress up to keep the hem out of the snow, and Jack checks his suit pocket for the rings before taking her hand. They steady each other and make their way to the candlelit cottage. The door swings open, voices fill the air, and the music begins to play.

♉ ACKNOWLEDGMENTS ✈

I am so fortunate to have worked with the fabulous team at Emily Bestler Books for almost ten years! I'm indebted to my brilliant editor Emily Bestler and to Hydia Scott-Riley, Lara Jones, Megan Rudloff, Dayna Johnson, Jane Elias, Sonja Singleton, Shelby Pumphrey, Paige Lytle, Suzanne Donahue, Dana Trocker, Libby McGuire, and everyone at EBB and Atria Books for all the work they do. And huge thanks to Ella Laytham for the consistently wonderful cover art.

I'm so grateful to Laurie Fox for being such a champion and advocate and for stepping up with such care and consideration when Linda Chester left us.

Thank you, Anika Streitfeld, for your patience, your tireless efforts to make my stories hold water, your sharp eyes, and your friendship.

And thank you to Liz Parker at Verve!

This book contains many subjects that I knew little about when I started writing. Karina Schultz not only suggested a house swap book, but also spent time with me in Berlin and provided a wealth of information about specific neighborhoods and (funny) German American cultural differences. *Herzlichen Dank,* Karina, along with Alex Savelyev and Sebastian d'Huc, for the walking tour and for the brainstorming session about solar panel squeegees, systems engineers, patents, and Mars simulations.

The painting in the book—*Girl with a Red Turban*—is fictional. But both Benjamin Binstock and his wonderful book *Vermeer's*

Family Secrets are very real. I met Ben twenty years ago at the American Academy in Berlin and was fascinated by his research on Maria Vermeer and the theory that she painted several works attributed to her father Johannes Vermeer. Thank you, Ben, for all your help and for being so interesting and convincing that I had to include you in *Far and Away*.

For talking through all things regarding young men and their frontal lobes, I thank my boys Luke, Andrew, and especially Alex for his knowledge of the music industry. And thank you to the best sisters ever, Laurie Mitchell and Wendy O'Sullivan, for always talking to me about my fictional families and their many problems. And thank you, Megan O'Sullivan, for editing my Dallas chapters.

I married into a German family, which is the only reason I was able to write this book at all. Thank you, David, for introducing me to Berlin, a city I truly love, and for indulging me in a trip to Heiligenhafen. And *vielen Dank* Julie and Domi, and Lili, Katharina, and Eliana for help with all things German, from the geography to the language, from teenage behavior to cultural *Missverständisse*.

Thank you to Calvin Woods and Mike Shelley for helping me with math. Thank you, Yasmin Rachid, for talking through vacation spots on the Baltic and Rebecca Jussen for discussing law schools in Germany. And thanks as always to Amy White for our conversations about all matters of life, including the ways teenage boys get themselves into trouble.

So much gratitude to my lovely Thursday authors/friends—Fiona Davis, Jamie Brenner, Lynda Cohen Loigman, Nicola Harrison, Susie Schnall, and Suzy Leopold—and to the many, many writers who make up our wonderful support network. Huge thanks to Suzanne Rindell for being an early reader and cheerleader, for talking through characters, and for always being supportive. Thanks to Annissa Joy Armstrong and the members of Beyond the Page book club for the *Far and Away* cover reveal. Thank you to April and Doug and Victor for feeding me and entertaining me during long, lonely stretches of writing and Pamela Klinger Horn for getting me to the theater (my happy place) whenever she's in town. Thank you to Ben, Mary, and the team at House of Books in Kent, CT, for supporting my books and keeping my TBR pile high. And finally, thank you to the many readers who show up at events, preorder books, and write me the loveliest emails. You are the BEST.